Jim Butcher is a ten-year student of martial arts, including Ryuku Kempo, Tae Kwan Do, Gojo Shorei Ryu, and a sprinkling of Kung Fu. He is a skilled rider and has worked as a summer camp horse wrangler and performed in front of large audiences in both drill riding and stunt riding exhibitions. He also enjoys fencing, singing, song-writing, and live-action gaming. He works as a computer support technician, although he has held a variety of jobs in the past, from fast-food management to door-to-door vacuum selling. Jim lives in Oklahoma with his wife and son and a houseful of computers.

Find out more about Jim Butcher and other Orbit authors by registering for the free monthly newsletter at www.orbitbooks.co.uk

D0452419

Grave Peril

The Dresden Files
Book Three

Jim Butcher

www.orbitbooks.co.uk

ORBIT

First published in Great Britain in October 2005 by Orbit
Reprinted 2006, 2007

A CIP catalogue record for this book is available from
the British Library.

ISBN 978-1-84149-400-5

Papers used by Orbit are natural, recyclable products made from
wood grown in sustainable forests and certified in accordance with
the rules of the Forest Stewardship Council.

Typeset in Garamond 3 by
Palimpsest Book Production Limited, Polmont, Stirlingshire.

Printed and bound in Great Britain by
Mackays of Chatham plc, Chatham, Kent
Paper supplied by Hellefoss AS, Norway

Orbit
An imprint of
Little, Brown Book Group
Brettenham House
Lancaster Place
London WC2E 7EN

A Member of the Hachette Livre Group of Companies

www.orbitbooks.co.uk

Grave Peril

1

There are reasons I hate to drive fast. For one, the Blue Beetle, the mismatched Volkswagen bug that I putter around in, rattles and groans dangerously at anything above sixty miles an hour. For another, I don't get along so well with technology. Anything manufactured after about World War II seems to be susceptible to abrupt malfunction when I get close to it. As a rule, when I drive, I drive, very carefully and sensibly.

Tonight was an exception to the rule.

The Beetle's tires screeched in protest as we rounded a corner, clearly against the NO LEFT TURN sign posted there. The old car growled gamely, as though it sensed what was at stake, and continued its valiant puttering, moaning, and rattling as we zoomed down the street.

'Can we go any faster?' Michael drawled. It wasn't a complaint. It was just a question, calmly voiced.

'Only if the wind gets behind us or we start going down a hill,' I said. 'How far to the hospital?'

The big man shrugged his shoulders and shook his head. He had that kind of salt-and-pepper hair, dark against silver, that some men seem lucky enough to inherit, though his beard was still a solid color of dark brown, almost black. There were worry and laugh lines at the corners of his leathery face. His broad, lined hands rested on his knees, which were scrunched up due to the dashboard. 'I don't know for certain,' he answered me. 'Two miles?'

I squinted out the Beetle's window at the fading light. 'The sun is almost down. I hope we're not too late.'

'We're doing all we can,' Michael assured me. 'If God wills it, we'll be there in time. Are you sure of your . . .' his mouth twisted with distaste, 'source?'

'Bob is annoying, but rarely wrong,' I answered, jamming on the brakes and dodging around a garbage truck. 'If he said the ghost would be there, it will be there.'

'Lord be with us,' Michael said, and crossed himself. I felt a stirring of something; powerful, placid energy around him – the power of faith. 'Harry, there's something I've been meaning to talk to you about.'

'Don't ask me to Mass again,' I told him, uncomfortable. 'You know I'm just going to say no.' Someone in a red Taurus cut me off, and I had to swerve around him, into the turn lane, and then ahead of him again. A couple of the Beetle's wheels lifted off the ground. 'Jerk!' I howled out the driver's window.

'That doesn't preclude asking,' Michael asked. 'But no. I wanted to know when you were going to marry Miss Rodriguez.'

'Hell's Bells, Michael,' I scowled. 'You and I have been chasing all over town for the past two weeks, going up against every ghost and spirit that has all of a sudden reared its ugly head. We still don't know what's causing the spirit world to go postal.'

'I know that, Harry, but—'

'At the moment,' I interrupted, 'we're going after a nasty old biddy at Cook County, who could kill us if we aren't focused. And you're asking me about my love life.'

Michael frowned at me. 'You're sleeping with her, aren't you,' he said.

'Not often enough,' I growled, and shifted lanes, swerving around a passenger bus.

The knight sighed. 'Do you love her?' he asked.

'Michael,' I said. 'Give me a break. Where do you get off asking questions like that?'

'Do you love her?' he pressed.

'I'm trying to drive, here.'

'Harry,' he asked, smiling. 'Do you love the girl or don't you? It isn't a difficult question.'

'Speaks the expert,' I grumbled. I went past a blue-and-white at about twenty miles an hour over the speed limit, and saw the police officer behind the wheel blink and spill his coffee as he saw me go past. I checked my rearview mirror, and saw the blue bulbs on the police car whirl to life. 'Dammit, that tears it. The cops are going to be coming in right after us.'

'Don't worry about them,' Michael assured me. 'Just answer the question.'

I flashed Michael a glance. He watched me, his face broad and honest, his jaw strong, and his grey eyes flashing. His hair was cropped close, Marine-length, on top, but he sported a short, warrior's beard, which he kept clipped close to his face. 'I suppose so,' I said, after a second. 'Yeah.'

'Then you don't mind saying it?'

'Saying what?' I stalled.

'Harry,' Michael scolded, holding on as we bounced through a dip in the street. 'Don't be a child about this. If you love the woman, say so.'

'Why?' I demanded.

'You haven't told her, have you. You've never said it.'

I glared at him. 'So what if I haven't? She knows. What's the big deal?'

'Harry Dresden,' he said. 'You, of all people, should know the power of words.'

'Look, she knows,' I said, tapping the brakes and then flattening the accelerator again. 'I got her a card.'

'A card?' Michael asked.

'A Hallmark.'

He sighed. 'Let me hear you say the words.'

'What?'

'Say the words,' he demanded. 'If you love the woman, why can't you say so?'

'I don't just go around *saying* that to people, Michael. Stars and sky, that's . . . I just couldn't, all right?'

'You don't love her,' Michael said. 'I see.'

'You know that's not—'

'*Say* it, Harry.'

'If it will get you off my back,' I said, and gave the *Beetle* every ounce of gas that I could. I could see the police in traffic somewhere behind me. 'All right.' I flashed Michael a ferocious, wizardly scowl and snarled, 'I love her. There, how's that?'

Michael beamed. 'You see? That's the only thing that stands between you two. You're not the kind of person who says what they feel. Or who is very introspective, Harry. Sometimes, you just need to look into the mirror and see what's there.'

'I don't like mirrors,' I grumbled.

'Regardless, you needed to realize that you *do* love the woman. After Elaine, I thought you might isolate yourself too much and never—'

I felt a sudden flash of anger and vehemence. 'I don't *talk* about Elaine, Michael. Ever. If you can't live with that, get the hell out of my car and let me work on my own.'

Michael frowned at me, probably more for my choice of words than anything else. 'I'm talking about Susan, Harry. If you love her, you should marry her.'

'I'm a wizard. I don't have *time* to be married.'

'I'm a knight,' Michael responded. 'And I have the time. It's worth it. You're alone too much. It's starting to show.'

I scowled at him again. 'What does that mean?'

'You're tense. Grumpy. And you're isolating yourself more all the time. You need to keep up human contact, Harry. It would be so easy for you to start down a darker path.'

'Michael,' I snapped, 'I don't need a lecture. I don't need the conversion speech again. I don't need the "cast aside your evil powers before they consume you" speech. *Again*. What I need is for you to back me up while I go take care of this thing.'

Cook County Hospital loomed into sight and I made an illegal U-turn to get the Blue Beetle up into the Emergency entrance lane.

Michael unbuckled his seat belt, even before the car had come to a stop, and reached into the back seat to draw an enormous sword, fully five feet long in its black scabbard, from the backseat. He exited the car and buckled on the sword. Then he reached back in for a white cloak with a red cross upon the left breast, which he tossed over his shoulders in a practiced motion. He clasped it with another cross, this one of silver, at his throat. It clashed with his flannel workman's shirt, blue jeans, and steel-toed work boots.

'Can't you leave the cloak off, at least?' I complained. I opened the door and unfolded myself from the Beetle's driver's seat, stretching my long legs, and reached into the backseat to recover my own equipment – my new wizard's staff and blasting rod, each of them freshly carved and still a little green around the edges.

Michael looked up at me, wounded. 'The cloak is as much a part of what I do as the sword, Harry. Besides, it's no more ridiculous than that coat you wear.'

I looked down at my black leather duster, the one with the large mantle that fell around my shoulders and spread out as it billowed in a most heavy and satisfactory fashion around my legs. My own black jeans and dark Western shirt were a ton and a half more stylish than Michael's costume. 'What's wrong with it?'

'It belongs on the set of *El Dorado*,' Michael said. 'Are you ready?'

I shot him a withering glance, to which he turned the other cheek with a smile, and we headed toward the door. I could hear police sirens closing in behind us, maybe a block or two away. 'This is going to be close.'

'Then we best hurry.' He cast the white cloak back from his right arm, and put his hand on the hilt of the great broadsword. Then he bowed his head, crossed himself, and murmured, 'Merciful Father, guide us and protect us as we go to do battle with the darkness.' Once more, there was that thrum of energy around him, like the vibrations of music heard through a thick wall.

I shook my head, and fetched a leather sack, about the size of my palm, from the pocket of my duster. I had to juggle staff, blasting rod, and sack for a moment, and wound up with the staff in my left hand, as was proper, the rod in my right, and the sack dangling from my teeth. 'The sun is down,' I grated out. 'Let's move it.'

And we broke into a run, knight and wizard, through

the emergency entrance of Cook County Hospital. We drew no small amount of stares as we entered, my duster billowing out in a black cloud behind me, Michael's white cloak spreading like the wings of the avenging angel whose namesake he was. We pelted inside, and slid to a halt at the first intersection of cool, sterile, bustling hallways.

I grabbed the arm of the first orderly I saw. He blinked, and then gawked at me, from the tips of my Western boots to the dark hair atop my head. He glanced at my staff and rod rather nervously, and at the silver pentacle amulet dangling at my breast, and gulped. Then he looked at Michael, tall and broad, his expression utterly serene, at odds with the white cloak and the broadsword at his hip. He took a nervous step back. 'M-m-may I help you?'

I speared him into place with my most ferocious, dark-eyed smile and said, between teeth clenched on the leather sack, 'Hi. Could you tell us where the nursery is?'

2

We took the fire stairs. Michael knows how technology reacts to me, and the last thing either of us wanted was to be trapped in a broken elevator while innocent lives were snuffed out. Michael led the way, one hand on the rail, one on the hilt of his sword, his legs churning steadily.

I followed him, huffing and puffing. Michael paused by the door and looked back at me, white cloak swirling around his calves. It took me a couple of seconds to come gasping up behind him. 'Ready?' he asked me.

'Hrkghngh,' I answered, and nodded, still clenching my leather sack in my teeth, and fumbled a white candle from my duster pocket, along with a box of matches. I had to set my rod and staff aside to light the candle.

Michael wrinkled his nose at the smell of smoke, and pushed open the door. Candle in one hand, rod and staff in the other, I followed, my eyes flicking from my surroundings to the candle's flame and back.

All I could see was more hospital. Clean walls, clean halls, lots of tile and fluorescent lights. The long, luminescent tubes flickered feebly, as though they had all gone stale at once, and the hall was only dimly lit. Long shadows stretched out from a wheelchair parked to the side of one door and gathered beneath a row of uncomfortable-looking plastic chairs at an intersection of hallways.

The fourth floor was a graveyard, bottom-of-the-well silent. There wasn't a flicker of sound from a television or radio. No intercoms buzzed. No air conditioning whirred. Nothing.

We walked down a long hall, our steps sounding out clearly despite an effort to remain quiet. A sign on the wall, decorated with a brightly colored plastic clown, read: NURSERY/MATERNITY, and pointed down another hall.

I stepped past Michael and looked down that hallway. It ended at a pair of swinging doors. This hallway, too, was quiet. The nurse's station stood empty.

The lights weren't just flickering here – they were altogether gone. It was entirely dark. Shadows and uncertain shapes loomed everywhere. I took a step forward, past Michael, and as I did the flame of my candle burned down to a cold, clear pinpoint of blue light.

I spat the sack out of my mouth and fumbled it into my pocket. 'Michael,' I said, my voice strangled to hushed urgency. 'It's here.' I turned my body, so that he could see the light.

His eyes flicked down to the candle and then back up, to the darkness beyond. 'Faith, Harry.' Then he reached to his side with his broad right hand, and slowly, silently, drew *Amoracchius* from its sheath. I found it a tad more encouraging than his words. The great blade's polished steel gave off a lambent glow as Michael stepped forward to stand beside me in the darkness, and the air fairly thrummed with its power – Michael's own faith, amplified a thousandfold.

'Where are the nurses?' he asked me in a hoarse whisper.

'Spooked off, maybe,' I answered, as quietly. 'Or maybe some sort of glamour. At least they're out of the way.'

I glanced at the sword, and at the long, slender spike of metal set into its cross guard. Perhaps it was only my imagination, but I thought I could see flecks of red still upon it. Probably rust, I reasoned. Sure, rust.

I set the candle down upon the floor, where it continued to burn pinpoint-clear, indicating a spiritual presence. A big one. Bob hadn't been lying when he'd said that the ghost of Agatha Hagglethorn was no two-bit shade.

'Stay back,' I told Michael. 'Give me a minute.'

'If what the spirit told you is correct, this creature is dangerous,' Michael replied. 'Let me go first. It will be safer.'

I nodded toward the glowing blade. 'Trust me, a ghost would feel the sword coming before you even got to the door. Let me see what I can do first. If I can dust the spook, this whole contest is over before it begins.'

I didn't wait for Michael to answer me. Instead, I took my blasting rod and staff in my left hand, and in my right I grasped the pouch. I untied the simple knot that held the sack closed, and slipped forward, into the dark.

When I reached the swinging doors, I pressed one of them slowly opened. I remained still for a long moment, listening.

I heard singing. A woman's voice. Gentle. Lovely.

Hush little baby, don't say a word. Mama's gonna buy you a mockingbird.

I glanced back at Michael, and then slipped inside the door, into total darkness. I couldn't see — but I'm not a wizard for nothing. I thought of the pentacle upon my breast, over my heart, the silver amulet that I had inherited from my mother. It was a battered piece of jewelry, scarred and dented from uses for which it was never intended, but I wore it still. The five-sided star within the circle was the symbol of my magic, of what I believed in, embodying the five forces of the universe working in harmony, contained inside of human control.

I focused on it, and slid a little of my will into it, and the amulet began to glow with a gentle, blue-silver light, which spread out before me in a subtle wave, showing me the shapes of a fallen chair, and a pair of nurses at a desk behind a counter, slumped forward over their stations, breathing deeply.

The soothing, quiet lullaby continued as I studied the nurses. Enchanted sleep. It was nothing new. They were out, they weren't going anywhere, and there was little sense in wasting time or energy in trying to break the spell's hold on them. The gentle singing droned on, and I found myself reaching for the fallen chair, with the intention of setting it upright so that I would have a comfortable place to sit down for a little rest.

I froze, and had to remind myself that I would be an idiot to sit down beneath the influence of the unearthly song, even for a few moments. Subtle magic, and strong. Even knowing what to expect, I had barely sensed its touch in time.

I skirted the chair and moved forward, into a room filled with dressing hooks and little pastel hospital gowns hung upon them in rows. The singing was louder, here, though it still drifted around the room with a ghostly lack of origin. One wall was little more than a sheet of Plexiglas, and behind it was a room that attempted to look sterile and warm at the same time.

Row upon row of little glass cribs on wheeled stands stood in the room. Tiny occupants, with toy-sized hospital mittens over their brand-new fingernails, and tiny hospital stocking caps over their bald heads, were sleeping and dreaming infant dreams.

Walking among them, visible in the glow of my wizard's light, was the source of the singing.

Agatha Hagglethorn had not been old when she died. She wore a proper, high-necked shirt, as was appropriate to a lady of her station in nineteenth-century Chicago, and a long, dark, no-nonsense skirt. I could see through her, to the little crib behind her, but other than that she seemed solid, real. Her face was pretty, in a strained, bony sort of way, and she had her right hand folded over the stump at the end of her left wrist.

If that mockingbird don't sing, mama's going to buy you . . .

She had a captivating singing voice. Literally. She lilted out her song, spun energy into the air that lulled listeners into deeper and deeper sleep. If she was allowed to continue, she could draw both infants and nurses into a sleep from which they would never awaken, and the authorities would blame it on carbon monoxide, or something a little more comfortably normal than a hostile ghost.

I crept closer. I had enough ghost dust to pin down Agatha and a dozen spooks like her, and allow Michael to dispatch her swiftly, with a minimum of mess and fuss – just as long as I didn't miss.

I hunkered down, kept the little sack of dust gripped loosely in my right hand, and slipped over to the door that led into the roomful of sleeping babies. The ghost did not appear to have noticed me – ghosts aren't terribly observant. I guess being dead gives you a whole different perspective on life.

I entered the room, and Agatha Hagglethorn's voice rolled over me like a drug, making me blink and shudder. I had to keep focused, my thoughts on the cool power of my magic flowing through my pentacle and coming out in its spectral light.

If that diamond ring don't shine . . .

I licked my lips and watched the ghost as it stooped over one of the rolling cradles. She smiled, loving-kindness in her eyes, and breathed out her song over the baby.

The infant shuddered out a tiny breath, eyes closed in sleep, and did not inhale.

Hush little baby . . .

Time had run out. In a perfect world, I would have simply dumped the dust onto the ghost. But it's not a perfect world: Ghosts don't have to play by the rules of reality, and until they acknowledge that you're there, it's tough, very, very tough, to affect them at all. Confrontation is the only way, and even then, knowing the shade's identity and speaking its name aloud is the only sure way to make it face you. And, better and better, most spirits can't hear just anyone – it takes magic to make a direct call to the hereafter.

I rose fully to my feet, bag gripped in my hand and shouted, forcing my will into my voice, 'Agatha Hagglethorn!'

The spirit started, as though a distant voice had come to her, and turned toward me. Her eyes widened. The song abruptly fell silent.

'Who are you?' she said. 'What are you doing in my nursery?'

I struggled to keep the details Bob had told me about the ghost straight. 'This isn't your nursery, Agatha Hagglethorn. It's more than a hundred years since you died. You aren't real. You are a ghost, and you are dead.'

The spirit drew itself up with a sort of cold, high-society

haughtiness. 'I might have known. Benson sent you, didn't he? Benson is always doing something cruel and petty like this, then calling me a madwoman. A madwoman! He wants to take my child away.'

'Benson Hagglethorn is long dead, Agatha Hagglethorn,' I responded, and gathered back my right hand to throw. 'As is your child. As are you. These little ones are not yours to sing to or bear away.' I steeled myself to throw, began to bring my arm forward.

The spirit looked at me with an expression of lost, lonely confusion. This was the hard part about dealing with really substantial, dangerous ghosts. They were almost human. They appeared to be able to feel emotion, to have some degree of self-awareness. Ghosts aren't alive, not really – they're a footprint in stone, a fossilized skeleton. They are shaped like the original, but they aren't it.

But I'm a sucker for a lady in distress. I always have been. It's a weak point in my character, a streak of chivalry a mile wide and twice as deep. I saw the hurt and the loneliness on the ghost-Agatha's face, and felt it strike a sympathetic chord in me. I let my arm go still gain. Perhaps, if I was lucky, I could talk her away. Ghosts are like that. Confront them with the reality of their situation, and they dissolve.

'I'm sorry, Agatha,' I said. 'But you aren't who you think you are. You're a ghost. A reflection. The true Agatha Hagglethorn died more than a century ago.'

'N-no,' she said, her voice shaking. 'That's not true.'

'It *is* true,' I said. 'She died on the same night as her husband and child.'

'No,' the spirit moaned, her eyes closing. 'No, no, no, no. I don't want to hear this.' She started singing to herself again, low and desperate – no enchantment to it this time, no unconscious act of destruction. But the infant girl still hadn't inhaled, and her lips were turning blue.

'Listen to me, Agatha,' I said, forcing more of my will into my voice, lacing it with magic so that the ghost could hear me. 'I know about you. You died. You remember. Your husband beat you. You were terrified that he would beat your daughter. And when she started crying, you covered her mouth with your hand.' I felt like such a bastard to be going over the woman's past so coldly. Ghost or not, the pain on her face was real.

'I didn't,' Agatha wailed. 'I didn't hurt her.'

'You didn't mean to hurt her,' I said, drawing on the information Bob had provided. 'But he was drunk and you were terrified, and when you looked down she was gone. Isn't that right?' I licked my lips, and looked at the infant girl again. If I didn't get this done quickly, she'd die. It was eerie, how still she was, like a little rubber doll. Something, some spark of memory caught a flame in the ghost's eyes. 'I remember,' she hissed. 'The axe. The axe, the axe, the axe.' The proportions of the ghost's face changed, stretched, became more bony, more slender. 'I took my axe, my axe, my axe and gave my Benson twenty whacks.' The spirit grew, expanding, and a ghostly wind rustled through the room, emanating from the ghost, and rife with the smell of iron and blood.

'Oh, crap,' I muttered, and gathered myself to make a dash for the girl.

'My angel gone,' screamed the ghost. 'Benson gone. And then the hand, the hand that killed them both.' She lifted the stump of her arm into the air. 'Gone, gone, gone!' She threw back her head and screamed, and it came out as a deafening, bestial roar that rattled the nursery walls.

I threw myself forward, toward the breathless child, and as I did the rest of the infants burst into terrified wails. I reached the child and smacked her little up-turned baby butt. She blinked her eyes open in sudden shock, drew in a breath, and joined the rest of her nursery mates in crying.

'No,' Agatha screamed, 'no, no, no! He'll hear you! He'll hear you!' The stump of her left arm flashed out toward me, and I felt the impact both against my body and against my soul, as though she had driven a chip of ice deep into my chest. The power of the blow flung me back against a wall like a toy, hard enough to send my staff and rod clattering to the floor. By some miracle or other, I kept hold of my sack of ghost dust, but my head vibrated like a hammer-struck bell, and cold shivers wracked my body in rapid succession.

'Michael,' I wheezed, as loudly as I could, but already I could hear doors being thrown open, heavy work boots pounding toward me. I struggled to my feet and shook my head to clear it. The wind rose to gale force, sending cribs skittering around the room on their little wheels, tearing at my eyes so that I had to shield them with one hand. Dammit. The dust would be useless in such a gale.

'Hush little baby, hush little baby, hush little baby.' Agatha's ghost bowed over the infant girl's cradle again, and thrust the stump of her left arm down and *into* the mouth of the child, her translucent flesh passing seamlessly into the infant's skin. The child jerked and stopped breathing, though she still attempted to cry.

I shouted a wordless challenge and charged the spirit. If I could not cast the dust upon her from across the room,

I could thrust the leather bag into her ghostly flesh and pin her into place from within – agonizing, but undoubtedly effective.

Agatha's head whipped toward me as I came, and she jerked away from the child with a snarl. Her hair had come free in the gale and spread about her face in a ferocious mane well suited to the feral features that had replaced her gentle expression. She drew back her left hand, and there suddenly appeared, floating just above the stump, a short, heavy-headed hatchet. She shrieked and brought the hatched down at me.

Ghostly steel chimed on true iron, and *Amoracchius's* light flared bright-white. Michael slid his feet into position on the floor, gritting his teeth with effort, and kept the spirit-weapon from touching my flesh.

'Dresden,' he called. 'The dust!'

I fought my way forward, through the wind, shoved my fist into Agatha's weapon-arm, and shook loose some of the ghost dust from the leather sack.

Upon contact with her immaterial flesh, the ghost dust flared into blazing motes of scarlet light. Agatha screamed and jerked back, but her arm remained in place as firmly as if it had been set in concrete.

'Benson!' Agatha shrieked. 'Benson! Hush little baby!' And then she simply tore herself away from her arm at the shoulder, leaving her spirit flesh behind, and vanished. The arm and hatchet collapsed to the floor in a sudden spatter of clear, semifluid gelatin, the remnants of spirit-flesh when the spirit was gone, ectoplasm that would swiftly evaporate.

The gale died, though the lights continued to flicker. My blue-white wizard light, and the lambent glow of

Michael's sword were the only reliable sources of illumination in the room. My ears shrieked with the sudden lack of sound, though the dozen or so babies, in their cribs, continued a chorus of steady, terrified little wails.

'Are the children all right?' Michael asked. 'Where did it go?'

'I think so. The ghost must have crossed over,' I guessed. 'She knew she'd had it.'

Michael turned in a slow circle, sword still held at the ready. 'It's gone, then?'

I shook my head, scanning the room. 'I don't think so,' I responded, and bent over the crib of the infant girl who had nearly been smothered. The name on her wrist bracelet read Alison Ann Summers. I stroked her little cheek, and she turned her mouth toward my finger, baby lips fastening on my fingertip, cries dying.

'Take your finger out of her mouth,' Michael chided. 'It's dirty. What happens now?'

'I'll ward the room,' I said. 'And then we'll get out of here before the police show up and arres—'

Alison Ann jerked and stopped breathing. Her tiny arms and legs stiffened. I felt something cold pass over her, heard the distant drone of mad lullaby.

Hush little baby . . .

'Michael,' I cried. 'She's still here. The ghost, she's reaching here from the Nevernever.'

'Christ preserve,' Michael swore. 'Harry, we have to step over.'

My heart skipped a beat at the very thought. 'No,' I said. 'No way. This is a big spook, Michael. I'm not going to go onto her home ground naked and offer to go two out of three.'

'We don't have a choice,' Michael snapped. 'Look.'

I looked. The infants were falling silent, one by one, little cries abruptly smothered in mid-breath.

Hush little baby . . .

'Michael, she'll tear us apart. And even if she doesn't, my godmother *will*.'

Michael shook his head, scowling. 'No, by God. I won't let that happen.' He turned his gaze on me, piercing. 'And neither will you. Harry Dresden. There is too much good in your heart to let these children die.'

I returned his stare, uncertain. Michael had insisted that I look him in the eyes on our first meeting. When a wizard looks you in the eyes, it's serious. He can see inside of you, all of your dark secrets and hidden fears of your soul – and you see his in return. Michael's soul had made me weep. I wished that my soul would look liked his had to me. But I was pretty damned sure that it didn't.

Silence fell. All the little babies hushed.

I closed the sack of ghost dust and put it away in my pocket. It wouldn't do me any good in the Nevernever.

I turned toward my fallen rod and staff, thrust out my hand, and spat, '*Ventas servitas.*' The air stirred, and then flung staff and rod into my open hands before dying away again. 'All right,' I said. 'I'm tearing open a window that will give us five minutes. Hopefully, my godmother won't have time to find me. Anything beyond that and we're going to be dead already or back here, in my case.'

'You have a good heart, Harry Dresden,' Michael said, a fierce grin stretching his mouth. He stepped closer to my side. 'God will smile on this choice.'

'Yeah. Ask Him not to Sodom and Gomorrah my apartment, and we'll be even.'

Michael gave me a disappointed glance. I shot him a testy glare. He clamped a hand onto my shoulder and held on.

Then I reached out, caught hold of reality in my fingertips, and with an effort of will and a whispered, *'Aparturum,'* tore a hole between this world and the next.

3

Even days that culminate in a grand battle against an insane ghost and a trip across the border between this world and the spirit realm usually start out pretty normally. This one, for example, started off with breakfast and then work at the office.

My office is in a building in midtown Chicago. It's an older building, and not in the best of shape, especially since there was that problem with the elevator last year. I don't care what anyone says, that wasn't my fault. When a giant scorpion the size of an Irish wolfhound is tearing its way through the roof of your elevator car, you get real willing to take desperate measures.

Anyway, my office is small — one room, but on the corner, with a couple of windows. The sign on the door reads, simply, HARRY DRESDEN, WIZARD. Just inside the door is a table, covered with pamphlets with titles like: *Magic and You*, and *Why Witches Don't Sink Any Faster Than Anyone Else — a Wizard's Perspective*. I wrote most of them. I think it's important for we practitioners of the Art to keep up a good public image. Anything to avoid another Inquisition.

Behind the table is a sink, counter, and an old coffee machine. My desk faces the door, and a couple of comfortable chairs sit across from it. The air conditioning rattles, the ceiling fan squeaks on every revolution, and the scent of coffee is soaked into the carpet and the walls.

I shambled in, put coffee on, and sorted through the mail while the coffee percolated. A thank you letter from the Campbells, for chasing a spook out of their house. Junk mail. And, thank goodness, a check from the city for my last batch of work for the Chicago P.D. That had been a nasty case, all in all. Demon summoning, human sacrifice, black magic – the works.

I got my coffee and resolved to call Michael to offer to split my earnings with him – even though the legwork had been all mine, he and *Amoracchius* had come in on the finale. I'd handled the sorcerer, he'd dealt with the demon, and the good guys won the day. I'd turned in my logs and at fifty bucks an hour had netted myself a neat two grand. Michael would refuse the money (he always did) but it seemed polite to make the offer; especially given how much time we'd been spending together recently, in an attempt to track down the source of all the ghostly happenings in the city.

The phone rang before I could pick it up to call Michael. 'Harry Dresden,' I answered.

'Hello there, Mr Dresden,' said a warm, feminine voice. 'I was wondering if I could have a moment of your time.'

I kicked back in my chair, and felt a smile spreading over my face. 'Why, Miss Rodriguez, isn't it? Aren't you that nosy reporter from the *Arcane*? That useless rag that publishes stories about witches and ghosts and Bigfoot?'

'Plus Elvis,' she assured me. 'Don't forget the King. And I'm syndicated now. Publications of questionable reputation all over the world carry my column.'

I laughed. 'How are you today?'

Susan's voice turned wry. 'Well, my boyfriend stood me up last night, but other than that . . .'

I winced a little. 'Yeah, I know. Sorry about that. Look, Bob found a tip for me that just couldn't wait.'

'Ahem,' she said, in her polite, professional voice. 'I'm not calling you to talk about my *personal* life, Mr Dresden. This is a business call.'

I felt my smile returning. Susan was absolutely one in a million, to put up with me. 'Oh, beg pardon, Miss Rodriguez. Pray continue.'

'Well. I was thinking that there were rumors of some more ghostly activity in the old town last night. I thought you might be willing to share a few details with the *Arcane*.'

'Mmmm. That might not be wholly professional of me. I keep my business confidential.'

'Mr Dresden,' she said. 'I would as soon not resort to desperate measures.'

'Why, Miss Rodriguez.' I grinned. 'Are you a desperate woman?'

I could almost see the way she arched one eyebrow. 'Mr Dresden. I don't want to threaten you. But you must understand that I am well acquainted with a certain young lady of your company – and that I could see to it that things became *very* awkward between you.'

'I see. But if I shared the story with you—'

'Gave me an exclusive, Mr Dresden.'

'An exclusive,' I amended, 'then you might see your way clear to avoiding causing problems for me?'

'I'd even put in a good word with her,' Susan said, her voice cheerful, then dropping into a lower, smokier register. 'Who knows. You might get lucky.'

I thought about it for a minute. The ghost Michael and I had nailed last night had been a big, bestial thing lurking in the basement of the University of Chicago library. I didn't have to mention the names of any people involved, and while the university wouldn't like it, I doubted it would be seriously hurt by appearing in a magazine that most people bought along with every other tabloid in the supermarket checkout lines. Besides which, just the thought of Susan's caramel skin and soft, dark hair under my hands . . . Yum. 'That's an offer I can hardly refuse,' I told her. 'Do you have a pen?'

She did, and I spent the next ten minutes telling her the details. She took them down with a number of sharp, concise questions, and had the whole story out of me in less time than I would have believed. She really was a good reporter, I thought. It was almost a shame that she was spending her time reporting the supernatural, which people had been refusing to believe in for centuries.

'Thank you very much, Mr Dresden,' she said, after she squeezed the last drips of information out of me. 'I hope things go well between you and the young lady tonight. At your place. At nine.'

'Maybe the young lady would like to discuss the possibilities with me,' I drawled.

She let out a throaty laugh. 'Maybe she would,' Susan agreed. 'But this is a business call.'

I laughed. 'You're terrible, Susan. You never give up, do you?'

'Never, ever,' she said.

'Would you really have been mad at me if I hadn't told you?'

'Harry,' she said. 'You stood me up last night without a word. I don't usually stand for that kind of treatment from any man. If you hadn't had a good story for me, I was going to think that you were out horsing around with your friends.'

'Yeah, that Michael.' I chuckled. 'He's a real party animal.'

'You're going to have to give me the story on him sometime. Have you come any closer to working out what's going on with the ghosts? Did you look into the seasonal angle?'

I sighed, closing my eyes. 'No, and yes. I still can't figure why the ghosts seem to be freaking out all at once – and we haven't been able to get any of them to hold still long enough for me to get a good look at them. I've got a new recipe to try out tonight – maybe that will do it. But Bob is sure it isn't a Halloweeny kind of problem. I mean, we didn't have any ghosts last year.'

'No. We had werewolves.'

'Different situation entirely,' I said. 'I've got Bob working overtime to keep an eye on the spirit world for any more activity. If anything else is about to jump, we'll know it.'

'All right,' she said. She hesitated for a moment and then said, 'Harry. I—'

I waited, but when she stalled I asked, 'What?'

'I, uh . . . I just want to be sure that you're all right.'

I had the distinct impression that she had been going to say something else, but I didn't push. 'Tired,' I said. 'A couple of bruises from slipping on some ectoplasm and falling into a card catalog. But I'm fine.'

She laughed. 'That creates a certain image. Tonight then?'

'I'm looking forward to it.'

She made a pleased little sound with more than a hint of sexuality in it, and let that be her goodbye.

The day went fairly quickly, with a bunch of the usual business. I whipped up a spell to find a lost wedding ring, and turned down a customer who wanted me to put a love spell on his mistress. (My ad in the Yellow Pages specifically reads 'No love potions,' but for some reason people always think that their case is special.) I went to the bank, referred a caller to a private detective I knew, and met with a fledgling pyromancer in an attempt to teach him to stop igniting his cat accidentally.

I was just closing down the office when I heard someone come out of the elevator and start walking down the hallway toward me. The steps were heavy, as though from boots, and rushed.

'Mr Dresden?' asked a young woman's voice. 'Are you Harry Dresden?'

'Yes,' I said, locking the office door. 'But I'm just leaving. Maybe we can set up an appointment for tomorrow.'

The footsteps stopped a few feet away from me. 'Please, Mr Dresden. I've got to talk to you. Only you can help me.'

I sighed, without looking at her. She'd said the exact words she needed to in order to kick off my protective streak. But I could still walk away. Lots of people got to thinking that magic could dig them out of their troubles, once they realized they couldn't escape. 'I'll be glad to, Ma'am. First thing in the morning.' I locked the door and started to turn away.

'Wait,' she said. I felt her step closer to me, and she grabbed by hand.

A tingling, writhing sensation shot up my wrist and over my elbow. My reaction was immediate and instinctive. I

threw up a mental shield against the sensation, jerked my
hand clear of her fingers, and took several steps back and
away from the young woman.

My hand and arm still tingled from brushing against
the energy of her aura. She was a slight girl in a black
knit dress, black combat boots, and hair dyed to a flat,
black matte. The lines of her face were soft and sweet, and
her skin was pale as chalk around eyes that were sunken,
shadowed, and glittering with alley-cat wariness.

I flexed my fingers and avoiding meeting the girl's eyes
for more than a fraction of a second. 'You're a practitioner,'
I said, quietly.

She bit her lip and looked away, nodding. 'And I need
your help. They said that you would help me.'

'I give lessons to people who want to avoid hurting
themselves with uncontrolled talent,' I said. 'Is that what
you're after?'

'No, Mr Dresden,' the girl said. 'Not exactly.'

'Why me, then? What do you want?'

'I want your protection.' She lifted a shaking hand, fidg-
eting with her dark hair. 'And if I don't have it . . . I'm
not sure I'll live through the night.'

4

I let us both back into the office, and flicked on the lights. The bulb blew out. It does that a lot. I sighed, and shut the door behind us, leaving stripes of golden autumn light pouring through the blinds, interweaving with shadows on the floor and walls.

I drew out a seat in front of my desk for the young woman. She blinked at me in confusion for a second before she said, 'Oh,' and sat. I walked around the desk, leaving my duster on, and sat down.

'All right,' I said. 'If you want my protection, I want a few things from you first.'

She pushed back her asphalt-colored hair with one hand and gave me a look of pure calculation. Then she simply crossed her legs, so that the cut of her dress left one pale leg bare to mid-thigh. A subtle motion of her back thrust out her young, firm breasts, so that their tips pressed visibly against the fabric. 'Of course, Mr Dresden. I'm sure we can do business.' The look she gave me was direct, sensual, and willing.

Nipple erection on command – now that's method acting. Oh, she was pretty enough, I suppose. Any adolescent male would have been drooling and hurling himself at her, but I'd seen acts a lot better. I rolled my eyes. 'That's not what I meant.'

Her sex-kitten look faltered. 'It . . . it isn't?' She frowned at me, eyes scanning me again, reassessing me. 'Is it . . . are you . . . ?'

'No,' I said. 'I'm not gay. But I'm not buying what you're selling. You haven't even told me your name, but you're willing to spread your legs for me? No thanks. Hell's Bells, haven't you ever heard of AIDS? Herpes?'

Her face went white, and she pressed her lips together until they were white, too. 'All right, then,' she said. 'What do you want from me?'

'Answers,' I told her, jabbing a finger at her. 'And don't try lying to me. It won't do you any good.' Which was only a marginal lie, in itself. Being a wizard doesn't make you a walking lie detector, and I wasn't going to try a soulgaze on her to find out if she was sincere – it wasn't worth it. But another great thing about being a wizard is that people attribute just about anything you do to your vast and unknowable powers. Granted, it only works with those who know enough to believe in wizards, but not enough to understand our limits – the rest of the world, the regular people who think magic is just a joke, just look at you like someone is going to stuff you into a little white coat any second now.

She licked her lips, a nervous gesture, not a sexy one. 'All right,' she said. 'What do you want to know?'

'Your name, for starters.'

She let out a harsh laugh. 'You think I'm going to give you that, wizard?'

Point. Serious spell-slingers like me could do an awful lot with a person's name, given by their own lips. 'All right, then. What do I call you?'

She didn't bother to cover her leg again. A rather pretty

leg, actually, with a tattoo of some kind encircling her ankle. I tried not to notice. 'Lydia,' she said. 'Call me Lydia.'

'Okay, Lydia. You're a practitioner of the Art. Tell me about that.'

'It doesn't have anything to do with what I want from you, Mr Dresden,' she said. She swallowed, her anger fading. 'Please. I need your help.'

'All right, all right,' I said. 'What kind of help do you need? If you're into some kind of gang-related trouble, I'm going to recommend that you head for the police. I'm not a bodyguard.'

She shivered, and hugged herself with her arms. 'No, nothing like that. It's not my body I'm worried about.'

That made me frown.

She closed her eyes and drew in a breath. 'I need a talisman,' she said. 'Something to protect me from a hostile spirit.'

That made me sit up and take notice, metaphorically speaking. With the city flying into spiritual chaos as it was, I had no trouble believing that a girl gifted with magical talent might be experiencing some bad phenomena. Ghosts and spooks are drawn to the magically gifted. 'What kind of spirit?'

Her eyes shifted left and right, never looking at me. 'I can't really say, Mr Dresden. It's powerful and it wants to hurt me. They . . . they told me you could make something that would keep me safe.'

True, in point of fact. Around my left wrist at that very moment was a talisman made from a dead man's shroud, blessed silver, and a number of other, more difficult to come by ingredients. 'Maybe,' I told her. 'That depends on why you're in danger, and why you feel you need protection.'

'I c-can't tell you that,' she said. Her pale face pinched into an expression of worry – real worry, the kind that makes you look older, uglier. The way she hugged herself made her look smaller, more frail. 'Please, I just need your help.'

I sighed, and rubbed at one eyebrow with my thumb. My first rampant instincts were to give her a cup of hot chocolate, put a blanket around her shoulders, tell her everything would be all right and strap my talisman onto her wrist. I tried to rein those in, though. Down, Quixote. I still knew nothing about her situation, or what she needed protection from – for all I knew, she was trying to stave off an avenging angel coming after her in retribution for some act so vile that it stirred the Powers that be to take immediate action. Even vanilla ghosts sometimes come back to haunt someone for a darned good reason.

'Look, Lydia. I don't like to get involved in anything without knowing something about what's going on.' *Which hadn't slowed me down before*, I noted. 'Unless you can tell me a little bit about your situation, convince me that you are in legitimate need of protection, I won't be able to help you.'

She bowed her head, her asphalt hair falling across her face for a long minute. Then she drew in a breath and asked, 'Do you know what Cassandra's Tears is, Mr Dresden?'

'Prophetic condition,' I said. 'The person in question has random seizures – visions of the future, but they're always couched in terms of conditions that make explanation of the dreams seem unbelievable. Doctors mistake it for epilepsy in children, sometimes, and prescribe a bunch of different drugs for it. Pretty accurate prophecy, as it goes, but no one ever buys into it. Some people call it a gift.'

'I'm not one of them,' she whispered. 'You don't know how horrible it is. To see something about to happen and to try to change it, only to have no one believe you.'

I studied her for a minute in silence, listening to the clock on my wall count down the seconds. 'All right,' I said. 'You say that you have this gift. I guess you want me to believe that one of your visions warned you about an evil spirit coming after you?'

'Not one,' she said. 'Three. *Three*, Mr Dresden. I only got one vision when they tried to kill the President. I got two for that disaster at NASA, and for the earthquake in Laos. I've never had three before. Never had something appear so clearly . . .'

I closed my eyes to think about this. Again, my instincts told me to help the girl, smash the bad ghost or whatever, and walk off into the sunset. If she was indeed afflicted with Cassandra's Tears, my actions could do more than save her life. My faith could change it for the better.

On the other hand, I'd been played for a sucker before. The girl was obviously a competent actress. She had shifted smoothly to the role of willing seductress, when she thought I had been asking for sex in payment. That she would immediately make that conclusion based on my own fairly neutral statement said something about her, all by itself. This wasn't a girl who was used to playing things fair and square. Unless I was grossly misreading her, she had bartered sex for goods and services before – and she was awfully young to be so jaded about the entire matter.

The entire Cassandra's Tears angle was a perfect scam,

and people had used it before, among the circles of the magically endowed. The story required no proof, no performance on the part of the person running the scam. All she would need would be a smidgen of talent to give her the right aura, maybe enough kinetomancy to tilt the dice a little on their way down. Then she could make up whatever story she wanted about her supposed prophetic gifts, put on a little-girl-lost act, and head straight for the local dummy, Harry Blackstone Copperfield Dresden.

I opened my eyes to find her watching me. 'Of course,' she said. 'I could be lying. Cassandra's Tears can't be analyzed or observed. I could be using it as an excuse to provide a reasonable explanation why you should help a lady in distress.'

'That's pretty much what's going through my mind, Lydia, yeah. You could just be a small-time witch who stirred up the wrong demon and is looking for a way out.'

She spread her hands. 'All I can tell you is that I'm not. I know that something's coming. I don't know what, and I don't know why or how. I just know what I see.'

'Which is?'

'Fire,' she whispered. 'Wind. I see dark things and a dark war. I see my death coming for me, out of the spirit world. And I see you at the middle of it all. You're the beginning, the end of it. You're the one who can make the path go different ways.'

'*That's* your vision? Iowa has less corn.'

She turned her face away. 'I see what I see.'

Standard carny procedure. Flatter the ego of the mark, draw him in, get him good and hooked, and fleece him for everything he's got. Sheesh, I thought, someone else trying to get something out of me. My reputation must be growing.

Still, there was no sense in being rude. 'Look, Lydia. I think maybe you're just overreacting, here. Why don't we meet again in a couple of days, and we'll see if you still think you need my help.'

She didn't answer me. Her shoulders just slumped forward and her face went slack with defeat. She closed her eyes, and I felt a nagging sensation of doubt tug at me. I had the uncomfortable impression that she wasn't acting.

'All right,' she said, softly. 'I'm sorry to have kept you late.' She got up and started walking toward the door of my office.

My better judgement propelled me up out of my chair and across the room. We reached the door at the same time.

'Wait a minute,' I said. I unbound the talisman from my arm, feeling the silent *pop* of energy as the knot came undone. Then I took her left wrist and turned her hand over to tie the talisman onto her. There were pale scars on her arm – the vertical kind that run along the big veins. The ones you get when you're really serious about killing yourself. They were old and faded. She must have gotten them when she was . . . what? Ten years old? Younger?

I shuddered and secured the little braid of musty cloth and silver chain about her wrist, willing enough energy into it to close the circle once the knot was tied. When I finished, I touched her forearm lightly. I could just feel the talisman's power, a tingling sensation that hovered a half-inch off of her skin.

'Faith magic works best against spirits,' I said quietly. 'If you're worried, get to a church. Spirits are strongest just after the sun goes down, around the witching hour, and again just before the sun comes up. Go to Saint Mary of the Angels. It's a church at the corner of Bloomingdale and Wood, down by Wicker Park. It's huge, you can't miss it. Go around to the delivery door and ring the bell. Talk to Father Forthill. Tell him that Michael's friend said that you need a safe place to stay for a while.'

She only stared at me, her mouth open. Tears formed in her eyes. 'You believe me,' she said. 'You believe me.'

I shrugged, uncomfortable. 'Maybe. Maybe not. But things have been bad, the past few weeks, and I would rather not have you on my conscience. You'd better hurry. It's going to be sundown soon.' I pressed some bills into her hand and said, 'Take a cab. Saint Mary of the Angels. Father Forthill. Michael's friend sent you.'

'Thank you,' she said. 'Oh, God. Thank you, Mr Dresden.' She seized my hand in both of hers and pressed a tearstained kiss to my knuckles. Her fingers were cold and her lips too hot. Then she vanished out the door.

I shut it behind her and shook my head. 'Harry, you idiot. Your one decent talisman that would protect you against ghosts and you just gave it away. She's probably a plant. They probably sent her to you just to get the talisman off you, so that they can eat you up the next time you go spoil their fun.' I glared down at my hand, where the warmth of Lydia's kiss and the dampness of her tears still lingered. Then I sighed, and walked to the cabinet where I kept fifty or sixty spare light-bulbs on hand, and replaced the one that had burned out.

The phone rang. I got down off my chair and answered it sourly. 'Dresden.'

There was silence and scratchy static on the other end of the line.

'Dresden,' I repeated.

The silence stretched on, and something about it made the hairs on the back of my neck stand up. There was a quality to it that is difficult to describe. Like something waiting. Gloating. The static crackled louder, and I thought I could hear voices underneath it, voices speaking in low, cruel tones. I glanced at the door, after the departed Lydia. 'Who is this?'

'Soon,' whispered a voice. 'Soon, Dresden. We will see one another again.'

'Who is this?' I repeated, feeling a little silly.

The line went dead.

I stared at the phone before hanging it up, then ran my hand back through my hair. A chill crawled neatly down my spine and took up residence somewhere a little lower than my stomach. 'All right, then,' I said, my own voice a little too loud in the office. 'Thank God that wasn't too creepy or anything.'

The antique radio on the shelf beside the coffee machine hissed and squalled to life and I almost jumped out of my shoes. I whirled to face it in a fury, hands clenched.

'Harry?' said a voice on the radio. 'Hey, Harry, is this thing working?'

I tried to calm my pounding heart, and focused enough will on the radio to let my voice carry through. 'Yeah, Bob. It's me.'

'Thank the stars,' Bob said. 'You said you wanted to know if I found out anything else ghostly going on.'

'Yeah, yeah, go ahead.'

The radio hissed and crackled with static – spiritual interference, not physical. The radio wasn't set up to receive AM/FM any more. Bob's voice was garbled, but I could understand it. 'My contact came through. Cook County Hospital, tonight. Someone's stirred up Agatha Hagglethorn. This is a bad one, Harry. She is one mean old biddy.'

Bob gave me the rundown on Agatha Hagglethorn's grisly and tragic death, and her most likely target at the hospital. I glanced down at my bare left wrist, and abruptly felt naked. 'All right,' I said. 'I'm on it. Thanks, Bob.'

The radio squalled and went silent, and I dashed out the door. Sundown would come in less than twenty minutes, rush hour had been going for a while now, and if I wasn't at Cook County by the time it got dark, all kinds of bad things could happen.

I flew out the front door, the sack of ghost dust heavy in my pocket, and all but slammed into Michael, tall and broad, toting a huge athletic bag over his shoulder, which I knew would contain nothing but *Amoracchius* and his white cloak.

'Michael!' I burst out. 'How did you get here?'

His honest face split into a wide smile. 'When there is a need, He sees to it that I am there.'

'Wow,' I said. 'You're kidding.'

'No,' he said, his voice earnest. Then he paused. 'Of course, you've gotten in touch with me every night for the past two weeks. Tonight, I just thought I'd save Him the trouble of arranging coincidence, so I came on over as soon as I got off work.' He fell into step beside me and we both got into the Blue Beetle – he got in the red door, I got in the white one, and we peered out over the grey hood as I pulled the old VW into traffic.

And that was how we ended up doing battle in the nursery at Cook County.

Anyway, you see what I mean about a day being fairly normal before it falls all to pieces. Or, well. Maybe it hadn't been all that normal. As we took off into traffic and I gave the Beetle all the gas it could take, I got that sinking feeling that my life was about to get hectic again.

5

Michael and I plunged through the hole I'd torn in reality and into the Nevernever. It felt like moving from a sauna into an air-conditioned office, except that I didn't feel the change my skin. I felt it in my thoughts and my feelings, and in the primitive, skin-crawling part of me at the base of my brain. I stood in a different world than our own.

The little leather sack of ghost dust in my duster pocket abruptly increased its weight, dragging me off balance and to the ground. I let out a curse. The whole point of the ghost dust was that it was something extra-real, that it was heavy and inert and locked spiritual matter into place when it touched it. Even inside its bag, it had become a sudden stress on the Nevernever. If I opened the bag here, in the world of spirit, it might tear a hole in the floor. I'd have to be careful. I grunted with effort and pulled the little pouch out of my pocket. It felt like it weighed thirty or forty pounds.

Michael frowned down at my hands. 'You know. I never really thought to ask before – but what *is* that dust made of?'

'Depleted uranium,' I told him. 'At least, that's the base ingredient. I had to add in a lot of other things. Cold iron, basil, dung from a—'

'Never mind,' he said. 'I don't want to know.' He turned away from me, his arms steadily holding the massive sword before him. I recovered staff and rod, and stood beside him, studying the lay of the as-it-were land.

This part of the Nevernever looked like Chicago, at the end of the nineteenth century – no, strike that. This was the ghost's demesne. It looked like a mishmash of Agatha Hagglethorn's memories of Chicago at the end of her life. Edison's bulbs were mounted in some of the streetlights, while others burned with flickering gas flames. All of them cast hazy spheres of light, doing little to actually illuminate their surroundings. The buildings stood at slightly odd angles to one another, with parts of them seamlessly missing. Everything – streets, sidewalks, buildings – was made of wood.

'Hell's bell,' I muttered. 'No wonder the real Chicago kept burning down. This place is a tinderbox.'

Rats moved in the shadows, but the street was otherwise empty and still. The rift that led back to our world wavered and shifted, fluorescent light and sterile hospital air pouring onto the old Chicago streets. Around us pulsed maybe a dozen shimmering disturbances in the air – the rich life forces of the infants back in the infirmary, showing through into the Nevernever.

'Where is she?' Michael asked, his voice quiet. 'Where's the ghost?'

I turned in a slow circle, peering at the shadows, and shook my head. 'I don't know. But we'd better find her, fast. And we need to get a look at this one if we can.'

'To try to find out what's gotten it stirred up,' Michael said.

'Exactly. I don't know about you, but I'm getting a little tired of chasing all over town every night.'

'Didn't you already get a look at her?'

'Not the right kind of look,' I said with a grimace. 'There could be spells laid on her, some kind of magic around her to clue me in on what's going on. I need to be not in mortal peril for a couple of minutes to examine her.'

'Provided she doesn't kill us first, all right,' Michael assented. 'But time is short, and I don't see her anywhere. What should we do?'

'I hate to say it,' I said, 'but I think we should—'

I was going to say 'split up,' but I didn't get the chance. The heavy wooden timbers of the roadway beneath us exploded up and out in a deadly cloud of splinters. I threw one leather-clad arm across my eyes and went tumbling one way. Michael went the other.

'My little angels! Mine, mine, MINE!' screamed a voice that roared against my face and chest and made my duster flap around as though made of gauze.

I looked up, to see the ghost, quite real and solid now, clawing its one-armed way up from the substreet. Agatha's face was lean and bony, twisted in rage, and her hair hung about her in a shaggy mane, sharply at odds with her crisp white shirt. Her arm was missing from its shoulder, and dark fluid stained the cloth beneath it.

Michael rose to his feet with a shout, one of his cheeks cut and bleeding, and went after her with *Amoracchius*. The spirit backhanded him away with her remaining arm as though he weighed no more than a doll. Michael grunted and went flying, rolling along the wooden street.

And then, snarling and drooling, her eyes wide with frenzied madness, the ghost turned toward me.

I scrambled to my feet and held out my staff across my body, a slender barrier between me and the ghost on its home turf. 'I guess it's too late to have a reasonable discussion, Agatha.'

'My babies!' the spirit screamed. 'Mine! Mine! Mine!'

'Yeah, that's what I thought,' I breathed. I gathered my forces and started channeling them through the staff. The pale wood began glowing with a gold-and-orange light, spreading out before me in a quarter-dome shape.

The ghost screamed again and hurtled toward me. I stood fast and shouted, *'Reflettum!'* at the top of my lungs. The spirit impacted against my shield with all the momentum of a bull rhinoceros on steroids. I've stopped bullets and worse with that shield before, but that was on my home turf, in the real world. Here, the Nevernever, Agatha's ghost overloaded my shield, which detonated with a thunderous roar and sent me sprawling to the ground. Again.

I jammed my scorched staff into the ground and groaned to my feet. Blood stained my tingling fingers, the skin swelling with dark bruises and burst blood vessels.

Agatha stood several paces away, shaking with rage, or if I was lucky, with confusion. Bits of my shield-fire played over her shape and slowly winked out. I fumbled for my blasting rod, but my fingers had gone numb and I dropped it. I bent over to pick it up, swayed, and stood up again, red mist and sparkling dots swimming through my vision.

Michael circled the stunned spirit and arrived at my side. His expression was concerned, rather than frightened. 'Easy, Harry, easy. Good Lord, man, are you all right?'

'I'll make it,' I croaked. 'There's good news and bad news.'

The knight brought his sword to guard again. 'I've always been partial to the good news.'

'I don't think she's interested in those babies anymore.'

Michael flashed me a swift smile. 'That *is* good news.'

I wiped some sweat from my eyes. My hand came away scarlet. I must have gotten a cut, somewhere along the way. 'The bad news is that she's going to come over here and tear us apart in a couple more seconds.'

'Not to be negative, but I'm afraid the news gets worse,' Michael said. 'Listen.'

I glanced at him, and cocked my head to one side. Distantly, but quickly growing nearer, I could hear haunting, musical baying, ghostly in the midnight air. 'Holy shit,' I breathed. 'Hellbounds.'

'Harry,' Michael said sternly. 'You know I hate it when you swear.'

'You're right. Sorry. Holy shit,' I breathed, 'heckhounds. Godmother's out hunting. How the hell did she find us so damned fast?'

Michael grimaced at me. 'She must have been close already. How long before she gets here?'

'Not long. My shield made a lot of noise when it buckled. She'll home in on it.'

'If you want to go, Harry,' Michael said, 'go on and leave. I'll hold the ghost until you can get back through the rift.'

I was tempted. There aren't a lot of things that scare me more than the Nevernever and my godmother in tandem. But I was also angry. I hate it when I get shown up. Besides, Michael was a friend, and I'm not in the habit of leaving friends to clean up my messes for me. 'No,' I said. 'Let's just hurry.'

Michael grinned at me, and started forward, just as Agatha's ghost extinguished the last residual bits of my magic that had been plaguing it. Michael send *Amoracchius* whistling at the ghost, but she was unthinkably swift, and dodged each blow with a circling, swooping sort of grace. I lifted my blasting rod and narrowed my focus. I tuned out the baying of the hell-hounds, now a lot nearer, and the sound of galloping hoofbeats that sent my pulse racing. I methodically blanked out everything but the ghost, Michael, and the power funneling into the blasting rod.

The ghost must have sensed the strike gathering, because she turned and flew at me like a bullet. Her mouth opened in a scream, and I could see jagged, pointed teeth lining her jaws, the empty white fire of her eyes.

'Fuego!' I shouted, and then the spirit hit me, full force. A beam of white fire spewed out from my blasting rod and across the wooden storefronts. They burst into flame as though soaked in gasoline. I went down, rolling, the spirit going after my throat with her teeth. I jammed the end of the blasting rod into her mouth and prepared to fire again, but she tore it from my hands with a ferocious dog-like worrying motion and it tumbled away. I swiped the staff at her awkwardly, to no avail. She went for my throat again.

I shoved a leather-clad forearm into her mouth and shouted, 'Michael!' The ghost ripped at me with her nails and clamped down on my forearm. I dropped the ghost dust and scrabbled furiously at her with my free hand, trying to lever her off of me, but didn't do much more than muss up her clothing.

She got her hand on my throat and I felt my breath cut off. I writhed and struggled to escape, but the snarling ghost was a lot stronger and faster than me. Stars swam in front of my eyes.

Michael shouted, and swept *Amoracchius* at the spirit. The great blade bit into her back with a wooden-sounding thunk and made her arch up, screaming in pain. It was a deathblow. The white light of the blade touched her spirit-flesh and set it alight, sizzling away from the edges of the wound. She twisted, screaming in fury, and the motion jerked the blade from Michael's hands. Agatha Hagglethorn's blazing ghost prepared to fly at his throat.

I sat up, seized the sack of ghost dust, and with a grunt of effort swept it at the back of her head. There was a sharp sound when the improvised cosh struck her, the superheavy matter I'd enchanted hitting like a sledge-hammer on china. The ghost froze in place for a moment, her feral mouth wide – and then toppled slowly to one side.

I looked up at Michael, who stood gasping for breath, staring at me. 'Harry,' he said. 'Do you see?'

I lifted a hand to my aching throat and looked around me. The sounds of baying hounds and thundering hooves had gone. 'See what?' I asked.

'Look.' He pointed at the smoldering ghost-corpse.

I looked. In my struggles with Agatha's ghost, I had torn aside the prim white shirt, and she must have ripped up the dress when she'd been crashing through sidewalks and strangling wizards and so on. I crawled a bit closer to the corpse. It was burning – not blazing, but steadily being eaten away by *Amoracchius*'s white fire, like newsprint slowly curling into flame. The fire didn't hide what Michael was talking about, though.

Wire. Strands of barbed wire ran about the ghost's flesh, beneath her torn clothing. The barbs had dug cruelly into her flesh every two inches or so, and her body was covered with small, agonizing wounds. I grimaced, picking away at the burning cloth in tentative jerks. The wire was a single strand that began at her throat and wrapped about her torso, beneath the arms, winding all the way down one leg to her ankle. At either end, the wire simply vanished into her flesh.

'Sun and stars,' I breathed. 'No wonder she went mad.'

'The wire,' Michael asked, crouching down next to me. 'It was hurting the ghost?'

I nodded. 'Looks like. Torturing it.'

'Why didn't we see this in the hospital?'

I shook my head. 'Whatever this is . . . I'm not sure it would be visible in the real world. I don't think we would have seen it if we hadn't come here.'

'God smiled on us,' Michael said.

I eyed my own injuries, then glowered at the bruises already spreading over Michael's arm and throat. 'Yeah, whatever. Look, Michael – this kind of thing doesn't just happen. Someone had to do it to this ghost.'

'Which implies,' Michael said, 'that they had a reason to want this ghost to hurt those children.' His face darkened into a scowl.

'Whether or not that was their goal, what it implies is that some*one* is behind all the recent activity – not some thing or condition. Someone is purposefully doing this to the ghosts in the area.' I stood up and brushed myself off, as the corpse continued to burn, like the buildings around us. Fire raged up the sides of anything vertical, and began to chew its way across the streets and sidewalks as well. A haze of smoke filled the air, as the spirit's demesne in the Nevernever crumbled along with its remains.

'Ow,' I complained. I keep my complaints succinct.

Michael took the handle of his sword and drew it out of the flames, shaking his head. 'The city is burning.'

'Thank you, Sir Obvious.'

He smiled. 'Can the flames hurt us?'

'Yes,' I said, emphatic. 'Time to go.'

Together, we headed back to the rift at a quick trot. At one point, Michael shouldered me out of the way of a tumbling chimney, and we had to skirt around the pile of shattered bricks and blazing timbers.

'Wait,' I said suddenly. 'Wait. Do you hear that?'

Michael kept me hustling over the ground, toward the rift. 'Hear what? I don't hear anything.'

'Yeah.' I coughed. 'No more hounds howling.'

A very tall, slender, inhumanly beautiful woman stepped out of the smoke. Reddish hair curled down past her hips in a riotous cascade, complementing her flawless skin, high cheekbones, and lush, full, bloodred lips. Her face was ageless, and her golden eyes had vertical slits instead of pupils, like a cat. Her gown was a flowing affair of deep green.

'Hello, my son,' Lea purred, evidently unaffected by the smoke and unconcerned about the fire. Three great shapes, like mastiffs built from shadows and soot, crouched about her feet, watching us with flat, black eyes. They stood between us and the rift that led back home.

I swallowed and forced down a sudden feeling of child-like panic that started gibbering down in my belly and threatened to come dancing up out of my throat. I stepped forward, between the faerie and Michael and said, in a rough voice, 'Hello, Godmother.'

6

My godmother looked around at the inferno and smiled. 'It reminds me of times gone by. Doesn't it remind you, my sweet?' She idly reached down and stroked the head of one of the hounds at her side.

'However did you find me so quickly, Godmother?' I asked.

She gave the hellhound a benign smile. 'Mmmm. I have my little secrets, sweet. I only wanted to greet my long-estranged godson.'

'All right. Hi, good to see you, have to do it again sometime,' I said. Smoke curled up into my mouth and I started coughing. 'We're kind of in a hurry here, so—'

Lea laughed, a sound like bells just a shade out of tune. 'Always in such a rush, you mortals. But we haven't seen each other in ages, Harry.' She walked closer, her body moving with a lithe, sensuous grace that might have been mesmerizing in other circumstances. The hounds spread out silently behind her. 'We should spend some time together.'

Michael lifted his sword again, and said, calmly, 'Madame, step from our path, if you please.'

'It does *not* please me,' she spat, sudden and vicious. Those rich lips peeled back from dainty, sharp canines, and at the same time the three shadowy hounds let out bubbling growls. Her golden eyes swept past Michael and back to me. 'He is mine, sir Knight, by blood right, by

Law, and by his own broken word. He has made a compact with me. You have no power over that.'

'Harry?' Michael shot me a quick look. 'Is what she says true?'

I licked my lips, and gripped my staff. 'I was a lot younger, then. And a lot more stupid.'

'Harry, if you have made a covenant with her of your own free will then she is right – there is little I can do to stop her.'

Another building fell with a roar. The fires gathered around us, and it got hot. Really, really hot. The rift wavered, growing smaller. We didn't have much time left.

'Come, Harry,' Lea purred, her voice gone, pardon the pun, smoky again. 'Let the good Knight of the White God pass on his way. And let me take you to waters that will soothe your hurts and balm your ills.'

It sounded like a good idea. It sounded *really* good. Her own magic saw to that. I felt my feet moving toward her in a slow, leaden shuffling.

'Dresden,' Michael said, sharply. 'Good Lord, man! What are you doing?'

'Go home, Michael,' I said. My voice came out thick, dull, as though I'd been drinking. I saw Lea's mouth, her soft, lovely mouth, curl upward in a triumphant smirk. I didn't try to fight the pull of the magic. I wouldn't have been able to stop my legs in any case. Lea'd had my number for years, and as far as I could tell she always would. I hadn't a prayer of taking control back for more than a few seconds. The air grew cooler as I got closer to her, and I could smell her – her body, her hair, like wildflowers and musky earth, intoxicating. 'There isn't much time before the rift closes. Go home.'

'Harry!' Michael shouted.

Lea placed one long-fingered, slender hand upon my cheek. A wash of tingling pleasure went through me. My body reacted to her, helpless and demanding at the same time, and I had to fight to keep thoughts of her beauty from preoccupying me altogether.

'Yes, my sweet man,' Lea whispered, golden eyes bright with glee. 'Sweet, sweet, sweet. Now, lay aside your rod and staff.'

I watched dully, as my fingers released both. They clattered to the ground. The flames grew closer, but I didn't feel them. The rift glowed and shrank, almost closed. I narrowed my eyes, gathering my will.

'Will you complete your bargain now, sweet mortal child?' Lea murmured, sliding her hands over my chest and then over my shoulders.

'I will go with you,' I answered, letting my voice come out thick, slow. Her eyes lit with malicious glee, and she threw her head back and laughed, revealing creamy, delicious expanses of throat and bosom.

'When Hell freezes over,' I added, and drew out the little sack of ghost dust for the last time. I dumped it all over and down the previously mentioned bosom. There isn't much lore about faeries and depleted uranium, yet, but there's a ton about faeries and cold iron. They don't like it, and the iron content of the dust's formula was pretty high.

Lea's flawless complexion immediately split into fiery scarlet welts, the skin drying and cracking before my eyes. Lea's triumphant laugh turned into an agonized scream, and she released me, tearing her silken gown away from her chest in a panic, revealing more gorgeous flesh being riven by the cold iron.

'Michael,' I shouted, 'now!' I gave my godmother a stiff shove, scooped up my staff and rod, and dove for the rift. I heard a snarl, and something fastened around one of my boots, dragging me to the ground. I thrust my staff down at one of the hellhounds, and the wood struck it in one of its eyes. It roared in rage, and its two pack mates came rushing toward me.

Michael stepped in the way and swept his sword at one of them. The true iron struck the faerie beast, and blood and white fire erupted from the wound. The second one leapt upon Michael and fastened its fangs onto his thigh, ripping and jerking.

I brought my staff down hard on the beast's skull, driving it off Michael's leg, and started dragging my friend back toward the swiftly vanishing line of the rift. More hellhounds appeared, rushing from the burning ruins around us. 'Come on!' I shouted. 'There's no time!'

'Treacher!' spat my godmother. She rose up from the ground, blackened and burned, her fine dress in tatters about her waist, her body and limbs stretched, knobby, and inhuman. She clenched her hands into fists at her sides, and the fire from the building around us seemed to rush down, gathering in her grasp in a pair of blazing points of violet and emerald light. 'Treasonous, poisonous child! You are mine as your mother swore unto me! As you swore!'

'You shouldn't make contracts with a minor!' I shouted back, and shoved Michael forward, into the rift. He wavered for a moment on the narrow opening, and then fell through and vanished back into the real world.

'If you will not give me your life, serpent child, then I will have your *blood*!' Lea took two huge strides toward me and hurled both hands forward. A thunderbolt of braided emerald and violet power rushed at my face.

I hurled myself backwards, at the rift, and prayed that it was still open enough to let me fall through. I extended my staff toward my godmother and threw up whatever weak shield I could. The faerie fire hammered into the shield, hurling me back into the rift like a straw before a tornado. I felt my staff smolder and burst into flames in my hand as I went sailing through.

I landed on the floor of the nursery back in Cook County Hospital, my leather duster trailing with it a shroud of smoke that swiftly converted itself to a thin, disgusting coating of residual ectoplasm, while my staff burned with weird green and purple fire. Babies, in their little glass cribs, screamed lustily all around me. Confused voices babbled from the next room.

Then the rift closed, and we were left back in the real world, surrounded by crying babies. The fluorescent lights all came back up, and we could hear more worried words from the nurses back at the duty station. I beat out the fires on my staff, and then sat there, panting and hurting. None of the matter of the Nevernever may have come back to the real world – but the injuries gained there were very real.

Michael got up, and looked around at the babies, making sure that they were all in satisfactory condition. Then he sat down next to me, wiped the patina of ectoplasm from his brow, and started pressing the material of his cloak against the oozing gashes in his leg, where the hellhound's fangs had sunk through his jeans. He gave me a pensive, frowning stare.

'What?' I asked him.

'Your godmother. You got away from her,' he said.

I laughed, weakly. 'This time, yeah. So what's bothering you?'

'You lied to her to do it.'

'I tricked her,' I countered. 'Classic tactics with faeries.'

He blinked, and then used another section of his cloak to clean the ecto-gook off of *Amoracchius*. 'I just thought you were an honest man, Harry,' he said, his expression injured. 'I can't believe you lied to her.'

I started to laugh, weakly, too exhausted to move. 'You can't believe I lied to her.'

'Well, no,' he said, his voice defensive. 'That's not the way we're supposed to win. We're the good guys, Harry.'

I laughed some more, and wiped a trickle of blood off of my face.

'Well, we are!'

Some kind of alarm started going off. One of the nurses stepped into the observation room, took one look at the pair of us, and ran out screaming.

'You know what bothers me?' I asked.

'What's that?'

I set my scorched staff and rod aside. 'I'm wondering how in the world my godmother happened to be right at hand, when I stepped through into Nevernever. It isn't like the place is a small neighborhood. I wasn't there five minutes before she showed up.'

Michael sheathed his sword and set it carefully aside, out of easy arm's reach. Then unfastened his cloak, wincing. 'Yes. It seems an unlikely coincidence.'

We both put our hands up on top of our heads, as a Chicago P.D. patrolman, his jacket and pants stained with spilled coffee, burst into the nursery, gun drawn. We both sat there with our hands on our head, and did our best to look friendly and non-threatening.

'Don't worry,' Michael said, quietly. 'Just let me do the talking.'

7

Michael rested his chin in his hands and sighed. 'I can't believe we're in jail.'

'Disturbing the peace,' I snorted, pacing the confines of the holding cell. 'Trespass. Hah. They'd have seen disturbed peace if we hadn't shown up.' I jerked a fistful of citations out of my pants pocket. 'Look at this. Speeding, failure to obey traffic signs, dangerous and reckless operation of a motor vehicle. And here's the best one. Illegal *parking*. I'm going to lose my license!'

'You can't blame them, Harry. It isn't as though we could explain what happened in terms that they would understand.'

I kicked at the bars in frustration. Pain lanced up my leg and I immediately regretted it – they'd taken away my boots when I'd been put through processing. Added to my aching ribs, the wounds on my head, and my stiffening fingers, it was too much. I sat down on the bench next to Michael with a *whuff* of expelled breath. 'I get so sick of that,' I said. 'People like you and me stand up to things that these jokers' – I made an all-encompassing gesture – 'would never even dream existed. We don't get paid for it, we hardly even get thanked for it.'

Michael's tone was unruffled, philosophical. 'It's the nature of the beast, Harry.'

'I don't mind it so much. I just hate it when something like this happens.' I stood up, frustrated again, and started pacing the interior of the cell. 'What really galls me is that we still don't know why the spirit world's been so jumpy. This is big, Michael. If we don't pin down what's causing it—'

'Who's causing it.'

'Right, who's causing it – who knows what could happen.'

Michael half-smiled. 'The Lord will never give you a burden bigger than your shoulders can bear, Harry. All we can do is face what comes and have faith.'

I gave him a sour glance. 'I need to get myself some bigger shoulders, then. Someone in accounting must have made a mistake.'

Michael let out a rough, warm laugh, and shook his head, then lay back on the bench, crossing his arms beneath his head. 'We did what was right. Isn't that enough?'

I thought of all those babies, snuffling and making cute, piteous little sounds as the nurses had rushed about, gathering them up and making sure that they were all right, carrying them off to their mommies. One, a fat little Gerber candidate, had simply let out an enormous burp and promptly fallen asleep on the nurse's shoulder. About a dozen little lives, all told, with an open future laid out before them – a future that would have abruptly ended if I hadn't acted.

I felt a stupid little smile playing at the corners of my mouth, and a very small, very concrete sense of satisfaction that my indignation hadn't managed to erase. I turned away from Michael, so that he wouldn't see the smile, and forced myself to sound resigned. 'Is it enough? I guess it's going to have to be.'

Michael laughed again. I flashed him a scowl, and it

only drew more merry laughter, so I gave up trying, and just leaned against the bars. 'How long before we get out of here, do you think?'

'I've never been bailed out of jail before,' Michael said. 'You'd be a better judge.'

'Hey,' I protested, 'what's that supposed to mean?'

Michael's smile faded. 'Charity,' he predicted, 'is not going to be very happy.'

I winced. Michael's wife. 'Yeah, well. All we can do is face what comes and have faith, right?'

Michael grunted, somehow making it wry. 'I'll say a prayer to Saint Jude.'

I leaned my head against the bars and closed my eyes. I ached in places I didn't know could ache. I could have dozed off right there. 'All I want,' I said, 'is to get home, get clean, and go to sleep.'

An hour or so later, a uniformed officer appeared and opened the door, informing us that we'd made bail. I got a sickly little feeling in my stomach. Michael and I shuffled out of the holding area into the adjacent waiting room.

A woman in a roomy dress and a heavy cardigan stood waiting for us, her arms folded over her seventh or eighth month of pregnancy. She was tall, with gorgeous, silken blonde hair that fell to her waist in a shining curtain, timelessly lovely features, and dark eyes smoldering with contained anger. 'Michael Joseph Patrick Carpenter,' she snapped, and stalked toward us. Well, actually she waddled, but the set of her shoulders and her determined expression made it seem like a stalk. 'You're a mess. This is what comes of taking up with bad company.'

'Hello, angel,' Michael rumbled, and leaned over to give the woman a kiss on the cheek.

She accepted it with all the loving tolerance of a Komodo dragon. 'Don't you hello angel me. Do you know what I had to go through to find a baby-sitter, get all the way out here, get the money together and then get the sword back for you?'

'Hi Charity,' I said brightly. 'Gee, it's good to see you, too. It's been, what, three or four years since we've talked?'

'Five years, Mr Dresden,' the woman said, shooting me a glare. 'And the Good Lord willing it will be five more before I have to put up with your idiocy again.'

'But I—'

She thrust her swollen stomach at me like the ram on a Greek warship. 'Every time you come nosing around, you get Michael into some sort of trouble. And now into jail! What will the children think?'

'Look, Charity, it was really imp—'

'*Missus* Carpenter,' she snarled. 'It's *always* really important, Mr Dresden. Well, my husband has engaged in many important activities without what I dubiously term your "help." But it's only when you're around that he seems to come back to me covered in blood.'

'Hey,' I protested. 'I got hurt too!'

'Good,' she said. 'Maybe it will make you more cautious in the future.'

I scowled down at the woman. 'I'll have you know—'

She grabbed the front of my shirt and dragged my face down to hers. She was surprisingly strong, and she could glare right at me without looking me square in the eyes. 'I'll have *you* know,' she said, voice steely, 'that if you *ever* get my Michael into trouble so deep that he can't come home to his family I will make you sorry for it.' Tears that had nothing to do with weakness made her eyes bright for a moment, and she shook with emotion. I have to admit, at that particular moment, her threat scared me, waddling pregnancy and all.

She finally released me and turned back to her husband, gently touching a dark scab on his face. Michael put his arms around her, and with a little cry she hugged him back, burying her face against his chest and weeping without making any sound. Michael held her very carefully, as if he were afraid of breaking her, and stroked her hair.

I stood there for a second like a floundering goob. Michael looked up at me and met my gaze for a moment. He then turned, keeping his wife under one arm, and started walking away.

I watched the two of them for a moment, walking in step beside one another, while I stood there alone. Then I stuck my hands into my pockets, and turned away. I hadn't ever noticed, before, how well the two of them matched one another – Michael with his quiet strength and unfailing reliability, and Charity with her blazing passion and unshakeable loyalty to her husband.

The married thing. Sometimes I look at it and feel like someone from a Dickens novel, standing outside in the cold and staring in at Christmas dinner. Relationships hadn't ever really worked for me. I think it's had something to do with all the demons, ghosts, and human sacrifice.

As I stood there, brooding, I sensed her presence before I smelled her perfume, a warmth and energy about her that I'd grown to know over the time we'd been together. Susan paused at the door of the waiting room, looking back over her shoulder. I studied her. I never got tired of that. Susan had dark skin, tanned even darker from our previous weekend at the beach, and raven-black hair cut off neatly at her shoulders. She was slender, but curved enough to draw an admiring look from the officer behind the counter as she stood there in a flirty little skirt and half-top which left her midriff bare. My phone call caught her just as she'd been leaving for our rendezvous.

She turned to me and smiled, her chocolate-colored eyes worried but warm. She tilted her head back toward the hallway behind her, where Michael and Charity had gone. 'They're a beautiful couple, aren't they?'

I tried to smile back, but didn't do so well. 'They got off to a good start.'

Susan's eyes studied my face, the cuts there, and the worry in her eyes deepened. 'Oh? How's that?'

'He rescued her from a fire-breathing dragon.' I walked toward her.

'Sounds nice,' she said, and met me halfway, giving me a long and gentle hug that made my bruised ribs ache. 'You okay?'

'I'll be okay.'

'More ghostbusting with Michael. What's his story?'

'Off the record. Publicity could hurt him. He's got kids.'

Susan frowned, but nodded. 'All right,' she said, and added a flair of melodrama to her words. 'So what is he? Some kind of eternal soldier? Maybe a sleeping Arthurian knight woken in this desperate age to battle the forces of evil?'

'As far as I know he's a carpenter.'

Susan arched a brow at me. 'Who fights ghosts. What, has he got a magic nailgun or something?'

I tried not to smile. The muscles at the corners of my mouth ached. 'Not quite. He's a righteous man.'

'He seemed nice enough to me.'

'No, not self-righteous. Righteous. The real deal. He's honest, loyal, faithful. He lives his ideals. It gives him power.'

Susan frowned. 'He looked average enough. I'd have expected . . . I'm not sure. Something. A different attitude.'

'That's because he's humble too,' I said. 'If you asked him if he was righteous, he'd laugh at the idea. I guess that's part of it. I've never met anyone like him. He's a good man.'

She pursed her lips. 'And the sword?'

'*Amoracchius,*' I supplied.

'He named his sword. How very Freudian of him. But his wife just about reached down that clerk's throat to get it back.'

'It's important to him,' I said. 'He believes that it is one of three weapons given by God to mankind. Three swords. Each of them has a nail that is supposed to be from the Cross worked into its design. Only one of the righteous can wield them. The ones who do call themselves the Knights of the Cross. Others call them the Knights of the Sword.'

Susan frowned. '*The* Cross?' she said. 'As in *the* Crucifixion, capital *C*?'

I shrugged, uncomfortably. 'How should I know? Michael believes it. That kind of belief is a power of its own. Maybe that's enough.' I took a breath and changed the subject. 'Anyway, my car got impounded. I had to drive fast and C.P.D. didn't like it.'

Her dark eyes sparkled. 'Anything worth a story?'

I laughed tiredly. 'Don't you ever give up?'

'A girl's got to earn a living,' she said, and fell into step beside me on the way out, slipping her arm through mine.

'Maybe tomorrow? I just want to get back home and get some sleep.'

'No date, I guess.' She smiled up at me, but I could see the expression was strained around the edges.

'Sorry. I—'

'I know.' She sighed. I shortened my steps a little and she lengthened hers, though neither of us moved quickly. 'I know what you're doing is important, Harry. I just wish, sometimes, that—' She broke off, frowning.

'That what?'

'Nothing. Really. It's selfish.'

'That what?' I repeated. I found her hand with my bruised fingers and squeezed gently.

She signed, and stopped in the hall, turning to face me. She took both of my hands, and didn't look up when she said, 'I just wish that I could be that important to you, too.'

An uncomfortable pang hit me in the middle of my sternum. Ow. It hurt to hear that, literally. 'Susan,' I stammered. 'Hey. Don't ever think that you're not important to me.'

'Oh,' she said, still not looking up, 'it's not that. Like I said, just selfish. I'll get over it.'

'I just don't want you to feel like . . .' I frowned and took a breath. 'I don't want you to think that I don't . . . What I mean to say is that I . . .' *Love you.* That should have been simple enough to say. But the words stuck hard in my throat. I'd never said them to anyone I didn't lose, and every time I told my mouth to make the sounds, something shut down somewhere along the way.

Susan looked up at me, her eyes flickering over my face. She reached up a hand and touched the bandage on my forehead, her fingers light, gentle, warm. Silence fell heavy on the hallway. I stood there staring stupidly at her.

Finally, I leaned down and kissed her, hard, like I was trying to push the words out of my useless mouth and into her. I don't know if she understood, but she melted to me, all warm, soft tension, smelling of cinnamon, the sweetness of her lips soft and pliant beneath mine. One of my hands drifted to the small of her back, to the smooth, rounded ridges of muscle on either side of her spine, and drew her against me a little harder.

Footsteps coming from the other direction made us both smile and break away from the kiss. A female officer walked by, her lips twisted into a knowing little smirk, and I felt my cheeks flush.

Susan took my hand from her back, bending her mouth to put a gentle kiss on my bruised fingers. 'Don't think you're getting off that easy, Harry Dresden,' she said. 'I'm going to get you to start talking if it kills you,' But she didn't press the issue, and together we reclaimed my stuff and left.

I fell asleep on the drive back to my apartment, but I woke up when the car crunched into the gravel parking lot beside the stone stairs leading down to my lair, in the basement of an old boardinghouse. We got out of the car, and I stretched, looking around the summer night with a scowl.

'What's wrong?' Susan asked.

'Mister,' I said. 'He's usually running right up to me when I come home. I let him out early this morning.'

'He's a cat, Harry,' Susan said, flashing me a smile. 'Maybe he's got a date.'

'What if he got hit by a car? What if a dog got him?'

Susan let out a laugh and walked over to me. My libido noted the sway of her hips in the little skirt with an interest that made my aching muscles cringe. 'He's as big as a horse, Harry. I pity the dog that tries something.'

I reached back into the car for my staff and rod, then slipped an arm around her. Susan's warmth beside me, the scent of cinnamon drifting up to me from her hair, felt incredibly nice at the end of a long day. But it just didn't feel right, to not have Mister run up to me and bowl into my shins in greeting.

That should have been enough to tip me off. I'll plead weariness, achiness, and sexual distraction. It came as a total shock to me to feel a wave of cold energy writhe into my face, in tandem with a shadowy form rising up from the steps leading down to my apartment. I froze and took a step back, only to see another silent shape step around the edge of the boardinghouse and start walking toward us. Gooseflesh erupted up and down my arms.

Susan caught on a second or two after my wizard's senses had given me warning. 'Harry,' she breathed. 'What is it? Who are they?'

'Take it easy, and get out your car keys,' I said, as the two shapes approached us, the waves of cool energy increasing as they did. Light from the distant street lamp reflected in the nearest figure's eyes, gleaming huge and black. 'We're getting out of here. They're vampires.'

8

One of the vampires let out a velvet laugh, and stepped out into the dim light. He wasn't particularly tall, and he moved with a casual and dangerous grace that belied his crystal-blue eyes, styled blond hair, and the tennis whites he wore. 'Bianca told us you'd be nervous,' he purred.

The second of the pair kept coming toward us from the corner of the boardinghouse. She, too, was of innocuous height and build, and possessed the same blue eyes and flawless golden hair as the man. She too was dressed in tennis whites. 'But,' she breathed, and licked her lips with a cat-quick tongue, 'she didn't tell us you would smell so delicious.'

Susan fumbled with her keys, and pressed up against me, tight with tension and fear. 'Harry?'

'Don't look them in the eyes,' I said. 'And don't let them lick you.'

Susan shot me a sharp look from beneath raven brows. 'Lick?'

'Yeah. Their saliva's some kind of addictive narcotic.' We reached her car. 'Get in.'

The male vampire opened his mouth, showing his fangs, and laughed. 'Peace, wizard. We're not here for your blood.'

'Speak for yourself,' the girl said. She licked her lips again, and this time I could see the black spots on her long, pink tongue. Ewg.

The male smiled and put a hand on her shoulder, a

gesture that was half affection, half physical restraint. 'My sister hasn't eaten tonight,' he explained. 'She's on a diet.'

'Vampires on a diet?' Susan murmured beneath her breath.

'Yeah,' I said back, sotto voce. 'Make hers a Blood Lite.'

Susan made a choking sound.

I eyed the male and raised my voice. 'Who are you, then? And why are you at my house?'

He inclined his head politely. 'My name is Kyle Hamilton. This is my sister, Kelly. We are associates of Madame Bianca's, and we are here to give you a message. An invitation, actually.'

'It only takes one of you to deliver a message.'

Kyle glanced at his sister. 'We were just on the way to our game of doubles.'

I snorted. 'Yeah, right,' I told him. 'Whatever it is you're selling, I don't want any. You can go now.'

Kyle frowned. 'I urge you to reconsider, Mr Dresden. You, of all people, should know Madame Bianca is the most influential vampire in the city of Chicago. Denying her invitation could have grave consequences.'

'I don't like threats,' I shot back. I hefted my blasting rod and leveled it at Kyle's baby blues. 'Keep it up and there's going to be a greasy spot right about where you're standing.'

The pair of them smiled at me – innocent angels with pointed teeth. 'Please, Mr Dresden,' Kyle said. 'Understand that I am only pointing out the potential hazards of a diplomatic incident between the Vampire Court and the White Council.'

Whoops. That changed things. I hesitated, and then lowered the blasting rod. 'This is court business? Official business?'

'The Vampire Court,' Kyle said, a measured cadence to his words, 'extends a formal invitation to Harry Dresden, Wizard, as the local representative of the White Council of Wizards, to attend the reception celebrating the elevation of Bianca St Claire to the rank of Margravine of the Vampire Court, three nights hence, reception to begin at midnight.' Kyle paused to produce an expensive-looking white envelope and to refresh his smile. 'The safety of all invited guests is assured, by word of the assembled court, of course.'

'Harry,' Susan breathed. 'What's going on?'

'Tell you in a minute,' I said. I stepped away from Susan. 'You are acting as an ordained herald of the court, then?'

'I am,' Kyle said.

I nodded. 'Bring me the invitation.'

The pair of them started toward me. I lifted my blasting rod and muttered a word. Power flooded through the rod, and the far tip began to glow with an incandescent light. 'Not her,' I said, nodding to the herald's sister. 'Just you.'

Kyle kept his smile, but his eyes had changed from blue to a shade of angry black that was rapidly expanding to cover the whites. 'Well,' he said, his voice tense, 'aren't we the little lawyer, Mr Dresden.'

I smiled back at him. 'Look, Sparky, you're the herald. You should know the accords as well as I do. You've license to deliver and receive messages and to have safe passage granted you so long as you don't start any trouble.' I waved the tip of the rod toward the girl beside him. 'She doesn't. And she's not obliged to keep the peace, either. Let's just say I'd rather we all walked away from this.'

They both made a hissing sound that no human could quite have duplicated. Kyle pushed Kelly roughly back

behind him, where she remained, her soft-looking hands
pressed to her stomach, her eyes flooded entirely black and
empty of humanity. Kyle stalked toward me and thrust
the envelope at me. I swallowed my fear, lowered my
blasting rod, and took it.

'Your business here is complete,' I told him. 'Blow.'

'You'd better be there, Dresden,' Kyle snarled, pacing
back to his sister's side. 'My lady will be most upset if
you are not.'

'I told you to blow, Kyle.' I lifted my hand, gathered
my anger and my fear as handy sources of fuel, and said,
quietly, 'Ventas servitas.'

Energy flowed out of me. Wind roared up in response
to my command, and whipped out toward the pair of
vampires, carrying a cloud of dust and dirt and debris with
it. They both staggered, lifting a hand to shield their eyes
against flying particles.

As the wind faded I sagged, wearied by the effort of
moving that much air, and watched the vampires gather
their wits and blink their eyes clear. Their perfect tennis
whites were stained, their beautiful complexions were
mussed, and best of all, their flawless hair was standing
up every which way.

They hissed at me and crouched, bodies oddly balanced
and held with an inhuman lightness. Then there was a
blur of tennis whites, and they were gone.

I didn't assume that they had left until I let my senses
drift out from me, tasting the air for the cold energy that
had surrounded them. It had faded, as well. Only then,
when I was absolutely sure they were gone, did I relax.
Well, it felt like simple relaxing – but generally when I
relax, I don't stagger and need to plant my staff firmly on

the ground to keep from falling over. I stood there like that for a second, my head swimming.

'Wow.' Susan came toward me, her face concerned. 'Harry, you sure know how to make friends.'

I wobbled a little, hardly able to stand. 'I don't need friends like that.'

She got close enough for me to lean on, and spared my ego by slipping underneath my arm as though for my protection. 'Are you all right?'

'Tired. I've been working too hard tonight. Must have gotten out of shape.'

'Can you walk?'

I gave her a smile that probably looked strained, and started walking toward the stairs leading down to my apartment. Mister, my grey cat, came flying over the ground from the darkness somewhere and threw himself fondly against my legs. Thirty pounds of cat is a lot of fondness, and I had to have Susan's help to keep from falling over. 'Eating small children again, Mister?'

My cat meowed, then padded down the stairs and pawed at the door.

'So,' Susan said. 'The vampires are throwing a party.'

I fished my keys out of my duster's pocket. I unlocked the door to the old place, and Mister bolted inside. I shut the door behind us, and stared wearily at my living room. The fire had died down to glowing embers, but still shed red-golden light over everything. I decorated my apartment in textures, not colors, in any case. I like the smooth grain of old woods, the heavy tapestries on the bare stone walls. The chairs are all thickly padded and comfortable looking, and rugs are strewn over the bare stone floor in a variety of materials, patterns, and weaves, from Arabian to Navajo.

Susan helped me hobble in until I could collapse on my plushly cushioned couch. She took my staff and blasting rod from me, wrinkling her nose at the charred smell, and set them in the corner next to my cane sword. Then she came back over to me and knelt down, flashing a lot of bare, pretty leg. She took my boots off, and I groaned as my feet came free.

'Thanks,' I said.

She plucked the envelope from my hand. 'Could you get the candles?'

I groaned, for an answer, and she sniffed. 'Big baby. You just want to see me walk around in this skirt.'

'Guilty,' I said. She quirked a smile at me, and went to the fireplace. She added a few logs to it from the old tin hod, and then stirred the embers with a poker until licks of flame came up. I don't have any electric lights in my apartment. Gadgets go out so often that there's no point in constantly replacing them. My refrigerator is an old-style icebox. The kind with ice. I shuddered to think of what I could do to gas lines.

So, I lived without heat, except for my fireplace, and without hot water, without electricity. The curse of a wizard. It saves on the utilities bills, I have to admit, but it can be damned inconvenient.

Susan had to bend down far over the fire to thrust a long candlestick's tip down into the small flames. The orange light curved around the lean muscles of her legs in a fashion I found positively fascinating, even as wearied as I was.

Susan rose with the lighted candle in her hand and cast a smirk at me. 'You're staring, Harry.'

'Guilty,' I said again.

She lit several candles on the mantel from the first, and then opened the white envelope, frowning. 'Wow,' she said, and held the invitation inside up to the light. I couldn't make out the words, but they had that white-yellow glint that you only get from true gold. 'The bearer, Wizard Harry Dresden, and an escort of his choosing are hereby courteously invited to a reception . . . I didn't think they used invitations like this anymore.'

'Vampires. They can be a couple hundred years out of style and not notice.'

'Harry,' Susan said. She flicked the invitation against the heel of her hand a couple of times. 'You know, something occurs to me.'

My brain tried to stir from its congealment. Some instinct twitched, warning me that Susan was up to something. 'Um,' I said, blinking my eyes in an effort to clear my thoughts. 'I hope you're not thinking what a great opportunity it would be for you to go to the ball.'

Her eyes glinted with something very much like lust. 'Think of it, Harry. There could be beings there hundreds of years old. I could get enough stories from a half hour of chat to last me—'

'Hang on, Cinderella,' I said. 'In the first place, I'm not going to the ball. In the second, even if I was I wouldn't take you with me.'

Her back straightened and she put one fist on her hip. 'And just what is that supposed to mean?'

I winced. 'Look, Susan. They're *vampires*. They eat people. You've got no idea how dangerous it would be for me there – or for you, for that matter.'

'What about what Kyle said? The guarantee of your safety?'

'Talk is cheap,' I said. 'Look, everyone in the old circles is big on the old laws of courtesy and hospitality. But you can only trust them to adhere to the letter of the law. If I happened to get served a bad batch of mushrooms, or someone drove by and filled the whole place with bullets and I was the only mortal there, they'd just say, "Oh my, what a terrible shame. So sorry, really, it won't happen again."'

'So you're saying they'd kill you,' Susan said.

'Bianca has a grudge against me,' I said. 'She couldn't just sneak up on me and tear my throat out, but she could arrange for something to happen to me more indirectly. It's probably what she has in mind.'

Susan frowned. 'I've seen you handle things a lot worse than those two out there.'

I let out a breath in exasperation. 'Maybe, sure. But what's the point in taking chances?'

'Can't you see what this might mean to me?' she said. 'Harry, that footage I shot of the werewolf—'

'Loup-garou,' I interrupted.

'Whatever. It was ten seconds of footage that was only aired for three days before it vanished – and it put me further ahead than five *years* of legwork. If I could publish actual interviews with vampires—'

'Sheesh, Susan. You're reading too much off the best-seller list. In the real world, the vampire eats you before you get to hit the record button.'

'I've taken chances before – so have you.'

'I don't go *looking* for trouble,' I said.

Her eyes flashed. 'Dammit, Harry. How long have I been putting aside the things that happen to you? Like tonight, when I was supposed to be spending the evening with my boyfriend and instead I'm bailing him out of jail.'

Ouch. I glanced down. 'Susan, believe me. If I could have done anything else—'

'This could be a fantastic opportunity for me.'

She was right. And she had bailed me out of trouble often enough before that maybe I owed her that opportunity, dangerous as it might be. She was a big girl and could make her own choices. But dammit, I couldn't just nod my head and smile and let her walk into that kind of danger. Better to try to sidetrack her. 'No,' I said. 'I've got enough problems without pissing off the White Council again.'

Her eyes narrowed. 'What's this White Council? Kyle talked to you as though it were some kind of ruling body. Is it like the Vampire Court, only for wizards?'

Exactly like that, I thought. Susan hadn't gotten as far as she had by being stupid. 'Not really,' I told her.

'You're a horrible liar, Harry.'

'The White Council is a group of the most powerful men and women in the world, Susan. Wizards. Their big currency is in secrets, and they don't like people knowing about them.'

Her eyes gleamed, like a hound on a fresh scent. 'And you're . . . some kind of ambassador for them?'

I had to laugh at the notion. 'Oh, God, no. But I'm a member. It's sort of like having a black belt. It's a mark of status, of respect. With the council, it means that I get to vote, when issues come up, and that I have to abide by their rules.'

'Are you entitled to represent them at a function like this?'

I didn't like the direction this conversation was headed. 'Um. Obligated to, really, in this case.'

'So if you *don't* show up, you'll be in trouble.'

I scowled. 'Not as much trouble as I'll be in if I go. The worst the council'd be able to accuse me of is being impolite. I can live with that.'

'And if you do show up? Come on, Harry. What's the worse that could happen?'

I threw up my hands. 'I could get myself killed! Or worse. Susan, you really don't understand what you're asking of me.' I pushed myself up off the couch, to go to her. Bad idea. My head swam and my vision blurred.

I would have fallen, but Susan dropped the invitation and caught me. She eased me back down to the couch, and I kept my arm around her, drawing her down with me. She felt soft and warm.

We lay there for a minute, and she rubbed her cheek against the duster. Leather creaked. I heard her sigh. 'I'm sorry, Harry. I shouldn't hit you with this right now.'

'It's all right,' I said.

'I just think that it's something big. If we—'

I turned a little, tangled my fingers in the dark softness of her hair, and kissed her.

Her eyelids opened wide for a second, and then lowered. Her words broke off into a low, growling sound, and her mouth softened beneath mine, warm and getting warmer. In spite of my aches and bruises, the kiss felt good. It felt really good. Her mouth tasted nice, the softness of her lips mobile and eager beneath mine. I felt her slide a few fingers in between the buttons of my shirt, caressing the skin there, and electric sensation thrilled through me.

Our tongues met, and I dragged her closer. She moaned

again, then abruptly pushed me back enough to straddle my hips with those long and lovely legs and begin to kiss me as though she meant to inhale me. I ran my hands over her hips, lingering on the small of her back, and she moved them, grinding against me. I moved my hands to the taut tension of her thighs and slid them up over the bare, smooth skin, lifting the skirt up, baring her legs, her hips.

I faltered in surprise for a half-second when I realized she wasn't wearing anything underneath – but then, we'd been planning on an evening in. A spasm of need and hunger pounded through all the exhaustion, and I clutched her, felt her gasp again, willing and as hungry as me, her body tensing against me, beneath my hands.

She started jerking at my belt, gasping, her breath hot in my face. 'Harry. You jerk. Don't you think this is going to distract me forever.'

Shortly after that, we made sure that neither of us could think of anything at all, and fell asleep a goodly while after that, tangled together in a sprawl of exhausted limbs, dark hair, and soft blankets in front of the fire.

All right, so. The *entire* day wasn't a living hell.

But, as it turned out, hell got up awfully early in the morning.

9

I dreamed.

The nightmare felt familiar, almost comfortable, though it had been years since I'd gone through it. It began in a cave, its walls made of translucent crystal, all but glowing in the dim light of the fire beneath the cauldron. The silver manacles were tight on my wrists, and I was too dizzy to keep my own balance. I looked to the left and right and watched my blood glide down over the manacles from where they pierced my wrists like thorns, then fall into a pair of earthen bowls set out beneath them.

My godmother came to me, pale and breathtaking in the firelight, her hair spilling down around her like a cloud of silk. The sidhe lady was beautiful beyond the pale of mortals, her eyes bewitching, her mouth more tempting than the most luscious fruit. She kissed my bare chest. Shudders of cold pleasure ran through me.

'Soon,' she whispered, between kisses. 'Only a few more nights of the dark moon, my sweetling, and you will be strong enough.'

She kept kissing me, and I began to lose my vision. Cold pleasure, faerie magic, coursed through her lips like a drug, so sweet that it was almost an agony of its own, and made the torment of the bonds, the blood loss, almost worthwhile. Almost. I felt myself gasping for breath, and stared at the fire, focusing on it, trying to keep from falling into the darkness.

The dream changed. I dreamt of fire. Someone I had once loved like a father stood in the middle of it, screaming in agony. They were black screams, horrible screams, high-pitched and utterly without pride or dignity or humanity. In the dream, as in life,

I forced myself to watch flesh blacken and flake away from
sizzling muscle and baking bone, watched muscles contract in
tortured spasms while I stood over the fire and, metaphorically
speaking, blew on the coals.

'Justin,' I whispered. In the end, I couldn't watch any longer.
I closed my eyes and bowed my head, listening to the thunder of
my own heart pounding in my ears. Pounding. My heart
pounding.

I came out of the dream, blinked opened my eyes. My
door rattled on its frame under a series of hammering
blows. Susan woke up at the same time, sitting up, the
blanket we'd been curled under gliding down over the
curves of her breasts. It was still dark outside. The longest
candle hadn't yet burned away, but the fire was down to
embers again.

My body ached all over, the day-after ache of tired joints
and muscles demanding time to recuperate. I rose as the
pounding went on, and went to the kitchen drawer. My
.38 had been lost in the battle with the gang of half-mad
lycanthropes the year before, and I'd replaced it with a
medium-barreled .357. I must have been feeling insecure
that day, or something.

The gun weighed about two thousand pounds in my
hand. I made sure that it was loaded and turned to face
the door. Susan pushed her hair out of her eyes, blinked
at my gun, and backed away, making damn sure she was
out of my line of fire. Smart girl, Susan.

'You're not going to have much luck breaking down
that door,' I called out. I didn't point the gun at the door,
yet. Never point a gun at anything you aren't sure you
want dead. 'I replaced the original one with a steel door
and a steel frame. Demons, you know.'

The pounding ceased. 'Dresden,' Michael called from the other side of the door. 'I tried to reach you on the phone, but it must be off the hook. We've got to talk.'

I frowned, and put the gun back in the drawer. 'Okay, okay. Sheesh, Michael. Do you know what time it is?'

'Time to work,' he answered. 'The sun will be up shortly.'

'Lunatic,' I mumbled.

Susan looked around at the remains of our clothing, scattered pretty much everywhere, the sprawl of blankets and pillows and cushions all over the floor. 'I think maybe I'll just wait in your room,' she said.

'Right, okay.' I opened the kitchen closet and got my heavy robe out, the one I usually save for working in the lab, and slipped into it. 'Stay covered up, all right? I don't want you to get sick.'

She gave me a sleepy half-smile and rose, all long limbs and grace and interesting tan lines, then vanished into my little bedroom and shut the door. I walked across the room, and opened the door for Michael.

He stood there in blue jeans, a flannel shirt, and a fleece-lined denim jacket. He had his big gym bag slung over his shoulder, and *Amoracchius* was a silent tension I could just barely feel within it. I looked from the bag to his face and asked, 'Trouble?'

'Could be. Did you send someone to Father Forthill last night?'

I rubbed at my eyes, trying to get the sleep out of them. Coffee. I needed coffee. Or a Coke. Just as long as there was caffeine somewhere. 'Yes. A girl named Lydia. She was worried that a ghost was after her.'

'He called me this morning. Something spent the night trying to get into the church.'

I blinked at him. 'What? Did it get inside?'

He shook his head. 'He didn't have time to tell me much. Can you come down there with me and take a look around?'

I nodded, and stepped back from the door. 'Give me a couple of minutes.' I headed for the icebox and got out a can of Coke. My fingers worked enough to open it, at least, though they still felt stiff. My stomach reminded me that I'd been ignoring it, and I got out the plate of cold cuts while I was there.

I swigged Coke and made myself a big sandwich. I looked up a minute later to see Michael eyeing the destruction that had been the living room. He nudged one of Susan's shoes with his foot, and glanced up at me apologetically. 'I'm sorry. I didn't know anyone was here.'

'It's okay.'

Michael smiled briefly, then nodded. 'Well. Do I need to lecture you on sexual involvement before marriage?'

I growled something about early morning and inconvenient visitors and toads. Michael only shook his head, smiling, while I wolfed down food. 'Did you tell her?'

'Tell her what?'

He lifted an eyebrow at me.

I rolled my eyes. 'Almost.'

'You almost told her.'

'Sure. Got distracted.'

Michael nudged Susan's other shoe with his foot and let out a delicate cough. 'So I see.'

I finished the sandwich and part of the Coke, then walked across the room and slipped into the bedroom. The room was freezing, and I could see Susan curled into a ball beneath the heavy blankets on my bed. Mister had lain down with his back against hers, and watched me with sleepy, self-satisfied eyes as I came in.

'Rub it in, fuzzball,' I growled at him, and dressed quickly. Socks, jeans, T-shirt, heavy flannel work shirt over that. Mom's amulet, around my neck, and a little silver charm bracelet with a half-dozen shields dangling off it, fixed to my left wrist in place of the charm I'd given to Lydia. A plain silver ring, its interior surface inscribed with a number of runes, went onto my right hand. Both pieces of jewelry tingled with the enchantments I'd laid on them, still fairly fresh.

I leaned over the bed and kissed Susan's cheek. She made a sleepy, murmuring sound, and snuggled a little deeper beneath the covers. I thought about getting under there with her and making sure she was nice and warm before leaving – but instead went out, shutting the door carefully behind me.

Michael and I left, piling into his truck, a white (of course) Ford pick-up with extra wheels and enough hauling power to move mountains, and headed for Saint Mary of the Angels.

Saint Mary of the Angels is a big church. I mean, a *big* church. It's been looming over the Wicker Park area for more than eighty years, and has seen the neighborhood grow up from a collection of cheap homes for immigrants mixed in with rich folks' mansions to Little Bohemia today, packed with yuppies and artsies, success stories, and wannabes. The church, I'm told, is modeled after St Peter's Basilica in Rome – which is to say, enormous and elegant and maybe a bit overdone. It takes up an entire city block. I mean, sheesh.

The sun came up as we entered the parking lot. I felt

the golden rays slice across the morning skies, the sudden, subtle shift of forces playing about the world. Dawn is significant, magically speaking. It is a time of new beginnings. Magic isn't as simple as good and evil, light and dark, but there's a lot of correlations between the powers particular to night and the use of black magic.

We drove around to the rear parking lot of the church and got out of the truck. Michael walked in front of me, carrying his bag. I stuffed my hands down in the pockets of my duster as I followed him. I felt uncomfortable, approaching the church – not for any weirdo quasi-mystical reason. Just because I'd never felt comfortable with churches in general. The Church had killed a lot of wizards in its day, believing them in league with Satan. It felt strange to just be strolling up on business. Hi, God, it's me, Harry. Please don't turn me into a pillar of salt.

'Harry,' Michael said, bringing me out of my reverie. 'Look.'

He had stopped beside a pair of worn old cars parked in the back lot. Someone had done one hell of a job on them. The windows had all been smashed, their safety glass fractured and dented. The hoods were dented as well. The headlights lay mostly on the ground in front of the cars, and all the tires were flat.

I walked around to the back of the cars, frowning. The taillights lay shattered on the ground. The antenna had been torn off each car, and were not in sight. Long scratches, in three parallel rows ran down the sides of both cars.

'Well?' Michael asked me.

I looked up at him and shrugged. 'Probably something got frustrated when it couldn't get inside the church.'

He snorted. 'Do you think?' He adjusted the gym bag

until *Amoracchius's* handle lay jutting outside the zipper. 'Any chances that it's still around?'

I shook my head. 'I doubt it. Come daylight, ghosts usually head back to the Nevernever.'

'Usually?'

'Usually. Almost without exception.'

Michael eyed me and kept one hand on the hilt of the sword. We walked on up to the delivery door. Compared to the grandeur of the church's front, it looked stunningly modest. On either side of the double doors, someone had gone to a lot of trouble to plant and care for a half-dozen rosebushes. Someone else had gone to a lot of trouble to tear them to shreds. Each plant had been uprooted. Thorny branches lay strewn across several dozen square yards around the door.

I crouched down beside several fallen branches, picking them up one at a time, squinting at them in the dawn dimness.

'What are you looking for?' Michael asked me.

'Blood on the thorns,' I said. 'Rose thorns can poke little holes in just about anything – and something that tore them up this hard would have been scratching itself on them.'

'Any blood?'

'No. No footprints in the earth, either.'

Michael nodded. 'A ghost, then.'

I squinted up at Michael. 'I hope not.'

He tilted his head and frowned at me.

I dropped a branch and spread my hands. 'A ghost can usually only manage to move things, physically, in bursts. Throwing pots and pans. Maybe really stretch things and stack up a bunch of books or something.' I gestured at the torn plants, and then back toward the wrecked cars. 'Not only that, but it's limited to a certain place, time, or event. The ghost, if it is one, followed Lydia here and rampaged around on blessed ground tearing things apart. I mean, wow. This thing is way stronger than any ghost I've ever heard about.'

Michael's frown deepened. 'What are you saying, Harry?'

'I'm saying we might be getting out of our depth, here. Look, Michael, I know a lot about spooks and nasties. But they aren't my specialty or anything.'

He frowned at me. 'We might need to know more.'

I stood up, brushing myself off. 'That,' I said, 'is my specialty. Let's talk to Father Forthill.'

Michael knocked on the door. It opened at once. Father Forthill, a greying man of slight build and only medium stature, blinked anxiously up at us through a pair of wire-rimmed spectacles. His eyes were normally a shade of blue so bright as to rival robin's eggs, but today they were heavily underlined, shadowed. 'Oh,' he said. 'Oh, Michael. Thank the Lord.' He opened the door wider, and Michael stepped over the threshold. The two embraced. Forthill kissed Michael on either cheek and stepped back to peer at me. 'And Harry Dresden, professional wizard. I've never had anyone ask me to bless a five-gallon drum into holy water before, Mr Dresden.'

Michael peered at me, evidently surprised that the priest and I knew each other. I shrugged, a little embarrassed, and said, 'You told me I could count on him in a pinch.'

'And so you can,' Forthill said, his blue eyes sparkling for a moment behind the spectacles. 'I trust you have no complaints about the blessed water?'

'None at all,' I said. 'Talk about your surprised ghouls.'

'Harry,' Michael chided. 'You've been keeping secrets again.'

'Contrary to what Charity thinks, Michael, I don't go running to the phone to call you every time I have a little problem.' I clapped Michael on the shoulder in passing and offered my hand to Father Forthill, who shook it gravely. No hug and kiss on each cheek for me.

Forthill smiled up at me. 'I look forward to the day when you give your life to God, Mr Dresden. He can use men with your courage.'

I tried to smile, but it probably looked a little sickly. 'Look, Father. I'd love to talk about it with you sometime, but we're here for a reason.'

'Indeed,' Forthill said. The sparkle in his eyes faded, and his manner became absolutely serious. He began to walk down a clean hallway with dark, heavy beams of old wood overhanging it and paintings of the Saints on the walls. We kept pace with him. 'The young woman arrived yesterday, just before sunset.'

'Was she all right?' I asked.

He lifted both eyebrows. 'All right? I should say not. All the signs of an abused personality. Borderline malnutrition. She had a low-grade fever as well, and hadn't bathed recently. She looked as though she might be going through withdrawal from something.'

I frowned. 'Yeah. She looked like she was in pretty bad shape.' I briefly recounted my conversation with Lydia and my decision to help her.

Father Forthill shook his head. 'I provided fresh clothes and a meal for her and was getting set to put her to bed on a spare cot at the back of the rectory. That's when it happened.'

'What happened?'

'She began to shake,' Forthill said. 'Her eyes rolled back into her head. She was still sitting at the dinner table, and spilled her soup onto the floor. I thought she was having a seizure of some sort, and tried to hold her down and to get something into her mouth to keep her from biting her tongue.' He sighed, clasping his hands behind his back as he walked. 'I'm afraid that I was of little help to the poor child. The fit seemed to pass in a few moments, but she still trembled and had gone absolutely pale.'

'Cassandra's Tears,' I said.

'Or narcotic withdrawal,' Forthill said. 'Either way, she needed help. I moved her to the cot. She begged me not to leave her, so I sat down and began to read part of St Matthew's gospel to her. She seemed to calm somewhat, but she had such a look in her eyes . . .' The old priest sighed. 'That resolved look that they get when they're sure that they're lost. Despair, and in one so young.'

'When did the attack begin?' I asked.

'About ten minutes later,' the priest said. 'It started with the most terrible howling of wind. Lord preserve me, but I was sure the windows would rattle out of their frames. Then we started to hear sounds, outside.' He swallowed. 'Terrible sounds. Something walking back and forth. Heavy footsteps. And then it started calling her name.' The priest folded his arms and rubbed his palms against either arm.

'I rose and addressed the being, and asked its name, but it only laughed at me. I began to compel it by the Holy Word, and it went quite mad. We could hear it crushing things outside. I don't mind telling you that it was quite the most terrifying experience I have ever had in my life.

'The girl tried to leave. To go out to it. She said that she didn't want me harming myself, that it would only find her in any case. Well, I forbade her, of course, and refused to let her past me. It kept on, outside, and I kept on reading the Word aloud to the girl. It waited outside. I could . . . feel it, but could see nothing outside the windows. Such a darkness. And every so often it would destroy something else, and we'd hear the sound of it.

'After several hours, it seemed to grow quiet. The girl went to sleep. I walked the halls to make sure all the doors and windows were still closed, and when I came back she was gone.'

'Gone?' I asked. 'Gone as in left or as in just gone?'

Forthill gave me a smile that looked a bit shaky. 'The back door was unlocked, though she'd shut it after herself.' The older man shook his head. 'I called Michael at once, of course.'

'We've got to find that girl,' I said.

Forthill shook his head, his expression grave. 'Mr Dresden, I am certain that only the power of the Almighty kept us safe within these walls last night.'

'I won't argue with you, Father.'

'But if you could have sensed this creature's anger, its . . . rage. Mr Dresden, I would not wish to encounter this being outside of a church without seeking God's help in the matter.'

I jerked a thumb at Michael. 'I *did* seek God's help. Heck, is one Knight of the Cross not enough? I could always put out the Bat-signal for the other two.'

Forthill smiled. 'That's not what I meant, and you know it. But as you wish. You must come to your own decision.' He turned to Michael and me both and said, 'I hope, gentlemen, that I can trust your discretion on this matter? The police report will doubtless reflect that persons unknown perpetuated the vandalism.'

I snorted. 'A little white lie, Father?' I felt bad the minute I'd said it, but heck. I get tired of the conversion efforts every time I show up.

'Evil gains power from fear, Mr Dresden,' Forthill replied. 'Within the Church, we have agencies for dealing with these matters.' He put a hand on Michael's shoulder, briefly. 'But spreading word of it to everyone, even to all of the brethren would accomplish nothing but to frighten many people and to make the enemy that much more able to do harm.'

I nodded at the priest. 'I like that attitude, Father. You almost sound like a wizard.'

His eyebrows shot up, but then he broke into a quiet, weary laugh. 'Be careful, both of you, and may God go with you.' He made the sign of the cross over both of us, and I felt the quiet stirring of power, just as I sometimes did around Michael. Faith. Michael and Forthill exchanged a few quiet words about Michael's family while I lurked in the background. Forthill arranged to christen the new baby, whenever Charity delivered. They exchanged hugs again; Forthill shook my hand, businesslike and friendly, and we left.

Outside, Michael watched me as we walked back to his truck. 'Well?' he asked. 'What's next?'

I frowned, and stuffed my hands into my pockets. The sun was higher now, painting the sky blue, the clouds white. 'I know someone who's pretty close to the spooks around here. That psychic in Oldtown.'

Michael scowled and spat. 'The necromancer.'

I snorted. 'He's no necromancer. He can barely call up
a ghost and talk to it. He's got to fake it most of the time.'
Besides. Had he been a real necromancer, the White
Council would already have hounded him down and
beheaded him. Doubtless, the man I was thinking of had
already been visited by at least one Warden and warned
of the consequences of dabbling too much into the dark
arts.

'If he's so inept, why speak to him at all?'

'He's probably closer to the spirit world than anyone
else in town. Other than me, I mean. I'll send out Bob,
too, and see what kind of information he can run down.
We're bound to have different contacts.'

Michael frowned at me. 'I don't trust this business of
communing with spirits, Harry. If Father Forthill and the
others knew about this familiar of yours—'

'Bob isn't a familiar,' I shot back.

'He performs the same function, doesn't he?'

I snorted. 'Familiars work for free. I've got to pay Bob.'

'Pay him?' he asked, his tone suspicious. 'Pay what?'

'Mostly romance novels. Sometimes I splurge on a—'

Michael looked pained. 'Harry, I really don't want to
know. Isn't there some way that you could work some kind
of spell here, instead of relying upon these unholy beings?'

I sighed, and shook my head. 'Sorry, Michael. If it was
a demon, it would have left footprints, and maybe some
kind of psychic trail I could follow. But I'm pretty sure
this was pure spirit. And a goddamned strong one.'

'Harry,' Michael said, voice stern.

'Sorry, I forgot. Ghosts don't usually inhabit a construct
– a magical body. They're just energy. They don't leave
any physical traces behind – at least none that last for

hours at a time. If it was *here*, I could tell you all kinds of things about it, probably, and work magic on it directly. But it's not here, so—'

Michael sighed. 'Very well. I will put out the word to those I know to be on the lookout for the girl. Lydia, you said her name was?'

'Yeah.' I described her to Michael. 'And she had a charm on her wrist. The one I'd been wearing the past few nights.'

'Would it protect her?' Michael asked.

I shrugged. 'From something as mean as this thing sounded . . . I don't know. We've got to find out who this ghost was when it was alive and shut it down.'

'Which still will not tell us who or what is stirring up the spirits of the city.' Michael unlocked his truck, and we got inside.

'That's what I like about you, Michael. You're always thinking so positively.'

He grinned at me. 'Faith, Harry. God has a way of seeing to it that things fall into place.'

He started driving, and I leaned back in my seat and closed my eyes. First off to see the psychic. Then to send Bob out to find out more about what looked to be the most dangerous ghost I'd seen in a long time. And *then* to keep on looking for whoever it was behind all the spooky goings-on and to rap them politely on the head until they stopped. Easy as one, two, three. Sure.

I whimpered, sunk down in my seat a little more, and wished that I had kept my aching, sore self in bed.

10

Mortimer Lindquist had tried to give his house that gothic feel. Greyish gargoyles stood at the corners of his roof. Black iron gates glowered at the front of his house and statuary lined the walk to his front door. Long grass had overgrown his yard. If his house hadn't been a red-roofed, white-walled stucco transplant from somewhere in southern California, it might have worked.

The results looked more like the Haunted Mansion at Disneyland than an ominous abode of a speaker to the dead. The black iron gates stood surrounded by plain chain-link fence. The gargoyles, on closer inspection, proved to be plastic reproductions. The statuary, too, had the rough outlines of plaster, rather than the clean, sweeping profile of marble. You could have plopped a pink flamingo down right in the middle of the unmowed weeds, and it would have somehow matched the decor. But, I supposed, at night, with the right lighting and the right attitude, some people might have believed it.

I shook my head and lifted my hand to rap on the door.

It opened before my knuckles touched it, and a well-rounded set of shoulders below a shining, balding head backed through the doorway, grunting. I stepped to one side. The little man tugged an enormous suitcase out onto the porch, never taking notice of me, his florid face streaked with perspiration.

I sidled into the doorway as he turned to lug the bag

out to the gate, muttering to himself under his breath. I shook my head and went on into the house. The door was a business entrance – there was no tingling sensation of crossing the threshold of a dwelling uninvited. The front room reminded me of the house's exterior. Lots of black curtains draped down over the walls and doorways. Red and black candles squatted all over the place. A grinning human skull leered from a bookshelf straining to contain copies of the *Encyclopedia Britannica* with the lettering scraped off their spines. The skull was plastic, too.

Morty had a table set up in the room, several chairs around it with a high-backed chair at the rear, wood that had actually been carved with a number of monstrous beings. I took a seat in the chair, folded my hands on the table in front of me, and waited.

The little man came back in, wiping at his face with a bandana handkerchief, sweating and panting.

'Shut the door,' I said. 'We need to talk, Morty.'

He squealed and whirled around.

'Y-you,' he stammered. 'Dresden. What are you doing here?'

I stared at him. 'Come in, Morty.'

He came closer, but left the door open. In spite of his pudginess, he moved with the nervous energy of a spooked cat. His white business shirt showed stains beneath his arms reaching halfway to his belt. 'Look, Dresden. I told you guys before – I get the rules, right? I haven't been doing *anything* you guys talked about.'

Aha. The White Council *had* sent someone to see him. Morty was a professional con. I hadn't planned on getting any honest answers out of him without a lot of effort. Maybe I could play this angle and save myself a lot of work.

'Let me tell you something, Morty. When I come into a place and don't say a thing except, "Let's talk," and the first thing I hear is "I didn't do it," it makes me think that the person I'm talking to must have done something. You know what I'm saying?'

His florid face lost several shades of red. 'No way, man. Look, I've got nothing to do with what's been going on. Not my fault, none of my business, man.'

'With what's been going on,' I said. I looked down at my folded hands for a moment, and then back up at him. 'What's the suitcase for, Morty? You do something that means you need to leave town for a while?'

He swallowed, thick neck working. 'Look, Dresden. Mister Dresden. My sister got sick, see. I'm just going to help her out.'

'Sure you are,' I said. 'That's what you're doing. Going out of town to help your sick sister.'

'I swear to God,' Morty said, lifting a hand, his face earnest.

I pointed at the chair across from me. 'Sit down, Morty.'

'I'd like to, but I got a cab coming.' He turned toward the door.

'*Ventas servitas*,' I hissed, nice and dramatic, and threw some will at the door. Sudden wind slammed it shut right in front of his eyes. He squeaked, and backed up several paces, staring at the door, then whirling to face me.

I used the remnants of the same spell to push out a chair opposite me. 'Sit down, Morty. I've got a few questions. Now, if you cut the crap, you'll make your cab. And, if not . . .' I left the words hanging. One thing about intimidation is that people can always think up something worse that you could do to them than you can, if you leave their imagination some room to play.'

He stared at me, and swallowed again, his jowls jiggling. Then he moved to the chair as though he expected chains to fly out of it and tie him down the moment he sat. He balanced his weight on the very edge of the chair, licked his lips, and watched me, probably trying to figure out the best lies for the questions he expected.

'You know,' I said. 'I've read your books, Morty. *Ghosts of Chicago*. *The Spook Factor*. Two or three others. You did good work, there.'

His expression changed, eyes narrowing in suspicion. 'Thank you.'

'I mean, twenty years ago, you were a pretty damn good investigator. Sensitivity to spiritual energies and apparitions – ghosts. What we call an ectomancer in the business.'

'Yeah,' he said. His eyes softened a little, if not his voice. He avoided looking directly in my face. Most people do. 'That was a long time ago.'

I kept my voice in the same tone, the same expression. 'And now what? You run séances for people. How many times do you actually get to contact a spirit? One time in ten? One in twenty? Must be a real letdown from the actual stuff. Playacting, I mean.'

He was good at covering his expressions, I'll give him that. But I'm used to watching people. I saw anger in the way he held his neck and shoulders. 'I provide a legitimate service to people in need.'

'No. You play on their grief to take them for all you can. You don't believe that you're doing right, Morty, deep down. You can justify it any way you want, but you don't *like* what you're doing. If you did, your powers wouldn't have faded like they have.'

His jaw set in a hard line, and he didn't try to hide the anger anymore — the first honest reaction I'd seen out of him since he'd cried out in surprise. 'If you've got a point, Dresden, get to it. I've got a plane to catch.'

I spread my fingers over the tabletop. 'In the past two weeks,' I said, 'the spooks have been going mad. You should see the trouble they've caused. That poltergeist in the Campbell house. The Basement Beast at U. of C. Agatha Hagglethorn, down at Cook County.'

Morty grimaced and wiped at his face again. 'Yeah. I hear things. You and the Knight of the Sword have been covering the worst of it.'

'What else has been happening, Morty? I'm getting a little cranky losing sleep, so keep it short and simple.'

'I don't know,' he said, sullen. 'I've lost my powers, remember.'

I narrowed my eyes. 'But you hear things, Morty. You've still got some sources in the Nevernever. Why are you leaving town?'

He laughed, and it had a shaky edge to it. 'You said you read all of my books? Did you read *They Shall Rise?*'

'I glanced over it. End-of-the-world-type stuff. I figured you had been talking to the wrong kind of spirits too much. They love trying to sell people on Armageddon. A lot of them are cons like you.'

He ignored me. 'Then you read my theory on the barrier between our world and the Nevernever. That it's slowly being torn away.'

'And you think it's falling to pieces, now? Morty, that

wall has been there since the dawn of time. I don't think it's going to collapse right now.'

'*Wall.*' He said the word with a sneer. 'More like Saran Wrap, wizard. Like Jell-O. It bends and wiggles and stirs.' He rubbed his palms on his thighs, shivering.

'And it's falling now?'

'Look around you!' he shouted. 'Good God, wizard. The past two weeks, the border's been waggling back and forth like a hooker at a dockworker's convention. Why the hell do you think all of these ghosts have been rising?'

I didn't let the sudden volume of his tone make me blink. 'You're saying that this instability has been making it easier for ghosts to cross over from the Nevernever?'

'And easier to form bigger, stronger ghosts when people die,' he said. 'You think you've got some pissed-off ghosts now? Wait until some honor student on her way out of the south side with a college scholarship gets popped by accident in a gang shootout. Wait until some poor sap who got AIDS from a blood transfusion breathes his last.'

'Bigger, badder ghosts,' I said. 'Superghosts. That's what you're talking about.'

He laughed, a nasty little laugh. 'New generation of viruses is coming, too. Things are going to hell all over. Eventually, that border's going to get thin enough to spit through, and you'll have more problems with demon attacks than gang violence.'

I shook my head. 'All right,' I said. 'Let's say that I buy that the barrier is fluid rather than concrete. There's turbulence in it, and it's making crossing over easier, both ways. Could something be causing the turbulence?'

'How the hell should I know?' he snarled. 'You don't know what it's like, Dresden. To speak to things that exist in the past and in the future as well as in the now. To have them walk up to you at the salad bar and start telling you how they murdered their wife in her sleep.

'I mean, you think you've got a hold on things, that you understand, but in the end it all falls to pieces. A con is simpler, Dresden. You *make* order. People don't give a flying fuck if Uncle Jeffrey really forgives them for missing his last birthday party. They want to know that the world is a place where Uncle Jeffrey *can* and *should* forgive them.' He swallowed, and looked around the room, at the fake tomes and the fake skull. 'That's what I sell them. Closure. Like on television. They want to know that it's all going to work out in the end, and they're happy to pay for it.'

A car honked outside. Morty glared at me. 'We're through.'

I nodded.

He jerked to his feet, splotches of color in his cheeks. 'God, I need a drink. Get out of town, Dresden. Something came across last night like nothing I've ever felt.'

I thought of ruined cars and rosebushes planted in consecrated ground. 'Do you know what it is?'

'It's big,' Morty said. 'And it's pissed off. It's going to start killing, Dresden. And I don't think you or anyone else is going to be able to stop it.'

'But it's a ghost?'

He gave me a smile that showed me his canines. It was creepy on that florid, eyes-too-wide face. 'It's a nightmare.' He started to turn away. I wanted to let him go, but I couldn't. The man had become a liar, a sniveling con, but he hadn't always been.

I rose and beat him to the door, taking his arm in one hand. He spun to face me, jerking his arm away, glaring defiantly at my eyes. I avoided locking gazes. I didn't want to take a look at Mortimer Lindquist's soul.

'Morty,' I said, quietly. 'Get away from your séances for a while. Go somewhere quiet. Read. Relax. You're older now, stronger. If you give yourself a chance, the power will come back.'

He laughed again, tired and jaded. 'Sure, Dresden. Just like that.'

'Morty—'

He turned away from me and stalked out the door. He didn't bother to lock the place up behind him. I watched him head out to the cab, which waited by the curb. He lugged his bag into the backseat, and then followed it.

Before the cab pulled out, he rolled down the window. 'Dresden,' he called. 'Under my chair there's a drawer. My notes. If you want to kill yourself trying to stand up to this thing, you might as well know what you're getting into.'

He rolled the window back up as the cab pulled away. I watched it go, then went back inside. I found the drawer hidden in the base of the carved wooden chair, and inside I found a trio of old leather-bound journals, vellum pages covered in script that started out neat in the oldest one and became a jerky scrawl in the most recent entries. I held the books up to my mouth and inhaled the smell of leather, ink, paper; musty and genuine and real.

Morty hadn't had to give me the notes. Maybe there was some root of the person he had been, deep down somewhere, that wasn't dead yet. Maybe I'd done him a little good with that advice. I'd like to think that.

I blew out a breath, found a phone and called a cab of my own. I needed to get the Beetle out of impound if I could. Maybe Murphy could fix it for me.

I gathered the journals and went to the porch to wait for the cab, shutting the door behind me. Something big was coming through town, Morty had said.

'A nightmare,' I said, out loud.

Could Mort be right? Could the barrier between the spirit world and our own be falling apart? The thought made me shudder. Something had been formed, something big and mean. And my gut instinct told me that it had a purpose. All power, no matter how terrible or benign, whether its wielder is aware of it or not, has a purpose.

So this Nightmare was here for something. I wondered what it wanted. Wondered what it would do.

And worried that, all too soon, I would find out.

11

An unmarked car sat in my driveway with two nonde-
script men inside.

I got out of the taxi, paid off the cabby, and nodded at
the driver of the car, Detective Rudolph. Rudy's clean-cut
good looks hadn't faded in the year since he'd started with
Special Investigations, Chicago's unspoken answer to the
officially unacknowledged world of the supernatural. But
the time had hardened him a bit, made him a little less
white around the eyes.

Rudolph nodded back, not even trying to hide his
glower. He didn't like me. Maybe it had something to do
with the bust several months back. Rudy had cut and run,
rather than stick it out next to me. Before that, I'd escaped
police custody while he was supposed to be watching me.
I'd had a darn good reason to escape, and it wasn't really
fair of him to hold that against me, but hey. Whatever
got him through the day.

'Heya, Detective,' I said. 'What's up?'

'Get in the car,' Rudolph said.

I planted my feet and shoved my hands in my pockets
with a certain nonchalance. 'Am I under arrest?'

Rudolph narrowed his eyes and started to speak again,
but the man in the passenger seat cut him off. 'Heya,
Harry,' Detective Sergeant John Stallings said, nodding at
me.

'How you doing, John? What brings you out today?'

'Murph wanted us to ask you down to a scene.' He reached up and scratched at several days' worth of unshaven beard beneath a bad haircut and intelligent dark eyes. 'Hope you got the time. We tried at your office, but you haven't been in, so she sent us down here to wait for you.'

I shifted Mort Lindquist's books in my arms. 'I'm busy today. Can it wait?'

Rudolph spat, 'The lieutenant says she wants you down there now, you get your ass down there. Now.'

Stallings gave Rudolph a look, and then rolled his eyes for my benefit. 'Look, Harry. Murphy told me to tell you that this one was personal.'

I frowned. 'Personal, eh?'

He spread his hands. 'It's what she said.' He frowned and then added, 'It's Micky Malone.'

I got a sickly little feeling in my stomach. 'Dead?'

Stallings's jaw twitched. 'You'd better come see for yourself.'

I closed my eyes and tried not to get frustrated. I didn't have time for detours. It would take me hours to grind through Mort's notes, and sundown, when the spirits would be able to cross over from the Nevernever, would come swiftly.

But Murphy did plenty for me. I owed her. She'd saved my life a couple of times, and vice versa. She was my main source of income, too. Karrin Murphy headed up Special Investigations, a post that had traditionally resulted in a couple of months of bumbling and then a speedy exit from the police force. Murphy hadn't bumbled – instead, she'd hired the services of Chicago's only professional wizard as a consultant. She was getting to where she had a pretty good grasp on the local preternatural predators, at least the most common of them, but when things got hairy she still called me in. Technically, I show up on the paperwork as an investigative consultant. I guess the computer records system doesn't have numerical codes for demon banishment, divination spells, or exorcisms.

S.I. had gone toe to toe with one of the worst things anyone but a wizard like me was ever likely to see, only the year before – a half-ton of indestructible loup-garou. They'd taken some serious casualties. Six dead, including Murphy's partner. Micky Malone had gotten hamstrung. He'd gone through therapy, and had come along for one last job when Michael and I took down that demon-summoning sorcerer. After that, though, he'd decided that his limp was going to keep him from being a good cop, and retired on disability.

I felt guilty for that – maybe irrational, true, but if I'd been a little smarter or a little faster, maybe I could have saved those people's lives. And maybe I could have saved Micky's health. No one else saw it that way, but I did.

'All right,' I said. 'Give me a second to put these away.'

The ride was quiet, except for a little meaningless chatter from Stallings. Rudolph ignored me. I closed my eyes and ached along the way. Rudolph's radio squawked and then fell abruptly silent. I could smell burnt rubber or something, and knew that it was likely my fault.

I opened one eye and saw Rudolph scowling back at me in the mirror. I half-smiled, and closed my eyes again. Jerk.

The car stopped in a residential neighborhood near West Armitage, down in Bucktown. The district had gotten its name from the number of immigrant homes once there, and the goats kept in people's front yards. The homes had been tiny affairs, stuffed with too-large families and children.

Bucktown had been lived in for a century and it was all grown up. Literally. The houses on their tiny lots hadn't had much room to expand out, so they'd grown up instead, giving the neighborhood a stretched, elongated look. The trees were ancient oaks and sycamores, and decorated the tiny yards in stately majesty, except where they'd been roughly hacked back from power lines and rooftops. Shadows fell in sharp slants from all the tall trees and tall houses, turning the streets and sidewalks into candy canes of light and darkness.

One of the houses, a two-story white-on-white number, had its small driveway full and another half-dozen cars parked out on the street, plus Murphy's motorcycle leaning on its kickstand in the front yard. Rudolph pulled the car up alongside the curb across the street from that house and killed the engine. It went on rattling and coughing for a moment before it died.

I got out of the car and felt something *wrong*. An uneasy feeling ran over me, prickles of sensation along the nape of my neck and against my spine.

I stood there for a minute, frowning, while Rudolph and Stallings got out of the car. I looked around the neighborhood, trying to pin down the source of the odd sensations. The leaves in the trees, all in their autumn motley, rustled and sighed in the wind, occasionally falling. Dried leaves rattled and scraped over the streets. Cars drove by in the distance. A jet rumbled overhead, a deep and distant sound.

'Dresden,' Rudolph snapped. 'Let's go.'

I lifted a hand, extending my senses out, pushing my

perception out along with my will. 'Hang on a second,' I
said. 'I need to . . .' I quit trying to speak, and searched
for the source of the sensation. What the hell was it?

'Fucking showboat,' Rudolph growled. I heard him start
toward me.

'Hang on, kid,' Stallings said. 'Let the man work. We've
both seen what he can do.'

'I haven't seen shit that can't be explained,' Rudolph
growled. But he stayed put.

I drifted across the street, to the yard of the house in
question, and found the first body in the fallen leaves, five
feet to my left. A small, yellow-and-white furred cat lay
there, twisted so that its forelegs faced one way, its
hindquarters the opposite. Something had broken its neck.

I felt a pang of nausea. Death isn't ever pretty, really.
It's worst with people, but with the animals that are close
to mankind, it seems to be a little nastier than it might
be elsewhere in the wild kingdom. The cat couldn't have
reached its full growth, yet – maybe a kitten from early
in the spring, roaming the neighborhood. There was no
collar on its neck.

I could feel a little cloud of disturbance around it, a
kind of psychic energy left by traumatic, agonizing, and
torturous events. But this one little thing, one animal's
death, shouldn't have been enough to make me aware of
it all the way over from my seat in the police car.

Five feet farther on, I found a dead bird. I found its
wings in two more places. Then two more birds, without
heads. Then something that had been small and furry, and
was now small and furry and squishy – maybe a vole or a
ground squirrel. And there were more. A lot more – all
in all, maybe a dozen dead animals in the front yard, a

dozen little patches of violent energies still lingering. No single one of them would have been enough to disturb my wizard's sense, but all of them together had.

So what the hell had been killing these animals?

I rubbed my palms over my arms, a sickly little feeling of dread rolling through me. I looked up to see Rudolph and Stallings following me around. Their faces looked kind of greenish.

'Jesus,' Stallings said. He prodded the body of the cat with one toe. 'What did this?'

I shook my head and rolled my shoulders in a shrug. 'It might take me a while to find out. Where's Micky?'

'Inside.'

'Well then,' I said, and stood up, brushing off my hands. 'Let's go.'

12

I stopped outside the doorway. Micky Malone owned a nice house. His wife taught elementary school. They wouldn't have been able to afford the place on his salary alone, but together they managed. The hardwood floors gleamed with polish. I saw an original painting, a seascape, hanging on one of the walls of the living room, adjacent to the entryway. There were a lot of plants, a lot of greenery that, along with the wood grain of the floors, gave the place a rich, organic glow. It was one of those places that wasn't just a house. It was a home.

'Come on, Dresden,' Rudolph snapped. 'The lieutenant is waiting.'

'Is Mrs Malone here?' I asked.

'Yes.'

'Go get her. I need her to invite me in.'

'What?' Rudolph said. 'Give me a break. Who are you, Count Dracula?'

'Drakul is still in eastern Europe, last time we checked,' I replied. 'But I need her or Micky to ask me in, if you want me to do anything for you.'

'What the hell are you talking about?'

I sighed. 'Look. Homes, places that people live in and love and have built a life in have a kind of power of their own. If a bunch of strangers had been trooping in and out all day, I wouldn't have any trouble with the threshold, but you're not. You guys are friends.' Like Murphy had said – this one was personal.

Stallings frowned. 'So you can't come in?'

'Oh, I could come in,' I said. 'But I'd be leaving most of what I can do at the door. The threshold would mess with me being able to work any forces in the house.'

'What shit,' Rudolph snorted. 'Count Dracula.'

'Harry,' Stallings said. 'Can't we invite you in?'

'No. Has to be someone who lives there. Besides, it's polite,' I said. 'I don't like to go places where I'm not welcome. I'd feel a lot better if I knew it was all right with Mrs Malone for me to be here.'

Rudolph opened his mouth to spit venom on me again, but Stallings cut him off. 'Just do it, Rudy. Go get Sonia and bring her back here.'

Rudolph glowered but did what he was told, going into the house.

Stallings tapped out a cigarette and lit up. He puffed for a second, thoughtfully. 'So you can't do magic inside a house unless someone asks you in?'

'Not a house,' I said. 'A home. There's a difference.'

'So what about Victor Sells's place? I hear you took him on, right?'

I shook my head. 'He'd screwed up his threshold. He was running his business out of it, using the place for dark ceremonies. It wasn't a home anymore.'

'So you can't mess with anything on its own turf?'

'Can't mess with mortals, no. Monsters don't get a threshold.'

'Why not?'

'How the hell should I know,' I said. 'They just don't. I can't know everything, right?'

'Guess so,' Stallings said, and after a minute he nodded. 'Sure, I see what you mean. So it shuts you down?'

'Not completely, but it makes it a lot harder to do anything. Like wearing a lead suit. That's why vampires have to keep out. Other nasties like that. If you give them that much of a handicap, they have trouble just staying alive, much less using any freaky powers.'

Stallings shook his head. 'This magic crap. I never would have believed it before I came here. I still have trouble with it.'

'Yeah? That's good. Means you aren't running into it too much.'

He blew out twin columns of smoke from his nostrils. 'Could be changing. Last couple of days, we've had some people go missing. Bums, street people, folks some of the cops and detectives know.'

I frowned. 'Yeah?'

'Yeah. It's all rumors so far. And people like that, they can just be gone the next day. But since I started working S.I., stuff like that makes me nervous.'

I frowned, and debated telling Stallings what I knew about Bianca's party. Doubtless, there would be a whole flock of vampires in from out of town for the event. Maybe she and her flunkies were rounding up hors d'oeuvres. But I had no proof of that – for all I knew, the disappearances, if they *were* disappearances, could be related to the turbulence in the Nevernever. If so, the cops couldn't do anything about it. And if it was something else, I could be starting a very nasty exchange with Bianca. I didn't want to sic the cops on her for no reason. I'm pretty sure Bianca had the resources to send them back at me – and she could probably make it look like I'd done something to deserve it, too.

Besides that, in the circles of the supernatural commu-
nity, an Old World code of conduct still ruled. When you
have a problem, you settle it face to face, within the circle.
You don't bring in the cops and the other mortals as
weapons. They're the nuclear missiles of the supernatural
world. If you show people a supernatural brawl going on,
it's going to scare the snot out of them and the next thing
you know, they're burning everything and everyone in
sight. Most people wouldn't care that one scary guy might
have been right and the other was wrong. Both guys are
scary, so you ace both of them and sleep better at night.

It had been that way since the dawn of the Age of
Reason and the rising power of mortal kind. And more
power to the people, I say. I hated all these bullies,
vampires, demons, and bloodthirsty old deities rampaging
around like they ruled the world. Never mind that, until
a few centuries ago, they really had.

In any case, I decided to keep my mouth shut about
Bianca's gathering until I knew enough to be certain, either
way.

Stallings and I made small talk until Sonia Malone
appeared at the door. She was a woman of medium height,
comfortably overweight and solid-looking. Her face would
have been gorgeous when she was a young woman, and it
still carried that beauty, refined by years of self-confidence
and steady reliability. Her eyes were reddened, and she
wore no makeup, but her features seemed composed. She
wore a simple dress in a floral print, her only jewelry the
wedding band on her finger.

'Mr Dresden,' she said, politely. 'Micky told me that
you saved his life, last year.'

I coughed and looked down. Though I guess that was

true, technically, I still didn't see it that way. 'We all did everything we could, ma'am. Your husband was very brave.'

'Detective Rudolph said that I needed to invite you in.'

'I don't want to go where I'm not welcome, ma'am,' I replied.

Sonia wrinkled up her nose and eyed Stallings. 'Put that out, Sergeant.'

Stallings dropped the cigarette and mushed it out with his foot.

'All right, Mr Dresden,' she said. For a moment, her composure faltered and her lips began to tremble. She closed her eyes and took a deep breath, smoothing over her features, then opened her eyes again. 'If you can help my Micky, please come in. I invite you.'

'Thank you,' I said. I stepped forward, through the door, and felt the silent tension of the threshold parting around me like a beaded curtain rimed with frost.

We went through a living room where several cops, people I knew from S.I., sat around talking quietly. It reminded me of a funeral. They looked up at me as I went by, and talk ceased. I nodded to them, and we went on past, to a staircase leading up to the second floor.

'He was up late last night,' she told me, her voice quiet. 'Sometimes he can't sleep, and he didn't come to bed until late. I got up early, but I didn't want to wake him, so I let him sleep in.' Mrs Malone stopped at the top of the stairs, and pointed down the hall at a closed door. 'Th-there,' she said. 'I'm sorry. I c-can't . . .' She took another deep breath. 'I need to see about lunch. Are you hungry?'

'Oh. Yes, sure.'

'All right,' she said, and retreated back down the stairs.

I swallowed and looked at the door at the end of the hall, then headed toward it. My steps sounded loud in my own ears. I knocked gently on the door.

Karrin Murphy opened it. She wasn't anyone's idea of a leader of a group of cops charged with solving every bizarre crime that fell between the lines of the law enforcement system. She didn't look like someone who would stand, with her feet planted, putting tiny silver bullets into an oncoming freight train of a loup-garou, either – but she was.

Karrin looked up at me from her five-foot-nothing in height. Her blue eyes, normally clear and bright, looked sunken. She'd shoved her golden hair under a baseball cap, and wore jeans and a white T-shirt. Her shoulder harness wrinkled the cotton around the shoulder where her side arm hung. Lines stood out like cracks in a sunbaked field, around her mouth, her eyes. 'Hi, Harry,' she said. Her voice too was quiet, gruff.

'Hiya, Murph. You don't look so good.'

She tried to smile. It looked ghastly. 'I . . . I didn't know who else to call.'

I frowned, troubled. On any other day, Murphy would have returned my mildly insulting comment with compounded interest. She opened the door farther, and let me in.

I remembered Micky Malone as an energetic man of medium height, balding, with a broad smile and a nose that peeled in the sun if he walked outside to get his morning paper. The cane and limp were additions too recent for me to have firmly stuck in my memory. Micky wore old, quality suits, and was careful never to get the jackets messy or his wife would never let him hear the end of it.

I didn't remember Micky with a fixed, tooth-baring grin and eyes spread out in that Helter-Skelter gleam of madness. I didn't remember him covered in small scratches, or his fingernails crusted with his own blood, or his wrists and ankles cuffed to the iron-framed bed. He panted, grinning around the neatly decorated little room. I could smell sweat and urine. There were no lights on in the room, and the curtains had been drawn over the windows, leaving it in a brownish haze.

He turned his head toward me and his eyes widened. He sucked in a breath and threw back his head in a long, falsetto-pitched scream like a coyote's. Then he started laughing and rocking back and forth, jerking on the steel restraints, making the bed shake in a steady, squeaking rhythm.

'Sonia called us this morning,' Murphy said, toneless. 'She'd locked herself into her closet and had a cellular. We got here right before Micky finished breaking down the closet door.'

'She called the cops?'

'No. She called me. Said she didn't want them to see Micky like this. That it would ruin him.'

I shook my head. 'Damn. Brave lady. And he's been like this ever since?'

'Yeah. He was just . . . crazy mean. Screaming and spitting and biting.'

'Has he said anything?' I asked.

'Not a word,' Murphy said. 'Animal noises.' She crossed her arms and looked up at me, at my eyes for a second, before looking away. 'What happened to him, Harry?'

Micky giggled and started bouncing his hips up and down on the bed as he rocked, making it sound as though a couple of hyperkinetic teenagers were coupling there. My stomach turned. No wonder Mrs Malone hadn't been willing to come back into this room.

'You better give me a minute to find out,' I said.

'Could he be . . . you know. Possessed? Like in the movies?'

'I don't know yet, Murph.'

'Could it be some kind of spell?'

'Murphy, I don't know.'

'Dammit, Harry,' she snapped. 'You'd damned well better find out.' She clenched her fists and shook with suppressed fury.

I put my hand on her shoulder. 'I will. Give me some time with him.'

'Harry, I swear, if you can't help him—' Her voice caught in her throat, and tears sparkled in her eyes. 'He's one of *mine*, dammit.'

'Easy, Murph,' I told her, making my voice as gentle as I knew how. I opened the door for her. 'Go get some coffee, all right? I'll see what I can do.'

She glanced up at me and then back at Malone. 'It's okay, Micky,' she said. 'We're all here for you. You won't be alone.'

Micky Malone gave her that fixed grin and then licked his lips before bursting out into another chorus of giggles. Murphy shivered and then walked out of the room, her head bowed.

And left me alone with the madman.

13

I drew up a chair beside the bed and sat down. Micky stared at me with white-rimmed eyes. I rummaged around in the inside pocket of my duster. I had some chalk there, in case I needed to draw a circle. A candle and some matches. A couple of old receipts. Not much, magically speaking, to work with.

'Hi, there, Micky,' I said. 'Can you hear me in there?'

Micky broke out in another fit of giggles. I made sure to keep my eyes away from his. Hells bells, I did *not* want to get drawn into a soulgaze with Micky Malone at the moment.

'All right, Micky,' I said, keeping my voice calm, low, like you do with animals. 'I'm going to touch you – okay? I think I'll be able to tell if there's anything inside of you if I do. I'm not going to hurt you, so don't freak out.' As I spoke, I reached out a hand toward his bare arm and laid it lightly upon Micky's skin.

He was fever-hot to the touch. I could sense some kind of force at work on him – not the tingling energy of a practitioner's aura, or the ocean-deep power of Michael's faith, but it was there, nonetheless. Some kind of cold, crawling energy oozed over him.

What the hell?

It didn't feel like any kind of spell I'd ever experienced. And it wasn't a possession, I was sure of that. I would have been able to sense any kind of spirit-being in him, through a physical touch.

Micky stared at me for a second and then thrust his head at my hand, his teeth making snapping motions. I jerked back even though he couldn't have reached me. Someone trying to bite you makes you react, more than if they take a punch at you. Biting is just more primal. Spooky.

Micky started giggling again, rocking the bed back and forth.

'All right,' I breathed. 'I'm going to have to get a little desperate, here. If you weren't a friend, Micky . . .' I closed my eyes for a moment, steeling myself, then focused my will into a spot right between my eyebrows, only a little higher. I felt the tension gather there, the pressure, and when I opened my eyes again, I'd opened my wizard's Sight, too.

The Sight is a blessing and a curse. It lets you see things, things you couldn't normally see. With my Sight, I can see even the most ethereal of spirits. I can see the energies of life stirring and moving, running like blood through the world, between the earth and the sky, between water and fire. Enchantments stand out like cords braided from fiber-optic cables, or maybe Las Vegas-quality neon, depending on how complicated or powerful they are. You can sometimes see the demons that walk among mankind in human form, this way. Or the angels. You see things the way they really are, in spirit and in soul, as well as in body.

The problem is that anything you see stays with you. No matter how horrible, no matter how revolting, no matter how madness-inducing or terrifying – it stays with you. Forever. Always right there in your mind in full technicolor, never fading or becoming easier to bear. Sometimes you see things that are so beautiful you want to keep them with you, always.

But more often, in my line of work, you see things like Micky Malone.

He was dressed in boxers and a white undershirt, stained with bits of blood and sweat and worse. But when I turned my Sight on him, I saw something different.

He had been ravaged. Torn apart. He was missing flesh, everywhere. Something had attacked him and taken out sections of him in huge bites. I'd seen pictures of people who'd been attacked by sharks, had hunks of meat just taken, gone. That's what Micky looked like. It wasn't visible to the flesh, but something had torn his mind, and maybe his soul, to bloody shreds. He bled and bled, endlessly, never staining the sheets.

And wound around him, starting at his throat and running down to one ankle was a strand of black wire, oversized barbs gouging into his flesh, the ends disappearing seamlessly into his skin.

Just like Agatha Hagglethorn.

I stared at him, horrified, my stomach writhing and heaving. I had to fight to keep from throwing up. Micky looked up at me and seemed to sense something was different, because he went abruptly still. His smile didn't look mad to me anymore. It looked agonized, like a grimace of pain twisted and cranked until the muscles of his face were at the snapping point.

His lips moved. Shook, his whole face writhing with the expression. 'Uh, uh, uh,' he moaned.

'It's all right, Micky,' I said. I clasped my hands together to keep from shaking. 'I'm here.'

'Hurts,' he breathed at last, barely a whisper. 'It hurts,

it hurts, it hurts, it hurts, it hurts, it hurts . . .' He went on and on repeating it until he ran out of breath. Then he squeezed his eyes shut. Tears welled out and he broke into another helpless, maddened giggle.

What the hell could I do for *that*? The barbed wire had to be a spell of some kind, but it didn't look like anything I had ever seen before. Most magic throbbed and pulsed with light, life, even if it was being used for malevolent purposes. Magic comes from life, from the energy of our world and from people, from their emotions and their will. That's what I had always been taught.

But that barbed wire was dull, flat, matte-black. I reached out to touch it, and it almost seared my fingers with how cold it was. Micky, God. I couldn't imagine what he must have been going through.

The smart thing to do would have been to fall back. I could get Bob and work on this, research it, figure out how to get the wire from around Micky without hurting him. But he had already been suffering through this for hours. He might not make it through many more – his sanity was going to be hard-pressed to survive the spiritual mauling he had taken. Adding another day of this torture onto it all might send him someplace from where he'd never come back.

I closed my eyes and took a breath. 'I hope I'm right, Micky,' I told him. 'I'm going to try to make it stop hurting.'

He let out a whimpering little giggle, staring up at me.

I decided to start at his ankle. I swallowed, steeling myself again, and reached down, getting my fingers between the burning cold barbed wire and his skin. I clenched my teeth, forcing will, power, into the touch, enough to be able to touch the material of the spell around him. Then I started pulling. Slowly, at first, and then harder.

The metal strands burned into me. My fingers never went numb – they just began to ache more and more violently. The barbed wire resisted, barbs clinging at Micky's flesh. The poor man screamed aloud, agonized, though there was that horrible, tortured laughter added to it as well.

I felt tears burn into my eyes, from the pain, from Micky's scream, but I kept pulling. The end of the wire tore free of his flesh. I kept pulling. Barb by barb, inch by inch, I tore the wire-spell free, drawing it up *through* his flesh at times, pulling that dead, cold energy away from Micky. He screamed until he ran out of breath and I heard whimpers coming from somewhere else in the room. I guess it was me. I started using both hands, struggling against the cold magic.

Finally, the other end slithered free from Micky's neck. His eyes flew open wide and then he sagged down, letting out a low, exhausted moan. I gasped and stumbled back from the bed, keeping the wire in my hands.

It suddenly twisted and spun like a serpent, and one end plunged into my throat.

Ice. Cold. Endless, bitter, aching cold coursed through me, and I screamed. I heard footsteps running down the hall outside, a voice calling out. The wire whipped and thrashed around, the other end darting toward the floor, and I seized it in both hands, twisted it up and away from attaching itself at the other end. The loose strands near my neck started rippling, cold barbs digging into me through my clothes, my skin, as the dark energy tried to attach itself to *me*.

The door burst open. Murphy came through it, her eyes living flames of azure blue, her hair a golden coronet around her. She held a blazing sword in her hand and she shone so bright and beautiful and terrifying in her anger that it was hard to see. The Sight, I realized, dimly. I was seeing her for who she was.

'Harry! What the hell?'

I struggled against the wire, knowing that she couldn't see it or feel it, gasping. 'The window. Murph, open the window!'

She didn't hesitate for a second, but crossed the floor and threw open the window. I staggered after her, winding the frozen wire around one hand, my mind screaming with the agony of it. I fought it down, dragged it into a coil, my face twisted into a snarl as I did it. Anger surged up, hot and bright, and I reached for that power as I jerked the wire from my throat and threw it out the window as hard as I could, sending it sailing into the air.

I snarled, jabbed a finger at it, took all that anger and fear and sent it coursing out of me, toward that dark spell. '*Fuego!*'

Fire came to my call, roared forth from my fingertips and engulfed the wire. It writhed and then vanished in a detonation that rattled the house around me and sent me tumbling back to the floor.

I lay there for a minute, stunned, trying to get a handle on what was happening. Damn the Sight. It starts blurring the lines between what's real and what isn't. A guy would go crazy that way. Fast. Just keep it open all the time and let everything pour in and really *know* what everything is like. That sounded like a good idea, really. Just bask in all the beauty and horror for a while, just drink it all in and let it erase everything else, all that bother and worry about people being hurt or not being hurt—

I found myself sitting on the floor, aching from cold that had no basis in physical reality, giggling to myself in a high-pitched stream, rocking back and forth. I had to struggle to close my Sight again, and the second I did, everything seemed to settle, to become clearer. I looked up, blinking tears out of my eyes, panting. Outside, dogs were barking all over the place, and I could hear several car alarms whooping, touched off by the force of the blast.

Murphy stood over me, her eyes wide, her gun held in one hand and pointed at the door. 'Jesus,' she said, softly. 'Harry. What happened?'

My lips felt numb and I was freezing, all over, shaking. 'Spell. S-something attacked him. L-laid a spell on him after. H-had to burn it. Fire even burns in the s-spirit world. S-sorry.'

She put the gun away, staring at me. 'Are you all right?'

I shook some more. 'H-how's Micky?'

Murphy crossed the room to lay a hand on Micky's brow. 'His fever's gone,' she breathed. 'Mick?' she called gently. 'Hey, Malone. It's Murph. Can you hear me?'

Micky stirred, and blinked open his eyes. 'Murph?' he asked quietly. 'What's going on?' His eyes fell closed again, exhausted. 'Where's Sonia? I need her.'

'I'll get her,' Murphy breathed. 'You wait here. Rest.'

'My wrists hurt,' Micky mumbled.

Murphy looked back at me, and I nodded to her. 'He should be all right, now.' She unfastened the cuffs from him, but it looked as though he had already fallen into a deep, exhausted sleep.

Murphy drew the covers up over him, and smoothed his hair back from his forehead. Then she knelt down on the floor beside me. 'Harry,' she said. 'You look like . . .'

'Hell,' I said. 'Yeah, I know. He's going to need rest, Murph. Peace. Something tore him up inside, real bad.'

'What do you mean?'

I frowned. 'It's like . . . when someone close to you dies. Or when you break off a relationship with someone. It tears you up inside. Emotional pain. That's kind of what happened to Micky. Something tore him up.'

'What did it?' Murphy asked. Her voice was quiet, steel-hard.

'I don't know yet,' I said. I closed my eyes, shaking, and leaned my head back against a wall. 'I've been calling it the Nightmare.'

'How do we kill it?'

I shook my head. 'I'm working on it. It's staying a couple steps ahead of me, so far.'

'Damn,' Murphy said. 'I get sick of playing catch-up, sometimes.'

'Yeah. So do I.'

More footsteps came pounding down the hall, and Sonia Malone burst into the room. She saw Micky, laying quietly, and went to him as if she feared to stir the air too much, each movement fragile. She touched his face, his thinning hair, and he awoke enough to reach for her hand. She held onto it tightly, kissed his fingers, and bowed her head to rest her cheek against his. I heard her crying, letting it out.

Murphy and I traded a look, and rose by mutual consent

to leave Sonia in peace. Murphy had to help me up. I ached, everywhere, felt as though my bones had been frozen solid. Walking was hard, but Murphy helped me.

I took a last look at Sonia and Micky, and then quietly closed the door.

'Thank you, Harry,' Murphy said.

'Any time. You're my friend, Murph. And I'm always up to helping a lady in distress.'

She glanced up at me, a sparkle in her eyes underneath the brim of the baseball cap. 'You are such a chauvinist pig, Dresden.'

'A hungry chauvinist pig,' I said. 'I'm starving.'

'You should eat more often, beanpole.' Murphy sat me down on the top step and said, 'Stay here. I'll get you something.'

'Don't take too long, Murph. I've got work to do. The thing that did this comes out to play at sundown.'

I leaned against the wall and closed my eyes. I thought of dead animals and smashed cars and frozen agonies wrapped around Micky Malone's tortured soul. 'I don't know what the hell this Nightmare is. But I'm going to find it. And I'm going to kill it.'

'That sounds about right,' Murphy said. 'If I can help, you've got it.'

'Thanks, Murph.'

'Don't mention it. Um, Harry?'

I opened my eyes. She was watching me, her expression uncertain. 'For a minute there, when I came in. You stared at me. You stared at me with the strangest damned expression on your face. What did you see?' she asked.

'You'd laugh in my face if I told you,' I said. 'Go get me something to eat.'

She snorted and turned to go down the stairs and sort things out with the excited S.I. officers roaming around on the first floor. I smiled, remembering the vision, sharp and brilliant in my mind's eye. Murphy, the guardian angel, coming through the door in a blaze of wrath. It was a picture I wouldn't mind keeping with me. Sometimes you get lucky.

And then I thought of that barbed wire, the hideous torment I'd seen and briefly felt. The ghosts rising of late had been suffering from the same thing. But who could be doing it to them? And how? The forces used in that torture-spell weren't like anything I had seen or felt before. I had never heard of any kind of magic that could be slapped on a spirit or a mortal with the same results. I wouldn't have thought it possible. How was it being done?

More to the point, who was doing it? Or *what*?

I sat there shivering and alone and aching. I was starting to take this business personally. Malone was an ally, someone who had stood up to the bad guys beside me. The more I thought about it, the more angry and the more certain I became.

I would find this Nightmare, this thing that had crossed over, and destroy it.

And then I would find whoever or whatever had created it.

Unless, Harry, I thought to myself, *they find you first.*

14

'No,' I said into the phone. I tossed my coat onto a chair and then sprawled out on the couch. My apartment lay covered in shadows, sunlight filtering in through the sunken windows high up on the walls. 'I haven't gotten the chance yet. I lost a couple of hours detouring to pull a spell off of Micky Malone, from S.I. Someone had wrapped barbed wire around his spirit.'

'Mother of God,' Michael said. 'Is he all right?'

'Will be. But it's four hours of daylight lost.' I filled him in on Mort Lindquist and his diaries, as well as the events at Detective Malone's house.

'There isn't much more time to find this Lydia, Harry,' Michael agreed. 'Sundown's in another six hours.'

'I'm working on it. And after I get Bob out the door looking, I'll see if I can hit the streets myself. I got the Beetle back.'

He sounded surprised. 'It's not impounded?'

'Murphy fixed it for me.'

'Harry,' he said, disappointed. 'She broke the law to get you your car back?'

'Darn tootin' she did,' I said. 'She owed me a favor. Hey man, the Almighty doesn't arrange for *me* to be anywhere on time. I need wheels.'

Michael sighed. 'There isn't time to debate this right now. I'll call you if I find her – but it doesn't look good.'

'I just can't figure it. What would this thing have to do with that girl? We need to find her and work out the connection.'

'Could Lydia be responsible for the recent disturbances?'

'I don't think so. That spell I ran into today – I've never seen anything like it. It was . . .' I shivered, remembering. 'It was wrong, Michael. Cold. It was—'

'Evil?' he suggested.

'Maybe. Yeah.'

'There is such a thing as evil, Harry, in spite of what many people say. Just remember that there's good, too.'

I cleared my throat, uncomfortable. 'Murphy put out the word to the folks in blue – so if one of her friends on patrol sees a girl matching Lydia's description, we'll hear about it.'

'Outstanding,' Michael said. 'You see, Harry? This detour of yours to help Detective Malone is going to help us a great deal. Isn't that a very positive coincidence?'

'Yeah, Michael. Divine fortune, yadda, yadda. Call me.'

'Don't *yadda yadda* the Lord, Harry. It's disrespectful. God go with you.' And he hung up.

I put my coat away, got out my nice, heavy flannel robe and slipped into it, then went over to the rug against the south wall. I dragged it away from the floor, and the hinged door there, then swung the door open. I fetched a kerosene lamp, lit it up and dialed the wick up to a bright flame, then got ready to descend the folding wooden ladder into the sub-basement.

The telephone rang again.

I debated ignoring it. It rang again, insistent. I sighed, closed the door, put the rug back in place, and got to the phone on the fifth ring.

'What?' I said, uncharitably.

'I have to hand it to you, Dresden,' Susan said. 'You certainly know how to charm a girl the morning after.'

I let out a long breath. 'Sorry, Susan. I've been working and . . . it's not going so well. Lots of questions and no answers.'

'Ouch,' she said back. Someone said something to her in the background, and she murmured a response. 'I don't want to add to your day, but do you remember the name of that guy you and Special Investigations took down a couple months ago? The ritual killer?'

'Oh, right. Him . . .' I closed my eyes, and grubbed about in my memory. 'Leo something. Cravat, Camner, Conner. Kraven the Hunter. I didn't really get his name. I tracked him down by the demon he was calling up and nailed him that way. Michael and I didn't hang around for the paperwork afterwards, either.'

'Kravos?' Susan asked. 'Leonid Kravos?'

'Yeah, that might have been it, I think.'

'Great,' she said. 'Super. Thank you, Harry.' Her voice sounded a little tense, excited.

'Uh. Do you mind telling me what's going on?' I asked her.

'It's an angle I'm working on,' she said. 'Look, all I've got right now are rumors. I'll try to tell you more as soon as I've got something concrete.'

'Fair enough. I'm sort of focused on something else right now, anyway.'

'Anything you need help with?'

'God, I hope not,' I said. I shifted the phone a little closer to my ear. 'Did you sleep all right, last night?'

'Maybe,' she teased. 'It's hard to get really relaxed, when

I'm that unsatisfied, but your apartment's so cold it's kind of like going into hibernation.'

'Yeah, well. Next time I'll make sure it's a hell of a lot colder.'

'I'm shivering already,' she purred. 'Call you tonight if I can?'

'Might not be here.'

She sighed. 'I understand. Potluck, then. Thanks again, Harry.'

'Any time.'

We said goodbye, hung up, and I went back to the stairs leading down into the sub-basement. I uncovered the trap door, opened it, got my lantern, and clumped on down the steep, folding staircase.

My lab never got any less cluttered, no matter how much more organization I imposed on it. The contents only grew denser. Counters and shelves ran along three walls. A long table ran down the center of the room, with enough space for me to slip sideways down its length on either side. Next to the ladder, a kerosene heater blunted the worst of the subterranean chill. On the far side of the table, a brass ring had been set into the floor – a summoning circle. I'd had to learn the hard way to keep it clear of the other debris in the lab.

Debris. Technically, everything in the lab was useful, and served some kind of purpose. The ancient books with their faded, moldering leather covers and their all-pervasive musty smell, the plastic containers with resealable lids, the bottles, the jars, the boxes – they all had something in them I either needed or had needed at one time. Notebooks, dozens of pens and pencils, paper clips and staples, reams of paper covered in my restless, scrawling handwriting, the dried corpses of small animals, a human skull surrounded by paperback novels, candles, an ancient battle axe, they all had some significance. I just couldn't remember what it was for most of them.

I took the cover off the lamp and used it to light up about a dozen candles around the room, and then the kerosene heater. 'Bob,' I said. 'Bob, wake up. Come on, we've got work to do.' Golden light and the smell of candle flames and hot wax filled the room. 'I mean it, man. There's not much time.'

Up on its shelf the skull quivered. Twin points of orangish flame flickered up in the empty eye sockets. The white jaws parted in a pantomime yawn, an appropriate sound coming out with it. 'Stars and Stones, Harry,' the skull muttered. 'You're inhuman. It isn't even sundown yet.'

'Stop whining, Bob. I'm not in the mood.'

'Mood. I'm exhausted. I don't think I can help you out anymore.'

'Unacceptable,' I said.

'Even spirits get tired, Harry. I need rest.'

'Time enough for rest when I'm dead.'

'All right then,' Bob said. 'You want work, we make a deal. I want to do a ridealong the next time Susan comes over.'

I snorted at him. 'Hell's bells, Bob, don't you ever think about anything besides sex? No. I'm not letting you into my head while I'm with Susan.'

The skull spat out an oath. 'There should be a union. We could renegotiate my contract.'

I snorted. 'Any time you want to head back to the homeland, Bob, feel free.'

'No, no, no,' the skull muttered. 'That's all right.'

'I mean, there's still that misunderstanding with the Winter Queen, but—'

'All right, I said.'

'You probably don't need my protection anymore. I'm sure she'd be willing to sit down and work things out, rather than putting you in torment for the next few hundred—'

'All *right*, I said!' Bob's eyelights flamed. 'You can be such an asshole, Dresden, I swear.'

'Yep,' I agreed. 'You awake yet?'

The skull tilted to one side in a thoughtful gesture. 'You know,' it said. 'I am.' The eye sockets focused on me again. 'Anger really gets the old juices flowing. That was pretty sneaky.'

I got out a relatively fresh notepad and a pencil. It took me a moment to clear off a space on the central table. 'I've run into some new stuff. Maybe you can help me out. And we've got a missing person I need to look for.'

'Okay, hit me.'

I took a seat on the worn wooden stool and drew my warm robe a little closer about me. Trust me, wizards don't wear robes for the dramatic effect. They just can't get *warm* enough in their labs. I knew some guys in Europe who still operated out of stone towers. I shudder to think.

'Right,' I said. 'Just give me whatever you can.' And I outlined the events, starting with Agatha Hagglethorn, through Lydia and her disappearance, through my conversation with Mort Lindquist and his mention of the Nightmare, to the attack on poor Micky Malone.

Bob whistled, no mean trick for a guy with no lips. 'Let me get this straight. This creature, this thing, has been torturing powerful spirits for a couple of weeks with this barbed-wire spell. It tore up a bunch of stuff on consecrated ground. Then it blew through somebody's threshold and tore his spirit apart, and slapped a torture-spell on him?'

'You got it,' I said. 'So. What kind of ghost are we dealing with, and who could have called it up? And what is this girl's connection to it?'

'Harry,' Bob said, his tone serious. 'Leave this one alone.'

I blinked at him. 'What?'

'Maybe we could go on a vacation – Fort Lauderdale. They're having this international swimsuit competition there, and we could—'

I sighed. 'Bob, I don't have time for—'

'I know a guy who's possessed a travel agent for a few days, and he could get us tickets cut rate. What do you say?'

I peered at the skull. If I didn't know any better, I would think that Bob sounded . . . nervous? Was that even possible? Bob wasn't a human being. He was a spirit, a being of the Nevernever. The skull was his habitat, his home away from home. I let him stay in it, protected him, and bought him trashy romance novels on occasion in exchange for his help, his prodigious memory, and his affinity for the laws of magic. Bob was a records computer and personal assistant all rolled into one, provided you could keep his mind on the issue at hand. He knew thousands of beings in the Nevernever, hundreds of spell recipes, scores of formulae for potions and enchantments and magical constructions.

No spirit could have that kind of knowledge without it translating into considerable power. So why was he acting so scared?

'Bob. I don't know why you're so upset, but we need to stop wasting time. Sundown's coming in a few hours, and this thing is going to be able to cross over from the Nevernever and hurt someone else. I need to know what it is, and where it might be going, and how to kick its ass.'

'You humans,' Bob said. 'You're never satisfied. You always want to find out what's behind the next hill, open the next box. Harry, you've got to learn when you know too much.'

I stared up at him for a moment, then shook my head. 'We'll start with basics and work our way through this step by step.'

'Dammit, Harry.'

'Ghosts,' I said. 'Ghosts are beings that live in the spirit world. They're impressions left by a personality at the moment of death. They aren't like people, or sentient spirits like you. They don't change, they don't grow – they're just *there*, experiencing whatever it is they were feeling when they died. Like poor Agatha Hagglethorn. She was loopy.'

The skull turned its eye sockets away from me and said nothing.

'So, they're spirit-beings. Usually, they aren't visible, but they can make a body out of ectoplasm and manifest in the real world when they want to, if they're strong enough. And sometimes, they can just barely have any physical existence at all – just kind of exist as a cold spot, or a breath of wind, or maybe a sound. Right?'

'Give it up, Harry,' Bob said. 'I'm not talking.'

'They can do all kinds of things. They can throw things around and stack furniture. There have been documented incidents of ghosts blotting out the sun for a while, causing minor earthquakes, all sorts of stuff – but it isn't ever random. There's always some purpose to it, something related to their deaths.'

Bob quivered, about to add something, but clacked his bony teeth shut again. I grinned at him. It was a puzzle. No spirit of intellect could resist a puzzle.

'So, if someone leaves a strong enough imprint when they go, you got yourself a strong ghost. I mean, badass. Maybe like this Nightmare.'

'Maybe,' Bob admitted, grudgingly, then spun his skull to face wholly away from me. 'I'm still not talking to you, Harry.'

I drummed my pencil on the blank piece of paper. 'Okay. We know that this thing is stirring up the boundary between here and the Nevernever. It's making it easier for spirits to come across, and that's why things have been so busy, lately.'

'Not necessarily,' Bob chirped up. 'Maybe you're looking at it from the wrong angle.'

'Eh?' I asked.

He spun to face me again, eyelights glowing, voice enthusiastic. 'Someone *else* has been stirring these spirits, Harry. Maybe they started torturing them in order to make them jump around in the pool and start causing waves.'

There was a thought. 'You mean, prodding the big spirits into moving so that they create the turbulence.'

'Exactly,' Bob said, nodding. Then he caught himself, mouth still open. He turned the skull toward the wall and started banging the bony forehead against it. 'I am such an idiot.'

'Stirring up the Nevernever,' I said thoughtfully. 'But who would do that? And why?'

'You got me. Big mystery. We'll never know. Time for a beer.'

'Stirring up the Nevernever makes it easier for something to cross over,' I said. 'So . . . whoever laid out those torture spells must have wanted to pave the way for something.' I thought of dead animals and smashed cars. 'Something big.' I thought of Micky Malone, quivering and mad. 'And it's getting stronger.'

Bob looked at me again, and then sighed. 'All right,' he said. 'Gods, do you ever give up, Harry?'

'Never.'

'Then I might as well help you. You don't know what you're dealing with, here. And if you walk into this with your eyes closed, you're going to be dead before the sun rises.'

15

'Dead before the sun rises,' I said. 'Stars, Bob, why don't you just go all the way over the melodramatic edge and tell me that I'm going to be sleeping with the fishes?'

'I'm not sure that much of you would be left,' Bob said, seriously. 'Harry, look at this thing. Look at what it's done. It crossed a threshold.'

'So what?' I asked. 'Lots of things can. Remember that toad demon? It came over my threshold and trashed my whole place.'

'In the first place, Harry,' Bob said, 'you're a bachelor. You don't have all that much of a threshold to begin with. This Malone, though – he was a family man.'

'So?'

'So it means his home has a lot more significance. Besides which – the toad demon came in and everything after that was pure physical interaction. It smashed things, it spat out acid saliva, that kind of thing. It *didn't* try to wrench your soul apart or enchant you into a magical sleep.'

'This is getting to be a pretty fine distinction, Bob.'

'It is. Did you ask for an invitation before you went into the Malone's house?'

'Yeah,' I said. 'I guess I did. It's polite, and—'

'And it's harder for you to work magic in a home you haven't been invited into. You cross the threshold without an invitation, and you leave a big chunk of your power at the door. It doesn't affect you as much because you're a mortal, Harry, but it still gets you in smaller ways.'

'And if I was an all-spirit creature,' I said.

Bob nodded. 'It hits you harder. If this Nightmare is a ghost, like you say, then the threshold should have stopped it cold – and even if it had gone past it, then it shouldn't have had the kind of power it takes to hurt a mortal that badly.'

I frowned, drumming my pencil some more, and made some notes on the paper, trying to keep everything straight. 'And certainly not enough to lay out a spell that powerful on Malone.'

'Definitely.'

'So what *could* do that, Bob? What are we dealing with, here?'

Bob's eyes shifted restlessly around the room. 'It could be a couple of things from the spirit world. Are you sure you want to know?' I glared at him. 'All right, all right. It could be something big enough. Something so big that even a fraction of it was enough to attack Malone and lay that spell on him. Maybe a god someone's dug up. Hecate, Kali, or one of the Old Ones.'

'No,' I said, flatly. 'Bob, if this thing was so tough, it wouldn't be tearing up people's cars and ripping kitty cats apart. That's not my idea of a godlike evil. That's just pissed off.'

'Harry, it went through the threshold,' Bob said. 'Ghosts don't *do* that. They *can't.*'

I stood up, and started pacing back and forth on the little open space of floor of my summoning circle. 'It isn't one of the Old Ones. Guardian spells all over the world would be freaking out, alerting the Gatekeeper and the Council of something like that. No, this is local.'

'Harry, if you're wrong—'

I jabbed a finger at Bob. 'If I'm *right*, then there's a monster out there messing with my town, and I'm obliged to do something about it before someone else gets hurt.'

Bob sighed. 'It blew through a threshold.'

'So . . .' I said, pacing and whirling. 'Maybe it had some other way to get around the threshold. What if it had an invitation?'

'How could it have gotten that?' Bob said. 'Dingdong, Soul Eater Home Delivery, may I come in?'

'Bite me,' I said. 'What if it took Lydia? Once she was out of the church, she could have been vulnerable to it.'

'Possession?' Bob said. 'Possible, I guess – but she was wearing your talisman.'

'If it could get around a threshold, maybe it could get around that too. She goes to Malone's, looks helpless, and gets an invite in.'

'Maybe.' Bob did a passable imitation of scrunching up his eyes. 'But then why were all those little animals torn up outside? We are going way out on a branch here. There are a lot of maybes.'

I shook my head. 'No, no. I've got a feeling about this.'

'You've said that before. You remember the time you wanted to make "smart dynamite" for that mining company?'

I scowled. 'I hadn't had much sleep that week. And anyway, the sprinklers kicked in.'

Bob chortled. 'Or the time you tried to enchant that broomstick so that you could fly? Remember *that*? I thought it would take a year to get the mud out of your eyebrows.'

'Would you focus, please,' I complained. I pushed my hands against either side of my head to keep it from exploding with theories, and whittled them down to the ones that fit the facts. 'There are only a couple of possibilities. A, we're dealing with some kind of godlike being in which case we're screwed.'

'And the Absurd Understatement Award goes to Harry Dresden.'

I glared at him. 'Or,' I said, lifting a finger, 'B, this thing is a spirit, something we've seen before, and it's using smoke and mirrors within the rules we already know. Either way, I think Lydia knows more than she's admitting.'

'Gee, a woman taking advantage of Captain Chivalry. What are the odds.'

'Bah,' I said. 'If I can find her and find out what she knows, I could nail it today.'

'You're forgetting the third possibility,' Bob said amiably. 'C, it's something new that neither of us understand and you're sailing off in ignorance to plunge into the mouth of Charybdis.'

'You're so encouraging,' I said, fastening on the bracelet, and slipping on the ring, feeling the quiet, humming power in them both.

Bob somehow waggled his eyebrow ridges. 'Hey, you never went out with Charybdis. What's the plan?'

'I loaned Lydia my Dead Man's Talisman,' I said.

'I still can't believe after all the work we did, you gave it to the first girl to wiggle by.'

I scowled at Bob. 'If she's still got it, I should be able to work up a spell to home in on it, like when I find people's wedding rings.'

'Great,' Bob said. 'Give 'em hell, Harry. Have fun storming the castle.'

'Not so fast,' I said. 'She might not have it with her. If she's in on this with the Nightmare, then she could have dumped it once she had it away from me. That's where you come in.'

'Me?' Bob squeaked.

'Yes. You're going to head out, hit the streets, and talk to all of your contacts, see if we can get to her before sundown. We've only got a couple of hours.'

'Harry,' Bob pointed out, 'the sun's up. I'm exhausted. I can't just flit around like some kinda dewdrop fairy.'

'Take Mister,' I said. 'He doesn't mind you riding around. And he could use the exercise. Just don't get him killed.'

'Hooboy,' Bob said. 'Once more into the breech, dear friends, eh? Harry, don't quit your job to become a motivational speaker. I have your permission to come out?'

'Yep,' I said, 'for the purposes of this mission only. And don't waste time prowling around in women's locker rooms again.'

I put out the candles and the heater and started up the stepladder. Bob followed, drifting out of the eye sockets of the skull as a glowing, candleflame-colored cloud, and flowed up the steps past me. The cloud glided over to where Mister dozed in the warm spot near the mostly dead fire, and seeped in through the cat's grey fur. Mister sat up and blinked his yellow-green eyes at me, stretched his back, and flicked his stump of a tail back and forth before letting out a reproachful meow.

I scowled at Mister and Bob, shrugging into my duster, gathering up my blasting rod and my exorcism bag, and

old black doctor's case full of stuff. 'Come on, guys,' I said.
'We're on the trail. We have the advantage. What could
possibly go wrong?'

16

Finding people is hard, especially when they don't want to be found. It's so difficult, in fact, that estimates run up near seven-digit figures on how many people disappear, without a trace, every year in the United States. Most of these people aren't ever found.

I didn't want Lydia to become one of these statistics. Either she was one of the bad guys and had been playing me for a sucker, or she was a victim who was in need of my help. If the former, then I wanted to confront her – I have this thing about people who lie to me and try to get me into trouble. If the latter, then I was probably the only one in Chicago who could help her. She could be possessed by one very big and very brawny spirit who needed to get some, pardon the pun, exorcise.

Lydia had been on foot when she left Father Forthill, and I don't think she'd had much cash. Assuming she hadn't come into any more resources, she'd likely still be in the Bucktown/Wicker Park area, so I headed the Blue Beetle that way. The Beetle isn't really blue any more. Both doors had to be replaced when they'd gotten clawed to shreds, and the hood had been slagged, with a big old hole melted in it. My mechanic, Mike, who can keep the Beetle running most days, hadn't asked any questions. He'd just replaced the parts with pieces of other Volkswagens, so that the Blue Beetle was technically blue, red, white, and green. But my appellation stuck.

I tried to keep my cool as I drove, at least as best as I could. My wizard's propensity for blowing out any kind of advanced technology seems to get worse when I'm upset, angry, or afraid. Don't ask me why. So I did my best to Zen out until I got to my destination – parking strips alongside Wicker Park.

A brisk breeze made my duster flap as I got out. On one side of the street, tall town houses and a pair of apartment buildings gleamed as the sun began to go down over the western plains. The shadows of the trees in Wicker Park, meanwhile, stretched out like black fingers creeping toward my throat. Thank God my subconscious isn't too symbolically aware or anything. The park had a bunch of people in it, young people, mothers with kids, while on the streets, business types began arriving in their business clothes, heading for one of the posh restaurants, pubs, or cafes that littered the area.

I got a lump of chalk and a tuning fork out of my exorcism bag. I glanced around, then squatted down on the sidewalk and drew a circle around myself, willing it closed as the chalk marks met themselves on the concrete. I felt a sensation, a crackling tension, as the circle closed, encasing the local magical energies, compressing them, stirring them.

Most magic isn't quick and dirty. The kind of stunts you can pull off when some nasty thing is about to jump up in your face are called evocations. They're fairly limited in what they can do, and difficult to master. I only had a couple of evocations that I could do very well, and most of the time I needed the help of artificial foci, such as my blasting rod or one of my other enchanted doodads, to make sure that I don't lose control of the spell and blow up myself along with the slobbering monster.

Most magic is a lot of concentration and hard work. That's where I was really good – thaumaturgy. Thaumaturgy is traditional magic, all about drawing symbolic links between items or people and then investing energy to get the effect that you want. You can do a lot with thaumaturgy, provided you have enough time to plan things out, and more time to prepare a ritual, the symbolic objects, and the magical circle.

I've yet to meet a slobbering monster polite enough to wait for me to finish.

I slipped my shield bracelet off of my wrist and laid it in the center of the circle – that was my channel. The talisman I'd passed off to Lydia had been constructed in a very similar manner, and the two bracelets would resonate on the same pitches. I took the tuning fork and laid it down beside the bracelet, with the two ends of the shield bracelet touching either tine, making a complete circle.

Then I closed my eyes, and drew upon the energy gathered in the circle. I brought it into me, molded it, shaped it into the effect I was looking for with my thoughts, fiercely picturing the talisman I'd given Lydia while I did. The energy built and built, a buzzing in my ears, a prickling along the back of my neck. When I was ready, I spread my hands over the two objects, opened my eyes and said, firmly, *'Duo et unum.'* At the words, the energy poured out of me in a rush that left me a little light-headed. There were no sparks, no glowing luminescence or anything else that would cost a special effects budget some money – just a sense of completion, and a tiny, almost inaudible hum.

I picked up the bracelet and put it back on, then took

up the tuning fork and smudged the circle with my foot, willing it broken. I felt the little *pop* of the residual energies being released, and I rose up and fetched my exorcism bag from the Beetle. Then I walked away, down the sidewalk, holding my tuning fork out in front of me. After I'd taken several paces away, I turned in a slow circle.

The fork remained silent until I'd turned almost all the way around – then it abruptly shivered in my hand, and emitted a crystalline tone when I had it facing vaguely northwest. I looked up and sighted along the tines of the fork, then walked a dozen paces farther and triangulated as best I could. The direction change on the way the fork faced when it toned the second time was appreciable, even without any kind of instruments – Lydia must have been fairly close.

'Yes,' I said, and started off at a brisk walk, sweeping the tuning fork back and forth, setting my feet in the direction that it chimed. I kept on like that to the far side of the park, where the tuning fork pointed directly at a building that had once been some kind of manufacturing facility, perhaps, but now stood abandoned.

The lower floor was dominated by a pair of garage doors and a boarded-up front door. On the lower two floors, most of the windows had been boarded up. On the third floor, truly bored or determined vandals had pitched stones through those windows, and their shattered edges stood sharp and dusty against the blackness behind them, like dirty ice.

I took two more readings, from fifty feet on either side of the first. All pointed directly to the building. It glowered down at me, silent and spooky.

I shivered.

I would be smart to call Michael. Maybe even Murphy. I could get to a phone, try to get in touch with them. It wouldn't take them long to get here.

Of course, it would be after sundown. The Nightmare, if it was inside Lydia, would be free to leave her then, to roam abroad. If I could get to her, exorcise this thing now, I could end the spree of destruction it was on.

If, if, if. I had a lot of ifs. But I didn't have much time. The sun was swiftly vanishing. I reached inside my duster and got out my blasting rod, transferring my exorcism bag to the same hand as the tuning fork. Then I headed across the street, to the garage doors of the building. I tested one, and to my surprise it rolled upwards. I glanced left and right, then slipped inside into the darkness, shutting the door behind me.

It took a moment for my eyes to adjust. The room was lit only by the fading light that slipped its fingers beneath the plyboard over the windows, the edges of the garage doors. It was a loading dock that encompassed almost the entire first floor, I judged. Stone pillars held the place up. Water dripped somewhere, from a broken pipe, and there were pools of it everywhere on the floor.

A brand-new side-panel van, its engine still ticking, cooling off, stood parked at the far side of the loading dock, next to a five-foot-high stone abutment, where trucks would once have backed up to load and unload goods. A sign hanging by one hinge, over the van, read SUMNER'S TEXTILES MFG.

I approached the van slowly, my blasting rod held loosely at my side. I swept the tuning fork, and my eyes, around the shadowed chamber. The fork hummed every time it swept past the van.

The white van all but glowed in the half-light. Its windows had been tinted, and I couldn't see inside of them, even when I came within ten feet or so.

Something, some sound or other cue that I hadn't quite caught on the conscious level made the hair on the back of my neck prickle up. I spun to face the darkness behind me, the tip of my blasting rod rising up, my bruised fingers wrapped tight around its haft. I focused my senses on the darkness, and listened, honing my attention to the area around me.

Darkness.

Drip of water.

Creak of building, above me.

Nothing.

I put the tuning fork in my duster pocket. Then I turned back to the van, closed the distance quickly, and hauled open the side door, leveling my rod on the inside.

A blanket-wrapped bundle, approximately Lydia-sized, lay inside the van. One pale hand lay limp outside of it, my talisman, scorched-looking and bloodstained, wrapped around the slender wrist.

My heart leapt into my throat. 'Lydia?' I asked. I reached out and touched her wrist. Felt the dull, slow throb of pulse. I let out a breath of relief, pulled the blankets from her pale face. Her eyes were open, staring, the pupils dilated until there was barely any color left in them at all. I waved my hand in front of her eyes and said again, 'Lydia.' She didn't respond. Drugged, I thought.

What the hell was she doing here? Laying in a van, covered up in blankets drugged and placed as neatly as could be. It didn't make sense, unless, she was . . .

Unless she was a distraction. The bait for a trap.

I turned, but before I got halfway around that cold energy I'd felt the night before flooded over the side of my face, my throat. Something blonde and incredibly swift slammed into me with the force of a rushing bull, throwing me off my feet and into the van. I spun around onto my elbows to see the vampire Kyle Hamilton coming for me, his eyes black and empty, his face screwed up into a grimace of hunger. He still wore his tennis whites. I kicked at his chest, and superhuman strength or no, it lifted him up off the ground for a second, brought me a half-breath of life. I lifted my right hand, the silver ring there gleaming, and cried, '*Assantius!*'

The energy stored in the ring, all kinetic stuff that it saved back a little every time I moved my arm, unloaded in a flood, right in the vampire's face, an unseen fury of motion. The raw force split his lips – but no blood flowed out. It dug into the corners of his eyes and tore the skin away, but there was still no blood. It ripped the skin from his cheekbones, all rubbery black beneath the Anglo-Saxon pink, strips of flesh flapping back in the wave of force like flags in a high wind.

The vampire's body flew back and up. It thudded hard against the ceiling and then fell to the floor with a thump. I struggled out of the van, my chest aching with a dull sort of pain. I left the doctor's bag behind, shook out the shield bracelet and extended my left arm in front of me.

Kyle stirred for a moment and then flung himself to all fours, his body weirdly contorted, shoulders standing up too much, his back bent at a crooked angle. Shreds of flesh dangled from his face, slick-looking, rubbery black beneath them. His eyes also had the skin torn away from them, like pieces of a rubber mask, and bulged out black and huge and inhuman. His jaws parted, showing dripping fangs, saliva pattering to the damp floor.

'You,' the vampire hissed, his voice calm, normal, disconcerting.

'Whoah, that was original,' I muttered, drawing in my will. 'Yeah, me. What the hell are you doing here? Where do you think you're going with Lydia?'

His inhuman expression flickered. 'Who?'

My chest panged, hard, sharp, hot, as if something was broken. Broken badly. I remained standing, though, not letting him see weakness. 'Lydia. Bad dye job, sunken eyes, in your van, wearing my talisman on her wrist.'

He hissed out a dripping runnel of laughter. 'Is that what she told you her name was? You've been used, Dresden.'

I got a shivery feeling again, and narrowed my eyes. I didn't have any warning but instinct to make me throw myself to one side in an abrupt leap.

The vampire's sister, Kelly, as blonde and pretty as he had been a moment before, landed in the space I had occupied. She too dropped to her knees with a drooling hiss, fangs showing, eyes bulging. She wore a white cat suit, clinging tight to her curves, along with white boots and gloves, and a short white cape with a deep hood. Her clothing was smudged, imperfect, spotted with flecks of scarlet, and her blonde hair in disarray. Blood stained her mouth, like smeared lipstick, or a child with a big cup of juice. A blood mustache. Hells bells.

I kept my blasting rod trained on Kelly, my left hand thrust out before me. 'So you two are putting the snatch on Lydia, eh? Why?'

'Let me kill him,' moaned the female, her eyes all black, empty and hungry. '*Kyle*. I'm *hungry*.'

So sue me, I weird out when someone starts talking about *eating* me. I swung the blasting rod right at Kelly's face and started sending power into it, setting the tip to glowing. 'Yeah, Kyle,' I said. 'Let her try.'

Kyle *rippled*, beneath his skin, and it was enough to make my stomach turn. Something like that just ain't right, even when you know what's underneath. 'This affair is none of yours, wizard.'

'The girl is under my protection,' I said. 'You two clear out, now, and I won't have to get rough with you.'

'That will not happen,' Kyle said, his voice deadly quiet.

'Kyle,' the female moaned again. More drool slithered out of her mouth, dripping to the floor. She started shaking, quivering, as if she were about to fly apart. Or at me. My mouth went dry, and I got ready to blast her.

I saw Kyle move out of the corner of my eye. I lifted the shield bracelet toward him, transferred my will to it, but in time only to partially deflect the broken chip of concrete that he threw at my head. It slammed against my temple and sent me spinning. I saw Kelly blur toward me, white cape flying, and I lifted the blasting rod toward her, shouting, '*Fuego!*'

Fire slammed out the end of the rod, missing Kelly by at least a foot, but still hot enough to set the hem of her cloak ablaze. The flame slewed in an arch across the ceiling and down the wall as I started falling, cutting through wood and brick and stone like an enormous arc-welder.

She flung herself atop me, straddling my hips with her thighs, moaning in excitement. I thrust the blasting rod toward her, but she batted it aside, laughing in a wild, hysterical tone, throwing her smoldering cloak off with the other hand. She plunged toward my throat, but I lifted my hands to catch at her mane of hair. I knew it was a futile gesture – she was just too damned strong. I wouldn't be able to hold her off of me for long, a few seconds at most. My heart pounded in my burning chest, and I struggled, gasping in air.

And then droplets of her spittle fell onto my throat, my cheek, into my mouth. And none of it mattered any more.

It was a glorious sensation that spread over me – warmth, security, peace Ecstasy began at my skin and spread through me, easing all the horrid tension from my muscles. My fingers slackened in Kelly's lovely hair, and she purred, her hips writhing against mine. She lowered her mouth toward me, and I felt her breath on my skin, her breasts press against me through the thin material of her bodysuit.

Something, some nagging thought, bothered me for a moment. Perhaps it was something about the perfect, lightless depths of her eyes, or the way her fangs rubbed against my throat – no matter how good it felt. But then I felt her lips on my skin, felt her draw in her breath in shivering anticipation, and it stopped mattering. I just wanted *more*.

Then there was a roaring sound, and I dimly perceived the west wall of the building collapsing, falling away in great, flaming sections of wood and brick. The blast I had sent spewing at Kelly had sliced through the ceiling, walls, and support beams. It must have weakened the structure of the entire building as it had.

Oops.

Sunlight flooded in, through the falling bricks and clouds of dust, the last rays of daylight, warm and golden on my face, painfully bright in my eyes.

Kelly screamed and, wherever her skin wasn't covered by cloth, from her chin up, mostly – she burst into flame. The light hit her like a physical blow, hurling her away from me. I became aware of a dull pain, uncomfortable heat on my cheek, my throat, where her saliva had coated my skin.

Everything was light and heat and pain for a few moments, and someone was screaming. I struggled up a moment later, peering around the inside of the building. Fire spread, a dull chewing sound on the floors above me, and through the missing section of wall I could hear sirens in the distance. There were smears of something black and greasy on the concrete floor, leading to the white van. The sunlight barely touched the back window of the vehicle. The side door stood wide open, and Kyle, his face still hanging in ragged strips, hauled something grotesque – his sister, her true form no longer shrouded by its mask of flesh. The vampire girl made keening sounds of agony while her brother pitched her into the back of the van. He slammed the door shut, a snarl rippling his split lips. He took a step toward me, then clenched his jaws in frustration, stopping just short of the sunlight.

'Wizard,' he hissed. 'You'll pay. I'll make you pay for this.' Then he spun back to the van, with its dark-tinted windows, and leapt in. A moment later, the engine roared to life, and the van sped toward the garage doors, plowed through one of them, sending shards of wood flying, jounced into the street, and vanished from sight, engine racing.

I remained in place, stunned, burnt, hurting, my brain clouded. Then I stumbled to my feet, and staggered toward the hole in the wall, and out into the fading daylight. Sirens got closer.

'Damn,' I mumbled, looking back at the spreading fires. 'I'm kinda hard on buildings.'

I shook my head, trying to clear my thoughts. Dark. It was getting dark. Had to get home. Vampires could come out after dark. Home, I thought. Home.

I started stumbling back toward the Beetle.

Behind me, as I did, the sun sank beneath the horizon – freeing all the things that go bump in the night to come out and play.

17

I don't remember how I managed to get home again. I have a vague image of all the cars around me going way too fast, and then of Mister's rumbling purr greeting me as I got into my apartment and locked the door behind me.

The vampire's narcotic saliva had soaked in through my skin in a matter of a second or three, spreading into my system in short order after that. I felt numb, light, all over. The room wasn't quite whirling, but when I moved my eyes, things almost seemed to blur a little, then to settle when I focused on something. I throbbed. Every time my heart beat, my entire body pulsed with a slow, gentle pang of pleasant sensation.

Something inside me couldn't help but love every second of it. Even counting the times I'd been juiced up in a hospital, it was the best drug I'd ever had.

I stumbled to my narrow bed and dropped onto it. Mister came and prowled around my face, waiting for me to get up and feed him. 'Go away,' I heard myself mumble. 'Stupid furball. Go on.' He put one paw on my throat, and touched the area of burned skin where the sunlight had struck the smear of Kelly Hamilton's saliva. Pain flared through me, and I groaned, forcing myself into the kitchen. I got some cold cuts out of the icebox and dropped them onto Mister's plate. Then I stumbled into the bathroom and flicked on the light.

It hurt.

I shielded my eyes and studied myself in the mirror. My pupils had dilated out nice and big. The skin on my throat, my cheek, was red and glowing, as though from falling asleep outside on a summer afternoon – painful, but not dangerous. I couldn't find any marks on my throat, so the vampire hadn't bitten me. I was pretty sure that was a good thing. Something about a bite being a link to a victim. If she'd bitten me, she could have gotten into my head. Usual mind-control enchantment. Breaking one of the Laws of Magic.

I stumbled back to my bed and sank down onto it, trying to sort out my thoughts. My lovely, throbbing body made this fairly difficult. Mister came nosing around again, but I shoved him away with one hand and forced myself to ignore him.

'Focus, Harry,' I mumbled to myself. 'Got to have focus.'

I'd learned to block out pain, when necessary. Studying under Justin, it had been a practical necessity. My teacher hadn't believed in sparing the rod and spoiling the potential wizard. You learn very quickly not to make mistakes given the correct incentive to avoid them.

Blocking out pleasure was a more difficult exercise, but I somehow managed. The first thing I had to do was separate my sense of enjoyment. It took me a while, but I slowly marked out the boundaries of the parts of me that liked all the wonderful, warm sensations, and walled them away. Then the actual pounding happiness itself. I found my heart rate and slowed it a bit, though it was already going too slowly, then started shutting down perception of my limbs, pushing them behind the walls with the rest of me that wasn't doing any good. Giddy delight went next, leaving only a dull fuzz across my thinking, chemically unavoidable.

I closed my eyes and breathed, and tried to sort through things.

Lydia had fled the shelter of the church, and Father Forthill's protection. Why? I thought back, over the details of everything I knew about her. Her sunken eyes. The tingle of touching her aura. Had her hands been shaking, just a little? I think they had, in retrospect. I thought of what I had seen of her in the van, of the bracelet on her wrist. Her beating pulse. Had it been slow? I'd thought so, at the time – but then my own had been racing. I focused on the moment I'd been touching her.

Sixty, I thought. She'd been around sixty beats per minute. My own heart rate was about a sixth of that at the moment. Had been half that, before I'd slowed it down to quiet the song of the drug in my blood.

(Song, pretty song, why the hell did I have it shut away, when I could just lower the walls, listen to the music, lay here all happy and quiet and just *feel*, just *be* . . .)

I took a moment to prop the walls up again. Lydia's heart rate had been at human normal, nominally. But she'd been laying limp and still, much as I was, now. Kyle and Kelly had poisoned her, as they had me, I was sure of it. Then why had her heart been beating so quickly, in comparison?

She left the church and had been taken, perhaps, by the Nightmare. Then gone to Malone's house under its guidance, and gotten an invitation in. But why go to Malone's house? What did he have to do with anything?

Malone and Lydia. They'd both been attacked by the Nightmare. What was the connection? What linked them together?

More questions. What did the vampires want with her? If Kyle and his sister had been after Lydia, that meant that Bianca wanted her. Why? Was Bianca in league with the Nightmare? If she was, why the hell would she need to use her most powerful goons to kidnap the girl, if she was possessed by Bianca's ally?

And how the hell had the Nightmare gone through the threshold? An even better question, how had it gotten through the protection offered to Lydia by my Dead Man's talisman? No ghost should have been able to offer her any direct harm or contact through that thing. It didn't make any sense.

(Why should it? Why should anything need to mean anything at all? Just sit back, Harry, lay back and feel good and relax and let your blood sing, let your heart beat, just ease down into the wonderful, warm, spinning dark and stop worrying, stop caring, drift and float and . . .)

The walls started to crumble.

I struggled, but sudden fear made my heartbeat quicken. I fought against the pull of the poison in my blood, but that struggle only made me more vulnerable, more susceptible. I couldn't fail, now. I *couldn't*. People were depending upon me. I had to fight—

The walls fell, and my blood surged up with a roar.

I drifted.

And it was nice.

Drifting turned into sleep. Gentle, dark sleep. And sleep, in time, turned into dreams.

In my dream, I found myself back at the warehouse down by Burnham Harbor. It was night, beneath a full moon. I was wearing my duster, my black shirt and jeans, my black sneakers, which were better for . . . well.

Sneaking. Michael stood beside me, his breath steaming in the winter air, dressed in his cloak, his full mail, his bloodred surcoat. *Amoracchius* rode his hip, a source of quiet, constant power. Murphy and the other members of Special Investigations all wore dark, loose clothing and their flack vests, and everyone had a gun in one hand and something else – like vials of holy water or silver crucifixes – in the other.

Micky Malone glanced up at the moon and shifted the shotgun in both hands – he was the only person relying upon raw, shredding firepower. Hey, the guy had a point. 'All right,' he said. 'We go in and then what?'

'Here's the plan,' Murphy said. 'Harry thinks that the killer's followers will be drugged out and dozing. We round them up, cuff them up, and move on.' Murphy grimaced, her blue eyes sparkling in the silver light. 'Tell them what's next, Harry.'

I kept my voice quiet. 'The guy we're after is a sorcerer. It's sort of like being a wizard, only he spends all his energy doing things that are mostly destructive. He isn't good at doing anything that doesn't fuck someone up.'

'Which makes him a badass as far as we're concerned,' Malone growled.

'Pretty much,' I confirmed. 'The guy's got power, but no class. I'm going to go in and lock down his magic. We think he might have a demon on a string – that's what the murders have been for. They're part of his payment to get the demon to work for him.'

'Demon,' breathed Rudolph. 'Jesus, can you believe this shit?'

'Jesus did believe in demons,' Michael said, his voice quiet. 'If the creature is there, do not get close to it. Don't shoot at it. Leave it to me. If it gets past me, throw your holy water at the thing and run while it screams.'

'That's pretty much the plan,' I confirmed. 'Keep any human flunkies with knives from giving them to me or Michael. I'll take Kravos's powers out, and you guys grab him as soon as we're sure the demon won't eat us. I deal with any other supernatural stuff. Questions?'

Murphy shook her head. 'Let's go.' She leaned out and pumped her arm in the air, signaling the rest of the S.I. team, and we headed into the warehouse.

Everything went according to plan. In the front of the warehouse, a dozen young people, all with that lost, lonely look to them, lay dozing amidst fumes that made me dizzy. The remnants of a serious party lay all over the place — beer cans, clothes, roaches, empty needles, you name it. The cops fell on the kids in a dark-clad swarm and had them cuffed and hauled out into a waiting wagon in under ninety seconds.

Michael and I moved forward, toward the back of the warehouse, through stacks of boxes and shipping crates. Murphy, Rudy, and Malone followed hard on our heels. I cracked the door at the back wall and peered through it.

I saw a circle of black, smoking candles, a red-lit figure dressed in feathers and blood kneeling beside it, and something dark and horrible crouching within.

'Bingo,' I whispered. I turned to Michael. 'He's got the demon in there with him.'

The Knight simply nodded, and loosened his sword in its sheath.

I drew the doll out of my duster's pocket. It was a Ken doll, naked, and not anatomically correct, but it would work. The single hair that forensics had recovered from the last victim's crime scene had been carefully Scotch-taped to the doll's head, and I had attired Ken in the general garb of someone delving into black magic – reversed pentagrams, some feathers, and some blood (from a hapless mouse Mister had nabbed).

'Murphy,' I hissed. 'Are you absolutely sure about this hair? That it belongs to Kravos?' If it didn't, the doll wouldn't do diddly to the sorcerer, unless I managed to throw it into his eye.

'We're reasonably sure,' she whispered, 'yes.'

'Reasonably sure. Great.' But I knelt down, and marked out the circle around me, then another around the Ken doll, and wrought my spell.

The hair was Kravos's. He became aware of the spell taking effect a few seconds before it could close off his power altogether – and with those few seconds he had, he reached out and broke the circle around the demon with his will and his hand, then in a screaming rage compelled it to attack.

The demon leapt toward us, all writhing darkness and shadows and glowing red eyes. Michael stepped into the doorway and drew *Amoracchius*, the sudden blaze of light and magical fury like a gale in that darkness.

In real life, I had completed the spell and shut Kravos away from his powers. Michael had carved the demon into chutney. Kravos had made a run for it, but Malone, at fairly long range, had fired his shotgun at the ground and at Kravos's feet, and done it perfectly, sweeping the man's legs out from beneath him and leaving him writhing, bleeding, but alive. Murphy had wrestled the knife out of the sorcerer's hands, and the good guys had won the day.

In my dream, it didn't happen that way.

I felt the fabric of the spell closing around Kravos start to slip. One minute, he was there, in the weaving I was spinning around him — the next, he was simply gone, the spell collapsing of its own unsupported weight.

Michael screamed. I looked up, to see him lifted high in the air, his sword sweeping through the shadows and darkness before him in impotent futility. Dark hands, fingers nightmarishly long, grabbed Michael's head, covering his face. There was a twist, a wet, crackling sound, and the Knight's neck broke cleanly. His body jerked, then went limp. *Amoracchius's* light died out. The demon screamed, a tinny, high-pitched sound, and let the body fall to the ground.

Murphy shouted and hurled her jar of holy water at the demon. The liquid flared into silver light as it struck something in that writhing darkness that was the demon. The shape turned toward us. Claws flashed out, and Murphy stumbled back, her eyes wide with shock where the talons had carved through her kevlar jacket, her shirt, her skin, leaving her belly torn open. Blood and worse rushed out, and she let out a weak gasp, pressing both hands against her own ruined side.

Malone started pumping rounds out of the shotgun. The demon-darkness turned toward him, a red-fanged leer spreading over it, and waited until the gun clicked empty. Then it simply laughed, grabbed the end of the shotgun, and slammed Malone against a wall, shoving the hard-wood stock against the man's belly until he screamed, until the flesh began to rip, until ribs started crackling, and then shoved harder, until I could clearly hear, even above the sound of Malone's retching, the bones in his spine start to splinter and break. Malone, too, fell to the ground, dying.

Rudolph screamed, pasty-faced and white, and ran away.

Leaving me alone with the demon.

My heart rushed with terror and I shook like a leaf before the creature. I was still inside of the circle. I still had the circle protecting me. I struggled to reach out for my power, to summon a strike that would annihilate this thing.

And found something in my way. A wall. The same spell I'd meant to lay on Kravos.

The demon stalked over to me and, as though my circle wasn't even there, reached out and backhanded me into the air. I landed with a thud upon the ground.

'No,' I stammered, and tried to struggle back from the thing. 'No, this isn't happening. This isn't the way it happened!'

The demon's red eyes glowed. I lifted my blasting rod toward it, pointed, and shouted, '*Fuego!*'

There was no stirring of heat. No fitful crackling of energy. Nothing.

The demon laughed again, reaching down toward me, and I felt myself lifted into the air.

'This is a dream!' I shouted. With that awareness, I started struggling to reach out to the fabric of the dream, to alter it – but I'd made no preparations before I'd slept, and was already too panicked, too distracted to focus. 'This is a dream! This isn't the way it happened!'

'That was then,' the demon purred, its voice silken. 'This is now.' Then its maw opened up and closed over my belly, horrible fangs sinking in, worrying me, stretching my guts. It shook its head, and I exploded, shreds of meat flying out of me, into it, my blood rushing out while I strained and struggled helplessly, screaming.

And then a grey tabby with a bobtail bounded out of nowhere and whipped one paw at me, lashing it across my nose, claws slashing like fire.

I screamed again and found myself in the far corner of my bedroom, back in my apartment, curled into a fetal ball. I had been puking my guts out. Mister hovered over me and then, almost judiciously, delivered another scratch to my cheek. I heard myself cry out and flinch from the blow.

Something rippled along my skin. Something cold and dark and nauseating. I sat up, blinking sleep from my eyes, struggling through the remnants of the vampire's poison and sleep to focus on the presence – but it was gone.

I shook, violently. I was terrified. Not frightened, not apprehensive – viciously and unremittingly terrified. Mindless, brain-stem terror, the kind that quite simply bypasses rational thought and heads straight for your soul. I felt horribly violated, somehow, used. Helpless. Weak.

I crawled down to my lab, fumbling in the dark. Dimly, I was aware of Mister coming along behind me. It was dark down here, dark and cold. I stumbled across the room, knocking things down left and right, to the summoning circle built into the floor. I threw myself into it, sobbing, fumbled with tingling fingers at the floor until I located the ring. Then I willed the circle closed. It struggled, resisted, and I pushed harder, forced myself on it harder, until finally I felt it snap shut around me in an invisible wall.

I curled on my side, keeping every part of myself within that circle, and wept.

Mister prowled around the circle, a rumbling, reassuring

purr in his throat. Then I heard the big grey cat hop up onto the work table, and over to one of the shelves. His dim shadow curled up by the pale bone of the skull. Orange light began to glide out of his mouth, into the skull's eye sockets, until Bob's candleflame eyes blinked, and the skull turned to focus on me.

'Harry,' Bob said, his voice quiet, solemn. 'Harry, can you hear me?'

Shaking, I looked up, desperately grateful to hear a familiar voice.

'Harry,' Bob said gently. 'I saw it, Harry. I think I know what went after Malone and the others. I think I know how it did it. I tried to help you, but you wouldn't wake up.'

My mind whirled, confused. 'What?' I asked. My voice came out a whimper. 'What are you talking about?'

'I'm sorry, Harry.' The skull paused, and though its expression couldn't really change, it somehow looked troubled. 'I think I know what just tried to eat you.'

18

'Eat me,' I whispered. 'I don't . . . I don't understand.'

'This thing you've been chasing, I think. The Nightmare. I think it was here.'

'Nightmare,' I said. I lowered my head and closed my eyes. 'Bob, I can't . . . I can't think straight. What's going on?'

'Well. You came in about five hours ago drugged to the gills on vampire spit, and muttering like a madman. I think you didn't realize that I was inside Mister. Do you remember that part?'

'Yeah. Sort of.'

'What happened?'

I relayed my experience with Kyle and Kelly Hamilton to Bob. Speaking seemed to help things stop spinning, my guts to settle. My heartbeat slowly eased down to something less than that of a terrified rabbit.

'Sounds weird,' Bob said. 'Got to be something important to make them risk going out in daylight like that. Even in a specially equipped van.'

'I realize that, Bob,' I said, and mopped at my face with one hand.

'You any steadier?'

'I . . . I guess.'

'I think you got torn up pretty good, spirit-wise. It's lucky you started screaming. I came as quick as I could, but you didn't want to wake up. The poison, I think.'

I sat up, cross-legged, staying inside the circle. 'I remember that I had a dream. God, it was a terrible dream.' I felt my guts turn to water, and I started shaking again. 'I tried to change it, but I wasn't ready. I couldn't.'

'A dream,' Bob said. 'Yeah, that figures.'

'Figures?' I asked.

'Sure,' Bob said.

I shook my head, rested my elbows on my knees, and put my face in my hands. I did not want to be doing this. Someone else could do it. I should go, leave town. 'It was a spirit that jumped me?'

'Yeah.'

I shook my head. 'That doesn't make any sense. How did it get past the threshold?'

'Your threshold isn't so hot to begin with, Bachelor Man.'

I worked up enough courage to scowl at Bob. 'The wards, then. I've got all the doors and windows warded. And I don't have any mirrors it could have used.'

If Bob had any hands, he would have been rubbing them together. 'Exactly,' he said. 'Yes, exactly.'

My stomach quailed again, and a fresh burst of shuddering made me put my hands in my lap. I felt like sprawling somewhere, crying my eyes out, puking up whatever shreds of dignity remained in my stomach, and then crawling into a hole and pulling it in after me. I swallowed. 'It . . . it never came in to me, then, is what you're saying. It never had to cross those boundaries.'

Bob nodded, eyes burning brightly. 'Exactly. You went out to it.'

'When I was dreaming?'

'Yes, yes, yes,' Bob bubbled. 'It makes sense now – don't you see?'

'Not really.'

'Dreams,' the skull said. 'When a mortal dreams, all kinds of strange things can happen. When a wizard dreams, it can be even weirder. Sometimes, dreams can be intense enough to create a little, temporary world of their own. Kind of a bubble in the Nevernever. Remember how you told me Agatha Hagglethorn was a strong enough ghost to have had her own demesne in the Nevernever?'

'Yeah. It looked kind of like old Chicago.'

'Well, people can do the same, at times.'

'But I'm not a ghost, Bob.'

'No,' he said. 'You're not. But you've got everything it takes to make a ghost inside you except for the right set of circumstances. Ghosts are only frozen images of people, Harry, last impressions made by a personality.' Bob paused, reflectively. 'People are almost always more trouble than anything you run into on the Other Side.'

'I hadn't noticed,' I said. 'All right. So you're saying that any time I dream, it creates my own little rent-by-the-hour demesne in the Nevernever.'

'Not every time,' Bob said. 'In fact, not even most times. Only really intense dreams, I suspect, bring the necessary energy out of people. But, with the border being so turbulent and easy to get through . . .'

'More people's dreams are making bubbles on the other side. That must have been how it got to poor Micky Malone, then. While he was sleeping. His wife said he'd had insomnia that night. So the thing hangs around outside his house waiting for him to fall asleep and starts killing fuzzy animals to fill up the time.'

'Could be,' Bob said. 'Do you remember your dream?'

I shuddered. 'Yeah. I . . . I remember it.'

'The Nightmare must have got inside with you.'

'While my spirit was in the Nevernever?' I asked. 'It should have ripped me to shreds.'

'Not so,' Bob beamed. 'Your spirit's demesne, remember? Even if only a temporary one. Means you have the home field advantage. It didn't help, since it got the drop on you, but you had it.'

'Oh.'

'Do you remember anything in particular, any figure or character in the dream that wouldn't have been acting the way you thought it should have?'

'Yeah,' I said. My shaking hands went to my belly, feeling for tooth marks. 'Hell's bells, yeah. I was dreaming of that bust a couple of months back. When we nailed Kravos.'

'That sorcerer,' Bob mused. 'Okay. This could be important. What happened?'

I swallowed, trying not to throw up. 'Um. Everything went wrong. That demon he'd called. It was stronger than it had been in life.'

'The demon was?'

I blinked. 'Bob. Is it possible for something like a demon to leave a ghost?'

'Oh, uh,' Bob said, 'I don't think so – unless it had actually died there. Eternally perished, I mean, not just had its vessel dispersed.'

'Michael killed it with *Amoracchius*,' I said.

Bob's skull shuddered. 'Ow,' he said. '*Amoracchius*. I'm not sure, then. I don't know. That sword might be able to kill a demon, even through a physical shell. That whole faith-magic thing is awfully strong.'

'Okay, so. We could be dealing with the ghost of a

demon, here,' I said. 'A demon that died while it was all fired up for a fight. Maybe that's what makes it so . . . so vicious.'

'Could be,' Bob agreed, cheerily.

I shook my head. 'But that doesn't explain the barbed-wire spells we've been finding on those ghosts and people.' I grabbed onto the problem, the tangled facts, with a silent kind of desperation, like a man about to drown who has no breath to waste on screaming. It helped to keep me moving.

'Maybe the spells are someone else's work,' Bob offered.

'Bianca,' I said, suddenly. 'She and her lackeys are all messed up in this somehow – remember that they put the snatch on Lydia? And they were waiting for me, that first night, when I came back from being arrested.'

'I didn't think she was that big time a practitioner,' Bob said.

I shrugged. 'She's not, horribly. But she just got promoted, too. Maybe she's been studying up. She's always had a little more than her share of freaky vampire tricks – and if she was over in the Nevernever when she did it, it would have made her stronger.'

Bob whistled through his teeth. 'Yeah, that could work. Bianca stirs things up by torturing a bunch of spirits, gets all the turbulence going so that she can prod this Nightmare toward you. Then she lets it loose, sits back, and enjoys the fun. She got a motive?'

'Regret,' I said, remembering a note I'd read more than a year ago. 'She blames me for the death of one of her people. Rachel. She wants to make me regret it.'

'Neat,' Bob said. 'And she could have been everywhere in question?'

'Yeah,' I said. 'Yeah, she could have been.'

'Means, opportunity, motive.'

'Damn shaky logic, though. Nothing I could justify to the Council in order to get their back-up, either. I don't have any proof.'

'So?' Bob said. 'Hat up, go kill her. Problem solved.'

'Bob,' I said. 'You can't just go around killing people.'

'I know. That's why you should do it.'

'No, no. *I* can't go around killing people, either.'

'Why not? You've done it before. And you've got a new gun and everything.'

'I can't arbitrarily end someone's life because of something they may have done.'

'Bianca's a vampire,' Bob pointed out cheerfully. 'She's not alive in the classic sense. I'll get Mister and go fetch the bullets and you—'

I sighed. 'No, Bob. She's got lots of people around her, too. I'd probably have to kill some of them to get to her.'

'Oh. Damn. This is one of those right and wrong issues again, isn't it.'

'Yeah, one of those.'

'I'm still confused about this whole morality thing, Harry.'

'Join the club,' I muttered. I took a shaking breath and leaned forward to put my hand over the circle, and will it broken. I almost cringed when its protective field faded from around me, but forced myself not to. I was as recovered as I was going to get. I needed to focus on work.

I stood up and walked to my work table, my eyes by now adjusted to the dimness. I reached for the nearest candle, but there weren't any matches handy. So, I pointed my finger at it, frowned, and muttered the words, '*Flickum bicus.*'

My spell, a tiny one I had used thousands of times, stuttered and coughed, the energy twitching instead of flowing. The candle's wick smoked, but did not flicker to life.

I frowned, then closed my eyes, made a little bit of an effort, and repeated the spell. This time, I felt a little surge of dizziness, and the candle flickered to life. I braced one hand on the edge of the table.

'Bob,' I asked. 'Were you watching that?'

'Yeah,' Bob said, a frown in his voice.

'What happened?'

'Um. You didn't put enough magic into the spell, the first time around.'

'I put as much as I always do,' I protested. 'Come on, I've done that spell a million times.'

'Seventeen hundred and fifty-six, that I've seen.'

I gave him a pale version of my usual glower. 'You know what I mean.'

'Not enough power,' Bob said. 'I call 'em like I see 'em.'

I stared at the candle for a second. Then muttered, to myself, 'Why did I have to work to make that thing light up?'

'Probably because the Nightmare took a big bite out of your powers, Harry.'

I turned around, very slowly, to blink at Bob. 'It . . . it did what?'

'When it attacked you, in your dream, did it go after a specific place on your body?'

I put my hand to the base of my stomach, pressing there, and felt my eyes go wide.

Bob winced. 'Oooooo, chakra point. That isn't good. Got you right in the chi.'

'Bob,' I whispered.

'Good thing he didn't go after your mojo though, right? I mean, you have to look on the bright side of these—'

'Bob,' I said, louder. 'Are you saying it . . . it *ate* my magic?'

Bob got a defensive look on his face. 'Not *all* of it. I woke you up as quick as I could. Harry, don't worry about it, you'll heal. Sure, you might be down for a couple of months. Or, um, years. Well, decades, possibly, but that's only a very outside chance—'

I cut him off with a slash of my hand. 'He ate part of my power,' I said. 'Does that mean that the Nightmare is stronger?'

'Well, naturally, Harry. You are what you eat.'

'Dammit,' I snarled, pressing one hand against my forehead. 'Okay, okay. We've really got to find this thing now.' I started pacing back and forth. 'If it's using my power, it makes me responsible for what it does with it.'

Bob scoffed. 'Harry, that's irrational.'

I shot him a look. 'That doesn't make it any less true,' I snapped.

'Okay,' Bob said, meekly. 'We have now left Reason and Sanity Junction. Next stop, Looneyville.'

'*Grrrr,*' I said, still pacing. 'We have to figure out where this thing is going to hit next. It's got all night to move.'

'Six hours, thirteen minutes,' Bob corrected me. 'Shouldn't be hard. I've been reading those journals you got from the ectomancer, while you were sleeping. The thing can show up in nightmares, but there's going to be commonality between all of it. Ghosts can only have the kind of power this Nightmare has while they are acting within the parameters of their specific bailiwick.'

'Baili-what?'

'Look at it this way, Harry. A ghost can only affect something that relates directly to its death somehow. Agatha Hagglethorn couldn't have terrorized a Cubs game. That wasn't where her power was. She could mess with infants, with abusive husbands, maybe with abused wives—'

'And meddling wizards,' I mumbled.

'You put yourself in the line of fire, sure,' Bob said. 'But Agatha couldn't just run somewhere willy-nilly and wreak havoc.'

'The Nightmare's got to have a personal beef in this,' I said. 'That's what you're saying.'

'Well. It has to be related to its demise, somehow. So, yeah. I guess that is what I'm saying. More specifically, it's what Mort Lindquist was saying, in his journals.'

'Me,' I said. 'And Lydia. And Mickey Malone. How the hell do all of those relate? I never saw Lydia before in my life.' I frowned. 'At least, I don't think I have.'

'She's kind of an oddball,' Bob agreed. 'Leave her out of the equation for a minute?'

I did, and it came to me as clearly as a beam of sunlight. 'Dammit,' I said. I turned and ran toward the stairs on my unsteady legs, started hauling myself up them and toward the phone.

'What?' Bob called after me. 'Harry, what?'

'If that thing is the demon's ghost, I know what it wants. Payback. It's after the people that took it down.' I yelled back down the stairs, 'I've got to find Murphy.'

19

There's a kind of mathematics that goes along with saving people's lives. You find yourself running the figures without even realizing it, like a medic on a battlefield. This patient has no chance of surviving. That one does, but only if you let a third die.

For me, the equation broke down into fairly simple elements. The demon, hungry for its revenge, would come after those who had struck it down. The ghost would only remember those who had been there, whom it had focused on in those last moments. That meant that Murphy and Michael would be its remaining targets. Michael had a chance of protecting himself against the thing – hell, maybe a better chance than me. Murphy didn't.

I got on the phone to Murphy's place. No answer. I called the office, and she answered with a fatigue-blurred, 'Murphy.'

'Murph,' I said. 'Look, I need you to trust me on this one. I'm coming down there and I'll be there in about twenty minutes. You could be in danger. Stay where you are and stay awake until I get to you.'

'Harry?' Murphy asked. I could hear her starting to scowl. 'You telling me you're going to be late?'

'Late? No, dammit. Look, just do what I said, all right?'

'I do not appreciate this crap, Dresden,' Murphy growled. 'I haven't slept in two days. You told me you'd be here in ten minutes, and I told you I'd wait.'

'Twenty. I said twenty minutes, Murph.'

I could feel her glare over the phone. 'Don't be an asshole, Harry. That's not what you said five minutes ago. If this is some kind of joke, I am not amused.'

I blinked, and a cold feeling settled into my gut, into the hollow place the Nightmare had torn out of me. The phone line snapped, crackled, and popped, and I struggled to calm down before the connection went out. 'Wait, Murphy. Are you saying you talked to me five minutes ago?'

'I am about two seconds short of killing the next thing that pisses me off, Harry. And everything keeping me out of bed is pissing me off. Don't get added to the list.' She hung up on me.

'Dammit!' I yelled. I hung up the phone and dialed Murphy's number again, but only got a busy signal.

Something had talked to Murphy and convinced her she was talking to me. The list of things that could put on someone else's face was awfully long, but the probabilities were limited: either another supernatural beastie had wandered onto the stage or, I gulped, the Nightmare had taken a big enough bite of me that it could put on a convincing charade.

Ghosts could take material form, after all – if they had the power to form a new shape out of material from the Nevernever, and if they were familiar enough with the shape. The Nightmare had eaten a bunch of my magic. It had the power it needed. And it had the familiarity it needed.

Hell's bells, it was pretending to be me.

I hung up the phone and tore around the house frantically, collecting car keys and putting together an improvised exorcism kit from stuff in my kitchen: Salt, a wooden spoon, a table knife, a couple of storm candles and matches, and a coffee cup. I stuffed them all into an old Scooby-Doo lunch box, then, as an afterthought, reached into a bag of sand that I keep in the kitchen closet for Mister's litter box, and tossed a handful into a plastic bag. I added the scorched staff and blasting rod to the accumulating pile of junk in my arms. Then I ran for the door.

I hesitated, though. Then went to the phone and dialed Michael's number, fingers dancing over the rotary. It was also busy. I let out a shriek of purest frustration, slammed down the phone, and ran out the door to the Blue Beetle.

It was late. Traffic could have been worse. I got there in less than the twenty minutes I'd promised Murphy and parked the car in one of the visitor's parking spaces.

The district station Murphy worked in crouched down amongst taller buildings that surrounded it, solid and square and a bit battered, like a tough old sergeant amongst a forest of tall, young recruits. I ran up the stairs, taking my blasting rod with me, with my Scooby-Doo lunch box in my right hand.

The grizzled old sergeant behind the desk blinked at me as I came panting through the doorway. 'Dresden?'

'Hi,' I panted. 'Which way did I go?'

He blinked. 'What?'

'Did I come through here a minute ago?'

His thick, grey moustache twitched in nervous little motions. He took a look at his clipboard. 'Yeah. You went up to see Lieutenant Murphy just a minute ago.'

'Great,' I said. 'I need to see her again. Buzz me through?'

He peered at me, a little closer, then reached forward to buzz me through. 'What's going on here, Mr Dresden?'

'Believe me,' I said, 'As soon as I work that out, I'll be sure to tell you.' I opened the door and headed through, up the stairs, and toward the S.I. offices on the fourth floor. I pounded through the doors and sprinted down the rows of desks toward Murphy's office. Stallings and Rudolph both started up from their chairs, blinking as I went past.

'What the hell?' Rudy blurted, his eyes widening.

'Where's Murphy?' I shouted.

'In her office,' Stallings stammered, 'with you.'

Murphy's office stood at the back of the room, with cheap walls and a cheap door that finally bore a genuine metallic nameplate with her name and title on it. I leaned back and drove my heel at the doorknob. The cheap door splintered, but I had to kick it again to send it swinging open.

Murphy sat at her desk, still wearing the clothes I'd last seen her in. She'd taken her hat off, and her short blonde hair was mussed. The circles beneath her eyes were almost as dark as bruises. She sat perfectly still, staring forward with her blue eyes set in an expression of horror.

I stood behind her, all in black – the same outfit I'd worn the night we'd stopped Kravos and his demon. The Nightmare looked like me. Its hands rested on either side of her face, fingertips on her temples – except that they had, somehow, pressed *into* her head, reaching down through skin and bone as though gently massaging her brain. The Nightmare was smiling, leaning down a bit toward her, head canted as though listening to music. I didn't know my face was capable of making an expression like that – serene and malicious and frightening.

I stared for a second in sheer horror at the weirdness of the sight. Then blurted, 'Get the hell off of her!'

The Nightmare's dark eyes snapped up, sparkling with a cold, calm intelligence. It lifted its lips away from its teeth in an abrupt snarl. 'Be thou silent, wizard,' it murmured, steel and razor blades in its words. 'Else I will tear thee apart, as I already have this night.'

A little gibbering shriek of terror started somewhere down in my quivering belly, but I refused to give it a voice. I heard Rudy and Stallings coming behind me. I lifted the blasting rod and leveled it at the Nightmare's head. 'I said to get off of her.'

The Nightmare's mouth twisted into a smile. It lifted its hands away from Murphy, fingers just sliding out of her skin as though from water, and showed me its palms. 'There is something thou hast forgotten, wizard.'

'Yeah?' I asked. 'What's that?'

'I have partaken of thee. I am what thou art,' the Nightmare whispered. He flicked his wrists toward me. '*Ventas servitas.*'

Wind roared up in a sudden fury and hurled me from my feet, back into the air. I collided with Rudolph and Stallings as they ran forward. We all went down in a heap upon the ground.

I lay there stunned for a moment. I heard the Nightmare walk out. It just walked past us, footsteps calm and quiet, and left the room. We gathered ourselves together slowly, sitting up.

'What the hell?' Rudolph said.

My head hurt, in back. I must have slammed it into something. I pressed a hand against my skull, and groaned. 'Oh, stars,' I muttered. 'I should have known better than to give him a straight line like that.'

Stallings had blood running out his nose and into his

greying moustache. Flecks of red spotted his white dress shirt. 'That . . . Good Lord, Dresden. What was that thing?'

I pushed myself to my feet. Everything wobbled for a moment. My whole body shook, and I felt like I might just fall over and start crying like a baby. It had used my magic. It had stolen my face and my magic and used them both to hurt people. It made me want to start screaming, to tear something apart with my bare hands.

Instead, I staggered toward Murphy's office. 'It's what got Malone,' I told Stallings. 'It's kind of complicated.'

Murphy still sat in her chair, her eyes wide and staring and horrified, her hands folded into her lap. 'Murph?' I asked. 'Karrin? Can you hear me?'

She didn't move. But her breath came out with a little edge to it, as though she had tried to speak. She breathed. Thank God. I knelt down and took her hands in mine. They felt ice cold.

'Murph,' I whispered. I waved my hand in front of her eyes, and snapped my fingers sharply. She didn't so much as blink.

Rudolph's handsome face was pale. 'I'll call downstairs. Tell them not to let him out.' I heard him go to the nearest phone and start calling down to the desk. I didn't bother to tell him that it wouldn't do any good. The Nightmare could walk out through the walls if it needed to.

Stallings joined me in the room, looking shaken and a little grey. He stared at Murphy for a long moment, and then asked, 'What is it? What's wrong with her?'

I peered at her eyes. They were dilated wide. I braced myself, and looked deeper into her eyes. When a wizard looks into your eyes, you cannot hide from him. He can see deep down into you, see the truest parts of your character, the dark places and the light – and you see him in return. Eyes are the windows to the soul. I searched for Murphy behind all of that terror, and waited for the soul-gaze to begin.

Nothing happened.

Murphy just sat there, staring ahead. Another low breath rattled out, not quite making a sound – but I recognized the effort she was making for what it was.

Murphy was screaming.

I had no idea what she was seeing, what horrors the Nightmare had set before her eyes. What it had taken from her. I touched her throat with gentle fingertips, but I couldn't feel the bone-chilling cold of the torment-spell like the one upon Malone. At least there was that much. But if I couldn't see inside of her, then Murphy was in another place. The lights were on, but no one was home.

'She's . . . This thing has messed with her head. I think it's making her see things. Things that aren't here. I don't think she knows where she is, and she can't seem to move.'

'Christ preserve,' Stallings whispered. 'What can we do?'

'John,' I said, quietly. 'I need you to pull the evidence files from the Kravos case. I need that big leather book that we found at his apartment.'

Stallings started, and then stared at me. 'You need what?'

I repeated my request.

He closed his eyes. 'Jesus, Dresden. I don't know. I don't know if I could get it. There's been some stuff come up lately.'

'I need that book,' I said. 'The thing that's doing this is a kind of demon. Kravos will have that demon's name written down in his spell book. If I can get that name, I can catch this thing and stop it. I can make it tell me how to help Murph.'

'You don't understand. It isn't going to be that easy for me. This has gotten complicated, and I'm not going to be able to just walk into storage and get the damn thing for you, Dresden.' He studied Murphy with worried eyes. 'It could cost me my job.'

I set my Scooby-Doo lunch box on the floor and opened it up. 'Listen to me,' I said. 'I'm going to try to help Murphy. I need someone to stay with her until dawn and then to take her back to her house – or better yet, to Malone's house.'

'Why?' Stallings asked. 'What are you doing?'

'I think this thing is making her live through some messed up stuff – like in a nightmare. I'm pretty sure I can stop it, but she'll still be vulnerable. So I'm going to set up a protection around her so that she'll be safe until dawn.' Once morning rolled around, the Nightmare would be trapped in whatever mortal body it possessed, or else would have to flee to the Nevernever. 'Someone will need to watch her, in case she wakes up.'

'Rudolph can do it,' Stallings said, and rose to his feet. 'I'll talk to him.'

I looked up at him. 'I need that book, John.'

He frowned, studying the ground in front of me. 'Are we going to be able to catch this thing, Dresden?' *We* meaning the police. I could hear that much in his voice.

I shook my head.

'If I get the book for you,' he said, 'can you help the lieutenant?'

I nodded at him.

He closed his eyes and let out a breath. 'All right,' he whispered. Then he walked out. I heard him talking to Rudolph a moment later.

I turned back to Murphy, taking the plastic sack of sand out of the lunch box. I got out a piece of chalk and pushed Murphy's chair back from the desk so that I could draw a circle around us both and will it closed. It took more effort than it usually did, leaving me dizzy for a second.

I swallowed and began to gather up energy, to focus it as carefully and precisely as I could. It built slowly, while Murphy continued to inhale, and to exhale whispered screams. I put my hand on her cold fingers, and thought about all the stuff we'd been through, the bond of friendship that had grown between us. Good times and bad, Murph's heart had always been in the right place. She didn't deserve this kind of torment.

A great fury began to stir in me – not some vaporous, swiftly dissipated flash of anger, but something deeper, darker, more calm and more dangerous. Rage. Rage that this sort of thing should happen to someone as selfless and caring as Murphy. Rage that the creature had used my power, my face, to trick its way close to her and to hurt her.

From that rage came the power I needed. I gathered it up carefully and shaped it with my thoughts into the softest-edged spell I could conceive. Gently, I sent the power coursing down my arm into the grains of sand I pinched between a single fingertip. Then I slowly lifted my arm, the spell holding in a precarious balance as I sprinkled a bit of sand over each of her eyes. *'Dormius, dorme,'* I whispered. 'Murphy, *dormius.'*

Power coursed out of me, flowed down my arm like

water. I felt it fall with the grains of sand. Murphy let out a long, shivering breath, and her staring eyes began to flutter closed. Her expression slackened, from horror to deep, silent sleep, and she slumped into her chair.

I let out my breath as the spell took hold, and bowed my head, trembling. I reached out and stroked my hand over Murphy's hair. Then I composed her into something that looked a little more comfortable. 'Down where there's no dreams,' I whispered to her. 'Just rest, Murph. I'll nail this thing for you.'

With an effort of will, I smudged the circle and broke it. Then I stepped outside it, used the chalk to close it again and willed it closed around Murphy. I had to strain, this time, more than I'd ever needed to since I was barely more than a child. But the circle closed around her, sealing her in. A small haze, only an inch or two high, danced around the chalk lines, like heat waves rising from summer roads. The circle would keep out anything from the Nevernever – and the enchanted sleep would hold until the dawn came, keep her from dreaming and giving the Nightmare a way to further harm her.

I shambled out of her office, to the nearest phone. Rudolph watched me. Stallings wasn't in evidence. I dialed Michael's number. It was still busy.

I wanted to crawl home and drop a sleep spell on myself. I wanted to hide somewhere warm and quiet and get some rest. But the Nightmare was still out there. It was still after its vengeance, after Michael. I had to get to it, find it, stop it. Or at least warn him.

I put the phone down and started gathering my stuff together. Someone touched my shoulder. I looked up at Rudolph. He looked uncertain, pale.

'You'd better not be a fake, Dresden,' he said, quietly. 'I'm not really sure what's going on here. But so help me God, if something happens to the lieutenant because of you . . .'

I studied his face numbly. And then nodded. 'I'll call back for Stallings. I need that book.'

Rudolph's expression was serious, earnest. He'd never much liked me, anyway. 'I mean it, Dresden. If you let Murphy get hurt, I'll kill you.'

'Kid, if anything happens to Murphy because of me . . .' I sighed. 'I think I'll let you.'

20

I wouldn't have thought you could find a peaceful, suburbanish neighborhood in the city of Chicago. Michael had managed, not too far west of Wrigley Field. Ancient old trees lined either side of the street in stately splendor. The homes were mostly old Victorian affairs, restored after a fluctuating economy and a century of wear and tear had reduced them to trembling firetraps. Michael's house looked like it was made of gingerbread. Fancy trim, elegant paint in ivory and burgundy – and, perhaps inevitably, a white picket fence around the house and its front yard. The porch light cast a circle of white radiance out onto the front lawn, almost to the edge of the property.

I slewed the Beetle up onto the curb in front of the house and pushed my way through the swinging gate, clomping up the stairs to rattle the knocker against the front door. I figured that it would take Michael a minute to stagger out of bed and come down the stairs, but instead I heard a thump, a pair of long steps, and then the curtains of the window beside the door stirred. A second later, the door opened, and Michael stood there, blinking sleep out of his eyes. He wore a pair of jeans and a T-shirt with JOHN 3:16 across his chest. He held one of his kids in his brawny arms, one I hadn't seen yet – maybe a year old, with a patch of curly, golden hair, her face pressed against her daddy's chest as she slept.

'Harry,' Michael said. His eyes widened. 'Merciful Father, what's happened to you?'

'It's been a long night,' I said. 'Have I been here yet?'

Michael peered at me. 'I'm not sure what you mean, Harry.'

'Good. Then I haven't. Michael, you've got to wake your family up, *now*. They could be in danger.'

He blinked at me again. 'Harry, it's late. What on earth—'

'Just listen.' In terse terms, I outlined what I'd learned about the Nightmare, and how it was getting to its victims.

Michael stared at me for a minute. Then he said, 'Let me get this straight. The ghost of a demon I killed two months ago is rampaging around Chicago, getting into people's dreams, and eating their minds from the inside.'

'Yeah,' I said.

'And now it's taken a part of you, manifested a body that looks like you, and you think it's coming here.'

'Yes,' I said. 'Exactly.'

Michael pursed his lips for a moment. 'Then how do I know that you aren't this Nightmare, trying to get me to invite you in?'

I opened my mouth. Closed it again. Then said, 'Either way, it's better if I stay out here. Charity would probably gouge out my eyes for showing up at this hour.'

Michael nodded. 'Come on in, Harry. Let me put the baby to bed.'

I stepped inside, into a small entry hall with a polished hardwood floor. Michael nodded toward his living room, to the right, and said, 'Sit down. I'll be back in a second.'

'Michael,' I said. 'You should wake your family up.'

'You said this thing is in a solid body, right?'

'It was a few minutes ago.'

'Then it's not in the Nevernever. It's here, in Chicago. It can't get into people's dreams from here.'

'I don't *think* so, but—'

'And it's going to be after the people who were near it when it died. It's going to come after me.'

I chewed on my lip for a second. Then I said, 'It's got a part of me in it, too.'

Michael frowned at me.

'If I was going to come after you, Michael,' I said. 'I wouldn't start with you.'

He looked down at the child he carried. His face hardened, and he said, in a very soft voice, 'Harry. Sit. I'll be down in a moment.'

'But it might—'

'I'll see to it,' he said in that same soft, gentle voice. It scared me. I sat down. He took the child, walking softly, and vanished up a stairway.

I sat for a moment in a big, comfortable easy chair, the kind that rocks back and forth. There was a towel and a half-emptied bottle off to my left, on the lamp table. Michael must have been rocking the little girl to sleep.

Beside the bottle was a note. I leaned forward and picked it up, reading:

Michael. Didn't want to wake you and the baby. The little one is demanding pizza and ice cream. I'll be back in a few minutes – probably before you wake up and read this. Love, Charity.

I stood up, and started toward the stairs. Michael appeared at the top of them, his face pale. 'Charity,' he said. 'She's gone.'

I held up the note. 'She went to the store for pizza and ice cream. Pregnant cravings, I guess.'

Michael came down the stairs and brushed past me. Then he reached into the entry hall closet and pulled out a blue Levi's jacket and *Amoracchius* in its black scabbard.

'What are you waiting for, Harry? Let's go find her.'

'But your kids—'

Michael rolled his eyes, took a step to the door, and jerked it open without looking away from me. Father Forthill stood on the other side, his thinning hair wind-blown, his bright blue eyes surprised behind his wire-rimmed spectacles. 'Oh. Michael. I didn't mean to stop by so late, but my car stalled only a block from here on the way back from taking Mrs Hamish home, and I thought I might borrow—' He paused, looking from me to Michael and then back to me again. 'You need a baby-sitter again, don't you.'

Michael shrugged into his jacket and slung the sword belt over his shoulder. 'They're already asleep. Do you mind?'

Father Forthill stepped in. 'Never.' He made the Cross over each of us again and murmured, 'God go with you.'

We started out of the house and to Michael's truck. 'You see, Harry?'

I scowled. 'Handy fringe benefit.'

Michael drove, the big white truck rumbling down the local streets toward a corner grocery on Byron Street, within a long sprint of the famous Graceland Cemetery. The lowering clouds rumbled and started dumping a steady, heavy rain down onto the city, giving all the lights golden halos and casting ghostly reflections on the wet streets.

'This time of night,' Michael said, 'Walsham's is the only place open. She'll be there.' Thunder rumbled again in growling punctuation to the statement. I drummed my fingers on my scorched staff, and made sure that my blasting rod was hanging loosely by its thong around my wrist.

'There's her van,' Michael said. He pulled the truck up into the row of parking spots in front of the grocery, next to the white Suburban troop transport. He barely took the time to take his keys with him – instead just snatching out *Amoracchius* and loosening the great blade in its sheath as he strode toward the store's front doors, his eyes narrowed, his jaw set. The rain pasted his hair down to his head after a few steps, soaking his Levi's jacket dark blue. I followed him, wincing at the damage to my leather duster, and reflecting that the old canvas job would have fared better in this weather.

Michael slammed the heel of his hand into the door, and it swept open with a jangling of tinny bells. He strode into the store, swept his eyes around the visible displays and the cash registers, and then bellowed, 'Charity! Where are you?'

A couple of teenage cashiers blinked at him, and an elderly woman perusing the vitamins turned to gawk at him through her spectacles. I sighed, then nodded to the nearest cashier, a too-skinny, too-blonde girl who looked as though she were impatient for her cigarette break. 'Uh, hi,' I said. 'Did you see me come in here a minute ago?'

'Or a pregnant woman,' Michael said. 'About this high.' He stuck his hand out flat about at the level of his own ear.

The female cashier traded a look with her counterpart. 'Seen you, mister?'

I nodded. 'Another guy, like me. Tall, skinny, all in black – jacket like mine, but all black clothes underneath.'

The girl licked her lips and gave us a calculating look. 'Maybe I have,' she said. 'What's in it for me?'

Michael rolled forward a step, a growl bubbling up out of his throat. I grabbed at his shoulder and leaned back. 'Whoah, whoah, Michael,' I yelped. 'Slow down, man.'

'There isn't *time* to slow down,' Michael muttered. 'You detect. I'm looking.' With that, he turned and strode off deeper into the store, casually carrying the sword in his left hand, his right upon the weapon's grip. 'Charity!'

I muttered something unflattering under my breath, then turned back to the cashier. I fumbled in my pockets for my billfold, and managed to produce a sorry trio of wrinkled fives. I held them up and said, 'Okay. My evil twin or else a pregnant woman. You seen either one?'

The girl looked at the bills and then back at me and rolled her eyes. Then she leaned out from her counter and plucked them from my hands. 'Yeah,' she said. 'She went down aisle five a few minutes ago. Back toward the freezer section.'

'Yeah?' I asked. 'Then what?'

She smiled. 'What? Is this your brother or something, running around with your woman? Am I going to see this on Larry Fowler tomorrow?'

I narrowed my eyes. 'It's complicated,' I said. 'What else did you see?'

She shrugged. 'She paid for some stuff, and went to that van out there. It wouldn't start. I saw you – or the guy that looks like you, come up to her and start talking to her. She looked pretty pissed at him, but she walked off with him. I didn't think anything of it.'

My stomach gave a little lurch. 'Walked off?' I said. 'Which way?'

The cashier shrugged. 'Look, mister, she just looked like she was getting a ride somewhere. She wasn't fighting or nothing.'

'Which way!' I thundered. The cashier blinked, and her jaded exterior wobbled for a moment. She pointed down the street – toward Graceland.

'Michael!' I shouted. 'Come on!' Then I turned around and banged my way back outside and into the rain and the dark. I stopped at Charity's van for a second, and tapped at the hood. It wobbled up without resistance, to reveal a mess of torn wires and shredded belts and broken pieces of metal. I winced, and shielded my eyes from the rain, trying to scan down the street toward the cemetery.

In the far distance, just barely, I saw two figures – one ungainly, with long hair. The other stood tall over her, slender, walking toward the cemetery holding her firmly by the hair.

They vanished into the shadows at the base of the stone wall around Graceland. I gulped, and looked around. 'Michael!' I shouted again. I peered through the grocery's windows, but I couldn't see him anywhere.

'Dammit!' I said, and kicked at the front bumper of the van. I was in no shape to go after the Nightmare on my own. It was full of power it had stolen from me. It had the booga booga factor going for it. And it had my friend's wife and unborn child as hostages.

Hell's bells, all I had was a headache, an hourglass quickly running out of sand, and a case of the shakes. Chicago's biggest cemetery, on a dark, rainy night, when the border between here and the spirit world was leaking

like a sieve. It would be full of spooks and crawlies, and
I would be alone.

'Yeah,' I muttered. 'That figures.'

I sprinted for the darkness into which I had seen the
Nightmare disappear with Charity.

21

I've done smarter things in my life. Once, for example, I threw myself out of a moving car in order to take on a truckload of lycanthropes singlehandedly. That had been nominally smarter. At least I had been fairly certain that I could kill them, if I had to, at the time.

Which put me one step ahead of where I was, now. I had already killed the Nightmare – or helped to kill it, at least. Something about that just didn't seem fair. There should be some kind of rule against needing to kill anything more than once.

Rain fell in sheets rather than drops, sluicing down into my eyes. I had to keep on wiping my brow, sweeping water away, only to have it fill my vision again. I started to give serious thought to what it might be like to drown, right there on the sidewalk.

I cut across the street toward the cemetery fence. Seven feet of red brick, the fence rose in a jagged stair-step fashion every hundred feet or so, keeping up with the slow slope of the street along its southern perimeter as it moved west. At one point, a gaping slash of darkness marred the fence's exterior, and I slowed as I approached it. The bricks had been torn like paper, and lay in rubble two feet deep around the hole in the wall. I tried to peer beyond it, and saw only more rain, green grass, the shadows of trees cast over the carefully tended grounds.

I paused, outside the graveyard. A dull, restless energy

pressed against me, like when weariness and caffeine mix around three-thirty in the morning. It rolled against my skin, and I heard, actually *heard* whispering voices, through the rain, dozens, hundreds of whispers, ghostly sussurance. I put my hand on the wall, and felt the tension there. There are always fences around cemeteries. Always, whether stone or brick or chainlink. It's one of those unwritten things that people don't really notice, they just do it by reflex. Any kind of wall is a barrier in more than merely a physical sense. Lots of things are more than what they seem in a purely physical sense.

Walls keep things out. Walls around cemeteries keep things in.

I looked back, hoping that Michael had followed me, but I didn't or couldn't see him in the rain. I still felt weak, shaken. The voices whispered, clustering around the weak point in the wall, where the Nightmare had torn its way in. Even if only one death in a thousand had produced a ghost (and more than that did) there might be dozens of restless spirits wandering the grounds, some even strong enough for nonpractitioners of the Art to experience.

Tonight, there weren't dozens. Dozens would have been a happy number. I closed my eyes and could feel the power they stirred up, the way the air wavered and shook with the presence of hundreds of spirits, easily crossed over from the turbulent Nevernever. It made my knees shake, my belly quiver – both from the wounds that had been inflicted on me by the Nightmare and from simple, primitive fear of darkness, the rain, and a place of the dead.

The inmates of Graceland felt my fear. They pressed close to the break in the wall, and I began to hear actual, physical moans.

'I should wait here,' I muttered to myself, shaking in the rain. 'I should wait for Michael. That would be the smart thing to do.'

Somewhere, in the darkness of the cemetery, a woman screamed. Charity.

What I wouldn't have given to have my Dead Man's talisman back, now. Son of a bitch.

I gripped my staff, knuckles white, and got out my blasting rod. Then I clambered through the break in the wall and headed into the darkness.

I felt them the moment I crossed into the cemetery, the second my shoes hit the ground. Ghosts. Shades. Haunts. Whatever you want to call them, they were dead as hell and they weren't going to take it anymore. They were weak spirits, each of them, something that would barely have given me a passing shiver on a normal night – but tonight wasn't.

A chill fell over me, abrupt as winter's first wind. I took a step forward and felt a resistance, but not as though someone was trying to keep me out. It felt more like those movies I've seen with tourists struggling through crowds of beggars in dusty Middle Eastern cities. That's what I experienced, in a chilling and spectral kind of way – people pushing against me, struggling to get something from me, something that I wasn't sure I had and that I didn't think would do any good even if I gave it to them.

I gathered in my will and slipped my mother's amulet from around my neck. I held it aloft in the smothering, clammy darkness, and fed power into it.

The blue wizard light began to glow, to cast out a dim radiance, not so bright as usual. The silver pentagram within the circle was the symbol of my faith, if that's what you wanted to call it, in magic. In the concept of power being controlled, ordered, used for constructive purpose. I wondered, for a minute, if the dimness was a reflection of my injuries or if it said something about my faith. I tried to think of how often I'd had to set something on fire, the past few years, how many times I'd had to blow something up. Or smash a building. Or otherwise wreak havoc.

I ran out of fingers and shivered. Maybe I'd better start being a little more careful.

The spirits fell back from that light, but for a few who still clustered close, whispering things into my ears. I didn't pay them any attention, or stop to listen. That way lay madness. I shoved forward, more an effort of the heart than of the body, and started searching.

'Charity!' I shouted. 'Charity, where are you?'

I heard a short sound, a call, off to my right, but it cut off swiftly. I turned toward it and began moving forward at a cautious lope, glowing pentacle held aloft like Diogenes's lamp. Thunder rumbled again. The rain had already soaked the grass, made the dirt beneath my feet soft and yielding. A brief, disturbing image of the dead tearing their way up through the softened earth brought me a brief chill and a dozen spirits clustering close as though to feed from it. I shoved both fear and clutching, unseen fingers aside, and pressed forward.

I found Charity laying upon a bier within a marble edifice that looked like nothing so much as a Greek temple, the roof open to the sky. Michael's wife lay upon her back, her hands clutched over her swollen belly, her teeth bared in a snarl.

The Nightmare stood over her, with my dark hair

plastered to its head, my dark eyes reflecting the gleam of my pentacle. It held one hand in the air over Charity's belly, its other over her throat. It tilted its head and watched me approach. In the edges of my wizard's light, shapes moved, flitted, spirits swirling around like moths.

'Wizard,' the Nightmare said.

'Demon,' I responded. I wasn't feeling much like any snapper patter.

It smiled, teeth showing. 'Is that what I am,' it said. 'Interesting. I wasn't sure.' It lifted its hand from Charity's throat, pointed a finger toward me, and murmured, 'Goodbye, wizard. *Fuego.*'

I felt the surge of power before any fire rose up and swept toward me through the rain. I lifted my staff in my left hand in front of me, horizontally, and slammed power recklessly into a shield. '*Riflettum!*'

Fire and rain met in a furious hiss and a cloud of steam a foot in front of my outstretched staff. The rain helped, I think. I would never have been stupid enough to try for a gout of flame in a downpour like this. It was too easily defeated.

Charity moved, the instant the Nightmare's attention was distracted. She spun her feet toward it and, with a furious cry, planted both her heels high in the thing's chest with a vicious shove.

Charity wasn't a weak woman. The thing grunted and flew back, away from her, and at the same time the motion pushed Charity's body off the bier. She fell to the other side, crying out, curling her body around her unborn child to protect it.

I sprinted forward. 'Charity,' I shouted. 'Get out! Run!'

She turned her head toward me and I saw how furious she was. She bared her teeth at me for a moment, but her face clouded with confusion. 'Dresden?' she said.

'No time!' I shouted. On the other side of the bier, the Nightmare rose to its feet again, dark eyes gone now, instead blazing with scarlet fury. I didn't have time to think about it, running forward. 'Run, Charity!'

I knew it would be suicide to wrestle with something that had torn down a brick wall a few minutes ago – but I had a sinking feeling that I was outclassed in the magic department. If he got another spell off, I didn't think I could counter it. I held my staff in both hands, planted it at the base of the bier and vaulted up, swinging my feet toward the Nightmare's face.

I had speed and surprise on my side. I hit it hard and it staggered back. My staff spun out of my hands and my hip struck painfully on the edge of the bier and scraped along my ribs as I continued forward, riding the thing into the marble flooring. My concentration gone, the blue wizard light died out and I fell in darkness.

I hit the ground with a wheeze, and scrambled back. If the Nightmare got hold of me, that would be it. I had just reached the edge of the bier when something seized my leg, right below the knee, a grip like an iron band around me. I struggled to draw myself back, but there was nothing to grab onto but rain-slicked marble.

The Nightmare stood up, and a flash of lightning somewhere overhead showed me its dark eyes, its face like mine. It was smiling. 'And so it ends, wizard,' it said. 'I am rid of thee at last.'

I tried to get away, but the Nightmare simply whirled me by one leg, whipping me into a circle in the air. Then

I flew upwards and saw one of the columns coming toward me.

Then there was a flash of light and a sharp pain in the center of my forehead. The impact with the ground came as a secondary sensation, relatively pleasant compared with the first.

Unconsciousness would have been a mercy. Cold rain instead kept me awake enough to experience every agonizing second of expanding pain in my skull. I tried to move my limbs and couldn't, and for a second I thought that my neck must have broken. Then, in the corner of my vision, I saw my fingers twitch, and thought with a flash of depression that I wasn't out of the fight yet.

A major effort got my hand down onto the ground. Another major effort pushed me up and made my head spin, my stomach heave. I leaned back against the column, gasping for breath through the rain, and tried to gather my strength.

It didn't take long – there just wasn't all that much strength left to gather. I opened my eyes, slowly focused them. I felt a sharp tang in my mouth. I touched my hand to my mouth, my cheek, and my fingers came away stained with something warm and dark. Blood.

I tried to rise up and couldn't. Just couldn't. Everything spun too much. Water coursed down over me, chilling me, pooling at the base of the little hill the Greek temple-cum-mausoleum stood upon, running a stream down toward another creek.

'So much water,' purred a female voice beside me. 'So many things flowing down, away. I wonder if some of them are not being wasted.'

I rolled my head enough to see my godmother standing

beside me in her green dress. Lea's skin had evidently recovered from the ghost dust I'd dumped upon her in Agatha Hagglethorn's demesne. Her golden cat-eyes studied me with their old, familiar warmth, her hair spilling around her in a mane that seemed unaffected by the rain. She didn't seem to mind it soaking her dress, though. It clung to the curves of her body, showed the perfection of her breasts, their tips clearly showing through the silken fabric as she knelt down beside me.

'What are you doing here?' I muttered.

She smiled, reached out a finger, and ran it over my forehead, then drew it back to her mouth and slipped it between her lips and suckled, gently, upon it. Her eyes closed, and she let out a long and shivering sigh. 'Such a sweet boy. You always were such a sweet boy.'

I tried to push myself to my feet and couldn't. Something in my head seemed broken.

She watched me with that same, benign smile. 'Thy strength is fading, my sweet. Here in the place of the dead, it may fail thee altogether.'

'This isn't the Nevernever, godmother,' I rasped. 'You don't have any power here.'

She pursed her lips in what would have been a seductive pout on a human. My blood had stained them even darker. 'My sweet. You know it is not true. I simply only have what I am given, here. What I have fairly traded for.'

I bared my teeth at her. 'You're going to kill me, then.'

She threw back her head in a rich laugh. 'Kill you? I *never* intended to kill you, my sweet, barring moments of frustration. Our bargain was for your life – not your death.' One of her hounds appeared out of the darkness, and crouched beside her, fastening its dark eyes upon me. She laid a fond hand upon its broad head, and it shivered in pleasure.

I felt myself grow colder, at that, staring at the hound. 'You don't want me dead. You want me . . .' I couldn't finish the sentence.

'Tamed.' Lea smiled. She scratched the dog's ears, fondly. 'But not like this.' Her mouth twisted into a contemptuous smirk. 'Not as you are. Pathetic. Really, Harry, allowing yourself to be *eaten*, so. Justin and I taught you better than that.'

Somewhere close, Charity shouted again. Thunder rolled overhead.

I groaned and struggled to push myself up. Lea watched me through golden, cat-slitted eyes, interested and uncaring. I managed to get to my feet, my back and most of my weight leaning against the column. In the rain, I could dimly see Charity on her knees. The Nightmare stood over her, one hand clutching her hair. It pushed the other toward her head. She fought it, uselessly, shuddering in the rain. Its fingers sunk into her skull, and Charity's struggles abruptly ceased.

I groaned and pushed myself forward, to get closer, to do something. Everything spun around and I fell to the earth again, hard.

'Sweet boy.' Lea sighed. 'Poor child.' She knelt down beside me again, and stroked my hair. It felt nice, through my nausea and pain. I think the nausea and pain definitely cut down on the seductive potential of it, though. 'Would you like me to help you?'

I managed to look up at her lovely face. 'Help me?' I asked. 'H-how?'

Her eyes sparkled. 'I can give you what you need to save the White Knight's Lady.'

I stared up at her. All the pain, the terror, the stupid, rainy cold made me ache horribly. I heard Charity whimper. I had tried. Dammit, I had done my best to help the woman. She didn't even like me. It wasn't my fault if she died, right? I had done everything in my power.

Hadn't I?

I swallowed down the sickly taste of bile and acid and asked, 'What do you want, Godmother?'

She shivered and drew in a swift breath. 'What I have always wanted, sweet boy. This bargain is no different than the one we made years ago. It is, in fact, a part of the same. I give you power. And in return, I get you.' Her eyes flashed. 'I want your promise, wizard. I want your promise that when the woman is safe, you will come to me. You will take my hand. Here, tonight.'

'You want me to go back with you,' I whispered. 'But you don't want me like this, Godmother. All torn up. I'm empty inside.'

She smiled, and stroked the hellhound's head. 'Yes. In time, you will heal. And I will make that time pass swiftly, my sweet.' She leaned closer to me, golden eyes burning. 'Such pleasures I will teach you. No man could wish for a merrier passing.' She looked up again, over the bier that hid my view of Charity and the Nightmare. 'The White Knight's Lady sees such things, now. Soon, she will be trapped, as is the police woman.'

'How did you know about Murphy?' I demanded.

'I know many things. I know that you may die, if you do nothing, my sweet. You may die here cold and alone.'

'I don't care about that,' I said. 'I . . .'

Charity let out a choking, sobbing sound nearby. Lea smiled, and murmured, 'Time is fleeting, child. It waits for no one, not man nor sidhe nor wizard.'

Lea already had me over a barrel. If I deepened our pact, reconfirmed it, I'd be letting her nail it closed with me inside. But I couldn't get up. I couldn't do a damned thing to save Charity without getting some help.

I closed my eyes, and saw Michael's little daughter. I thought of her growing up without a mother.

Damn it.

'I accept your bargain, Godmother.' When I spoke the words, I felt something stir against me, something that sealed closed.

Lea gasped, eyes closing as she shuddered again, then opening with a feral glow. She leaned down and murmured, 'The answer, my sweet, is all around you.' Then she kissed my forehead and was gone in a flicker of shadows.

I found myself thinking clearly again. It still hurt to move – stars, did it hurt, but I managed it. I clambered to my feet, leaned against the bier, and looked up to let the rain wash the blood from my eyes.

The answer was all around me. What the hell kind of idiotic advice was that? I glared around, but saw nothing but rolling lawns, trees, and graves. Lots of graves. Plain tombstones and marble markers, graves with ponds beside them, graves with lights, graves with small fountains. Dead people. That's what was all around.

I focused my eyes on Charity and the Nightmare, and felt cold anger inside. I moved around the edge of the bier, gaining a little stability and balance as I went, and shouted, 'Hey! You! Ugly!'

The Nightmare turned its head to blink in my direction,

surprised. Then it smiled again and said, 'Thou art not yet dead. How interesting.' It released Charity, fingers gliding out of her as they had from Murphy, and she fell limply to her side. 'I can finish that one at leisure. But thou, wizard, I will make an end to at once.'

'Yadda yadda yadda,' I muttered. I bent down and recovered my staff, standing again with it in both hands. 'People don't *talk* like that anymore. All those thous and thees. Hells bells, at least the faeries can keep up with the dialect.'

The Nightmare frowned at me, and started walking toward me. 'Dost thou not realize it, fool? This is thy death come upon thee.'

A boot planted itself heavily on the marble beside me. Then another. *Amoracchius* cast a glowing white light upon my shoulder, and Michael said, 'I think not.'

I glanced aside at Michael. 'You,' I groaned, 'have very good timing.'

He bared his teeth in an unpleasant, fierce expression. 'My wife?'

'She's alive,' I said. 'But we'd better get her out of here.'

He nodded. 'I'll kill it again,' he said. He passed me something hard and cool – a crucifix. 'You get her. Give her this.'

The Nightmare came to a halt, its eyes narrowing upon the pair of us. 'Thou,' it said to Michael. 'I knew it would come to this.'

'Oh, shut *up*!' I shouted, exasperated. 'Michael, killing this thing already!'

Michael started forward, the sword's white fire lighting the night like a halogen torch. The Nightmare screamed in fury and threw itself to one side, avoiding the blade, then rushed back in toward Michael, fingers raking like claws. Michael ducked under them, planted a shoulder in the thing's gut, and shoved it away, spun, and whipped the sword at it. *Amoracchius* cut into the Nightmare's midsection, and white fire erupted from the wound.

I hurried forward, around Michael's back to Charity. Already, she was stirring, trying to sit up. 'Dresden,' she whispered to me. 'My husband?'

'He's busy kicking ass,' I said, and pressed the crucifix into her fingers. 'Here. Take this. Can you walk?'

'Mind your tongue, Mr Dresden.' She grasped the crucifix and bowed her head for a second. 'I don't know,' she said. 'Oh, Lord help me. I think—' Her whole body tightened, and she let out a low gasp, pressing her hand against her belly.

'What?' I said. Had she been injured? Behind me, I could hear Michael grunting, see the sweep of *Amoracchius's* white fire making shadows dance. 'Charity, what is it?'

She let out a low groan. 'The baby,' she said. 'Oh, I think . . . I think my water broke earlier. When I fell.' Her face twisted up, flushing bright red, and she groaned again.

'Oh,' I said. 'Oh. Oh, no. No, this is *not* happening.' I put the heel of my hand to my forehead. 'This is just *wrong*.' I shot an accusing glance skywards. 'Someone up there has a *sick* sense of humor.'

'*Nnngggrhhh!*' Charity groaned. 'Oh, Lord preserve. Mr Dresden, I don't have much time.'

'No.' I sighed. 'Naturally not.' I bent down to pick her up and all but fell on my face. I managed to keep from sprawling onto her, but wobbled as I stood up again. Charity was not a dainty flower. There was no way I could carry her out of there.

'Michael!' I shouted. 'Michael, we've got a problem!'

Michael threw himself behind one of the biers as a stone whistled out of the darkness and shattered to powder against it. 'What?'

'Charity!' I shouted. 'Her baby's coming!'

'Harry!' Michael shouted. 'Look out!'

I turned and the Nightmare appeared from the darkness behind me, moving almost more swiftly than I could see. It reached down and simply tore a marble headstone from the earth, lifting it high. I threw myself between it and Charity, but even as I did, I knew it would be a futile gesture – it was strong enough to crush her right through me. But I did it anyway.

'Now!' screamed the Nightmare. 'Put down your sword, Knight! Put it down, or I crush them both!'

Michael started towards us, his face pale. 'Not a step closer,' the Nightmare snarled. 'Not an inch.'

Michael stopped. He stared at Charity, who groaned again, panting, eyes forced shut. 'H-Harry?' he said.

I could get out of the thing's way. I could draw its fire, maybe. But if I moved, it could simply crush Charity. She'd have no chance at all.

'The sword,' the Nightmare said, voice cool. 'Drop it.'

'Oh Lord,' Michael whispered.

'Don't do it, Michael,' I said. 'It's only going to kill us anyway.'

'Be thou silent,' the Nightmare said. 'My quarrel is with thee, wizard, and with the knight. The woman and her child are nothing to me, so long as I have both of you.'

Rain sleeted down for a long and otherwise silent moment. Then Michael closed his eyes. 'Harry,' he said. He lowered the great sword. Then gave it a gentle toss to one side, letting it fall on the ground. 'I'm sorry. I can't do it.'

The Nightmare met my eyes with its own, glowing faint scarlet, and its lips curled up into a gleeful smile. 'Wizard,' it said, in a whisper. 'Thy friend should have listened to thee.' I saw the gravestone start to come down toward me.

Charity's arm abruptly swept up, the crucifix I'd passed her held in it. The symbol flickered, and then kindled with white fire that threw harsh, horror-movie shadows up over the Nightmare's face. It twisted and recoiled from that light, screaming, and the tombstone crashed down to the earth, rending the damp, vulnerable soil.

Everything slowed down and came into crystalline focus. I could clearly see the grounds, the shadows of the trees. I could hear Charity beside me, uttering something in harsh Latin, and out of the corner of my eye, could see the restless shades moving about the cemetery. I could feel the cold sharpness of the rain, feel it coursing down over me, flowing down the gentle slopes to run in rivulets and streams to the nearby pond.

Running water. The answer was all around me.

I moved forward, toward the Nightmare. It swung at me with one flailing arm, and I felt it clip my shoulder as it swept down. Then I threw myself into the Nightmare's body, hit it hard. We tumbled together down the slope, toward the newly forming stream.

You ever hear the Legend of Sleepy Hollow? Remember the part with poor old Ichabod riding like blazes for the covered bridge and safety? Running water grounds magical energies. Creatures of the Nevernever, spirit bodies, cannot cross it without losing all the energy required to keep those bodies here. That was the answer.

I rolled down the slope with the Nightmare, and felt its hands tearing at me. We went down into the stream together, as one of its hands clenched my throat and shut off my breath.

And then it began to scream. It jerked and twisted atop me in eight or nine inches of running water, shrieking. The thing's body just started melting away, like sugar in water, starting at its feet and moving up. I watched it, watched myself dissolve with a morbid kind of fascination. It writhed, it bucked, it thrashed.

'Wizard,' it said, voice bubbling. 'This is not over. Not over. When the sun sets again, wizard, I will be back for thee!'

'Melt already,' I mumbled. And, seconds later, the Nightmare vanished, leaving only sticky gook behind, on my coat, my throat.

I stood up out of the water, drenched and shivering, and slogged my way back up the little hill. Michael had gone to his wife and crouched down beside her. He got his arms underneath her and lifted her as though she were a basket of laundry. Like I said before, Michael's buff.

'Harry,' he said. 'The sword.'

'I got it,' I replied. I trudged up to where he'd let *Amoracchius* fall and picked it up. The great blade weighed less than I would have thought, and it fairly hummed with power, vibrating in my fingers. I didn't have a sheath for it, so I just slung it up on one shoulder and hoped I wouldn't fall and cut my head off or something. I recovered my other stuff, too, and turned to walk out with Michael.

That was when Lea arrived, appearing before me with a trio of her hellhounds around her. 'My sweet,' she said. 'It is time to fulfill your bargain.'

I yelped and jumped back from her. 'No,' I said. 'No, wait. I beat this thing, but it's still loose. It will be able to come back from the Nevernever tomorrow night.'

'That is of no concern to me,' Lea said, and shrugged. 'Our bargain was for you to save the woman with what I gave you.'

'You didn't give me *anything*,' I said. 'You just blanked out some of the pain. It isn't as though you made the water, Godmother.'

She shrugged, smiling. 'Semantics. I pointed it out to you, did I not?'

'I would have realized it on my own,' I said.

'Perhaps. But we have a bargain.' She lowered her face, eyes gleaming gold and dangerous. 'Are you going to attempt to escape it once more?'

I'd given my word. And broken promises add up to trouble. But the Nightmare hadn't been defeated. Driven back, sure, but it would only be back the next night.

'I'll go with you,' I said. 'When I've beaten the Nightmare.'

'You'll go now.' Lea smiled. 'This instant. Or pay the price.' The three hellhounds took a pace toward me, baring their teeth in a silent snarl.

I fumbled everything out of my grasp but the sword, and gripped it tightly. I don't know a thing about broadswords, but it was heavy and sharp, and even without its vast power, I was pretty sure I could stick the pointy part into one of those hounds. 'I can't do that,' I said. 'Not yet.'

'Harry!' Michael shouted. 'Wait! It can't be used like that!'

One of the hounds leapt toward me, and I lifted the

blade. Then there was a flash of light and a jolt of pain that lanced up through my hands and arms. The blade twisted in my grasp, fell out of it and spun to the ground. The hellhound snapped at me, and I stumbled back, my hands gone numb and useless.

Lea's laughter rang out through the graves like silver bells. 'Yes!' she caroled, stepping forward. She bent and with a casual motion picked up the great sword. 'I knew you would try to cheat me again, sweet boy.' She smiled at me, a flash of dainty canines. 'I must thank you, Harry. I would never have been able to touch this had not the one who held it betrayed its purpose.'

I felt a flash of anger at my own stupidity. 'No,' I stammered. 'Wait. Can't we talk about this, Godmother?'

'We'll talk again, sweet boy. I'll see you both very soon.' Lea laughed again, eyes gleaming. And then she turned, her hellhounds gathering at her feet, and took a step forward, vanishing into the night. The sword went with her.

I stood there in the rain, feeling tired and cold and stupid. Michael stared at me for a second, his expression shocked, eyes wide. Charity curled against him, shuddering and moaning quietly.

'Harry,' Michael whispered. I think he was crying, but I couldn't see the tears in the rain. 'Oh my God. What have you done?'

22

All hospital emergency rooms have the same feel to them. They're all decorated in the same dull, muted tones and softened edges, which are meant to be comforting and aren't. They all have the same smell too: one part tangy antiseptics, one part cool dispassion, one part anxiety, and one part naked fear.

They wheeled Charity away first, Michael at her side. Triage being what it is, I got bumped to the front of the line. I felt like apologizing to the five-year-old girl holding a broken arm. Sorry, honey. Head trauma before fractured limbs.

The doctor who examined me wore a nameplate that read SIMMONS. She was broadly built and tough-looking, hair going grey in sharp contrast to her rich, dark skin. She sat down on a stool in front of me and leaned over, putting her hands on either side of my head. They were large, warm, strong. I closed my eyes.

'How are you feeling?' she asked, releasing me after a moment, and reaching for some supplies on a table next to her.

'Like a supervillain just threw me into a wall.'

She let out a soft chuckle. 'More specifically. Are you in pain? Dizzy? Nauseous?'

'Yes, no, and a little.'

'You hit your head?'

'Yeah.' I felt her start to daub at my forehead with a

cold cloth, cleaning off grime and dried blood, though there wasn't much left, thanks to the rain.

'Mmmm. Well. There's some blood here. Are you sure it's yours?'

I opened my eyes and blinked at her. 'Mine? Whose else would it be?'

The doctor lifted an eyebrow at me, dark eyes glittering from behind her glasses. 'You tell me, Mister . . .' she checked her charts. 'Dresden.' She frowned and then peered up at me. 'Harry Dresden? The wizard?'

I blinked. I'm not really famous, despite being the only wizard in the phone book. I'm more infamous. People don't tend to spontaneously recognize my name. 'Yeah. That's me.'

She frowned. 'I see. I've heard of you.'

'Anything good?'

'Not really.' She let out a cross sigh. 'There's no cut here. I don't appreciate jokes, Mister Dresden. There are people in need to attend to.'

I felt my mouth drop open. 'No cut?' But there had been a nice, flowing gash in my head at some point, pouring blood into my eyes and mouth. I could still taste some of it, almost. How could it have vanished?'

I thought of the answer and shivered. Godmother.

'No cut,' she said. 'Something that might have been cut a few months ago.'

'That's impossible,' I said, more to myself than to her. 'That just can't be.'

She shone a light at my eyes. I winced. She peered at each eye (mechanically, professionally – without the intimacy that triggers a soulgaze) and shook her head. 'If you've got a concussion, I'm Winona Ryder. Get off that bed and get out of here. Make sure to talk to the cashier on the way out.' She pressed a moist towelette into my hand. 'I'll let you clean up this mess, Mister Dresden. I have enough work to do.'

'But—'

'You shouldn't come into the emergency room unless it's absolutely necessary.'

'But I didn't—'

Dr Simmons didn't stop to listen to me. She turned around and strode off, over to the next patient – the little girl with the broken arm.

I got up and made my bruised way into the bathroom. My face was a mess of faint, dried blood. It had settled mostly into the lines and creases, making me look older, a mask of blood and age. I shivered and started cleaning myself off, trying to keep my hands from shaking.

I felt scared. Really, honestly scared. I would have been much happier to have needed stitches and painkillers. I wiped away blood and peered at my forehead. There was a faint, pink line beginning about an inch below my hair and slashing up into it at an angle. It felt very tender, and when I accidentally touched it with the rag, it hurt so much that I almost shouted. But the wound was closed, healed.

Magic. My godmother's magic. That kiss on the forehead had closed the wound.

If you think I should have been happy about getting a nasty cut closed up, then you probably don't realize the implications. Working magic directly on a human body is difficult. It's *very* difficult. Conjuring up forces, like my shield, or elemental manifestations like the fire or wind is a snap compared to the complexity and power required to change someone's hair a different color – or to cause the cells on either side of an injury to fuse back together, closing it.

The healing cut was a message for me. My godmother had power over me on earth now, too, as well as in the Nevernever. I'd made a bargain with one of the Fae and broken it. That gave her power over me, which she demonstrated aptly by the way she'd wrought such a powerful and complex working on me – and I'd never even felt it happening.

That was the part that scared me. I'd always known that Lea had outclassed me – she was a creature with a thousand years or more of experience, knowledge, and she had been born to magic like I had been born to breathing. So long as I remained in the real world, though, she'd had no advantage over me. Our world was a foreign place to her, just as hers was to me. I'd had the home field advantage.

Had being the operative word. Had.

Hell's bells.

I gave up and let my hands shake while I wiped off my face. I had a good reason to be afraid. Besides, my clothes were soaked from the rain and I felt desperately cold. I finished washing the blood away, and went to stand in front of the electric hand dryer. I had to slam the button a dozen times before it started.

I had the nozzle of the thing turned up, directing the hot air up my shirt, when Stallings came in sans, for once, Rudolph. He looked as though he hadn't slept since I'd seen him last. His suit was rumpled, his grey hair a little greyer, and his moustache was almost the same color as the bags underneath his eyes. He went to the sink and splashed cold water on his face without looking at me.

'Dresden,' he said. 'We got word you were in the hospital.'

'Heya, John. How's Murphy?'

'She slept. We just brought her in.'

I blinked at him. 'Christ. Is it dawn already?'

'About twenty minutes ago.' He moved over to the dryer next to mine. His started on the first slap of the button. 'She's sleeping, still. The docs are arguing about whether she's in a coma or on some kind of drug.'

'You tell them what happened?' I asked.

He snorted. 'Yeah. I'll just tell them that a wizard put her under a spell, and she's sleepy.' He glanced over at me. 'So when's she going to wake up?'

I shook my head. 'My spell won't hold her for long. Maybe a couple more days, at the most. Each time the sun comes up, it's going to degrade it a little more.'

'What happens then?'

'She starts screaming. Unless I find the thing that got her and figure out how to undo what it did.'

'That's what you want Kravos's book for,' Stallings said.

I nodded. 'Yeah.'

He reached into his pocket and produced the book – a little journal, thick but not broad, bound in dark leather. It was sealed in a plastic evidence bag. I reached for it, but Stallings pulled it away.

'Dresden. If you touch this, if you open it up, you're going to be leaving your prints on it. Skin cells. All sorts of things. Unless it disappears.'

I frowned at him. 'What's the big deal? Kravos is all but put away, right? Hell, we caught him with the murder weapon, with a body at the scene. There isn't anything in the journal to beat that, is there?'

I got a sick little feeling, and glanced aside at him. 'Michael?'

When he spoke, his voice was exhausted, numb. labor was complicated. She was cold, and might hav getting sick with something. Her water did brea'e at the graveyard. I guess it makes it a lot harde he baby.'

I just listened to him, feeling sicker.

'They had to go ahead and do a C-section. Bu think there might be damage. She got hit in the stomach at one point, they think. They don't know if she'll be able to have children again.'

'The baby?'

Silence.

'Michael?'

He stared at the infants and said, 'The doctor says that if he lasts thirty-six hours, he might have a chance. But he's weakening. They're doing everything they can.' Tears started at his eyes and rolled down his cheeks. 'There were complications. Complications.'

I tried to find something to say, and couldn't. Dammit. Tired frustration stirred my already unsteady belly. This shouldn't have happened. If I'd been faster, or smarter, or made a better decision, maybe I could have stopped Charity from getting hurt. Or the baby. I put my hand on Michael's shoulder and squeezed tight. Just trying to let him know that I was there. For all the good I'd done.

He took in a breath. 'The doctor thinks I beat her. That's how she got the bruises. He never said anything, but . . .'

'That's ridiculous,' I said, at once. 'Stars and stones, Michael, that's the stupidest thing I've ever heard.'

His voice came out hard, bitter. He stared at his faint reflection in the glass. 'It might as well have been me, ▮▮. If I hadn't gotten myself involved, this demon ▮▮n't have gone after her.' I heard his knuckles pop as ▮▮nched his fists. 'It should have come after me.'

▮▮u're right,' I said. 'Holy hell, Michael, you're right.'

▮ shot me a look. 'What are you talking about?'

▮▮bbed my hands together, trying to sort through the ▮▮ flashing across my brain in neon lights. 'It's a demon, this thing we're after, right? It's a demon's ghost.' An orderly, walking by pushing a tray, gave me an odd look. I smiled at him, feeling rather manic. He hurried along.

'Yes,' Michael said.

'Demons are tough, Michael. They're dangerous and they're scary, but they're really kind of clueless in a lot of ways.'

'How so?'

'They just don't get it, about people. They understand things like lust and greed and the desire for power, but they just don't get things like sacrifice and love. It's alien to most of them – doesn't make any sense at all.'

'I don't understand what you're driving at.'

'Remember what I said, about how I knew the worst way to get to you would be through your family?'

His frown darkened, but he nodded.

'I know that because I'm human. I know what it's like to care about someone other than myself. Demons don't – especially the thug-type demons who make pacts with two-bit sorcerers like Kravos. Even knowing that I thought the best way to get to you would be through someone close to you, I don't think a demon would have understood the context of that information.'

'So what you're saying is that this demon would have had no reason to go after my wife and child.'

'I'm saying it's inconsistent. If it was just a question of a demon's ghost going after the people who had killed it, then it should have just hammered on us all until we died and been done with it. I don't think it ever would have occurred to it to take a shot at someone that we care about – even if it did have my knowledge about you. There's got to be something else going on here.'

Michael's eyes widened a bit. 'The Nightmare is a cat's-paw,' he said. 'Someone else is using it to hit at us.'

'Someone who can cast those barbed-wire torment spells,' I said. 'And we've been chasing around after the tool instead of going after the hand that's wielding it.'

'Blood of God,' Michael swore. It was about the second-most powerful oath he used. 'Who could it be?'

I shook my head. 'I don't know. Someone who has us both in common, I guess. How many enemies do we share?'

He wiped his eyes on his sleeve, expression intent. 'I'm not sure. I've made enemies with pretty much every creature in the country.'

'Ditto,' I said, morosely. 'Even some of the other wizards wouldn't mind seeing me fall down a few flights of stairs. Not knowing our attacker's identity doesn't bother me as much as something else, though.'

'What's that?'

'Why he hasn't taken us out already.'

'They want to hurt us, first. Vengeance.' His brow beetled. 'Could your godmother be behind this?'

I shook my head. 'I don't think so. She's a faerie. They aren't usually this methodical or organized. And they aren't impatient, either. This thing's been active every night, like it couldn't wait to get going.'

Michael looked at me for a moment. Then he said, 'Harry, you know that I don't think it's my place to judge another person.'

'I hear a "but" coming.'

He nodded. 'But how did you get mixed up with the likes of that faerie? She's bad, Harry. Some of them are merely alien, but that one is . . . malevolent. She enjoys causing pain.'

'Yeah,' I said. 'I didn't exactly pick her.'

'Who did?'

I shrugged. 'My mother, I think. She was the one with power. My father wasn't a wizard. Wasn't into their world.'

'I don't understand why she would do that to her child.'

Something inside me broke with a little snapping sensation, and I felt tears at my eyes. I scowled. They were a child's tears, to go with a child's old pain. 'I don't know,' I said. 'I know that she was mixed up with some bad people. Bad beings. Whatever. Maybe Lea was one of her allies.'

'Lea. It's short for Leanandsidhe, isn't it.'

'Yeah. I don't know her real name. She takes blood from mortals and gives them inspiration in return. Artists and poets and things. That's how she amassed most of her power.'

Michael nodded. 'I've heard of her. This bargain you have with her. What is it?'

I shook my head. 'It isn't important.'

Something shifted in Michael, became harder, more resolute. 'It is important to me, Harry. Tell me.'

I stared at the babies for a minute, before I said, 'I was

a kid. Things fell out with my old teacher, Justin. He sent a demon to kill me, and I went on the run. I made a bargain with Lea. Enough power to defeat Justin in exchange for my service to her. My loyalty.'

'And you broke faith with her.'

'More or less.' I shook my head. 'She's never pushed it before now, and I've been careful to stay out of her way. She doesn't usually get this involved with mortal business.'

Michael moved his hand to *Amoracchius's* empty scabbard. 'She did take the sword though.'

I winced. 'Yeah. I guess that was my fault. If I hadn't have tried to use it to weasel out of the deal . . .'

'You couldn't have known,' Michael said.

'I should have,' I said. 'It isn't as though it as a tough one to figure out.'

Michael shrugged, though his expression was less casual than the gesture. 'What's done is done. But I don't know how much help to you I can be without the sword.'

'We'll get it back,' I said. 'Leah can't help herself. She makes deals. We'll figure out a way to get it back from her.'

'But will we do it in time,' Michael said. He shook his head, grim. 'The sword won't stay in her hands forever. The Lord won't allow that. But it may be that my time to wield it has passed.'

'What are you talking about?' I asked.

'Perhaps it was a sign. Perhaps that I am no longer worthy to serve Him in this way. Or that the burden of it has passed on to someone else.' He grimaced, staring at the glass, the infants. 'My family, Harry. Perhaps it's time they had a full-time father.'

Oh, great. All I needed, now, was a crisis of faith and bad case of career doubt from the Fist of God. I needed Michael. I needed someone to watch my back, someone who was used to dealing with the supernatural. Sword or no sword, he had a steady head, and his faith had a subtle power of its own. He could be the difference between me getting killed and defeating whoever was out there.

Besides, he had wheels.

'Let's get going. Time's a-wasting.'

He frowned. 'I can't. I'm needed here.'

'Michael, look. Is someone with your kids at home?'

'Yes. I called Charity's sister last night. She went over. Father Forthill was going to get some sleep, and then stay on.'

'Is there anything more you can do for Charity here?'

He shook his head. 'Only pray. She's resting, now. And her mother is on the way here.'

'Okay, then. We've got work to do.'

'You expect me to leave them again?'

'No, not leave them. But we need to find the person behind the Nightmare and take care of them.'

'Harry. What are we going to do? Kill someone?'

'If we have to. Hell's bells, Michael, they might have murdered your son.'

His face hardened, and I knew then that I had him, that he'd followed me into Hell to get at whoever had hurt his wife and child. I had him all right – and I hated myself for it. Way to go, Harry. Jerk those heartstrings like a fucking puppeteer.

I held up the book. 'I think I've got a line on the Nightmare's name. I'll bet you anything that Kravos recorded it in his book of shadows, here. If I'm right, I

might be able to use it to make contact with the Nightmare and then trace his leash back to whoever's holding it.'

Michael stared at the glass, at the kids beyond it.

'I need you to drive me home. From my lab, I might be able to sort out what's going on before things get any more out of hand. Then we go handle it.'

He didn't say anything.

'Michael.'

'All right,' he said, voice quiet. 'Let's go.'

23

Back in my lab, it felt a little creepy to be working by candlelight. Intellectually, I knew that it was still full daylight outside, but last night had brought out the instinctive fear of the dark that is a part of being human. I had been wounded. Everything, every shadow, every small sound made me twitch and jerk and look aside.

'Steady, Harry,' I told myself. 'You have time before sundown. Just relax and get it over with.'

Good advice. Michael and I had driven around most of the morning, collecting what I would need for the spell. I'd read through Kravos's journal while Michael drove. Sick stuff. He'd been careful about listing out every step of his rituals, complete with notes on the physical ecstasy he'd experienced during the killings – nine in all. Most of them had been women or children he'd killed with a cruelly curved knife. He'd roped a bunch of young people into his fold with drugs and blackmail, and then thrown orgies where he'd either participate or else channel the energy raised by all that lust into his magic. That seemed to be standard operating procedure for guys like Kravos. Win-win situation.

A thorough man. Thorough in his efforts to kill and corrupt lives to acquire more power, thorough in the documentation of his sick pleasures – and thorough in the listing of his efforts to secure a familiar demon by the name of Azorthragal.

The name had been carefully written, each syllable marked for specific emphasis.

Magic is a lot like language: it's all about stringing things together, linking one thing with another, one idea with another. After you establish links, then you pour power into them and make something happen. That's what we call thaumaturgy in the business — creating links between small things and big things. Then, you make something happen on the small scale and it happens on the large scale, too. Voodoo dolls are the typical example for that one.

But simulacra, like a voodoo doll, aren't the only way to create links. A wizard can use fingernail clippings, or hair, or blood, if it's fresh enough, or just about any other body part to create a link back to the original being.

Or you can use its name. Or maybe I should say, its Name.

Names have power. Everyone's Name says something about them, whether they're aware of it or not. A wizard can use that Name to forge a link to someone. It's difficult with people. People's self-concepts are always changing, evolving, so even if you get someone to tell you their full name, if you try to establish the link when they're in a radically different mood, or after some life-changing event that alters the way they see themselves, it might not work. A wizard can get a person's name only from their own lips, but if he doesn't use it fairly quickly, it's likely to get stale.

Demons, however, are a different matter. Demons aren't people. They don't have the problem of having a soul, and they don't worry about silly things like good and evil, or right and wrong. Demons are. If a demon is going to be inclined to eat your face, it's going to eat your face then, and now, and a thousand years from now.

It's almost comforting, in a way — and it makes them vulnerable. Once you know a demon's Name, you can get to it whenever you want to. I had Azorthragal's Name. Even though it was a ghost now, instead of a demon, it ought to respond to the memory of its Name, if nothing else.

Time to get to it.

Five white candles surrounded my summoning circle, the points of an invisible pentacle. White for protection. And because they're the cheapest color at Wal-Mart. Hey, being a wizard doesn't make money grow on trees.

Between each candle was an object from someone the Nightmare had touched. My shield bracelet was there. Michael had given me his wedding ring, and Charity's. I'd gone by the station, and grabbed the hand-lettered name-plate Murphy had kept stubbornly on her office door until the publicity last year had driven the municipal politicians into getting her a real one. It lay on the floor beside them. A visit to a grateful Malone household had turned up Micky's retirement watch. It completed the circle, between the last pair of candles.

I drew in a breath, and checked my props. You don't need all the candles and knives and whatnot to work magic. But they help. They make it easier to focus. In my weakened condition, I needed all the help I could get.

So I lit the incense and paced around the outside of the summoning circle, leaving myself enough room to work with inside the circle of incense and outside the circle of copper. I put out a little willpower as I did, just enough to close the circle, and felt the energy levels rise as random magic coalesced.

'Harry,' Michael called down from the room above. 'Are you finished?'

I suppressed a flash of irritation. 'Just getting started.'

'Forty-five minutes until sundown,' he said.

I couldn't keep the annoyance out of my voice. 'Gee, thanks. No pressure, Michael.'

'Can you do it or not, Harry? Father Forthill is staying at my house with the children. If you can't stop this thing now, I've got to go back to Charity.'

'I sure as hell can't do it with you breathing down my neck. Hell's bells, Michael, get out of the way and let me work.'

He growled something to himself about patience or turning the other cheek or something. I heard his feet on the floor above as he retreated from the door leading down to my lab.

Michael didn't come down into the lab with me because the whole concept of using magic without the Almighty behind it didn't sit well with him, regardless of what we'd been through together. He could tolerate it, but not approve of it.

I got back to work, closing my eyes and forcing myself to clear my thoughts, to focus on the task at hand. I started to draw my concentration toward the copper circle. The incense smoke tickled at my senses, and swirled about inside the perimeter of the outer circle, not leaving it. The energy grew slowly, as I concentrated, and then I picked up the knife in my right hand, and a handful of water from a bowl on my left.

Now for the three steps. 'Enemy, mine enemy,' I spoke, slipping power into the words, 'I seek you.' I passed the knife over the copper circle, straight down. I couldn't see it, without opening my Sight, but could feel the silent tension as I cut a slit between the mortal world and the Nevernever.

'Enemy, mine enemy,' I spoke again. 'I search for you. Show me your face.' I cast the water up, over the circle, where the energy of the spell atomized it into a fine, drifting mist, filled with rainbows from the surrounding candles, shifting shapes and colors.

Now for the hard part. 'Azorthragal!' I shouted, 'Azorthragal, Azorthragal! *Appare!*' I used the knife to cut my finger, and smeared the blood onto the edge of the copper circle.

Power surged out of me, into the circle, through the rent in the fabric of reality, and as it did, the circle sprang up like a wall around the band of copper in the floor. I felt the cut as an acute, vicious pain, enough to make me blink tears out of my eyes as the power quested out, fueled by the energy of the circle, guided by the articles spread around it.

The spell quested about in the Nevernever, like the blind tentacle of the Kraken scouring the deck, looking for some hapless soul to grab. It shouldn't have happened like that. It should have zipped to the Nightmare like a lariat and brought it reeling in. I reached out and put more power into the spell, picturing the thing that I had been fighting, the results of its work, trying to give the spell more guidance. It wasn't until I hit upon the *sense* of the Nightmare, for lack of a better word, the terror it had inspired that the spell latched onto something. There was a moment of startled stillness, and then a wild, bucking energy, a resistance, that made my heart pound in my chest, the cut in my finger burn as though someone had poured salt over it.

'*Appare!*' I shouted, forcing will into my voice, reeling back in on the spell. 'I command thee to appear!' I slip into the archaic at dramatically appropriate moments. So sue me.

The swirling mist of rainbows swayed and wavered, as though some kind of half-solid thing were stirring the air within the summoning circle. It struggled like a maddened bull, trying to tear away from my spell. '*Appare!*'

Upstairs, the telephone rang. I heard Michael walk across the floor while I struggled through several silent, furious seconds, the Nightmare trying to escape the web of my concentration.

'Hello,' Michael said. He'd left the door open and I heard him clearly.

'*Appare!*' I grated again. I felt the thing slip, and I jerked it closer in vicious triumph. The mists and lights swirled, began to take on shape, vaguely humanoid.

'Oh. Yes, but he's . . . a little busy,' Michael said. 'Uh-huh. No, not exactly. I think – Yes, but—' Michael sighed. 'Just a minute.' I heard his feet cross to the trap door again.

'Harry,' Michael called. 'Susan's on the phone. She says she needs to talk to you.'

I all but screamed, struggling to hold onto the Nightmare. 'I'll call her back,' I managed to gasp.

'She says it's really important.'

'Michael!' I half-screamed. 'I'm a little *busy* here!'

'Harry,' Michael said, his voice serious. 'I don't know what you're doing down there, but she sounds very upset. Says she's been trying to get in touch with you for a while without any luck.'

The Nightmare started slipping away from me. I gritted my teeth and hung on. 'Not now!'

'All right,' Michael said. He retreated from the door down to the lab, and I heard him speaking quietly on the phone again.

I blocked it out, blocked out everything but my spell, the circle, and the thing on the other end of it. I was tiring, but so was it. I had all the props, the power and focus of the circle – it was strong, but I had the leverage on it, and after another minute, minute and a half, I shouted, *'Appare!'* for the last time.

The mist in the circle swirled and trembled, taking on a vaguely humanoid shape. The shape screamed, a faint and bubbly sound, still trying to escape.

'You can't get away!' I shouted at it. 'Who brought you over! Who sent you!'

'Wizard,' the thing screamed. 'Release me!'

'Yeah, right. Who sent you!' I forced more energy into my voice, compulsion.

It screamed, a distorted sound, like a radio getting interference. The shape refused to clarify or solidify anymore. 'No one!'

'Who sent you!' I said, hammering on the spell and the Nightmare, with my will. 'Who has compelled you to harm these people? Hell's bells, you *will* answer me!'

'No one,' the Nightmare snarled. Its struggling redoubled, but I grabbed on tightly.

And then I felt it – a third party, intruding from the other side. I felt that cold, horrible power that had been behind the torment-spell on Micky Malone and on Agatha Hagglethorn's ghost. It poured into the Nightmare like nitrous into an engine, supercharging it. The Nightmare went from raging bull to frenzied elephant, and I felt it begin to tear free of my spell, to get loose.

'Wizard!' it howled in triumph. 'Wizard, the sun is sinking! I will tear out thy heart! I will hunt thy friends and their children! I will slay them all!'

'It's thine heart,' I muttered. 'And no you won't.' I lifted my left hand and slashed it at the sparkling mist, sprinkling droplets of blood at it. 'Bound, thou art,' I snarled. I reached out toward the thing, and found the part of me that was still inside of it, a warm sensation, like coming home again after a long trip. I could only barely brush it, but it was enough for what I wanted to do. 'No other souls wilt thou harm, no other blood wilt thou spill. Thy quarrel is now with *me*. Bound, I make thee! Bound!' And with the third repetition of the word, I felt the spell lock, felt it settle around the Nightmare like steel coils. I couldn't keep it from getting away, I couldn't forbid it from the mortal world altogether, but I could damn well make sure that the only person it could mess with would be me. 'Now let's see how you do in a fair fight, asshole.'

It screamed, all but bursting the bonds of my spell, the sound reverberating through the room. I lifted the knife in my other hand and ripped it at the air over the circle, releasing the holding spell, pouring everything I had left into the strike. I saw the magic lance out into the circle, even as the Nightmare faded. It split the rainbow mist like the sweep of some invisible woodsman's axe, and once more, the Nightmare screamed.

Then the mist gathered together in a horrible rush, an implosion of space, and the creature was gone. A handful of water splattered the ground, and the candles went out.

I collapsed forward, to my forearms, wheezing and gasping for breath, my muscles shaking. I'd hurt the bastard. It wasn't invincible. I'd hurt it. Maybe nothing much more inconvenient than the cut on my finger, or a slap in the face, but it hadn't expected that.

I hadn't been able to get to the person behind it, but I'd felt something – I'd sensed their presence, gotten a clear whiff of their perfume, in a metaphysical sense. Maybe I could use that.

'Take that, jerk,' I mumbled. I lay there gasping for several minutes, my head spinning from the effort of the spell. Then I put my things away and shambled up out of my lab, into the room above.

Michael helped me to a seat. He'd built up the fire, and I soaked in its warmth gratefully. He went to the kitchen and brought me a Coke, a sandwich. I drank and ate greedily. Only after I'd finished the last of the drink did he ask, 'What happened?'

'I called it up. The Nightmare. Someone helped it get away, but not before I laid a binding on it.'

He frowned at me, grey eyes studying my face. 'What kind of binding?'

'I kept it from going after you. Or Murphy. Or your family. I couldn't keep it out, but I could limit its targets.'

Michael blinked at me for a moment. Then said, slowly, 'By making it come after you.'

I grinned at him, a fierce show of teeth, and nodded. A touch of pride filled my voice. 'I had to do it at the last second, on the fly. I hadn't really planned it, but it worked. So long as I'm alive, it can't mess with anyone else.'

'So long as you're alive,' Michael said. He frowned, and leaned his thick forearms on his knees, pressing his palms together. 'Harry?'

'Yeah?'

'Doesn't that mean it's certainly going to try to kill you? No torment, no sadistic tortures — just flat-out mayhem and death.'

I nodded, sobering. 'Yeah.'

'And . . . whatever person is behind the Nightmare, whoever helped it escape — that means that you've just put yourself in their way. They can't use their weapon until they've removed you.'

'Yeah.'

'So . . . if they didn't need you dead before, they're going to stop at nothing else now.'

I was quiet for a moment, thinking about that. 'I made my choice, man,' I said, finally. 'But hell, I'm already in water so deep, it doesn't matter if it gets any deeper. Let the Nightmare and my godmother duke it out for who gets to be first in line.'

His eyes flickered up at mine. 'Oh, Harry. You shouldn't have done that.'

I scowled at him. 'Hey. It's better than anything else we've managed, so far. You'd have done the same thing, if you could.'

'Yes,' Michael said. 'But my family is well provided for.' He paused, and then added, in a gentle voice, 'And I'm sure of my soul's destination, when it's time for me to go.'

'I'll worry about Hell later. Besides, I think I have a plan.'

He grimaced. 'You aren't concerned about your soul, but you have a plan.'

'I don't intend to get killed just yet. We've got to take the offensive, Michael. If we just sit back and wait, it's going to be able to take us apart.'

'Take *you* apart, you mean,' he said. His expression grew

more troubled. 'Harry, without *Amoracchius* . . . I'm not sure how much help I'll be to you.'

'You know what you're doing, Michael. And I don't think the Almighty is going to quit the team just because we fumbled the ball, right?'

'Of course not, Harry. He is ever faithful.'

I leaned toward him, put a hand on his shoulder, and looked him right in the eyes. I don't do that to people very often. There aren't many I can. 'Michael. This thing is big, and it's bad, and it scares the hell out of me. But I might be the only one who can stop it, now. I need you. I need your help. Hell, man. I need to know that you're at my back, that you believe in what I'm doing here. Are you with me or not?'

He studied my face. 'You've lost much of your power, you say. And I don't have the sword anymore. Our enemies know it. We could both be killed. Or worse.'

'If we stay here doing nothing, we're going to get killed anyway. And maybe Murphy and Charity and your kids with us.'

He bowed his head, and nodded. 'You're right. There's not really any choice.' His hand covered mine for a moment, big and calloused and strong, and then he stood up again, his back straight and his shoulders squared. 'We just have to have faith. The good Lord wouldn't give us more than we could bear.'

'I hope you're right,' I said.

'So what's the plan, Harry? What are we going to do?'

I got up and went to the mantel over the fire, but what I needed wasn't there. I frowned, looking around the room, and spied it on the coffee table. I bent down and plucked

up the white envelope, taking the gold-lettered invitation
Kyle and Kelly Hamilton had delivered.

'We're going to a party.'

24

Michael parked his truck on the street outside Bianca's mansion. He put the keys in his leather belt pouch, and buttoned it with the silver cross button. Then he straightened the collar of his doublet, which showed through the neck of the mail, and reached behind the seat for the steel helmet that slipped on over his head. 'Tell me again, Harry, why this is a good idea. Why are we going to a masquerade ball with a bunch of monsters?'

'Everything points us this way,' I said.

'How?'

I took a breath, trying to be patient, and passed him the white cloak. 'Look. We know that someone's been stirring up the spirit world. We know that they did it in order to create this Nightmare that's been after us. We know that the girl, Lydia, was connected to the Nightmare somehow.'

'Yes,' Michael said. 'All right.'

'Bianca,' I said, 'sent out her thugs to take Lydia. And Bianca's hosting a party for the nastiest bad guys in the region. Stallings told me that people have been going missing off the streets. They've probably been taken for food or something. Even if Bianca isn't behind it, and I'm not saying she isn't, chances are that anyone who could be is going to be at the party tonight.'

'And you think you'll be able to spot them?' Michael asked.

'Pretty sure,' I responded. 'All I'll have to do is get close enough to touch them, to feel their aura. I felt whoever was backing the Nightmare when they helped it get away from me. I should be able to tell when I feel them again.'

'I don't like it,' Michael said. 'Why didn't the Nightmare come after you the minute the sun went down?'

'Maybe I scared it. I cut it up a little.'

Michael frowned. 'I still don't like it. There are going to be dozens of things in there that have no right to exist in this world. It will be like walking into a roomful of wolves.'

'All you have to do,' I said, 'is keep your mouth shut and watch my back. The bad guys have to play by the rules tonight. We've been given the protection of the old laws of hospitality. If Bianca doesn't respect that, it's going to kill her reputation in front of her guests and the Vampire Court.'

'I will protect you, Harry,' Michael said. 'As I will protect anyone who these . . . things threaten.'

'We don't need any fights, Michael. That's not why we're here.'

He looked out the truck window and set his jaw.

'I mean it, Michael. It's their turf. There's probably going to be bad stuff inside, but we have to keep the big picture in focus here.'

'The big picture,' he said. 'Harry, if there's someone in there that needs my help, they're getting it.'

'Michael! If *we* break the truce first, we're open game. You could get us both killed.'

He turned to look at me, and his eyes were granite. 'I am what I am, Harry.'

I threw my arms up in the air, and banged my hands on the roof of the truck. 'There are people who could get killed if we mess this up. It isn't only our own lives we're talking about, here.'

'I know,' he said. 'My family are some of them. But that doesn't change anything.'

'Michael,' I said. 'I'm not asking you to smile and chat and get cozy. Just keep quiet and stay out of the way. Don't shove a crucifix down anyone's throat. That's all I'm asking.'

'I won't stand by, Harry,' he said. 'I can't.' He frowned and said, 'I don't think you can, either.'

I glared at him. 'Hell's bells, Michael. I don't want to die, here.'

'Nor do I. We must have faith.'

'Great,' I said. 'That's just great.'

'Harry, will you join me in prayer?'

I blinked at him. 'What?'

'A prayer,' Michael said. 'I'd like to talk to Him for a moment.' He half smiled at me. 'You don't have to say anything. Just be quiet and stay out of the way.' He bowed his head.

I squinted out the window of the truck, silent. I don't have anything against God. Far from it. But I don't understand Him. And I don't trust a lot of the people that go around claiming that they're working in His best interests. Faeries and vampires and what-not – those I can fathom. Even demons. Sometimes, even the Fallen. I can understand why they do what they do.

But I don't understand God. I don't understand how he could see the way people treat one another, and not chalk up the whole human race as a bad idea.

I guess he's just bigger about it than I would be.

'Lord,' Michael said. 'We walk into darkness now. Our enemies will surround us. Please help to make us strong enough to do what needs to be done. Amen.'

Just that. No fancy language, no flashy beseeching the Almighty for aid. Just quiet words about what he wanted to get done, and a request that God would be on his side – on our side. Simple words, and yet power surrounded him like a cloud of fine mist, prickling along my arms and my neck. Faith. I calmed down a little. We had a lot going for us. We could do this.

Michael looked up at me and nodded. 'All right,' he said. 'I'm ready.'

'How do I look?' I asked him.

He smiled, white teeth showing. 'You're going to turn heads. That's for sure.'

I had to smile back at him. 'Okay,' I said. 'Let's party.'

We got out of the truck, and started walking toward the gates around Bianca's estate. Michael buckled on the white cloak with its red cross as he went. He had a matching surcoat, boots, and armored guards on his shoulders. He had a pair of heavy gauntlets tucked through his boots, and wore a pair of knives on his belt, one on either side. He smelled like steel and he clanked a little bit when he walked. It sounded comforting, in a friendly, dreadnought kind of way.

It would have been more stylish to drive up through the gates and have a valet park the truck, but Michael didn't want to hand over his truck to vampires. I didn't blame him. I wouldn't trust a bloodsucking, night stalking, fiend of the shadows valet, either.

The gate had an honest-to-goodness guard house, with

a pair of guards. Neither one of them looked like they were carrying guns, but they held themselves with an armed arrogance that neither myself nor Michael missed. I held up the invitation. They let us in.

We walked up the drive to the house. A black limo pulled up along the drive as we did, and we had to step off to the side to let it past. When we got to the front of the house, the occupants were just getting out of the car.

The driver came around to the rear door of the limo and opened it. Music washed out, something loud and hard. There was a moment's pause, and then a man glided out of the limo.

He was tall, pale as a statue. Sable hair fell in tousled curls to his shoulders. He was dressed in a pair of opalescent butterfly wings that rose from his shoulders, fastened to him by some mysterious mechanism. He wore white leather gloves, their gauntlet cuffs decorated in winding silver designs, and similar designs were set around his calves, down to his sandals. At his side hung a sword, delicately made, the handle wrought as though out of glass. The only other thing he had on was a loincloth of some soft, white cloth. He had the body for it. Muscle, but not too much of it, good set of shoulders, and the pale skin wasn't darkened anywhere by hair. Hell's bells, *I* noticed how good he looked.

The man smiled, bright enough for a toothpaste commercial, and then reached a hand back down to the car. A pair of gorgeous legs in pink high heels slid out of the car, followed by a slender and scrumptious girl barely covered in flower petals. She had a short, tight skirt made out of them, and more petals cupped her breasts like delicate hands. Other than that, and the baby's breath woven into the tumbled mass of her black hair, she wore nothing. And she wore it well. In the heels, she might have been five-seven, and she had a face that made me think that she was both lovely and sweet. Her cheeks were flushed in a delicate pink blush, vibrant and alive, her lips parted, and she had a look to her eyes that told me she was on something.

'Harry,' Michael said. 'You're drooling.'

'I'm not drooling,' I said.

'That girl can't be nineteen years old.'

'I'm not drooling!' I scowled, gripped my cane in hand, and stalked on up the driveway to the house. And wiped at my mouth with my sleeve. Just in case.

The man turned toward me, and both his eyebrows lifted. He looked me and my costume up and down, and burst out into a rich, rolling laugh. 'Oh, my,' he said. 'You must be Harry Dresden.'

That got my hackles up. It always bugs me when someone knows me and I don't know them. 'Yeah,' I said. 'That's me. Who the hell are you?'

If the hostility bothered him, it didn't bother his smile. The girl with him slipped beneath his left arm and nestled against him, watching me with stoned eyes. 'Oh, of course,' he said. 'I forget that you probably know very little of the intricacies of the Court. My name is Thomas, of House Raith, of the White Court.'

'White Court,' I said.

'Three vampire Courts,' Michael supplied. 'Black, Red, and White.'

'I knew that.'

Michael shrugged one shoulder. 'Sorry.'

Thomas smiled. 'Well. Only two, for all practical

purposes. The Black Court has fallen on hard times of late, the poor darlings.' His tone of voice suggested muted glee rather than pity. 'Mister Dresden, allow me to introduce Justine.'

Justine, the girl beneath his arm, gave me a sweet smile. I half-expected her to extend her hand to me to be kissed, but she didn't. She just molded her body to Thomas's in what looked like a most pleasant fashion.

'Charmed,' I said. 'This is Michael.'

'Michael,' Thomas mused, and studied the man up and down. 'Dressed as a Knight Templar.'

'Something like that,' Michael said.

'How ironic,' Thomas said. His eyes returned to me, and that smile widened. 'And you, Mister Dresden. Your costume is . . . going to make quite a stir.'

'Why, thank you.'

'Shall we go inside?'

'Oh, let's.' We all trouped up the front stairs, affording me an uncomfortably proximate view of Justine's legs along the way, lean and lovely and made for doing things that had nothing to do with locomotion. A pair of tuxedo-clad doormen who looked human swung open the mansion's doors for us.

The entry hall to Bianca's mansion had been redecorated since the last time I'd been there. The old-style decor had been lavishly restored. She'd had marble laid out instead of gleaming hardwood. All the doorways stood in graceful arches rather than stolid rectangles. Alcoves every ten feet or so sported small statuary and other pieces of art. It was lit only by the spots on each alcove, creating deep pools of shadow in between.

'Rather tacky,' Thomas sniffed, his butterfly wings

quivering. 'Have you been to any Court functions before, Mister Dresden? Are you aware of the etiquette?'

'Not really,' I said. 'But it had better not involve anyone drinking anyone's bodily fluids. Particularly mine.'

Thomas laughed, richly. 'No, no. Well,' he admitted, 'not formally, in any case, though there will be ample opportunity to indulge, if you wish.' His fingers caressed the girl's waist again, and she focused her eyes on me in a disconcertingly intent fashion.

'I don't think so. What do I need to know?'

'Well, we're all outsiders, not being members of the Red Court, and this is a Red function. First, we'll be presented to the company and they'll have the chance to come meet us.'

'Mingle, eh?'

'Just so. Afterwards, we'll be presented to Bianca herself, and she, in turn, will give us a gift.'

'A gift?' I asked.

'She's the hosting party. Of course she'll be giving gifts.' He smiled at me. 'It's only civilized.'

I eyed him. I wasn't used to vampires being so chatty. 'Why are you being so helpful?'

He laid his fingers upon his chest, lifting his eyebrows in a perfectly executed 'who me?' expression. 'Why, Mister Dresden. Why should I not help you?'

'You're a vampire.'

'So I am,' he said. 'But, I'm afraid, I'm not a terribly good one.' He gave me a sunny smile and said, 'Of course, I could also be lying.'

I snorted.

'So, Mister Dresden. Rumor had it you had refused Bianca's invitation.'

'I had.'

'What changed your mind?'

'Business.'

'Business?' Thomas asked. 'You're here on business?'

I shrugged. 'Something like that.' I stripped off my gloves, trying to look casual, and offered him my hand. 'Thanks again.'

His head tilted to one side and he narrowed his eyes. He looked down at my hand and then back up at me, his gaze calculating, before trading grips with me.

There was a faint, flickering aura about him. I felt it dance and glide over my skin like a soft, cool wind. It felt odd, different than the energy that surrounded a human practitioner – and nothing like the sense of whatever had been pumping up the Nightmare.

Thomas wasn't my man. I must have relaxed visibly, because he smiled and said, 'I pass the test, eh?'

'I don't know what you're talking about.'

'Whatever you say. You're an odd duck, Harry Dresden. But I like you.' And with that, he and his escort turned and glided together down the length of the entry hall, and through the curtained doors at the far end.

I glowered after them.

'Anything?' Michael asked.

'He's clean,' I said. 'Relatively speaking. Must be someone else here.'

'You'll get the chance to do some handshaking, it sounds like,' Michael said.

'Yeah. You ready?'

'Lord willing,' Michael said.

We started together down the hall, and through the curtained doorway, and emerged into Vampire Party Central.

We stood on a concrete deck, elevated ten feet off the rest of a vast, outdoor courtyard. Music flowed up from below. People crowded the courtyard in a blur of color and motion, talk and costume, like some kind of Impressionist painting. Glowing globes rested on wire stands, here and there, giving the place a sort of torch-lit mystique. A dias, opposite the entryway we stood in, rose up several feet higher in the air, a suspiciously throne-like chair upon it.

I had just started to take in details when a brilliant white light flooded my eyes, and I had to lift a hand against it. The music died down a bit, and the chatter of people quieted some. Evidently, Michael and I had just become the center of attention.

A servant stepped forward and asked, calmly, 'May I have your invitation, sir?' I passed it over, and a moment later heard the same voice, over a modest public address system.

'Ladies and gentlemen of the Court. I am pleased to present Harry Dresden, Wizard of the White Council, and guest.'

I lowered my hands, and the voices fell completely silent. From either side of the throne opposite, a pair of spotlights glared at me.

I shrugged my shoulders to get my cape to fall into place correctly, tattered red lining flashing against the black cotton exterior. The collar of the thing came up high on either side of my face. The spot glared off of the painted gold plastic medallion I wore at my throat. The worn powder-blue tux beneath it could have made an appearance at someone's prom, in the seventies. The servants at the party had better tuxes than I did.

I made sure to smile, so that they could see the cheap

plastic fangs. I suppose the spotlight must have bleached my face out to ghostly whiteness, especially with the white clown makeup I had on. The fake blood drooling out the corners of my mouth would be standing out bright red against it.

I lifted a white-gloved hand and said, slurring a little through the fangs. 'Hi! How are you all doing?'

My words rang out on deathly silence, from below.

'I still can't believe,' Michael said, *sotto voce*, 'that you came to the Vampires' Masquerade Ball dressed as a vampire.'

'Not just a vampire,' I said, 'a *cheesy* vampire. Do you think they got the point?' I managed to peer past the spotlights enough to make out Thomas and Justine at the foot of the stairs. Thomas was staring around at the courtyard with undisguised glee, then flashed me a smile and a thumbs-up.

'I think,' Michael said, 'that you've just insulted everyone here.'

'I'm here to find a monster, not make nice with them. Besides, I never wanted to come to this stupid party in the first place.'

'All the same. I think you've peeved them off.'

'Peeved? Come on. How bad could that be? Peeved.'

From the courtyard below came several distinctive sounds: A few hisses. The rasp of steel as several someones drew knives. Or maybe swords. The nervous *click-clack* of someone with a semiautomatic working the slide.

Michael shrugged in his cloak, and I sensed, more than saw him put his hand on the hilt of one of his knives. 'I think we're about to find out.'

25

Silence lay heavy over the courtyard. I gripped my cane and waited for the first gunshot, or whistle of a thrown knife, or blood-curdling scream of fury. Michael was a steel-smelling presence beside me, silent and confident in the face of the hostility. Hell's bells. I'd meant to give the vamps a little thumb of the nose with the costume, but wow. I didn't think I'd net *this* much of a reaction.

'Steady, Harry,' Michael murmured. 'They're like mean dogs. Don't flinch or run. It will only set them off.'

'Your average mean dog doesn't have a gun,' I murmured back. 'Or a knife. Or a sword.' But I remained where I stood, my expression bland.

The first sound to ring out was neither gunshot nor battle cry, but rich, silvery laughter. It drifted up, masculine, somehow merry and mocking, bubbling and scornful all at once. I squinted down through the lights, to see Thomas, posed like some bizarre postchrysalis incarnation of Errol Flynn, one foot up on the stairs, hand braced, his other hand on the crystalline hilt of his sword. His head was thrown back, every lean line of muscle on him displayed with the casual disregard of skilled effort. The butterfly wings caught the light at the edges of the spots and threw them back in dazzling colors.

'I've always heard,' Thomas drawled, his voice loud enough to be heard by all, artfully projected, 'that the Red Court gave its guests a warm welcome. I hadn't thought I'd get such a picturesque demonstration, though.' He turned toward the dias and bowed. 'Lady Bianca, I'll be sure to tell my father all about this dizzying display of hospitality.'

I felt my smile harden, and I peered past the spotlights to the dias. 'Bianca, dear, there you are. This *was* a costume party, was it not? A masquerade? And we were all supposed to come dressed as something we weren't? If I misread the invitation, I apologize.'

I heard a woman's voice murmur something, and the spotlights flicked off. I was left in the dark for a minute, until my eyes could adjust, and I could regard the woman standing across from me, upon the dias.

Bianca wasn't tall, but she was statuesque in a way you only find in erotic magazines and embarrassing dreams. Pale of skin, dark of hair and eye, full of sensuous curves, from her mouth to her hips, everything possessed of luscious ripeness coupled with slender strength that would have caught the eye of any man. She wore a gown of flickering flame. I don't mean that she wore a red dress – she *wore* flame, gathered about her in the shape of an evening gown, blue at its base fading through the colors of a candle to red as it cupped her full, gorgeous breasts. More flame danced and played through the elegant piles of her dark hair, flickering over her like a tiara. She had on a pair of real heels at least, adding several inches to her rather unimpressive height. The shoes did interesting things to the shape of her legs. The curve of her smile promised things that were probably illegal, and bad for you, and would carry warnings from the Surgeon General, but that you'd still want to do over and over again.

I wasn't interested. I had seen what was underneath her mask, once before. I couldn't forget what was there.

'Well,' she purred, her voice carrying over the whole of the courtyard. 'I suppose I shouldn't have expected any more taste from you, Mister Dresden. Though perhaps we will see about your taste, later in the evening.' Her tongue played over her teeth, and she gave me a dazzling smile.

I watched her, watched behind her. A pair of figures in black cloaks, hardly more than vague shapes behind her stood quietly, as though ready to attack if she snapped a finger. I suppose every decent flame casts shadows. 'I think you'd better not try it.'

Bianca laughed again. Several in the courtyard joined in with her, though it was a nervous thing. 'Mister Dresden,' she said. 'Many things can change a man's mind.' She crossed her legs, slowly, flashing naked skin up to her taut, silky thigh as she did. 'Perhaps we'll find something that changes yours.' She waved her hand, lazy and arrogant. 'Music. We are here to celebrate. Let us do so.'

The music began again while I sorted out the meaning behind what Bianca had just said. She had given her tacit permission for her people to try to get to me. They couldn't just walk up and bite me, maybe, but yeesh. I'd have to be on my guard. I thought of Kelly Hamilton's narcotic kisses on my throat, the glowing warmth that had surrounded me, infused me, and shivered. Some part of me wondered what it might be like to let the vamps catch me, and if it would be all that bad. Another chewed furiously over everything I'd seen so far that evening – Bianca clearly had something in mind.

I shook my head and glanced back at Michael. He nodded to me, a slight motion beneath the great helm, and we both descended the stairs. My legs were shaking, making the trip down unsteady. I prayed that none of the vamps noticed it. Wouldn't do to let them see weakness. Even if I was as nervous as a bird in a coal mine.

'Do what you need to do, Harry,' Michael said, low. 'I'll be a couple steps behind you, to your right. I'll watch your back.'

Michael's words steadied me, calmed me, and I felt profoundly grateful for them.

I expected the vamps to descend on me in a charming and dangerous cloud when I reached the courtyard, but they didn't. Instead, Thomas was waiting for me with one hand on the hilt of his sword, his pale body on shameless display. Justine stood a bit behind him. His face practically glowed with glee.

'Oh, *my*, that was marvelous, Harry. May I call you Harry?'

'No,' I said. I caught myself, though, and tried to soften the answer. 'But thanks. For what you said, when you did. Things might have gotten ugly.'

Thomas's eyes danced. 'They still might, Mister Dresden. But we couldn't have it descending into a general brawl, now could we?'

'We couldn't?'

'No, of course not. There would be far fewer opportunities to seduce and deceive and backstab.'

I snorted. 'I suppose you've got a point.'

The tip of his tongue touched his teeth when he smiled. 'I usually do.'

'Um, thanks, Thomas.'

He glanced aside, and frowned. I followed his gaze. Justine had drifted away from him, and now stood with a bright smile on her sweet face as she spoke to a lean, smiling man dressed in a scarlet tux and a domino mask.

While I watched, the man reached out and stroked his fingers over her shoulder. He made some comment that made the lovely girl laugh.

'Excuse me,' Thomas said with distaste. 'I can't abide poachers. Do enjoy the party, Mister Dresden.'

He drifted off toward them, and Michael stepped up to me. I half-turned my head toward him, to hear him murmur, 'They're surrounding us.'

I looked around. The courtyard was full of people. Many of them were young, pretty folk, dressed in all manner of black, poster children for the Goth subculture. Leather, plastic, and fishnet seemed to be the major themes in display, complete with black domino masks, heavy hoods upon cloaks, and a variety of different kinds of face paint. They talked and laughed, drank and danced to the music. Some of them wore a band of scarlet cloth about their arm, or a bloodred choker around their throats.

While I watched, I saw a too-lean young man bend over a table to inhale something through one nostril. A trio of giggling girls, two blondes and a brunette, all dressed up like Dracula's cheerleading squad, complete with black-and-red pom-poms, counted to three together and washed down a pair of pills with glasses of dark wine. Other young people pressed together in sensual motion, or simply sat or stood kissing, touching. A few, already partied out, lay upon the courtyard, smiling dreamily, their eyes closed.

I scanned the crowd with my eyes, and picked out the differences at once. Drifting among the young people clad in black were lean figures in scarlet – perhaps two or three dozen, in all. Male and female, of a variety of appearances and costumes, all shared the scarlet clothes, beauty, and a confident, stalking kind of motion that marked them as predators.

'The Red Court,' I said. I licked my lips, and looked around some more. The vampires were being casual about it, but they had wandered into a ring around us. If we remained there any longer, we wouldn't be able to walk out of the courtyard without coming within a few feet of one of them. 'The kids with the red bands are what? Junior vampires?'

'Marked cattle, I'd say,' Michael rumbled. There was anger in it, steady and slow anger.

'Easy, Michael. We need to move around a little. Make it harder for them to hem us in.'

'Agreed.' Michael nodded toward the drink table, and we headed that way, our pace brisk. The vamps tried to adjust to follow us, but they couldn't make it look casual.

A couple in red moved to intercept us, meeting Michael and me just before we reached the table. Kyle Hamilton wore a harlequin's outfit, all in shades of scarlet. Kelly followed along with him, dressed in a scarlet body stocking that left nothing to the imagination, but with a long cloak covering her shoulders and collarbones, the hood up high around her face. A scarlet mask hid her features, except for her chin and luscious mouth. I thought I could see a puckering of the skin at one side of her mouth – perhaps the burns she'd suffered.

'Harry Dresden.' Kyle greeted me in a too-loud voice, with a too-wide smile. 'How pleasant to see you again.'

I chucked him boisterously on the shoulder, making his balance waver. 'I wish it was mutual.'

The smile became brittle. 'And of course you remember my sister, Kelly.'

'Sure, sure,' I said. 'Hit that tanning bed a little too long, did we?'

I expected her to snarl or hiss or go for my throat. But instead she turned to the table, collected a silver goblet and a crystal wineglass from the attendant there, and offered them to us with a smile that mirrored her brother's. 'It's so pleasant to see you, Harry. I'm sorry that we didn't get to see the lovely Miss Rodriguez tonight.'

I accepted the goblet. 'She had to wash her hair.'

Kelly turned to Michael and offered him the glass. He accepted it with an inclination of his head, stiffly polite. 'I see,' she purred. 'I had no idea you were into men, Mister Dresden.'

'What can I say? They're just so big and strong.'

'Of course,' Kyle said. 'If I was surrounded by people who wanted to kill me as badly as I want to kill you, I'd want a bodyguard about, too.'

Kelly sidled up to Michael, her breasts thrust forward, straining the sheer fabric of the body stocking. She walked in a slow circle around him, while Michael remained standing just as he was. 'He's gorgeous,' she purred. 'May I give him a kiss, Mister Dresden?'

'Harry,' Michael said.

'He's married, Kelly. Sorry.'

She laughed, pressing close to Michael, and tried to catch his eyes. Michael frowned, and stared at nothing, avoiding her. 'No?' she asked. 'Well. Don't worry, pretty man. You'll love it. Everyone wants to party like it's their last night on earth.' She flashed a wicked smile up at him. 'Now you get to.'

'The young lady is too kind,' Michael said.

'So stiff. I admire that in a man.' She shot me a glance

from behind her mask. 'You really shouldn't drag poor defenseless mortals into these things, Mister Dresden.' She looked Michael up and down again, admiring. 'This one will be delicious, later.'

'Don't bite off more than you can chew,' I advised her.

She laughed, as though delighted. 'Well, Mister Dresden. I see his crosses, but we all know the value of them to most of the world.' She reached her hand toward Michael's arm, possessively. 'For a moment, you almost had me thinking that he might be a true Knight Templar.'

'No,' I said judiciously. 'Not a Knight Templar.'

Kelly's hand touched Michael's steel-clad arm – and erupted into sudden, white flame, as brief and violent as a stroke of lightning. She screamed, a piercing wail, and fell back from him to the ground. She lay there, curled helplessly around her blackened hand, struggling to get enough breath back to scream. Kyle flew to her side.

I looked at Michael and blinked. 'Wow,' I said. 'Color me impressed.'

Michael looked vaguely embarrassed. 'It happens like that sometimes,' he said, apologetically.

I nodded and took that in stride. I turned my gaze back to the vampire twins. 'Let that be a lesson to you. Hands off the Fist of God.'

Kyle shot me a murderous look, his face rippling.

My heart sped up, but I couldn't let the fear show. 'Go ahead, Kyle,' I dared him. 'Start something. Break the truce your own leader set up. Violate the laws of hospitality. The White Council will burn this place down so fast, people will call it Little Pompeii.'

He snarled at me, and picked Kelly up. 'This isn't over,' he promised. 'One way or another, Dresden. I'll kill you.'

'Uh-huh.' I flicked my wrist at him, my hand right in his face. 'Shoo, shoo. I have to mingle.'

Kyle snarled. But the pair withdrew, and I turned my gaze slowly around the courtyard. Everything in the immediate vicinity had stopped while people, black- and red-clad alike, stared at us. Some of the vampires in scarlet looked at Michael, swallowed, and took a couple of steps back.

I grinned, as cocky and as confident as I could appear, and lifted my glass. 'A toast,' I said. 'To hospitality.'

They were quiet for a moment, then hurriedly mumbled an echo to my toast and sipped from their drinks. I drained my goblet in a single gulp, hardly noticing the delightful flavor of it, and turned to Michael. He lifted his glass to the mouth of his helm in a token sip, but didn't take any.

'All right,' I said. 'I got to touch Kyle. He's out, too, though I didn't expect him to be our man. Or woman. Or monster.'

Michael looked slowly around as the scarlet-clad vampires continued to withdraw. 'It looks like we've cowed them for now.'

I nodded, still uneasy. The crowd parted at one side, and Thomas and Justine came to us, blazes of pale skin and brilliant color amidst the scarlet and black. 'There you are,' Thomas said. He glanced down at my goblet and let out a sigh. 'I'm glad I found you in time.'

'In time for what?' I asked.

'To warn you,' he said. He flicked a hand at the refreshments table. 'The wine is poisoned.'

26

'Poisoned?' I said, witlessly.

Thomas peered at my face and then down at my goblet. He leaned over it enough to see that it was empty and said, 'Ah. Oops.'

'Harry.' Michael stepped up beside me, and set his own glass aside. 'I thought you said that they couldn't try anything so overt.'

My stomach kept churning. My heart beat more quickly, though whether this was from the poison or the simple, cold fear that Thomas's words had brought to me, I couldn't say. 'They can't,' I said. 'If I pitch over dead, the Council would know what happened. I sent word in today that I was coming here tonight.'

Michael shot Thomas a hard look. 'What was in the wine?'

The pale man shrugged, slipping his arm around Justine once more. The girl leaned against him and closed her eyes. 'I don't know what they put in it,' he said. 'But look at these people.' He nodded to those black-clad folk who were already stretched out blissfully upon the ground. 'They all have wineglasses.'

I looked a bit closer and it was true. The servants moved about the courtyard, plucking up glasses from the fallen. As I watched, another young couple, dancing slowly together, sank down to the ground in a long, deep kiss that faded away into simple stillness.

'Hell's bells,' I swore. 'That's what they're doing.'

'What?' Michael asked.

'They don't want me dead,' I said. 'Not from this.' I didn't have much time. I stalked past the refreshments table to a potted fern and bent over it. I heard Michael take up a position behind me, guarding my back. I shoved a finger down my throat. Simple, quick, nasty. The wine burned my throat coming back up, and the fern's fronds tickled the back of my neck as I spat it back out into the base of the plant. My head spun as I sat back up again, and when I looked back toward Michael, everything blurred for a moment before it snapped back into focus. A slow, delicious numbness spread over my fingers.

'Everyone,' I mumbled.

'What?' Michael knelt down in front of me and gripped my shoulder with one arm. 'Harry, are you all right?'

'I'm fuzzy,' I said. Vampire venom. Naturally. It felt good to have it in me again, and I wondered, for a moment, what I was so worried about. It was just that nice. 'It's for everyone. They're drugging everyone's wine. Vamp venom. That way they can say they weren't just targeting me.' I wobbled, and then stood up. 'Recreational poisoning. Put everyone in the party mood.'

Thomas mused. 'Rather ham-handed, I suppose, but effective.' He looked around at the growing numbers of young people joining the first few upon the ground in ecstatic stupor. His fingers stroked Justine's flank absently, and she shivered, pressing closer to him. 'I suppose I'm prejudiced. I prefer my prey a little more lively.'

'We've got to get you out of here,' Michael said.

I gritted my teeth, and tried to push the pleasant sensations aside. The venom had to have an enormously quick absorption rate. Even if I'd brought the wine back up, I must have gotten a fairly good dose. 'No,' I managed after a moment. 'That's what they want me to do.'

'Harry, you can barely stand up,' Michael objected.

'You are looking a bit peaked,' Thomas said.

'Bah. If they want me incapacitated, it means they've got something to hide.'

'Or just that they want you to get killed,' Michael said. 'Or drugged enough to agree to let one of them feed on you.'

'No,' I disagreed. 'If they wanted to seduce me, they'd have tried something else. They're trying to scare me off. Or keep me from finding something out.'

'I hate to point out the obvious,' Thomas said, 'but why on earth would Bianca invite you if she didn't want you to be here?'

'She's obligated to invite the Council to witness. That means me, in this town. And she didn't expect me to actually show – pretty much everyone was surprised to see me at all.'

'They didn't think you'd come,' Michael murmured.

'Yeah. Ain't I a stinker.' I took a couple of deep breaths and said, 'I think the one we're after is here, Michael. We've got to stick this out for a little while. See if I can find out exactly who it is.'

'Exactly who is what?' Thomas asked.

'None of your beeswax, Thomas,' I said.

'Has anyone ever told you, Mister Dresden, that you are a thoroughly annoying man?' That made me grin, to which he rolled his eyes. 'Well,' he said, 'I'll not intrude on your business any further. Let me know if there's anything I can do for you.' He and Justine sauntered off into the crowd.

I watched Justine's legs go, leaning on my cane a bit to help me balance. 'Nice guy,' I commented.

'For a vampire,' Michael said. 'Don't trust him, Harry. There's something about him I don't like.'

'Oh, I like him,' I said. 'But I sure as hell don't trust him.'

'What do we do now?'

'Look around. So far we've got food in black, the vampires in red, and then there's you and me, and a handful of other people in different costumes.'

'The Roman centurion,' Michael said.

'Yeah. And some Hamlet-looking guy. Let's go see what they are.'

'Harry,' Michael asked. 'Are you going to be okay?'

I swallowed. I felt dizzy, a little sickened. I had to fight to get clear thoughts through, bulldogging them against the pull of the venom. I was surrounded by things that looked at people like we look at cows, and felt fairly sure that I was going to get myself killed if I stayed.

Of course, if I didn't stay, other people could get killed. If I didn't stay, the people who had already been hurt remained in danger: Charity. Michael's infant son. Murphy. If I didn't stay, the Nightmare would have time to recuperate, and then it and its corporate sponsor, who I thought was here at this party, would feel free to keep taking pot shots at me.

The thought of remaining in that place scared me. The thought of what could happen if I gave up now scared me a lot more.

'Come on,' I said. 'Let's get this over with.'

Michael nodded, looking around, his grey eyes dark, hard. 'This is an abomination before the Lord, Harry. These people. They're barely more than children . . . what they're doing. Consorting with these *things*.'

'Michael. Chill *out*. We're here to get information, not bring the house down on a bunch of nasties.'

'Samson did,' Michael said.

'Yeah, and look how well things turned out for him. You ready?'

He muttered something, and fell in behind me again. I looked around and oriented on the man dressed as a Roman centurion, then headed toward him. A man of indefinite years, he stood alone and slightly detached from the rest of the crowd. His eyes were an odd color of green, deep and intense. He held a cigarette between his lips. His gear, right down to the Roman short sword and sandals, looked awfully authentic. I slowed a little as I approached him, staring.

'Michael,' I murmured, over my shoulder. 'Look at his costume. It looks like the real thing.'

'It *is* the real thing,' said the man in a bored tone of voice, not looking at me. He exhaled a plume of smoke, then put the cigarette back between his lips. Michael would have barely been able to hear my question. This guy had picked it right out. Gulp.

'Interesting,' I said. 'Must have cost you a fortune to put together.'

He glanced at me. Smoke curled from the corners of his mouth as he gave me a very slight, very smug smirk. And said nothing.

'So,' I said, and cleared my throat. 'I'm Harry Dresden.'

The man pursed his lips and said, thoughtfully and precisely, 'Harry. Dresden.'

When someone, anyone, says your name, it touches you.

You almost feel it, that sound that stands out from a crowd of others and demands your attention. When a wizard says your Name, when he says it and *means* it, it has the same effect, amplified a thousandfold. The man in the centurion gear said my part of my Name and said it exactly right. It felt like someone had just rung a tuning fork and pressed it against my teeth.

I staggered, and Michael caught my shoulder, keeping me upright. Dear God. He had just used one *part* of my full name, my true Name, to reach out to me and casually backhand me off my feet.

'Hell's bells,' I whispered. Michael propped me back up. I planted my cane, so that I would have an extra support, and just stared at the man. 'How the hell did you *do* that?'

He rolled his eyes, took the cigarette in his fingers and blew more smoke. 'You wouldn't understand.'

'You're not White Council,' I said.

He looked at me as though I had just stated that objects fall toward the ground; a withering, scathing glance. 'How very fortunate for me.'

'Harry,' Michael said, his voice tense.

'Just a minute.'

'Harry. Look at his cigarette.'

I blinked at Michael. 'What?'

'Look at his cigarette,' Michael repeated. He was staring at the man with wide, intent eyes, and one hand had fallen to the hilt of a knife.

I looked. It took me a minute to realize what Michael was talking about.

The man blew more smoke out of the corner of his mouth, and smirked at me.

The cigarette wasn't lit.

'He's,' I said. 'He's, uh.'

'He's a dragon,' Michael said.

'A what?'

The man's eyes flickered with interest for the first time, and he narrowed his focus – not upon me, but upon Michael. 'Just so,' he said. 'You may call me Mister Ferro.'

'Why don't I just call you Ferrovax,' Michael said.

Mister Ferro narrowed his eyes, and regarded Michael with a dispassionate gaze. 'You know something of the lore, at least, mortal.'

'Wait a minute,' I said. 'Dragons . . . dragons are supposed to be *big*. Scales, claws, wings. This guy isn't big.'

Ferro rolled his eyes and said, impatient, 'We are what we wish to be, Master Drafton.'

'Dresden,' I snapped.

He waved a hand. 'Don't tempt me to show you what I can do by speaking your name and making an effort, mortal. Suffice to say that you could not comprehend the kind of power I have at my command. That my true form here would shatter this pathetic gathering of monkey houses and crack the earth upon which I stand. If you gazed upon me with your wizard's sight, you would see something that would awe you, humble you, and quite probably destroy your reason. I am the eldest of my kind, and the strongest. Your life is a flickering candle to me, and your civilizations rise and fall like grass in the summer.'

'Well,' I said. 'I don't know about your true form, but the weight of your ego sure is pushing the crust of the earth toward the breaking point.'

His green eyes blazed. 'What did you say?'

'I don't like bullies,' I said. 'You think I'm going to stand here and offer you my firstborn and sacrifice virgins to you or something? I'm not that impressed.'

'Well,' Ferro said. 'Let's see if we can't make an impression.'

I clutched my cane and gathered up my will, but I was way, way too slow. Ferro just waved a hand vaguely in my direction, and something crushed me down to the earth, as though I suddenly had gained about five thousand pounds. I felt my lungs strain to haul in a breath, and my vision clouded over with stars and went black. I tried to gather up my magic, to thrust the force away from me, but I couldn't focus, couldn't speak.

Michael looked down at me dispassionately, then said, to Ferro, 'Siriothrax should have learned that trick. It might have kept me from killing him.'

Ferro's cold regard swept back to Michael, bringing with it a tiny lessening in the pressure – not much, but enough that I could gasp out, *'Riflettum,'* and focus my will against it. Ferro's spell cracked and began to flake apart. I saw him look at me, sensed that he could have renewed the effort without difficulty. He didn't. I climbed back to my feet, gasping quietly.

'So,' Ferro said. 'You are the one.' He looked Michael up and down. 'I thought you'd be taller.'

Michael shrugged. 'It wasn't anything personal. I'm not proud of what I did.'

Ferro tapped a finger against the hilt of his sword. Then said, quietly, 'Sir Knight. I would advise you to be more humble in the face of your betters.' He cast a disdainful glance at me. 'And you might consider a gag for this one, until he can learn better manners.'

I tried for a comeback, but I still couldn't breathe. I just leaned against my cane and wheezed. Ferro and Michael exchanged a short nod, one where neither of them looked away from the other's eyes. Then Ferro turned and . . . well, just vanished. No flicker of light, no puff of flame. Just gone.

'Harry,' Michael chided. 'You're not the biggest kid on the block. You've got to learn to be a little more polite.'

'Good advice,' I wheezed. 'Next time, you handle any dragons.'

'I will.' He looked around and said, 'People are thinning out, Harry.' He was right. As I watched, a vampire in a tight red dress tapped the arm of a young man in black. He glanced over to her and met her eyes. They stared at one another for a while, the woman smiling, the man's expression going slowly slack. Then she murmured something and took his hand, leading him out into the darkness beyond the globes of light. Other vamps were drawing more young people along with them. There were fewer scarlet costumes around, and more people blissed out on the ground.

'I don't like the direction this is going,' I said.

'Nor do I.' His voice was hard as stone. 'Lord willing, we can put a stop to this.'

'Later. First, we talk to the Hamlet guy. Then there's just Bianca herself to check.'

'Not one of the other vampires?' Michael asked.

'No way. They're all subordinate to Bianca. If they were that strong, they'd have knocked her off by now, unless they were in her inner circle. That's Kyle and Kelly. She doesn't have the presence of mind for it, and he's already out. So if it's not a guest, it's probably Bianca.'

'And if it's not her?'

'Let's not go there. I'm floundering enough as it is.' I squinted around. 'Do you see Hamlet anywhere?'

Michael squinted around, taking a few paces to peer around another set of ferns.

I saw the flash of red out of the corner of my eye, saw a form in a red cloak heading for Michael's back, from around the ferns. I turned toward Michael and threw myself at his attacker.

'Look out!' I shouted. Michael spun, a knife appearing in his hand as though conjured. I grabbed the red cloaked-figure and whirled it around to face me.

The hood fell back from Susan's face, revealing her startled dark eyes. She'd pulled her hair into a ponytail. She wore a low-cut white blouse and a little pleated skirt, complete with white knee socks and buckle-down shoes. White gloves covered her hands. A wicker basket dangled in the crook of her elbow, and round, mirror-toned spectacles perched upon the bridge of her slender nose.

'Susan?' I stammered. 'What are you doing here?'

She let out a breath, and drew her arm out of my hand. 'God, Harry. You scared me.'

'What are you *doing* here?' I demanded.

'You know why I'm here,' she said. 'I came to get a story. I tried to call you and talk you into it, but *no*, you were way too busy doing whatever you were doing to even spare five minutes to talk to me.'

'I don't believe this,' I muttered. 'How did you get in here?'

She looked at me coolly and flicked open her basket. She reached inside and came out with a neat white invitation, like my own. 'I got myself an invitation.'

'You *what*?'

'Well. I had it made, in any case. I didn't think you'd mind me borrowing yours for a few minutes.'

Which explained why the invitation hadn't been on the mantel, back at my apartment. 'Hell's bells, Susan, you don't know what you've done. You've got to get out of here.'

She snorted. 'Like hell.'

'I mean it,' I said. 'You're in danger.'

'Relax, Harry. I'm not letting anyone lick me, and I'm not looking anyone in the eyes. It's kind of like visiting New York.' She tapped her specs with a gloved finger. 'Things have gone all right so far.'

'You don't get it,' I said. 'You don't understand.'

'Don't understand what?' she demanded.

'You don't understand,' purred a dulcet voice, behind me. My blood ran cold. 'By coming uninvited, you have waived any right you had to the protection of the laws of hospitality.' There came a soft chuckle. 'It means, Little Red Riding Hood, that the Big, Bad Wolf gets to eat you all up.'

27

I turned to find Lea facing me, her hands on her hips. She wore a slender, strapless dress of pale blue, which flowed over her curves like water, crashing into white foamy lace at its hem. She wore a cape of some material so light and sheer that it seemed almost unreal, and it drifted around her, catching the light in an opalescent sheen that trapped little rainbows and set them to dancing against her pale skin. When people talk about models or movie stars being glamorous, they take it from the old word, from *glamour*, from the beauty of the high sidhe, faerie magic. Supermodels wish they had it so good as Lea.

'Why, Godmother,' I said, 'what big eyes you have. Are we straining the metaphor or what?'

She drifted closer to me. 'I don't make metaphors, Harry. I'm too busy being one. Are you enjoying the party?'

I snorted. 'Oh, sure. Watching them drug and poison children and getting roughed up by every weird and nasty thing in Chicagoland is a real treat.' I turned to Susan and said, 'We have to get you out of here.'

Susan frowned at me and said, 'I didn't come here so that you could hustle me home, Harry.'

'This isn't a game, Susan. These thing are dangerous.' I glanced over at Lea. She kept drawing closer. 'I don't know if I can protect you.'

'Then I'll protect myself,' Susan said. She laid her hand over the picnic basket. 'I came prepared.'

'Michael,' I said. 'Would you get her out of here?'

Michael stepped up beside us, and said, to Susan, 'It's dangerous. Maybe you should let me take you home.'

Susan narrowed her dark eyes at me. 'If it's so dangerous, then I don't want to leave Harry here alone.'

'She has a point, Harry.'

'Dammit. We came here to find out who's behind the Nightmare. If I leave before I do that, we might as well never have come. Just go, and I'll catch up with you.'

'Yes,' Lea said. 'Do go. I'll be sure to take good care of my godson.'

'No,' Susan said, her tone flat. 'Absolutely not. I'm not some kind of child for you to tote around and make decisions for, Harry.'

Lea's smile sharpened, and she reached a hand toward Susan, touching her chin. 'Let me see those pretty eyes, little one,' she purred.

I shot my hand toward my godmother's wrist, jerking it away from Susan before the faerie could touch her. Her skin was silk-smooth, cool. Lea smiled at me, the expression stunning. Literally. My head swam, images of the faerie sorceress flooding my thoughts: those berry-sweet lips pressing to my naked chest, smeared with my blood, rose-tipped breasts bared by the light of fire and full moon, her hair a sheet of silken flame on my skin.

Another flash of image came then, accompanied by intense emotion: myself, looking up at her as I lay at her feet. She stretched out her hand and lightly touched my head, an absently fond gesture. An overwhelming sense of well-being filled me like shining, liquid light, poured into me and filled every empty place within me, calmed every fear, soothed every pain. I almost wept at the simple relief, at the abrupt release from worry, from hurt. My whole body trembled.

I was just so damned tired. So tired of hurting. Of being afraid.

'So it will be when you are with me, poor little one, poor lonely child.' Lea's voice coursed over me, as sweet as the drug already within me. I knew she spoke the truth. I knew it on a level so deep and simple that a part of me screamed at myself for struggling to avoid her.

So easy. It would be so easy to lay down at my lady's feet, now. So easy to let her make all the bad things go away. She would care for me. She would comfort me. My place would be there, in the warmth at her feet, staring up at her beauty—

Like a good dog.

It's tough to say no to peace, to the comfort of it. All through history, people have traded wealth, children, land, and lives to buy it.

But peace can't be bought, can it, chief, prime minister? The only ones offering to sell it always want something more. They lie.

I shoved the feelings away from me, the subtle glamour my godmother had cast. I could have taken a cheese grater to my own skin with less pain. But my pain, my weariness, my worries and fear – they were at least my own. They were honest. I gathered them back to me like a pack of mud-spattered children and stared at Lea, hardening my jaw, my heart. 'No,' I said. 'No, Lea.'

Surprise touched those delicate features. Dainty copper brows lifted. 'Harry,' she said, her voice gentle, perplexed, 'the bargain is already made. So mote it be. There is no reason for you to go on hurting.'

'There are people who need me,' I said. My balance wavered. 'I still have a job to do.'

'Broken faiths weaken you. They bind you tighter, lessen you every time you go against your given oath.' She sounded concerned, genuinely compassionate. 'Godson, I beg of you – do not do this to yourself.'

I said, struggling to be calm, 'Because if I do that, there will be less for you to eat, yes? Less power for you to take.'

'It would be a terrible waste,' she assured me. 'No one wants that.'

'We're under *truce* here, Godmother. You're not allowed to work magic on me without violating hospitality.'

'But I didn't,' Lea said. 'I've not worked any magic on you this night.'

'Bullshit.'

She laughed, silver and merry. 'Such language, and in front of your lover too.'

I stumbled. Michael was there at once, supporting my weight with his shoulder, drawing my arm across it. 'Harry,' he said. 'What is it? What's wrong?'

My head kept on spinning and my limbs started to shake. The drug already coursing through me, plus this new weakness, almost took me out. Blackness swam in front of my eyes and it was only with an effort of will that I kept myself from drowning in that darkness or giving in to the mad desire to throw myself down at Lea's feet. 'I'm okay,' I stammered. 'I'm fine.'

Susan moved to my other side, her anger pouring off of her like heat from a desert highway. 'What have you done to him?' she snapped at Lea.

'Nothing,' Lea replied in a cool voice. 'He has done this to himself, the poor little one. One always risks dire consequences should one not keep a bargain with the sidhe.'

'What?' Susan said.

Michael grimaced, and said, 'Aye. She's telling the truth. Harry made a bargain last night, when we fought the Nightmare and drove it away from Charity.'

I struggled to speak, to warn them not to let Lea trick them, but I was too busy trying to sort out where my mouth was, and why my tongue wasn't working.

'That doesn't give her the right to put a spell on him,' Susan snapped.

Michael rumbled, 'I don't think she has. I can usually feel it, when someone's done something harmful.'

'Of course I haven't,' Lea said. 'I have no need to do so. He's already done it himself.'

What? I thought. What was she talking about?

'What?' Susan said. 'What are you talking about?'

Lea's voice took on a patient, faux-sympathetic tone. 'Poor little poppet. All of your efforts to learn and you still know so little. Harry made a bargain with me long ago – and broke it, once then, and once a few nights past. He swore to uphold it again, last night, and broke it thrice. Now he reaps the consequences of his actions. His own powers turn against him, the poor dear, to encourage him to fulfill his word, to keep his promise.'

'They weren't doing it a minute ago,' Susan said. 'Only when you came up to him.'

Lea laughed, warmly. 'It's a party, dear poppet. We're here to mingle, after all. And I have lifted no weapon or spell against him. This is of his own doing.'

'So back off,' Susan said. 'Leave him alone.'

'Oh, this won't ever leave him alone, poppet. It's a small

thing now, but it will grow, in time. And destroy him, the poor, dear boy. I'd hate so much for that to happen.'

'So stop it!'

Lea focused her eyes on Susan. 'Do you offer to purchase his debt away from me? I don't think you could afford it, dear poppet . . . though I think surcease could be arranged.'

Susan shot a quick glance at me, and then Michael. 'Surcease? Purchase?'

Michael watched Lea, grimly. 'She's a faerie—'

Lea's voice crackled with irritation. 'A *sidhe*.'

Michael looked at my godmother and continued, 'A faerie, Miss Rodriguez, and they're prone to making bargains. And to getting the better of mortals when they do.'

Susan's mouth hardened. She was silent for a moment, and then said, 'How much, witch? How much for you to make this stop hurting Harry?'

I struggled to say something, but my mouth didn't work. Things spun faster instead of slowing down. I sagged more, and Michael labored to keep me on my feet.

'Why, poppet,' Lea purred. 'What do you offer?'

'I don't have much money,' Susan began.

'Money. What is money.' Lea shook her head. 'No, child. Such things mean nothing to me. But let me see.' She walked in a slow circle around Susan, frowning at her, looking her up and down. 'Such pretty eyes, even though they are dark. They will do.'

'My *eyes*?' Susan stammered.

'No?' Lea asked. 'Very well. Your Name, perhaps? Your whole Name?'

'Don't,' Michael said at once.

'I know,' Susan answered him. She looked at Lea and

said, 'I know better than that. If you had my Name, you could do anything you wanted.'

Lea thrust out her lip. 'Her eyes and her Name are too precious to allow her beloved to escape his trap. Very well, then. Let us ask of her a different price.' Her eyes gleamed and she leaned toward Susan. 'Your love,' she murmured. 'Give me that.'

Susan arched her brows and peered over her spectacles. 'Honey, you want me to love you? You've got a lot of surprises coming, if you think it works like that.'

'I didn't ask you to love me,' Lea said, her tone offended. 'I asked for your love. But well enough, if that is also too steep a price, perhaps memory will do instead.'

'My memory?'

'Not all of it,' Lea said. She tilted her head to one side and purred, 'Indeed. Only some. Perhaps the worth of one year. Yes, I think that would suffice.'

Susan looked uncertain. 'I don't know . . .'

'Then let him suffer. He won't live the night, with those arrayed against him. Such a loss.' Lea turned to leave.

'Wait,' Susan said, and clutched at Lea's arm. 'I . . . I'll make the trade. For Harry's sake. One year of my memory, and you make whatever is happening stop.'

'Memory for relief. Done,' Lea purred. She leaned forward and placed a gentle kiss upon Susan's forehead, then shivered, drawing in her breath in a swift inhalation, the tips of her breasts hardening against the silky fabric of her dress. 'Oh. Oh, sweet poppet. What a dear thing you are.' Then she turned and slapped me across the face with a sharp sound of impact, and I tumbled down to the ground despite Michael's best efforts.

My head abruptly cleared. The narcotic throb of the

vampire venom lessened a bit, and I found my thoughts running again, slowly, like a train gathering momentum.

'Witch,' Michael hissed up at Lea. 'If you hurt either of them again—'

'For shame, Sir Knight,' Lea said, her voice dreamy. ''Tis no fault of mine that Harry made the agreement he did, nor fault of mine that the girl loves him and would give anything for him. Nor was it my doing that the Sword fell ownerless to the ground before me and that I picked it up.' She fixed Michael with that dazzling smile. 'Should you wish to bargain to have it returned to you, you have only to ask.'

'Myself, for the Sword,' Michael said. 'Done.'

She let her head fall back and laughed. 'Oh, oh my, dear Knight, no. For once the Redeemer's blade was in your hands again, you would find the shattering of our pact a simple enough matter.' Her eyes glittered again. 'And you are, in any case, far too . . . restricted, for my tastes. You are set in your ways. Unbendable.'

Michael stiffened. 'I serve the Lord as I may.'

Lea made a face. 'Faugh. Just so. Holy.' Her smile turned sly again. 'But there are others whose lives you hold and can bargain with. You have children, do you not?' She shivered again and said, 'Mortal children are so sweet. And can be bent and shaped in so many, many ways. Your eldest daughter, I think, would—'

Michael didn't snarl, didn't roar, didn't make any sounds at all. He simply seized the front of Lea's dress and lifted her clear off the ground by it. His voice came out in a vicious growl. 'Stay away from my family, faerie. Or I will set such things in motion against you as will destroy you for all time.'

Lea laughed, delighted. '"Vengeance is mine, saith the Lord," is how the phrase runs, is it not?' There was a liquid shimmering in the air, and she abruptly stood upon the ground again, facing Michael, out of his grasp. 'Your power weakens with rage, dear man. You will not bargain – but I suppose I had plans for the Sword in any case. Until then, good Knight, adieu.' She gave me one last smile and a mocking laugh. Then she vanished into the shadows and the darkness.

I gathered myself back to my feet, and mumbled, 'That could have gone better.'

Michael's eyes glittered with anger beneath his helmet. 'Are you all right, Harry?'

'I'm better,' I said. 'Stars and stones, if this is some kind of self-inflicted spell . . . I'll have to talk to Bob about this one, later.' I rubbed at my eyes and asked, 'What about you, Michael? Are you all right?'

'Well enough,' Michael said. 'But we still don't have a culprit, and it's getting late. I've got a bad feeling that we're going to run into trouble if we don't get out of this place soon.'

'I've got a feeling you're right,' I said. 'Susan? Are you okay? You ready to get out of here?'

Susan brushed her hair idly back from her face with one hand, and turned to stare at me, frowning slightly.

'What?' I asked. 'Look, you didn't have to do what you did, but we can work on getting it taken care of. Let's just get out of here. Okay?'

'Okay,' she said. Then her frown deepened and she peered at me. 'This is going to sound odd, but – do I know you?'

28

I stared at Susan in mute disbelief.

She looked apologetic. 'Oh, I'm sorry. I mean. I didn't mean to upset you, Mister . . .'

'Dresden,' I supplied in a whisper.

'Mister Dresden, then.' She frowned down at herself, and smoothed a hand uncomfortably over the skirt, then looked around her. 'Dresden. Aren't you the guy who just opened a business as a wizard?'

Anger made me clench my teeth. 'Son of a—'

'Harry,' Michael said. 'I think we need to leave, rather than stand about cursing.'

My knuckles whitened as I tightened my fingers on my cane. No time for anger. Not now. Michael was right. We had to move, and quickly. 'Agreed,' I said. 'Susan, did you drive here?'

'Hey,' she said, squaring off against me. 'I don't know you, okay? My name is Miss Rodriguez.'

'Look, Su— Miss Rodriguez. My faerie godmother just stole a year's worth of your memory.'

'Actually,' Michael put in, 'you traded it away to her to keep some kind of spell from leaving Harry helpless.'

I shot him a glare and he subsided. 'And now you don't remember me, or I guess, Michael.'

'Or this faerie godmother, either,' Susan said, her face and stance still wary.

I shot Lea a look. She glanced over at me and her lips

curved up into a smirk, before she turned back to her conversation with Thomas. 'Oh, damn. She's such a bitch.'

Susan rolled her eyes a little. 'Look, guys. It's been nice chatting with you, but this has got to be the lamest excuse for a pickup line I've ever heard.'

I reached a hand toward her again. Her own flashed down into the picnic basket and produced a knife, a G.I.-issue weapon from the last century, its edge gleaming. 'I told you,' she said calmly, 'I don't know you. Don't touch me.'

I drew my hand back. 'Look. I just want to make sure you're all right.'

Susan's breathing was a little fast, but other than that she concealed her tension almost completely. 'I'm perfectly fine,' she said. 'Don't worry about me.'

'At least get out of here. You're not safe here. You came in on an invitation you had made up. Do you remember that?'

She screwed up her face into a frown. 'How did you know that?' she asked.

'You told me so about five minutes ago,' I said, and sighed. 'That's what I'm trying to tell you. You've had a bunch of your memories taken.'

'I remember coming here,' Susan said. 'I remember having the counterfeit invitation made.'

'I know,' I said. 'You got it off of my living room table. Do you remember that?'

She frowned. 'I got it . . .' Her expression flickered, and she swallowed, glancing around. 'I don't remember where I got it.'

'There,' I said. 'Do you see? Do you remember driving out to bail me out of jail a couple of nights ago?'

She'd lowered the knife by now. 'I . . . I remember that I went down to the jail. And paid the bail money, but . . . I can't think . . .'

'Okay, okay,' I said. My head hurt, and I pinched the bridge of my nose between my thumb and forefinger. 'It looks like she took all of your memories that had me directly in them. Or her. What about Michael, do you remember him?'

She looked at Michael and shook her head.

I nodded. 'Okay. Then I need to ask you to trust me, Miss Rodriguez. You've been affected by magic and I don't know how we can get it fixed yet. But you're in danger here and I think you should leave.'

'Not with you,' she said at once. 'I have no idea who you are. Other than some kind of psychic consultant for Special Investigations.'

'Okay, okay,' I said. 'Not with me. But at least let us walk you out of here, so that we can make sure you get out okay. You can't swing a cat without hitting a vampire in here. So let us get you out to your car and then you can go wherever you like.'

'I didn't get my interview,' she said. 'But . . . I feel so strange.' She shook her head, and replaced her knife in her picnic basket. I heard the click of a tape recorder being switched off. 'Okay,' she said. 'I guess we can go.'

I nodded, relieved. 'Wonderful. Michael, shall we?'

He chewed on his lip. 'Maybe I should stay, Harry. If your godmother's here, the Sword might be here too. I might get the chance to take it back.'

'Yeah. And you might get the chance to get taken from behind without someone here to cover for you. There's too much messed up stuff here, man. Even for me. Let's go.'

Michael fell in behind me, to my right. Susan walked beside him, on my left, keeping us both in careful view, and one hand still inside her picnic basket. I briefly wondered what kind of goodies she'd been bringing in case the big, bad wolf tried to head her off from grandma's house.

We reached the foot of the stairs that led back up into the house. Something prickled the hairs at the back of my neck, and I stopped.

'Harry?' Michael asked. 'What is it?'

'There's someone . . .' I said, and closed my eyes. I brought up my Sight, just for a moment, and felt the pressure just a little above the spot between my eyebrows. I looked up again. The Sight cut through the enchantment in front of me like sunlight through a wispy cloud. Behind me, Michael and Susan both took in sharp breaths of surprise.

The Hamlet lookalike stood three stairs up, half smiling. I realized only then that the figure was a woman rather than a man, the slender shape of her slim hips and breasts obscured by the sable doublet she wore, giving her an odd, androgynous appearance. Her skin was pallid – not pale, not creamy. Pallid. Translucent. Almost greyish. Her lips were tinged very faintly blue, as though she'd been recently chilled. Or dead. I shivered, and lowered the Sight before it showed me something that I didn't want to keep with me.

It didn't change her appearance one bit. She wore a cap, which hid her hair completely, one of those puffy ones that fell over to one side, and stood with one hip cocked out, a rapier hanging from her belt. She held a skull in her other hand – it was a real one. And the bloodstains on it couldn't have been more than a few hours old.

'Well done, wizard,' she said. Her voice sounded raspy, a quiet, hissing whisper, the kind that comes from throats and mouths which are perfectly dry. 'Very few can see me when I do not wish to be seen.'

'Thank you. And excuse me,' I said. 'We were just leaving.'

Bluish lips curved into a chill little smile. Other than that, she didn't move. Not an inch. 'Oh, but this is the hour for all to mingle and meet. I have a right to introduce myself to you and to hear your names and exhange pleasantries in return.' Her eyes fastened calmly on my face, evidently not fearing to meet my gaze. I figured that whatever she was, she probably had an advantage on me in the devastating gaze department. So I kept my own eyes firmly planted on the tip of her nose, and tried very hard not to notice that her eyes had no color at all, just a kind of flaccid blue-grey tinge to them, a filmy coating like cataracts.

'And what if I don't have time for the pleasantries?' I said.

'Oh,' she whispered. 'Then I might be insulted. I might even be tempted to call for satisfaction.'

'A duel?' I asked, incredulous. 'Are you kidding me?'

Her eyes drifted to my right. 'Of course, if you would rather a champion fought in your place, I would gladly accept.'

I glanced back at Michael, who had his eyes narrowed, focused on the woman's doublet or upon her belt, perhaps. 'You know this lady?'

'She's no lady,' Michael said, his voice quiet. He had a hand on his knife. 'Harry Dresden, Wizard of the White Council, this is Mavra, of the Black Court of Vampires.'

'A real vampire,' Susan said. I heard the click of her tape recorder coming on again.

'A pleasure,' Mavra whispered. 'To meet you, at last, wizard. We should talk. I suspect we have much in common.'

'I'm failing to see anything we might possibly have in common, ma'am. Do you two know each other?'

'Yes,' Michael said.

Mavra's whisper became chill. 'The good Knight here murdered my children and grandchildren, some small time ago.'

'Twenty years ago,' Michael said. 'Three dozen people killed in the space of a month. Yes, I put a stop to it.'

Mavra's lips curved a little more, and showed yellowed teeth. 'Yes. Just a little time ago. I haven't forgotten, Knight.'

'Well,' I said. 'It's been nice chatting, Mavra, but we're on our way out.'

'No you're not,' Mavra said, calmly. But for her lips and her eyes, she still hadn't moved. It was an eerie stillness, not real. Real things move, stir, breathe. Mavra didn't.

'Yes, we are.'

'No. Two of you are on your way out.' Her smile turned chilly. 'I know that the invitations said only one person could be brought with you. Therefore, one of your companions is not under the protection of the old laws, wizard. If the Knight is unprotected, then he and I will have words. A pity you do not have *Amoracchius* with you, Sir Knight. It would have made things interesting, at least.'

I got a sinking feeling in my gut. 'And if it isn't Michael?'

'Then you keep offensive company, wizard, and I am

displeased with you. I will demonstrate my displeasure decisively.' Her gaze swept to Susan. 'By all means. Choose which two are leaving. Then I will have a brief conversation with the third.'

'You mean you'll kill them.'

Mavra shrugged, finally breaking her stillness. I thought I heard a faint crackling of tendons, as though they'd protested moving again. 'One must eat, after all. And these little, dazzled morsels the Reds brought tonight are too sweet and insubstantial for my taste.'

I took a step back, and turned to Michael, speaking in a whisper. 'If I get Susan out of here, can you take this bitch?'

'You might as well not whisper, Harry,' Michael said. 'It can hear you.'

'Yes,' Mavra said. 'It can.'

Way to go, Harry. Endear yourself to the monsters, why don't you. 'Well,' I asked Michael. 'Can you?'

Michael looked at me for a moment, his lips pressed together. Then he said, 'Take Susan and go. I'll manage here.'

Mavra laughed, a dry and raspy sound. 'So very noble. So pure. So self-sacrificing.'

Susan stepped around me, to close a triangle with Michael and me. As she did, I noticed that Mavra leaned back from her, just slightly. 'Now just a minute,' Susan said. 'I'm a big girl. I knew the risks when I came here.'

'I'm sorry, Miss Rodriguez,' Michael said, his tone apologetic. 'But this is what I do.'

'Save me from chauvinist pigs,' Susan muttered. She turned her head around to me. 'Excuse me. What do you think you're doing?'

'Looking in your pick-a-nick basket,' I responded, as I flipped open one cover. I whistled. 'You came armed for bear, Miss Rodriguez. Holy water. Garlic. Two crosses. Is that a thirty-eight?'

Susan sniffed. 'A forty-five.'

'Garlic,' Michael mused.

Above us on the stairs, Mavra hissed.

I glanced up at her. 'The Black Court was nearly wiped out, Thomas said. I wonder if that's because they got a little too much publicity. Do you mind, Miss Rodriguez?' I reached into the basket and produced a nice, smelly clove of garlic, then idly flicked it through the air, toward Mavra.

The vampire didn't retreat — she simply blurred, and then stood several steps higher than she had been a moment before. The garlic clove bounced against the stairs where she'd been, and tumbled back down toward us. I bent down and picked it up.

'I'd say that's a big yes.' I looked up at Mavra. 'Is that what happened, hmm? Stoker published the *Big Book of Black Court Vampire Slaying*?'

Those drowned-blue lips peeled back from her yellowed teeth. No fangs. 'It matters little. You are beings of paper and cotton. I could tear apart a dozen score of your kind.'

'Unless they'd had an extra spicy pizza, I guess. Let's get out of here, guys.' I started up the stairs.

Mavra spread her hands out to either side, and gathered darkness into her palms. That's the only way I can explain it. She spread out her hands, and blackness rushed in to fill them, gathering there in a writhing mass that shrouded her hands to the wrists. 'Try to force your way past me with that weapon, wizard, and I will take it as an attack upon my person. And defend myself appropriately.'

Cold washed over me. I extended my senses toward that darkness, warily. And it felt familiar. It felt like frozen chains and cruel twists of thorny wire. It felt empty and black, and like everything that magic isn't.

Mavra was our girl.

'Michael,' I said, my voice strangled. Steel rasped as he drew one of his knives.

'Um,' Susan said. 'Why are her hands doing that? Can vampires do that?'

'Wizards can,' I said. 'Get behind me.'

They both did. I lifted my hand, my face creasing in concentration. I reached out and tried to call in my will, my power. It felt shaky, uncertain, like a pump that has lost its prime. It came to me in dribs and drabs, bit by bit, stuttering like a nervous yokel. But I gathered it around my upraised hand, in a crystalline azure glow, beautiful and fragile, casting harsh shadows over Mavra's face.

Her dead man's eyes looked down at me, and I had an abrupt understanding of why Michael had called her 'it.' Mavra wasn't a woman anymore. Whatever she was, she wasn't a person. Not like I understood people, in any case. Those eyes pulled at mine, pulled at me with a kind of horrid fascination, the same sickly attraction that makes you want to see what's under the blanket in the morgue, to turn over the dead animal and see the corruption beneath. I fought and kept my eyes away from hers.

'Come, wizard,' Mavra whispered, her face utterly without expression. 'Let us test one another, thou and I.'

I hardened the energy I held. I wouldn't have enough juice to take two shots at her. I'd have to take her out the

first time or not at all. Cold radiated off of her, little wisps
of steam curling up as ice crystals formed on the steps at
her feet.

'But you won't take the first shot, will you.' I didn't
realize I'd spoken my thoughts aloud until after I had.
'Because then you'd be breaking the truce.'

I saw an emotion in that face, finally. Anger. 'Strike,
wizard. Or do not strike. And I will take the mortal of
your choice from you. You cannot claim the protection of
hospitality to them both.'

'Get out of the way, Mavra. Or don't get out of the way.
If you try to stop us from leaving, if you try to hurt anyone
under my protection, you'll be dealing with a Wizard of
the Council, a Knight of the Sword and a girl with a basket
full of garlic and holy water. I don't care how big bad and
ugly you are, there won't be anything left of you but a
greasy spot on the floor.'

'You dare,' she whispered. She blurred and came at me.
I took a breath, but she'd caught me on the exhale, and I
had no time to unleash the crystalline blast I'd prepared.

Michael and Susan moved at the same time, hands
thrusting past me. She held a wooden cross, simple and
dark, while he clutched his dagger by its blade, the
crusader-style hilt turned up into a cross as well. Both
wood and steel flared with a cold white light as Mavra
closed, and she slammed into that light as if it were a
solid wall, the shadows in her hand scattering and falling
away like sand between her fingers. We stood facing her,
my azure power and two blazing crosses, which burned
with a kind of purity and quiet power I had never seen
before.

'Blood of the Dragon, that old Serpent,' Michael said,

quietly. 'You and yours have no power here. Your threats are hollow, your words are empty of truth, just as your heart is empty of love, your body of life. Cease this now, before you tempt the wrath of the Almighty.' He glanced aside at me and added, probably for my benefit, 'Or before my friend Harry turns you into a greasy spot on the floor.'

Mavra walked slowly back up the steps, tendons creaking. She bent and gathered up the skull she'd dropped at some point during the discussion. Then turned back to us, looking down with a quiet smile. 'No matter,' she said. 'The hour is up.'

'Hour?' Susan asked me, in a tight whisper. 'What hour is she talking about, Dresden?'

'The hour of socialization,' Mavra whispered back. She continued up to the top of the stairs, and gently shut the doors leading out. They closed with an ominous boom.

All the lights went out. All but the blue nimbus around my hand, and the faded glory of the two crosses.

'Great,' I muttered.

Susan looked frightened, her expression hard and tightly controlled. 'What happens now?' she whispered, her eyes sweeping around in the dark.

Laughter, gentle and mocking, quiet, hissing, thick with something wet and bubbling, came from all around us. When it comes to spooky laughter, it's tough to beat vampires. You're going to have to trust me on this one. They know it well.

Something glimmered in the dark, and Thomas and Justine appeared in the glow of the power gathered in my hand. He lifted both hands at once, and said, 'Would you mind terribly if I stood with you?'

I glanced at Michael, who frowned. Then at Susan, who was looking at Thomas in all his next-to-naked glory . . . somewhat intently. I nudged her with my hip and she blinked and looked at me. 'Oh. No, not at all. I guess.'

Thomas took Justine's hand, and the two of them stood off to my right, where Michael kept a wary eye on them. 'Thank you, wizard. I'm afraid I'm not well loved here.'

I glanced over at him. There was a mark on his neck, black and angry red, like a brand, in the shape of lovely, feminine lips. I would have thought it lipstick, but I sensed a faint odor of burnt meat in the air.

'What happened to your neck?'

His face paled a few shades. 'Your godmother gave me a kiss.'

'Damn,' I said.

'Well put. Are you ready?'

'Ready for what?'

'For Court to be held. To be given our gifts.'

The tenuous hold I had on the power faltered, and I lowered my trembling hand, let go of the tension gently, before I lost control of it. The last light flickered and went out, leaving us in a darkness I wouldn't have believed possible.

And then the darkness was shattered by light – the spotlights again, shining up on the dias, upon the throne there, and Bianca in her flaming dress upon it. Her mouth and throat and the rounded slopes of her breasts were smeared in streaks of fresh blood, her lips stained scarlet as she smiled, down at the darkness, at the dozens of pairs of glowing eyes in it, gazing up at the dias in adoration, or terror, or lust, or all three.

'All rise,' I whispered, as soft whispers and moans, rustled up out of the darkness around us, not at all human. 'Vampire Court is now in session.'

29

Fear has a lot of flavors and textures. There's a sharp, silver fear that runs like lightning through your arms and legs, galvanizes you into action, power, motion. There's heavy, leaden fear that comes in ingots, piling up in your belly during the empty hours between midnight and morning, when everything is dark, every problem grows larger, and every wound and illness grows worse.

And there is coppery fear, drawn tight as the strings of a violin, quavering on one single note that cannot possibly be sustained for a single second longer – but goes on and on and on, the tension before the crash of cymbals, the brassy challenge of the horns, the threatening rumble of the kettle drums.

That's the kind of fear I felt. Horrible, clutching tension that left the coppery flavor of blood on my tongue. Fear of the creatures in the darkness around me, of my own weakness, the stolen power the Nightmare had torn from me. And fear for those around me, for the folk who didn't have the power I had. For Susan. For Michael. For all the young people now laying in the darkness, drugged and dying, or dead already, too stupid or too reckless to have avoided this night.

I knew what these things could do to them. They were predators, vicious destroyers. And they scared the living hell out of me.

Fear and anger always come hand in hand. Anger is my

hiding place from fear, my shield and my sword against it. I waited for the anger to harden my resolve, put steel into my spine. I waited for the rush of outrage and strength, to feel the power of it coalesce around me like a cloud.

It never came. Just a hollow, fluttering sensation, beneath my belt buckle. For a moment, I felt the fangs of the shadow demon from my dream once again. I started shaking.

I looked around me. All around, the large courtyard was surrounded by high hedges, cut with crenelated squares, in imitation of castle walls. Trees rose up at the corners, trimmed to form the shapes of the guard towers. Small openings in the hedge led out into the darkness of the house's grounds, but were closed with iron-barred doors. The only other way out that I saw was at the head of the stairs, where Mavra leaned against the doors leading back into the manor and out front. She looked at me with those corpse-milk eyes and her lips cracked as she gave me a small, chill smile.

I gripped my cane with both hands. A sword cane, of course – one made in merry old Jack the Ripper England, not a knock-off from one of those men's magazines that sells lava lamps and laser pointers. Real steel. Clutching it didn't do much to make me feel better. I still shook.

Reason. Reason was my next line of defense. Fear is bred from ignorance. So knowledge is a weapon against it, and reason is the tool of knowledge. I turned back to the front as Bianca started speaking to the crowd, some vainglorious bullshit I didn't pay any attention to. Reason. Facts.

Fact one: Someone had engineered the uprising of the dead, the torment of the restless souls. Most likely Mavra had been the one to actually work the magic. The spiritual turbulence had allowed the Nightmare, the ghost of a demon Michael and I had slain, to cross over and come after me.

Fact two: The Nightmare was out to get me and Michael, personally, by taking shots at us and all of our friends. Mavra might even have been directing it, controlling it, using it as a cat's-paw. Optionally, Bianca could have been learning from Mavra, and used it herself. Either way, the results had been the same.

Fact three: It hadn't come after us at sundown, the way we'd half expected.

Fact four: I was surrounded by monsters, with only the strength of a centuries-old tradition keeping them from tearing my throat out. Still, it seemed to be holding. For now.

Unless . . .

'Hell's bells,' I swore. 'I hate it when I don't figure out the mystery that it's too late.'

Dozens of gleaming red eyes turned toward me. Susan jabbed her elbow into my ribs. 'Shut *up*, Dresden,' she hissed. 'You're making them look at us.'

'Harry?' Michael whispered.

'That's their game,' I said, quietly. 'We've been set up.'

Michael grunted. 'What?'

'This whole thing,' I said. The facts started falling into place, about two hours too late. 'It's been a setup from the very beginning. The ghosts. The Nightmare demon. The attacks on our family and friends. All of it.'

'For what?' Michael whispered. 'What's it a setup for?'

'She meant to force us to show here from the very beginning. She's getting set to take a lesson from history,' I said. 'We have to get out of here.'

'A lesson from history?' Michael said.

'Yeah. Remember what Vlad Tepesh did at his inauguration?'

'Oh Lord,' Michael breathed. 'Lord preserve us.'

'I don't get it,' Susan said, voice quiet. 'What did this guy do?'

'He invited all of his political and personal enemies to a feast. Then he locked them in and burned them all alive. He wanted to start off his administration on a high note.'

'I see,' Susan said 'And you think this is what Bianca's doing?'

'Lord preserve us,' Michael murmured again.

'I'm told that He helps those who help themselves,' I said. 'We've got to get out of here.'

Michael's armor clinked as he looked around. 'They've blocked the exits.'

'I know. How many of them can you handle without the Sword?'

'If it was only a question of holding them off . . .'

'But it isn't. We may have to punch a hole through them.'

Michael shook his head. 'I'm not sure. Maybe two or three, Lord willing.'

I grimaced. Only one vampire guarded each way out, but there were another two or three dozen in the courtyard – not to mention my godmother or any of the other guests, like Mavra.

'We'll head for that gate,' Michael said, nodding toward one of the gates in the hedges.

I shook my head. 'We'd never make it.'

'You will,' he said. 'I think I can manage that much.'

'Ixnay on that upidstay anplay,' I said. 'We need an idea that gets us all out alive.'

'No, Harry. I'm supposed to stand between people and the harm things like these offer. Even if it kills me. It's my job.'

'You're supposed to have the Sword to help. It's my fault that it's gone, so until I get it back for you, ease off on the martyr throttle. I don't need anyone else on my conscience.' Or, I thought, a vengeful Charity coming after me for getting her children's father killed. 'There's got to be a way out of this.'

'Let me get this straight,' Susan said, quietly, as Bianca's speech went on. 'We can't leave now because it would be an insult to the vampires.'

'And all the excuse they would need to call for instant satisfaction.'

'Instant satisfaction,' Susan said. 'What's that?'

'A duel to the death. Which means that one of them would tear my arms off and watch me bleed to death,' I said. 'If I'm lucky.'

Susan swallowed. 'I see. And what happens if we just wait around?'

'Bianca or one of the others finds a way to make us cross the line and throw the first punch. Then they kill us.'

'And if we don't throw the first punch?' Susan asked.

'I figure she'll have a backup plan to wipe us out with, just in case.'

'Us?' Susan asked.

'I'm afraid so.' I looked at Michael. 'We need a distraction. Something that will get them all looking the other way.'

He nodded and said, 'You might be better for that than me, Harry.'

I took a breath and looked around to see what I had to work with. We didn't have much time. Bianca was bringing her speech to a close.

'And so,' Bianca said, her voice carrying ably, 'we stand at the dawn of a new age for our kind, the first acknowledged Court this far into the United States. No longer need we fear the wrath of our enemies. No longer shall we meekly bow our heads and offer our throats to those who claim power over us.' At this point, her dark eyes fastened directly upon me. 'Finally, with the strength of the entire Court behind us, with the Lords of the Outer Night to empower us, we will face our enemies. And bring them to their knees.' Her smile widened, curving fangs, blood red.

She trailed a fingertip across her throat, then lifted the blood to her mouth to suckle it from her finger. She shivered. 'My dear subjects. Tonight, we have guests among us. Guests brought here to witness our ascension to real power. Please, my friends. Help me welcome them.'

The spotlights swivelled around. One of them splashed onto my little group; me, Michael, Susan, with Thomas and Justine just a little apart. A second illuminated Mavra, at the head of the stairs, in all her stark and unearthly pallor. A third settled upon my godmother, who glowed with beauty in its light, casually tossing her hair back and casting a glittering smile around the courtyard. At my godmother's side was Mister Ferro, unlit cigarette still between his lips, smoke dribbling out his nostrils, looking martial and bland in his centurion gear, and utterly unconcerned with everything that was going on.

Applause, listless and somehow sinister, came out of the dark around us. There should be some kind of law. Anything that is so bad that its *applause* is sinister should be universally banned or something. Or maybe I was just that nervous. I coughed, and waved my hand politely.

'The Red Court would like to take this opportunity to present our guests with gifts at this time,' Bianca said, 'so that they may know how very, very deeply we regard their goodwill. So, without further ado, Mister Ferro, would you honor me by stepping forward and accepting this token of the goodwill of myself and my Court.'

The spotlight followed Ferro as he walked forward. He reached the foot of the dias, inclined his head in a shallow but deliberate nod, then ascended to stand before Bianca. The vampire bowed to him in return, and made a gesture with one hand. One of the hooded figures behind her stepped forward, holding a small cask, about as big as a breadbox. The figure opened it, and the lights gleamed on something that sparkled and shone.

Ferro's eyes glittered, and he stretched his hand down into the cask, sinking it to the wrist. A small smile stretched his lips, and he withdrew his hand with slow reluctance. 'A fine offering,' he murmured. 'Especially in this age of paupers. I thank you.'

He and Bianca exchanged bows where she dipped her head just a fraction lower than his own. Ferro closed the cask and took it beneath one arm, withdrawing a polite step before turning and descending the stairs.

Bianca smiled and faced the courtyard again. 'Thomas, of House Raith, of our brothers and sisters in the White Court. Please step forward, that I may give you a token of our regard.'

I glanced over at Thomas. He took a slow breath and then said, to me, 'Would you stand with Justine for me, while I'm up there.'

I glanced at the girl. She stood looking up at Thomas, one hand on his arm, her eyes worried, one sweet little lip between her teeth. She looked small, and young, and frightened. 'Sure,' I said.

I held out a rather stiff arm. The girl's hands clutched at my forearm, as Thomas turned with a brilliant smile, and swaggered into the spotlight and up the steps. She smelled delicious, like flowers or strawberries, with a low, heady musky smell underneath, sensual and distracting.

'She hates him,' Justine whispered. Her fingers tightened on my arm, through my sleeve. 'They all hate him.'

I frowned and glanced down at the girl. Even worried, she was terribly beautiful, though her proximity to me lessened the impact of her outfit. Or lack thereof. I focused on her face and said, 'Why do they hate him?'

She swallowed, then whispered, 'Lord Raith is the highest Lord of the White Court. Bianca extended her invitation to him. The Lord sent Thomas in his stead. Thomas is his bastard son. Of the White Court, he is the lowest, the least regarded. His presence here is an insult to Bianca.'

I got over my surprise that the girl had spoken that many words all together. 'Is there some kind of grudge between them?'

Justine nodded, as on the dias, Thomas and Bianca exchanged bows. She presented him with an envelope, speaking too quietly for the crowd to hear. He responded in kind. Justine said, 'It's me. It's my fault. Bianca wanted me to come be hers. But Thomas found me first. She hasn't forgiven him for it. She calls him a poacher.'

Which made sense, in a way. Bianca had risen to where she was by being Chicago's most infamous Madame. Her Velvet Room provided the services of girls most men only got to daydream about, for a hefty price. She had enough dirt and political connections that she could protect herself from legal persecution, even without counting any of her vampire tricks, and she'd always had more than her share of those. Bianca would want someone like Justine – sweet looking, gorgeous, unconsciously sexy. Probably dress her up in a plaid skirt and a starched white shirt with—

Down, Harry. Hell's bells. 'Is that why you stay with him?' I asked her. 'Because you feel that it's your fault he has enemies?'

She looked up at me, for a moment, and then away, her expression more sad than anything. 'You wouldn't understand.'

'Look. He's a vampire. I know that they can affect people, but you could be in danger—'

'I don't need rescuing, Mr Dresden,' she said. Her lovely eyes sparkled with something hard, determined. 'But there is something you can do for me.'

I got an edgy feeling and watched the girl warily. 'Yeah? Like what?'

'You can take Thomas and me with you when you leave.'

'You guys showed up in a limo, and you want a ride home with me?'

'Don't be coy, Mr Dresden,' she said. 'I know what you and your friends were talking about.'

I felt my shoulders creak with tension. 'You heard us. You aren't human, either.'

'I'm very human, Mister Dresden. But I read lips. Will you help him or not?'

'It isn't my business to protect him.'

Her soft mouth compressed into a hard line. 'I'm making it your business.'

'Are you threatening me?'

Her face flushed as pink as the dress she was almost wearing, but she stood her ground. 'We need friends, Mister Dresden. If you won't help us, then I'll try to buy Bianca's favor by exposing your plans to escape and claiming that I heard you talking about killing her.'

'That's a lie,' I hissed.

'It's an exaggeration,' she said, her voice gentle. She lowered her eyes. 'But it will be enough for her to call duel. Or to force you to shed blood. And if that happens, you will die.' She took a breath. 'I don't want it to be like that. But if we don't do something to protect ourselves, she'll kill him. And make me into one of her pet whores.'

'I wouldn't let that happen to you,' I said. The words poured out of my mouth before I'd had time to run them past the thinking part of my brain, but they had that solid, certain ring of truth. Oh, hell.

She looked up at me, uncertain again, catching one of those soft lips between her teeth. 'Really?' she whispered. 'You really mean that, don't you.'

I grimaced. 'Yeah. Yeah, I guess I do.'

'Then you'll help me? You'll help us?'

Michael, Susan, Justine, Thomas. Before long, I was going to need a secretary just to keep track of everyone I was supposed to be looking out for. 'You. But Thomas can look out for himself.'

Justine's eyes filled with tears. 'Mister Dresden, please. If there's anything I can do or say to convince you, I—'

'Dammit,' I swore, earning a glare from Michael.

'Dammit, dammit, dammit, woman. All women, for that matter.' That earned me a glare from Susan. 'He's a *vampire*, Justine. He's *eating* you. Why should you care if something happens to him?'

'He's also a person, Mister Dresden,' Justine said. 'A person who's never done you any harm. Why shouldn't you care what happens to him?'

I hate it when a woman asks me for help and I witlessly decide to go ahead and give it, regardless of dozens of perfectly good reasons not to. I hate it when I get threatened and strong-armed into doing something stupid and risky. And I hate it when someone takes the moral high ground on me and wins.

Justine had just done all three, but I couldn't hold it against her. She just looked too sweet and helpless.

'All right,' I said, against my better judgment. 'All right, just stay close. You want my protection, then you do what I say, when I say, and maybe we can all get out of this alive.'

She let out a little shudder that ran through her most attractively, and then she pressed herself against me. 'Thank you,' she murmured, nuzzling her face into the hollow of my throat so that little lightning-streaks of sensation flickered down my spine. 'Thank you, Mister Dresden.'

I coughed, uncomfortably, and firmly shoved back any ideas of extracting a more thorough thanks from her later, despite the clamoring of my sex drive. Probably the vampire venom, I reasoned, making me notice things like that even more. Sure. I pushed Justine gently away, and looked up to see Thomas returning from his visit to the dias, holding an envelope in his hand.

'Well,' I greeted him quietly, as he returned. 'That looks like it went well enough.'

He gave me a rather pallid smile. 'It . . . she can be rather frightening, when she wishes, can't she.'

'Don't let her get to you,' I advised him. 'What did she give you?'

Thomas accepted Justine into the circle of his arm, and she pressed her body to his as though she wanted to wallow in him and leave one of those angel shapes. He lifted the envelope and said, 'A condo in Hawaii. And a ticket there, on a late flight tonight. She suggested that I might want to leave Chicago. Permanently.'

'One ticket,' I said, and glanced at Justine.

'Mmmm.'

'Friendly of her,' I commented. 'Look, Thomas. We both want to get out of here tonight. Just stay close to me and follow my lead. All right?'

He frowned a bit, and then shot Justine a reproachful look. 'Justine. I asked you not to—'

'I had to,' she said, her face earnest, frightened. 'I had to do something to help you.'

He coughed. 'I apologize, Mister Dresden. I didn't want to involve anyone else in my problems.'

I rubbed at the back of my neck. 'It's okay. We can help each other, I guess.'

Thomas closed his eyes for a moment. Then he said, very simply and very openly, 'Thank you.'

'Sheesh,' I said. I glanced up at Bianca, who was in converse with one of the robed and hooded shadows. The pair of them vanished to the back of the dias while Bianca watched, and then returned, lugging something that evidently weighted a good deal. They settled the fairly large object, hidden beneath a dark red cloth, on the dias beside Bianca.

'Harry Dresden,' Bianca purred. 'Old and esteemed acquaintance, and wizard of the White Council. Please come forward so that I can give you some of what I've been longing to for so long.'

I gulped, and shot a glance back at Michael and Susan. 'Look sharp,' I said. 'If she's going to do something, I guess it will be now, when we're separated.'

He put his hand on her shoulder, and said, 'God go with you, Harry.' Energy thrummed along my skin, and the nearest vampires shifted about uneasily and took a few steps away. He saw me notice, and gave me a small, sheepish smile.

'Be careful, Mister Dresden,' Susan said.

I bobbed my eyebrows at them, nodded to Thomas and Justine, and then walked forward, my cane in one hand, my cheesy cape flowing in the night air as I mounted the stairs to the dias. A bit of sweat stung in the corner of my eye, smearing my makeup, probably. I ignored it, meeting Bianca's gaze as I came level with her.

Vampires don't have souls. She didn't have to fear my gaze. And she wasn't good enough to sucker me into her eyes. Or at least, she hadn't been, a couple years ago. She met my gaze, steady, her eyes dark and lovely and so very, very deep.

I took the better course of valor, and focused upon the tip of her perfectly upturned nose. I saw her breasts rise and fall in pleasure beneath the flames that gowned her, and she let out a small, purring sound of satisfaction. 'Oh, Harry Dresden. I had looked forward to seeing you tonight.

You are a very handsome man, after all. But you look utterly ridiculous.'

'Thanks,' I said. No one, except maybe the pair of robed attendants at the back of the dias, could hear us. 'How did you plan on killing me?'

She fell quiet for a moment, thoughtful. Then she asked me, as she formally inclined her head, for the benefit of the crowd below, 'Do you remember Paula, Mister Dresden?'

I returned the gesture, only more shallowly, just to throw the little zing of insult into it. 'I remember. She was pretty. Polite. I didn't really get to meet her much.'

'No. She was dead within an hour of you setting foot in my house.'

'I thought she might have gone that way,' I said.

'That you might have killed her, you mean?'

'Isn't my fault if you lost control and ate her, Bianca.'

She smiled, teeth blinding white. 'Oh, but it *was* your fault, Mister Dresden. You'd come to my house. Provoked me to near madness. Forced me to go along with you under threat of my destruction.' She leaned forward, giving me a glimpse down the flame-dress. She was naked beneath. 'Now I get to return the favor. I'm not someone you can simply walk over, slap around, whenever you have a need. Not anymore.' She paused and then said, 'In a way, I'm grateful to you, Dresden. If I hadn't wanted so very badly to kill you, I would never have amassed the power and the contacts that I have. I never would have been elevated to the Court.' She gestured to the crowd of vampires below, the courtyard, the darkness. 'In a way, all of this is your doing.'

'That's a lie,' I said, quiet. 'I didn't make you rope Mavra into working for you. I didn't make you order her to torture those poor ghosts, stir up the Nevernever and bring Kravos's pet demon back across to send after a bunch of innocents while you tried to get to me.'

Her smile widened. 'Is *that* what you think happened? Oh, my, Mister Dresden. You have an unpleasant surprise awaiting you.'

Anger made me lift my eyes to meet her gaze, gave me the strength not to get pulled in by it – no mistaking. She had grown stronger in the past couple of years. 'Can we just get this over with.'

'Anything worth doing is worth doing slowly,' she murmured, but she reached out a hand and tugged on the dark red cloth, uncovering the object there. 'For you, Mister Dresden. With all of my most fervent sincerities.'

The cloth slid away from a white marble tombstone, set with a pentacle of gold in its center. Block letters carved into it read HERE LIES HARRY DRESDEN, above the pentacle. Below it, they read HE DIED DOING THE RIGHT THING. An envelope had been taped to the side of the tombstone.

'Do you like it?' Bianca purred. 'It comes complete with your own plot at Graceland, near to dear little Inez. I'm sure you'll have ever so much to talk about. When your time comes, of course.'

I looked from the tombstone back up to her. 'Go ahead,' I said. 'Make your move.'

She laughed, a rich sound that spilled back down into the crowd below. 'Oh, Mister Dresden,' she said, lowering her voice. 'You really don't understand, do you. I can't openly strike you down. Regardless of what you may have done to me. But I can defend myself. I can stand by while my guests defend themselves. I can watch you die. And if things are hectic and confusing enough, and a few others die along with you, well. That's hardly to be blamed upon me.'

'Thomas,' I said.

'And his little whore. And the Knight, and your reporter friend. I'm going to enjoy the rest of the evening, Harry.'

'My friends call me Harry,' I said. 'Not you.'

She smiled, and said, 'Revenge is like sex, Mister Dresden. It's best when it comes on slow, quiet, until it all seems inexorable.'

'You know what they say about revenge. I hope you got a second tombstone, Bianca. For the other grave.'

My words stung her, and she stiffened. Then she beckoned the attendants forward, to lift my tombstone in their gloved hands and carry it back. 'I'll have it delivered to Graceland, Mister Dresden. They'll have your bed all ready for you, before the sun rises.' She flicked her wrist at me, curt dismissal.

I bowed my head, a bare, stark motion, cold. 'We'll see.' How's that for a comeback? Then I turned and descended the stairs, my legs shaking a little, my back rigid and straight.

'Harry,' Michael said, as I drew close. 'What happened?'

I held up my hand and shook my head, trying to think. The trap was already closing around me. I could feel that much. But if I could figure out Bianca's plan, see it coming, maybe I could think my way out ahead of her.

I trusted Michael and the others to keep an eye out for trouble while I furiously pondered, tried to work through Bianca's logic. My godmother glided forward at Bianca's bidding, and I paused for a moment, to glance up to the dias.

Bianca presented her with a small black case. Lea opened it, and a slow tremble ran down her body, made her flame-red hair shift and glisten. My godmother closed it again and said, 'A princely gift. Happily, as is the custom of my people, I have brought a matter of equal worth, to exchange with you.'

Lea beckoned the attendant forward, and was given a long, dark case. She opened it, displaying it for a moment to Bianca, and then turned, showing it to the gathered Court.

Amoracchius. Michael's sword. It lay gleaming in the dark box, casting back the ruddy light with a pure, argent radiance. Michael went stiff beside me, stifling a shout.

A murmur went up from the assembled vampires and sundry creatures. They recognized the sword as well. Lea basked in it for a moment, until she folded the case closed and passed it over to Bianca. Bianca settled it across her lap, and smiled down at me and, I thought, at Michael.

'A worthy reply to my gift,' Bianca said. 'I thank you, Lady Leanandsidhe. Let Mavra of the Black Court come forward.'

My godmother retreated. Mavra glided out of the night and onto the dias.

'Mavra, you have been a most gracious and honorable guest in my house,' Bianca said. 'And I trust that you have found your treatment here fair and equitable.'

Mavra bowed to Bianca, silent, her rheumy eyes gleaming, glancing down towards Michael.

'Oh, Jesus,' I whispered. 'Son of a *bitch*.'

'He didn't mean it, Lord,' Michael said. 'Harry? What did you mean?'

I clenched my teeth, eyes flickering around. Everyone

was watching me, all the vampires, Mister Ferro, everyone. They all knew what was coming. 'The tombstone. It was written on my damned tombstone.'

Bianca watched the realization come over me, still smiling. 'Then please, Mavra, accept these minor tokens of my goodwill, and with them my hopes that vengeance and prosperity will belong to you and yours.' She offered forth the case, containing the sword, which Mavra accepted. Bianca then beckoned to the background, and the attendants brought out another covered bundle.

The attendants jerked the cover off of the bundle – Lydia. Her dark, tousled hair had been trimmed into an elegant cut, and she wore a halter and shorts of black Lycra that emphasized her hips, the beauty of her pale limbs. Her eyes stared into the lights, glazed, drugged, and she sagged helplessly between the attendants.

'My God,' Susan said. 'What are they going to do with that girl?'

Mavra turned to Lydia, reaching into the case as she did. 'Sweet,' her hissing voice rasped. Her eyes went to Michael again. 'Now to open my gift. It may tarnish the steel a bit, but I'm sure I'll get over it.'

Michael drew in a sudden breath.

'What's going on?' Susan blurted.

'The blood of innocents,' he snarled. 'The Sword is vulnerable. She means to unmake it. Harry, we cannot allow it.'

All around me, vampires dropped their wineglasses, slid out of their jackets, bared their scarlet-smeared fangs in slow smiles to me. Bianca started laughing, up above me, as Mavra opened the case and withdrew *Amoracchius*. The sword seemed to almost chime with an angry sound as the vampire touched it, but Mavra only sneered down at the blade as she lifted the sword.

Thomas moved closer to us, pushing Justine behind him as he drew his sword. 'Dresden,' he hissed. 'Dresden, don't be a fool. It's only one life – one girl's life and a sword balanced against all of us. If you act now, you condemn us all.'

'Harry?' Susan asked, her voice shaking.

Michael too turned to look at me, his expression grim. 'Faith, Dresden. Not all is lost.'

All looked pretty damned lost to me. But I didn't have to do anything. I didn't have to lift a finger. All I had to do, to get out of here alive, was to sit still. To do nothing. All I had to do was stand here and watch while they murdered a girl who had come to me a few days before, begging me for protection. All I had to do was ignore her screams as Mavra gutted her. All I had to do was let the monsters destroy one of the major bastions standing against them. All I had to do was let Michael go to his death, claim the protection of the laws of hospitality upon Susan, and I could walk away.

Michael nodded at me, then drew both knives and turned toward the dias.

I closed my eyes. *God forgive me for what I'm about to do.*

I grabbed Michael's shoulder before he could start walking. Then I drew the sword blade forth from the cane, holding the cane in my left hand, reversing it in my grip as I drew in my will, sent it coursing down the haft of the cane, caused blue-white light to flare in the runes etched there.

Michael flashed me a fighting grin and took position at my right. Thomas took one look at me and whispered,

'We're dead.' But he fell in at my left, crystalline sword glittering in his hand. A howl went up from the vampires, a sudden wave of deafening sound. Mavra turned her eyes to us, gathering night into the fingers of her free hand again. Bianca slowly rose, dark eyes glowing in triumph. Over to one side, Lea laid her hand on Mister Ferro's arm, frowning faintly, standing well out of the way.

Mavra hissed, lifting *Amoracchius* up high.

'Harry?' Susan asked. Her shaking hand touched my shoulder. 'What are we going to do?'

'Stay behind me, Susan.' I clenched my teeth. 'I guess I'm going to do the right thing.'

Even if it kills me, I thought. *And all of you too.*

30

In games and history books and military science lectures, teachers and old warhorses and other scholarly types lay out diagrams and stand up models in neat lines and rows. They show you, in a methodical order, how this division forced a hole in that line, or how these troops held their ground when all others broke.

But that's an illusion. A real struggle between combatants, whether they number dozens or thousands, is something inherently messy, fluid, difficult to follow. The illusion can show you the outcome, but it doesn't impress upon you the surge and press of bodies, the screams, the fear, the faltering rushes forward or away. Within the battle, everything is wild motion and sound and a blur of impressions that flash by almost before they have time to register. Instinct and reflex rule everything – there isn't time to think, and if there's a spare second or two, the only thought in your head is 'How do I stay alive?' You're intensely aware of what is happening around you. It's an obscure kind of torture, an acute and temporary hell – because one way or another, it doesn't last long.

A tide of vampires came toward us. They rushed in, animal-swift, a blur of twisted, bulging faces and staring black eyes. Their jaws hung too far open, fangs bared, hissing and howling. One of them held a long spear and shoved it toward Thomas's pale belly. Justine screamed. Thomas swept the crystalline sword he bore down in an arc, parrying the spear's tip aside and cutting through the haft.

Undeterred, the spear-wielding vampire came on, and sank its fangs into Thomas's forearm. Thomas shoved the vamp back, but it held firm. Thomas switched tactics, abruptly lifting the vampire up and clear of the ground, and then rolled the sword's blade around its belly, splitting it open in a welter of gore. The vampire fell to the ground, a sound bubbling up from his throat that was one part fury and one part agony.

'Their bellies!' Thomas shouted. 'Without the blood they're too weak to fight!'

Michael caught a descending machete's blade on the metal guard around his forearm, and whipped one of his knives across the belly of the vamp who held it. Blood splattered out of the vamp, and it went down in convulsions. 'I know,' Michael snapped back, flashing Thomas an irritated look.

And then he was buried in a swarm of red-clad bodies.

'Michael!' I shouted. I tried to push toward him, but found myself jostled aside. I saw him struggle and drop to one knee, saw the vampires shoving knives at him, and fangs, teeth tearing and worrying, and if any of them were burning, like before, I couldn't see it.

Kyle Hamilton appeared, across the dogpile over the fallen knight. He bared his fangs at me, and lifted a semi-automatic, one of the expensive models. Gold-plated. 'Fare thee well, Dresden.'

I lifted the cane, its runes shimmering blue and white, and snapped. 'Venteferro!'

The magic whispered silently out through the runes on the cane. Earth magic isn't really my forte, but I like to keep my hand in. The runes and the power I willed into the staff reached out and caught the gun in invisible waves of magnetism. I had been worried that the spells I'd laid on the cane might have gone stale, but they were still hanging in there. The gun flew from Kyle's hands.

I whipped it through the air, into the face of another vamp coming toward Justine. It hit at something just this side of the speed of sound, and sent the thing flying back into the darkness. Justine whirled, as a second vampire came at her, only to have its legs literally scythed out from beneath it by Thomas's blade.

'*Iesu domine!*' Michael's voice rang out from beneath the vampires like a brass army bugle, and with a sudden explosion of pressure and unseen force, bodies flew back and up, away from him, flesh ripped and torn from them, hanging in ragged, bloodless strips like cloth, showing gleaming, oily black flesh beneath. '*Domine!*' Michael shouted, rising, slewing gutted vamps off of him like a dog shakes off water. '*Lava quod est sordium!*'

'Come on!' I called, and strode forward, toward the stairs leading up to the dias. Michael had parted the scarlet sea, as it were – stunned vampires gathered themselves from the ground or slowed their attack, hovering several feet away, hissing. Susan and Justine caught one of them starting to creep in closer, and discouraged the others from following its example by splattering it with holy water from Susan's basket. The thing howled and fell back, clawing at its eyes, flopping and wriggling like a half-crushed bug.

'Bianca!' Thomas shouted. 'Our only chance is to take out their leader!' A knife flew out of the dark, too fast for me to see. But Thomas did. He reached out and flicked the blade of his sword across its path with a contemptuous swat, deflecting it out.

We reached the foot of the stairs. 'Thomas, hold them here. Michael, we go up.' I didn't wait to see who was listening – I just turned and headed up the stairs, sword and cane out and ready, my stomach sinking. There was no way we would be in time to save Lydia.

But we were. The carnage had evidently drawn Mavra's attention, and she stared at the blood, withered lips pulled back from yellow teeth. She looked at me, and her expression twisted in malice. She spun back to Lydia, sword held high.

'Michael,' I snapped, and stretched out my cane. '*Venteferro!*'

Amoracchius burst into conflicting shades of blue and golden light, as my power wrapped around it, a coruscation of sparks that made Mavra howl in surprise and pain. The vampire retreated, but kept her pale hands clenched on the blade.

'Suit yourself, sparky,' I muttered. I gritted my teeth as the cane smoked and shook in my hand. '*Vente! Venteferro!*' I whipped the cane in a wide arc, and with a hiss the vampire found herself lifted clear of the ground by her grip on the sword, and flung like a beach ball toward the courtyard below. She smacked into the stones of the courtyard hard, brittle popping sounds a gruesome accompaniment. The sword exploded in another cloud of vengeful argent sparks and went spinning away from Mavra, the blade flashing where hit the ground.

A wave of exhaustion and dizziness swept over me, and I nearly fell. Even using a focus, the rune-etched cane, that effort had nearly been more than I could manage. I had to clench my teeth and hope I wouldn't simply pitch to one side. I was getting down to the bottom of the barrel, as far as magic went.

'Harry!' Michael shouted. 'Look out!'

I looked up to see Mavra bound up onto the dias again, not bothering to take the stairs, landing a few feet from me. Michael strode forward, one hand holding a dagger up reversed, point down, a cross extended toward Mavra. The vampire flung her hands at Michael, and darkness spilled out of them like oil, splattering toward the knight. It sizzled and spat against him, going up in puffs of steam, and Michael came on forward through it, white fire gathering around the upheld cross. Mavra let out a dusty, hissing scream and fell back from him, forced away from me.

'Harry,' Thomas shouted up the stairs, 'hurry up! We can't last much longer!'

My eyes swept the dias, but I could see no sign of Bianca or her attendants in the shadows cast by the halogen-brightness of Michael's blazing cross. I hurried to Lydia, sheathing my slender blade before scooping her up. 'Longer? I'm amazed we're still alive now!'

'Light shines brightest in the deepest dark!' Michael shouted, a fierce joy on his face, his eyes alight with a passion and a vengeance I had never seen in him. He kept forcing Mavra back before the paralyzing fire of the cross, until with a scream she fell from the dias. 'Let come the forces of night! We will stand!'

'We will get the hell out of here is what we will do,' I muttered, but louder I said, 'back down the stairs. Let's go!'

I turned to see Thomas, Susan, and Justine holding off

a ring of vampires, at the base of the stairs to the dias, between the pair of spotlights. Only scraps of skin and cloth clung to the vampires. Some of the Red Court still had partially human faces, but most stood naked, now, free of the flesh masks they wore. Black, flabby creatures, twisted, horrible faces, bellies bulging, mostly, tight with fresh blood. Black eyes, empty of anything but hunger, glittered in the light. Long, skinny fingers ended in black claws, as did the grasping toes of their feet. Membranes stretched between their arms and flanks, horribly slime-covered, the beautiful bodies and shapes of before given way to the horror beneath.

A vampire lurched toward Thomas, while another reached out to grasp Susan. She thrust her cross in its face, but unlike with Mavra, the wood did not blaze to light. Faith magic isn't always easy to work, even on vampires, and the Red Court, creatures with a more solid hold on reality than the more magical denizens of the Black, were not so easily repelled. The vampire howled, mouth yawning open, foaming slaver spattering Susan's red hood.

She twisted and fought, and with her other hand swept up another baby food jar of holy water – not at the vampire, but at the spotlight beside them. With a screaming hiss, the water vaporized against the heat of the light, bursting out in a sudden cloud of steam that enfolded the vampire completely. It let out a screech that swept upward through the range of human hearing, vanishing above it, and fell away from Susan, its skin sloughing off, the black, stringy muscles and bones beneath showing through.

Susan fumbled her basket open and drew her gun. She fired for the vampire's belly, the rapid *thump-thump-thump* of panic fire, and the vampire's abdomen ruptured, blood spraying out in a cloud. The vamp fell to the ground, and I remember thinking that she'd just killed the thing — really and truly taken one of them out. A fierce pride shot through me, and I headed down the stairs.

And then our streak of luck ended.

Justine took a step too far to one side, and Bianca appeared out of nowhere, seizing the girl by the hair and dragging her away from Thomas. Thomas whirled, but too late. Bianca held the girl's back against her front, her fingers wound with deceptive gentleness around Justine's throat. With the other hand, Bianca, still quite human-seeming and calm, caressed the girl's belly. Justine struggled, but Bianca simply turned her head to one side and drew her tongue slowly, sensuously over Justine's throat. The girl's eyes widened, panicked. Then they grew heavy. She shuddered, her body relaxing toward Bianca, arching slowly. Bianca's rich mouth quirked, and she murmured something into Justine's ear that made the girl whimper.

'Enough,' Bianca said. And as quickly as that, the court-yard grew silent. Michael and I stood on the stairs a bit above Thomas and Susan. The vampires ringed them in, just out of reach of Thomas's sword. I held Lydia unmoving in my arms. Bianca looked up at me and said, 'The game has ended, wizard.'

'You haven't taken us down yet,' I shot back. 'Smart for you and your people to get out of my way, before I get cranky.'

Bianca laughed, idly plucking some of the petals from Justine's top, baring a bit more of her breasts. 'Surely you don't think me so stupid as to be bluffed now, Dresden. You have already had a measure of your strength taken. What remains barely keeps you standing. If you could force your way out, you'd have done it already.' Her eyes moved to Michael. 'And you, Sir Knight. You will die gloriously and take many of the horrid creatures of the night with you. But you are outnumbered and alone, and without the sword. You will die.'

I glanced at Thomas and Susan and said, 'Well, then. I guess it's a good thing we brought help. Your whole Court, Bianca, and you couldn't take us down.' I swept my eyes back and forth over the vampires below, and said, 'All of your little minions here have eternity laid out before them. Eternity is a bad thing to lose. And maybe you would get us, eventually. But whichever one of you would like to lose eternity first, please. Just go ahead and step on up.'

Silence reigned over the courtyard for a moment. I allowed a bit of hope to seep into my pounding heart. Kenny Rogers, eat your heart out. If this bluff worked, I'd be more of a gambler than he'd ever dreamed.

Bianca only smiled, and said, to Thomas, 'She's so beautiful, my cousin of the White Court. I've wanted her ever since the moment I saw her.' Bianca licked her lips. 'What would you say to a bargain?'

I sneered. 'You think we would do business with you?'

Thomas glanced back up at me. Incredibly, he was clean – but for a sprinkling of scarlet droplets on his pale flesh, unmarred, loincloth, wings, and all. 'Go ahead,' he said. 'I'm listening.'

'Give them to us, Thomas Raith,' Bianca said. 'Give us these three, and take the girl as your own, uncontested. I will have as many little pets as I wish, now. What is one over another?'

'Thomas,' I said. 'I know we just met, but don't listen to her. She set you up to get killed already.'

Thomas glanced back and forth between us. He met my eyes for a moment – almost long enough to let me see inside him. Then looked away. I had the impression that he was trying to tell me something. I don't know what. His expression seemed apologetic, maybe. 'I know, Mister Dresden,' he said. 'But . . . I'm afraid the situation has changed.' He didn't kick Susan, so much as he simply planted his sandaled foot against her and shoved her into the crowd of vampires. She let out a short, startled scream, and then they took her, and dragged her into the darkness.

Thomas lowered his sword and turned toward me, his back to the vampires. Leering, hissing, they crept closer to Michael and me, around Thomas, one of them rubbing up against his legs. His mouth twisted in distaste, and he sidestepped. 'I'm sorry, Mister Dresden. Harry. I do like you quite a bit. But I'm afraid that I like myself a whole lot more.'

Thomas faded back, while the vampires crowded around the bottom of the stairs. Somewhere, in the dark, Susan let out a short, terrified scream. And then it faded to a moan. And then silence.

Bianca smiled sweetly at me, over Justine's lolling head. 'And so, wizard, it ends. The pair of you will die. But don't worry. No one will ever find the bodies.' She glanced back, toward where Thomas had faded into the background and said, aside, 'Kyle, Mavra. Kill the white-bellied little bastard, too.'

Thomas's head whipped around toward Bianca and he snarled, 'You bitch!'

My mouth worked and twisted, but no words came out. How could they? Words couldn't possibly contain the frustration, the rage, the fear that poured through me. It cut through my weariness, sharp as thorns and barbed wire. It wasn't fair. We'd done everything we could. We'd risked everything.

Not we. The choices had been mine.

I'd risked everything.

And I'd lost.

Michael and I couldn't possibly fight them all alone. They'd taken Susan. The help we thought we'd found had turned against us.

They had Susan.

And it was my fault. I hadn't listened to her, when I should have. I hadn't protected her. And now she was going to die, because of me.

I don't know how that realization would make someone else feel. I don't know if the despair, and the self-loathing and the helpless fury would crumble them like too-brittle concrete, or melt them like dirty lead, or shatter them like cheap glass.

I only know what it did to me.

It set me on fire.

Fire in my heart, in my thoughts, in my eyes. I burned, burned down deep in my gut, burned in places I hadn't known I could hurt.

I don't remember the spell, or the words I said. But I remember reaching for that pain. I remember reaching for it, and thinking that if we had to go, then so help me God, weakened or not, hopeless or not, I was going to take these murdering, bloodsucking sons of bitches with me. I would show them that they couldn't play lightly with the powers of creation, of life itself. That it wasn't smart to cross a wizard of the White Council when someone has stolen his girlfriend.

I think Michael must have sensed something and taken the girl from my arms, because the next thing I remember is thrusting my hands toward the night sky and screaming, '*Fuego! Pyrofuego*! Burn, you greasy bat-faced bastards! Burn!'

I reached for fire – and fire answered me.

The tree-towers of the topiary castle exploded into blazes of light, and the hedge-walls, complete with their crenelated tops, went up with them. Fire leapt up into the air, forty, fifty feet, and the sudden explosion of it lifted everyone but me up and off the ground, sent wind roaring around us in a gale.

I stood amidst it, my mind brilliantly lit by the power coursing through me. It burned me, and some part of me screamed out in joy that it did. My cloak flapped and danced in the gale, spreading out around me in a scarlet and sable cloud. The abrupt glare fell on the scene of the vampires' revelry, lighting it harshly. The young people of earlier lay about, out in the darkness near the hedges, near the fires, pathetic little lumps. Some of them twitched. Some of them breathed. A few whimpered and tried to crawl away from the heat – but most lay dreadfully, perfectly still.

Pale. Pretty.

Dead.

The fury in me grew. It swelled and burned and I reached out to the fires again. Flames flew out, caught one of the more cowardly of the vampires, huddled at the back, scrabbling to slip his flesh mask back over his squashed bat face. The fire touched him and then twined about him, searing and blackening his skin, then dragging him back, winding and rolling him toward the blaze.

The magic danced in my eyes, my head, my chest, flying wild and out of control. I couldn't follow everything that happened. More vampires got too close to the flames, and began screaming. Tendrils of fire rose up from the ground and began to slither over the courtyard like serpents. Everything exploded into motion, shadows flashing through the brightness, seeking escape, screaming.

I felt my heart clench in my chest and stop beating. I swayed on my feet, gasping. Michael got to me, Lydia slung over his shoulder in a fireman's carry. He'd torn his cloak off, and it lay to one side, burning. He dragged my arm across his shoulder, and half carried me down the stairs.

Smoke gathered on us, thick and choking. I coughed and retched, helpless. The magic coursed through me, slower now, a trickle – not because the floodgates had closed, but because I had nothing left to pour out. I hurt. Fire spread out from my heart, my arms and legs clenching and twitching. I couldn't get a breath, couldn't think, and I knew, somewhere amidst all that pain, that I was about to die.

'Lord!' Michael coughed. 'Lord, I know that Harry hasn't always done what You would have done!' He staggered forward, carrying me, and the girl. 'But he's a good man! He's fought against Your foes! He deserves better than to die here, Lord! So if you could be kind enough to show me how to get us out of here, I'd really appreciate it.'

And then, abruptly, the smoke parted, and sweet, untainted air hit us in the face like a bucket of ice water.

I fell to the ground. Michael dropped the girl somewhere near me and tore the cheap tuxedo open. He laid his hand over my heart and let out a short cry. After that,

I don't remember much more than pain, and a series of dull, hard thumps on my chest.

And then my heart lurched and began to beat again. The red haze of agony receded.

I looked up.

The smoke had parted in a tunnel, as though someone had shoved a glass tube of clean air through it and around us. At the far end of the tunnel stood a slender, willowy figure, tall, feminine. Something like wings spread out behind the figure, though that might have been an illusion, light falling on it from many angles, so that it was all shadow and color.

'I thought He wasn't so literal,' I choked.

Michael drew back from me, his soot-stained face breaking into a brief smile. 'Are you complaining?'

'H − Heck, no. Where's Susan?'

'I'll come back in for her. Come on.' Too tired to argue, I let him haul me back to my feet. He picked up Lydia, and we staggered forward and out, to the figure at the tunnel's far end.

Lea. My faerie godmother.

We both drew up short. Michael fumbled for his knife, but it was gone.

Lea quirked one delicate brow at us. Her dress, still blue, unsoiled, flowed around her, and her silken mane matched the bloody fires consuming the courtyard. She looked almost good enough to drink, and she still held the black box Bianca had given her beneath one slender arm.

'Godmother,' I said, startled.

'Well, fool? What are you waiting for. I took the trouble to show you a way to escape. Do it.'

'*You* saved us?' I coughed.

She sighed and rolled her eyes. 'Though it pains me in ways I could not explain, yes, child. How am I supposed to have you if I let this Red Court hussy kill you? Stars above, wizard, I thought you had better sense than this.'

'You saved me. So *you* could get me.'

'Not like *this*,' Lea said, holding a silken cloth to her nose, delicately. 'You're a husk, and I want the whole fruit. Go rest, child. We will speak again soon enough.'

And then she withdrew and was gone.

Michael got me out of the house. I remember the smell of his old truck, sawdust and sweat and leather. I felt its worn seat creak beneath me.

'Susan,' I said. 'Where's Susan?'

'I'll try.'

Then I drifted in darkness for a while, dimly conscious of a lingering pain in my chest, of Lydia's warm skin pressed against my hand. I tried to move, to make sure the girl was all right, but it was too much effort.

The truck door opened and slammed closed. Then came the rumble of its engine.

And then everything went mercifully black.

31

The darkness swallowed me and kept me for a long time. There was nothing but silence where I drifted, nothing but endless night. I wasn't cold. I wasn't warm. I wasn't anything. No thought, no dreams, no anything.

It was too good to last.

The pain of the burns came to me first. Burns are the worst injuries in the world. I'd been scorched on my right arm and shoulder, and it throbbed with a dull persistence that dragged me out of the peace. All the other assorted scrapes and bruises and cuts came back to me. I felt like a collection of complaints and malfunctions. I ached everywhere.

Memory came through the haze next. I started remembering what had happened. The Nightmare. The vampire ball. The kids who had been seduced into being there.

And the fire.

Oh, God. What had I done?

I thought of the fire, towering up in walls of solid flame, reaching out with hungry arms to drag the vampires screaming back into the pyre I had made of the hedges and the trees.

Stars and stones. Those children had been helpless in that. In the fire and the smoke that I'd needed a major sidhe sorceress's assistance to escape. I had never stopped to think about that. I had never even considered the consequences of unleashing my power that way.

I opened my eyes. I lay in my bed in my room. I stumbled out of the bed and into my bathroom. Someone must have fed me soup at some point, because when I started throwing up, there was something left to come out.

Killed them. I killed those kids. My magic, the magic that was the energy of creation and life itself had reached out and burned them to death.

I threw up until my belly ached with the violence of it, wild grief running rampant over me. I struggled, but I couldn't force the images out of my head. Children burning. Justin burning. Magic defines a man. It comes from down deep inside you. You can't accomplish anything with magic that isn't in you, somewhere, to do.

And I had burned those children alive.

My power. My choice. My fault.

I sobbed.

I didn't come to myself until Michael came into the bathroom. By the time he did, I lay on my side, curled up tight, the water of the shower pouring down over me, the cold making me shiver. Everything hurt, inside and out. My face ached, from being twisted up so tightly. My throat had closed almost completely as I wept.

Michael picked me up as though I weighed no more than one of his children. He dried me with a towel and shoved me into my heavy robe. He had on clean clothes, a bandage on his wrist and another on his forehead. His eyes looked a little more sunken, as though short on sleep. But his hands were steady, his expression calm, confident.

I gathered myself again, very slowly. By the time he was finished, I lifted my eyes to his.

'How many?' I asked. 'How many of them died?'

He understood. I saw the pain in his eyes. 'After I got

the pair of you out, I called the fire department and let them know that people needed a rescue. They got there pretty quickly, but—'

'How many, Michael?'

He drew in a slow breath. 'Eleven bodies.'

'Susan?' My voice shook.

He hesitated. 'We don't know. Eleven was all they found. They're checking dental records. They said the heat was so intense that the bones hardly look human.'

I let out a bitter laugh. 'Hardly human. There were more kids than that there—'

'I know. But that's all they found. And they rescued a dozen more, alive.'

'It's something, at least. What about the ones unaccounted for?'

'They were gone. Missing. They're . . . they're presumed dead.'

I closed my eyes. Fire had to burn hot to reduce bones to ash. Had my spell been that powerful? Had it hidden most of the dead?

'I can't believe it,' I said. 'I can't believe I was so stupid.'

'Harry,' Michael said. He put his hand on my shoulder. 'We've no way to know. We just don't. They could have been dead before the fires came. The vampires were feeding from them indiscriminately, where we couldn't see.'

'I know,' I said. 'I know. God, I was so arrogant. Such an *idiot* to go walking in there like that.'

'Harry—'

'And those poor, stupid kids paid the price. Dammit, Michael.'

'A lot of the vampires didn't make it out, either, Harry.'

'It isn't worth it. Not if it wiped out all the vamps in Chicago.'

Michael fell quiet. We sat that way for a long time.

Finally, I asked him, 'How long have I been out?'

'More than a day. You slept through last night and yesterday and most of tonight. The sun will rise soon.'

'God,' I said. I rubbed at my face.

I could hear Michael's frown. 'I thought we'd lost you for a while. You wouldn't wake up. I was afraid to take you to the hospital. Any place where there'd be a record of you. The vampires could trace it.'

'We need to call Murphy and tell her—'

'Murphy's still sleeping, Harry. I called Sergeant Stallings, last night, when I called the fire department. S.I. tried to take over the investigation, but someone up the line called the police department off of it altogether. Bianca has contacts in City Hall, I guess.'

'They can't stop the missing persons investigations that are going to start cropping up as soon as people start missing those kids. But they can stick a bunch of things in the way of it. Crap.'

'I know,' Michael said. 'I tried to find Susan, the girl Justine, and the sword, after. Nothing.'

'We almost pulled it off. Sword and captives and all.'

'I know.'

I shook my head. 'How's Charity? The baby?'

He looked down. 'The baby – they still don't know about him. They can't find out what's wrong. They don't have any idea why he is getting weaker.'

'I'm sorry. Is Charity—?'

'She's stuck in bed for a while, but she'll be fine. I called her yesterday.'

'Called. You didn't go see her?'

'I guarded you,' Michael said. 'Father Forthill was with my family. And there are others who can watch them, when I'm away.'

I winced. 'She didn't like that, did she. That you stayed with me.'

'She's not speaking to me.'

'I'm sorry.'

He nodded. 'So am I.'

'Help me up. I'm thirsty.'

He did, and I only swayed a little as I stood. I tottered out into the living area of my apartment. 'What about Lydia?' I asked.

Michael remained silent, and my eyes answered my own question a few seconds later. Lydia lay on the couch in my living room, under a ton and a half of blankets, curled up, her eyes closed and her mouth a little open.

'I recognize her,' Michael said.

I frowned. 'From where?'

'Kravos's lair. She was one of the kids they hauled away, early on.'

I whistled. 'She must have known him. Known what he was going to do, somehow.'

'Try not to wake her up,' Michael said, his voice soft. 'She wouldn't sleep. I think they'd drugged her. She was panicky, gabbling. I just got her quieted down half an hour ago.'

I frowned a little and went into the tiny kitchen. Michael followed. I got a Coke out of the icebox, thought better of it with my stomach the way it was, and fetched a glass of water instead. I drank unsteadily. 'I've got hell to pay now, Michael.'

He frowned at me. 'How do you mean?'

'What you do comes back to you, Michael. You know that much. Roll a stone and it rolls back upon you. Sow the wind and reap the whirlwind.'

Michael lifted his eyebrows. 'I didn't realize you'd read much of the Bible.'

'Proverbs always made a lot of sense to me,' I said. 'But with magic, things like that come a lot sharper and cleaner than with other things. I killed people. I burned them. It's going to come back to haunt me.'

Michael frowned, and looked out at Lydia. 'The Law of Three, eh?'

I shrugged.

'I thought you told me once that you didn't believe in that.'

I drank more water. 'I didn't. I don't. It's too much like justice. To believe that what you do with magic comes back to you threefold.'

'You've changed your mind?'

'I don't know. All I know is that there's going to be justice, Michael. For those kids, for Susan, for what's happened to Charity and your son. If no one else is going to arrange it, I'll damn well do it myself.' I grimaced. 'I just hope that if I'm wrong, I can dodge karmic paybacks long enough to finish this.'

'Harry, the ball was the whole point. It was Bianca's chance to put you down while staying within the terms of the Accords. She laid her trap and missed. Do you think she's going to keep pushing it?'

I gave him a look. 'Of course. And so do you. Or you wouldn't have played watchdog here for the past day.'

'Good point.'

I raked my fingers through my hair, and reached for the Coke, my stomach be damned. 'We just have to decide what our next move is going to be.'

Michael shook his head. 'I don't know. I need to be with Charity. And my son. If he's . . . if he's sick. He needs me near him.'

I opened my mouth to object, but I couldn't. Michael had already risked his neck for me more than once. He'd given me a lot of good advice that I hadn't listened to. Especially about Susan. If I'd only paid more attention, told her what I felt, maybe . . .

I cut off that line of thought before the hysterical sob that rose in my throat became more than a blur of tears in my eyes. 'All right,' I said. 'I . . . thank you. For your help.'

He nodded, and looked down, as though ashamed. 'Harry. I'm sorry. I've done all that I could. But I'm not as young as I used to be. And . . . I lost the sword. Maybe I'm not the one to hold it anymore after all. Maybe this is how He is telling me that I need to be at home now. Be there for my wife, my children.'

'I know,' I said. 'It's all right. Do what you think is best.'

He touched the bandage on his forehead, lightly. 'If I had the sword, maybe I'd feel differently.' He fell quiet.

'Go on,' I said. 'Look, I'll be all right, here. The Council will probably give me some help.' If they didn't hear about the people who'd died in the fire, that is. If they heard about that, that I'd broken the First Law of Magic, they'd take my head off my neck faster than you could say 'capital offense.' 'Just go, Michael. I'll take care of Lydia.'

'All right,' he said. 'I'll . . .'

A thought occurred to me, and I didn't hear what Michael said next.

'Harry?' he asked. 'Harry, are you all right?'

'I'm having a thought,' I said. 'I . . . something feels *off* about this to me. Doesn't it to you?'

He just blinked at me.

I shook my head. 'I'll think about it. Make some notes. Try to sort this mess out.' I started toward the door. 'Come on. I'll let you out.'

Michael followed me to the door, and I had my hand on the knob when the door abruptly rattled under several rapid blows that could only loosely be construed as knocking. I shot him a glance over my shoulder, and without a word, he retreated to the fireplace and picked up the poker that had been laying against some of the logs. The tip glowed orange-red.

When a fresh barrage hammered against my door, I jerked it open, slipping to one side.

A slender figure of medium height stumbled into the room. He wore a leather jacket, jeans, tennis shoes, and a Cubs ball cap. He carried a rifle case made of black plastic, and he smelled of sweat and feminine perfume.

'You,' I snarled. I grabbed the man's shoulder before he could get his balance and spun his shoulders hard, sending him back against the wall. I drove my fist hard at his mouth, felt the bright *smack-thud* of impact on my knuckles. I grabbed the front of his jacket in both hands, and with a snarl hurled him away from the wall, to the floor of my living room.

Michael stepped forward, put his work boot on the back of the intruder's neck, and pressed the glowing tip of the poker close to his eyes.

Thomas released the rifle case and jerked his hands up, pale fingers spread. 'Jesus!' he gasped. His full lower lip had split, and was smeared with something pale and pinkish, not much like human blood. I glanced down at my knuckles, and they were smeared with the same substance. It caught the light of the fire and refracted in an opalescent sheen. 'Dresden,' Thomas stammered. 'Don't do anything hasty.'

I reached down and plucked the hat off of his head, letting his dark hair spill out and down in an unkempt mane. 'Hasty? Like, maybe, turn traitor on you all of a sudden and let a bunch of monsters eat your girlfriend?'

His eyes rolled back to Michael and then over to me. 'God, wait. It wasn't like that. You didn't see all that happened afterwards. At least shut the door and listen to me.'

I glanced over at the open doorway, and after a hesitation shut it. No sense in leaving my back open just to be contrary. 'I don't want to listen to him, Michael.'

'He's a vampire,' Michael said. 'And he betrayed us. He's probably come here to try to trick us again.'

'You think we should kill him?'

'Before he hurts someone,' Michael said. His tone was flat, disinterested. Scary, actually. I shivered a little, and drew my robe closed around me a little more tightly.

'Look, Thomas,' I said. 'I've had a really bad day, and I only woke up half an hour ago. You're adding to it.'

'We're all having a bad day, Dresden,' Thomas said. 'Bianca's people were after me all day and all night, too. I just barely got here without getting myself torn to pieces.'

'The night is young,' I said. 'Give me one good reason

why I shouldn't kill you like the lying, treacherous vampire sleaze you are?'

'Because you can trust me,' he said. 'I want to help you.'

I snorted. 'Why the hell should I believe you?'

'You shouldn't,' he said. 'Don't. I'm a good liar. One of the best. I'm not asking you to believe me. Believe the circumstances. We have a common interest.'

I scowled. 'You're kidding me.'

He shook his head, and offered me a wry smile. 'I wish I was. I thought I would get the chance to help you out once Bianca had taken her eyes off me, but she double crossed me.'

'Well, Thomas. I don't know how new you are to all of this, but Bianca is what we colloquially refer to as a 'bad guy.' They do that. That's one way you can tell they're bad guys.'

'God save me from idealists,' Thomas muttered. Michael growled, and Thomas shot him a hopeful, puppy-like smile. 'Look, both of you. They have Dresden's woman.'

I took a step forward, my heart fluttering. 'She's alive?'

'For now,' Thomas said. 'They've got Justine, too. I want her back. You want Susan back. I think we can make a deal. Work together. What do you say?'

Michael shook his head. 'He's a liar, Harry. I can tell just by being this close to him.'

'Yes, yes, yes,' Thomas said. 'I confess to it. But at the moment, it isn't a part of my agenda to lie to anyone. I just want her back.'

'Justine?'

Thomas nodded.

'So he can keep on draining the life out of her,' Michael

said. 'Harry, if we aren't going to kill him, let's at least put him out.'

'If you do,' Thomas said. 'You'll be making a huge mistake. And I swear to you, by my own stunning good looks and towering ego, that I'm not lying to you.'

'Okay,' I said to Michael. 'Kill him.'

'Wait!' Thomas shouted. 'Dresden, please. What do you want me to pay you? What do you want me to do? I don't have anywhere else to go.'

I studied Thomas's expression. He looked weary, desperate, beneath the cool facade he was barely holding onto. And beneath the fear, he looked resigned. Determined.

'Okay,' I said. 'It's all right, Michael. Let him up.'

Michael frowned. 'You sure?'

I nodded. Michael fell back from Thomas, but he kept the poker gripped loosely in one hand.

Thomas sat up, running his fingers lightly over his throat, where Michael's boot had left a dark mark, and then touched his split lip, and winced. 'Thank you,' he said, quietly. 'Look in the case.'

I glanced at the black rifle case. 'What's in it?'

'A deposit,' he said. 'A down payment, for your help.'

I quirked an eyebrow and leaned over the case. I ran my fingertips lightly over it. There was no spiny buzz of energy around it to herald a sorcerous booby trap, but a good one would be hard to notice. There was something inside, though. Something that hummed quietly, a silent vibration of power that ran through the plastic and into my hand. A vibration I recognized.

I flicked open the latches on the rifle case, fumbling in my hurry, and swung it open.

Amoracchius lay gleaming against the grey foam inside the case, unmarked from the inferno at Bianca's town house.

'Michael,' I said, quietly. I reached out and touched the blade's hilt, again. Still, it buzzed with that quiet, deep power, at once reassuring and intimidating. I withdrew my fingers.

Michael paced over to the case and leaned down, staring at the sword. His expression wavered and became difficult to read. His eyes filled with tears, and he reached a broad, scarred hand down to the weapon's hilt. He took it in hand and closed his eyes.

'It's all right,' he said. 'They didn't hurt it.' He blinked his eyes open, and looked upwards. 'I hear you.'

I glanced up toward my ceiling and said, 'I hope you meant that in a figurative sense. Because I didn't hear anything.'

Michael smiled and shook his head. 'I was weak for a while. The swords are a burden. A power, yes, but at a price. I thought that perhaps the loss of the sword was His way of telling me it was time to retire.' He ran his other hand over the twisted metal nail set into the blade at the weapon's crossguard. 'But there's still work to be done.'

I glanced up, at Thomas. 'You say they've got Susan and Justine, huh? Where?'

He licked his lips. 'The town house,' he said. 'The fire ruined the back of the house, but only the exterior. The inside was fine, and the basement was untouched.'

'All right,' I said. 'Talk.'

Thomas did, laying out facts in rapid order. After the havoc of the fire, Bianca and the Court had retreated into the mansion. Bianca had ordered the other vampires to each carry one of the helpless mortals out. One of them had brought Susan. When the police and fire crews had arrived, most of the action was over, and the fire marshal had been worked up into a lather over the deaths. He'd gone inside to speak to Bianca, and come out calm and collected, and ordered everyone to pack up and leave, that he was satisfied that it had been a terrible accident and that everything was over.

After that, the vampires had been able to relax and enjoy their 'guests.'

'I think they're turning some of them,' Thomas said. 'Bianca has the authority to allow it, now. And they lost too many in the fight and the fire. I know Mavra took a couple and took them with her when she left.'

'Left?' I asked.

Thomas nodded. 'She skipped town just after sunset, word is. Couple of hungry new mouths to feed, you know?'

'And how do you know all of this, Thomas? The last I heard, Bianca's people were trying to kill you.'

He shrugged. 'There's more to a good liar than meets the eye, Dresden. I was able to keep an eye on things for a while.'

'Okay,' I said. 'So they've got our people at the manor house. We just need to get inside, get them, and get out again.'

Thomas shook his head. 'We need something else. She's brought in mortal security. Guards with machine guns. It would be a slaughter.'

'That's the spirit,' I said, with a grim smile. 'Where in the house are they keeping the captives?'

Thomas looked at me rather blankly for a moment. Then he shook his head. 'I don't know.'

'You've known everything so far,' Michael said. 'Why are you drying up on us now?'

Thomas gave the Knight a wary look. 'I'm serious. I haven't seen any more of that house than you two.'

Michael frowned. 'Even if we do get in, we can't go blundering around checking every broom closet. We need to know about the inside of the house.'

Thomas shrugged. 'I'm sorry. I'm tapped.'

I waved a hand. 'Don't worry. We just need to talk to someone who *has* seen the inside of the house.'

'Capture a prisoner?' Michael asked. 'I don't know how much luck we'd have with that.'

I shook my head, and glanced over at the sleeping figure of Lydia, who hadn't stirred in all that time. 'We just need to talk to her. She was inside. She might have some useful insights for us, in any case. She's got a gift for it.'

'Gift?'

'Cassandra's Tears. She can see bits of the future.'

I got dressed, and we gave Lydia another hour or so. Thomas went into the bathroom to shower, while I sat out in the living room with Michael. 'What I can't figure,' I said, 'is how we managed to get out of there so easily.'

'You call that easy?' Michael said.

I grimaced. 'Maybe. I would have expected them to come after us by now. Or to have sent the Nightmare to get us.'

Michael frowned, rolling the hilt of the sword between his two hands as though it were a golf club. 'I see what you mean.' He was quiet for a minute, and then said, 'You really think the girl will be of help?'

'I hope so.'

At that moment, Lydia started coughing. I moved to

her side, and helped her drink some water. She seemed groggy, though she started to stir. 'Poor kid,' I commented to Michael.

'At least she got a little sleep. I don't think she'd had any for days.'

Michael's words froze me solid.

I started to push myself away from Lydia, but her fingers reached out and dug into the sweater I was wearing. I jerked against them, but she held me, easily, not at all moved. The pale girl opened her sunken eyes, and they were flooded with blood, all through the whites, scarlet. She smiled, slow and malicious. She spoke, and her voice came out in a low, harsh sound totally unlike her natural tones, alien and malevolent. 'You should have kept her from sleeping. Or killed her before she woke.'

Michael started to his feet. Lydia rose, and with one arm she lifted me clear of the ground, bloody eyes glaring up at me with wicked exultation. 'I've waited long enough for this,' the alien voice, that of the Nightmare, purred. 'Goodbye, wizard.' And the slender girl flung me like a baseball at the stone of my fireplace.

Some days, it just doesn't pay to get out of bed.

32

I flailed my arms and legs and watched the fireplace get closer to breaking open my head. At the last second, I saw a blur of white and pink, and then I slammed into Thomas, driving him into the stones of the fireplace. He let out a grunt, and I bounced off of him, and back to the floor, momentarily breathless. I shoved myself up to my hands and knees and looked at him. He'd wrapped a pink bath towel around his hips, but either the sheer speed of his movement or else the impact had knocked it mostly askew. His ribs jutted out on one side, oddly misshapen.

Thomas looked up at me, his face twisted into a grimace. 'I'll be all right,' he said. 'Look out.'

I looked up to find Lydia stalking toward me. 'Idiot,' she seethed at Thomas. 'What did you think you could accomplish? So be it. You just got added to the list.'

Michael slipped in between the possessed girl and me, the sword glittering in the low light of the room. 'That's far enough,' he said. 'Get back.'

I struggled back to my feet, and wheezed, 'Michael, be careful.'

Lydia let out another twisted laugh, and leaned forward, pressing her sternum against *Amoracchius's* tip. 'Oh yes, Sir Knight. Get back or what? You'll murder this poor child? I don't think so. I seem to remember, there was something about this sword not being able to draw innocent blood, wasn't there?'

Michael blinked, and darted a glance back at me. 'What?'

I got to my feet. 'This is really Lydia. It isn't a magical construct, like we saw before. The Nightmare is possessing her. Anything we do to Lydia's body, she's going to have to live with, later.'

The girl ran a hand over her breasts, beneath the taut Lycra, licking her lips and staring at Michael with bloody eyes. 'Yes. Just a sweet little innocent lamb, wandered astray. You wouldn't want to hurt her, would you, Knight?'

'Harry,' Michael said, 'how do we handle this?'

'You die,' Lydia purred. She rushed Michael, one hand reaching out to strike the sword's blade aside.

When she rushed me, I just got grabbed. But Michael had training, experience. He let the sword fall to the floor and rolled back with Lydia's rush. He grabbed her forearms as she reached for his throat, whirled, and sent her tumbling into the couch, knocking it over backwards and sending her into a sprawl on the far side.

'Keep her busy!' I shouted to him. 'I can get it out of her!' And then I rushed back into my bedroom, searching for the ingredients for an exorcism. My room was a mess. I scrambled through it, while out in the living room, Lydia screamed again. There was another thump, this one rattling the wall beside the bedroom door, and then the sounds of panting, scuffling.

'Hurry up, Harry!' Michael gasped. 'She's strong!'

'I know, I know!' I jerked open the door to my closet and started knocking things off the shelves, rather than hunt through them.

Behind the spare cans of shaving cream, I located five trick birthday candles, the kind that you can't blow out, and a five-pound bag of salt. 'Okay!' I called. 'I'm coming!'

Michael and Lydia lay on the floor, his legs wrapped around hers, while his arms pinned hers back behind her in some kind of modified full Nelson hold.

'Hold her there!' I shouted. I rushed in a circle around them, shoving back a chair and a footrest, kicking rugs and carpets aside, finally jerking the last one out from beneath Michael. Lydia fought him, twisting like an eel and screaming at the top of her lungs.

I tore open the salt and ran about the pair of them, dumping it out into a white mound in a circle. Then I ran about again, setting the candles down, piling up enough salt around them to keep them from being turned over. Lydia saw what I was doing and screamed again, redoubling her efforts.

'*Flickum bicus!*' I shouted, shoving a hurried effort of will into the little spell. The effort made me dizzy for a moment, but the candles burst to light, the circle of candles and salt gathering power.

I rose, reaching out my right hand and feeding more energy into the circle, setting it up in a spinning vortex winding about the three beings inside it – Lydia, Michael, and the Nightmare. Energy gathered in the circle, spinning around, whirling magic down into the earth, grounding and dispersing it. I could almost see the Nightmare clutching tighter to Lydia, holding on. All I needed was the right move to stun the Nightmare, to lock it up for a second, so that the exorcism could sweep it away.

'Azorthragal!' I shouted, bellowing out the demon's name. 'Azorthragal! Azorthragal!' I stretched out my right hand again, concentrating fiercely. 'Begone!'

Energy rushed out of my body as I completed the spell, swept toward the Nightmare within Lydia like a wave lifting a sleeping seal off a rock—

—and passed over, leaving it untouched.

Lydia began to laugh wildly, and managed to catch one of Michael's hands in hers. She gave a twist, and bones snapped with sharp pops and crackles. Michael let out an agonized scream, twisting and jerking. He knocked the circle of salt askew, and Lydia escaped him, rising to face me.

'Such a *fool*, wizard,' she said. I didn't banter. I didn't even stand there, stunned that my spell had failed so miserably. I wound back a hand and threw a punch at her as hard as I could, hoping to stun the body the demon was riding in, to keep it from reacting.

The possessed Lydia glided from the path of my punch, caught my wrist, and dumped me onto my back. I started to push myself up, but she threw herself astride me, and slammed my head back against the floor, twice. I saw stars.

Lydia stretched above me, purring, and thrusting her hips down against mine. I tried to escape during the moment of gloating, but my arms and legs just didn't respond. She reached down, laying both of her hands almost delicately on my throat, and murmured, 'Such a shame. All this time, and you didn't even know who it was after you. You didn't even know who else wanted revenge.'

'I guess sometimes you find out the hard way,' I slurred.

'Sometimes,' Lydia agreed, smiling And then her hands closed over my throat, and I didn't have any more air.

Sometimes, when you're facing death, it feels like everything slows down. Everything stands out sharply in detail, almost freezes. You can see it all, feel it all, as though your brain has decided, in sheer defiance, to seize the last few moments of life and to squeeze them for every bit of living left.

My brain did that, but instead of showing me my trashed apartment and how I really needed a new coat of paint on the ceiling, it started frantically shoving puzzle pieces together. Lydia. The shadow demon. Mavra. The torment spells. Bianca.

One thing stood out in my mind, a piece that didn't fit anywhere. Susan had been gone for a day or two, where I had barely been able to talk to her. She'd said she was working on something. That something was happening. It fit, somehow, somewhere.

Stars swam in my vision and fire started to spread through my lungs. I struggled to pry her arms off of me, but it was no use — possessed, she was simply too strong to deal with.

Susan had been asking me about something, some insignificant part of the phone conversation we had, between sexual innuendos. What had it been?

I heard myself making a very slight sound, something like, 'Gaghk. Aghk.' I tried to lever Lydia's weight up and off of me, but she simply rolled with me, taking my weight onto her and then continuing the motion, slamming me to the floor again. My vision began to darken, though I opened my eyes wide. It was like staring down a dark tunnel, looking up at Lydia's blood-filled eyes.

I saw Michael struggle to his knees, his face white as a fresh dusting of snow. He moved toward Lydia, but she turned her head slightly and kicked him, lashing out with one heel. I heard something else snap as the force of the kick drove Michael back.

Murphy had been distracted about something, too. Something she'd hurriedly changed subjects on. Intuition drew a line between them. And then an equal sign.

And then I had it: the last piece of the puzzle. I knew what had happened, where the Nightmare had come from, why it was after me, in particular. I knew how to stop it, knew what its limits were, how Bianca had enlisted it, and why my spells had been so hard-pressed to affect it.

Almost a pity, really. I'd figured things out just in time to die.

Vision faded altogether.

And a moment later, so did the pain in my throat.

Instead of drifting off into whatever lay beyond, though, I sucked in a breath of air, choking and gasping. My vision became red for a moment, as blood rushed back through my head, and then started to clear.

Lydia still crouched over me, up on her knees, straddling me – but she'd released my throat. Instead, she had arched her arms up and back, over her head, to caress Thomas's naked shoulders.

The vampire had pressed up against Lydia's back. His mouth nuzzled her throat, slow kisses, strokes of his tongue that made the girl shudder and quiver. His hands roamed slowly over her body, always touching skin, fingers roaming up beneath the brief Lycra top to caress her breasts. Lydia gasped, blood-filled eyes distant, unfocused, body responding with a slow, sensual grace.

Thomas looked past her, through the dark fall of his hair, to me. His eyes weren't blue-grey anymore. They were empty, white, no color to them at all. I felt cold coming off of him, something I sensed more than felt on my skin, a horrible and seductive cold. He continued, spreading a line of kisses up Lydia's neck, to her ear, making her whimper and shake.

I swallowed, and crawled back on my elbows, dragging my hips and legs out from beneath the pair of them.

Thomas murmured, so softly that I wasn't sure I'd heard him. 'I don't know how long I can distract her, Dresden. Quit gawking and do something. I'll put on afternoon theater for you later, if you want to watch that bad.' Then his mouth covered the girl's, and she stiffened, eyes flying open wide before they languidly closed, deepening the kiss.

I flushed at Thomas's words, which made my head pound painfully. I rooted around the floor and recovered the candles, still lit, and the bag of salt. I spread the salt in a circle around Lydia and Thomas, as Lydia drew the Lycra shorts down and reached back to grasp at Thomas, to urge him toward her.

Thomas let out a groan of pure anguish and said, 'Dresden. *Hurry.*'

I settled the candles into place and gathered up whatever power I had left to close the circle and to begin the vortex again. If I was right, I would free Lydia, maybe permanently. If I was wrong, this was the last of my energy, and I'd dump it into the earth for nothing. The Nightmare would presumably kill us — and I didn't think any of us were in shape to do anything about it.

Energy gathered in the circle, rising in a growing whirl of invisible, tingling power. I stretched out my hand and willed more energy into it, feeling dizzy.

The Nightmare finally seemed to take notice of what was around it again. Lydia shivered and leaned a little away from Thomas, breaking some of the contact between them

– then the bloodred eyes snapped open, and focused on me. Lydia began to rise, but Thomas clutched onto her hard, holding her.

The power rose again, a second vortex whirling around the pair of them, tugging at spiritual energies within. Lydia screamed.

'Leonid Kravos!' I thundered. I repeated the name, and saw Lydia's eyes fly open wide in shock. 'Begone, Kravos! You secondrate firecaller! Begone! Begone!' And with the last word, I stamped my foot down, releasing the power of the exorcism down, into the earth.

Lydia screamed, her body arching, her mouth dropping open wide. Within the whirling vortex, glittering motes of silver and gold light gathered into a funnel, centered on Lydia's gaping mouth. Scarlet energy flooded out of her screaming mouth, and for a moment there was an unnerving overlap of screams – one high-pitched, young, feminine, terrified, while the other was inhuman, otherworldly. More scarlet light lashed forth from Lydia's eyes, stolen away by the vortex's power.

And then with a rush and an implosion of suddenly empty air, the vortex swirled into an infinitely thin line and vanished, dropping down into the floor, lower, deep into the earth.

Lydia let out a low, exhausted cry, and dropped limply to the floor. Thomas, still clutching her, tumbled down with her. Silence fell on the room, but for the four of us, gasping for breath.

Finally, I managed to sit up. 'Michael,' I called, my voice hoarse. 'Michael. Are you okay?'

'Did you stop it?' he asked. 'Is the girl all right?'

'I think so.'

'Thank God,' he said. 'It kicked me, got one of my ribs. I'm not sure I can sit up.'

'Don't,' I said, and mopped sweat from my brow. 'Broken ribs could be bad. Thomas? Are you— Hey! What the hell do you think you're doing?'

Thomas lay with his arms around Lydia, his pale, naked body pressed against hers, his lips nuzzling her ear. Lydia's eyes were open, colored naturally again, but not focused on anything. She didn't look conscious, but she was making tiny, aroused motions of her body, her hips, leaning back to him. Thomas blinked up at me when I spoke, eyes still empty and white.

'What?' he asked. 'She's not unwilling. She's probably just grateful to me, for my help.'

'Get away from her,' I snapped.

'I'm *hungry*,' he said. 'It won't kill her, Dresden. Not the first time. You'd be dead right now without me. Just let me—'

'No,' I said.

'But—'

'No. Get off of her, or you and I are going to have words.'

A snarl split the air between us, Thomas's full lips peeling back from his teeth. They looked like human teeth, not vampire fangs. Whiter and more perfect than human teeth, but other than that, normal.

I returned his stare coolly.

Thomas looked away first. He closed his eyes for a moment, and when he opened them again, there were pale rings of color in them once more, slowly darkening. He released Lydia and rolled away from her. His ribs still looked dented, but not as much as before. He got to his feet and wrapped the towel around his hips again, then stalked back toward the bathroom without another word.

I checked Lydia's pulse, blushed, and tugged her shorts back into place. Then I righted the couch and put her back onto it, beneath the blankets. After that, I went to Michael.

'What was that all about?' he asked.

I told him what had happened, in terms as PG rated as possible. He scowled, flicking a glance back toward the bathroom. 'They're like that. The White Court. Seducers. They feed on lust, fear, hatred. Emotions. But they always use lust to seduce their victims. They can force them to feel it, indulge in sex. It's how they feed.'

'Sex vampires, I know,' I muttered. 'Still. It's interesting.'

'Interesting?' Michael sounded skeptical. 'Harry, I wouldn't call it *interesting*.'

'Why not?' I said. I squinted after Thomas, thoughtfully. 'Whatever he used, it worked on the Nightmare. Caught it up. That means that it's either some kind of ambient magic, maybe that cold I felt, that works on everything around, or else it's something chemical – like Red Court venom. Something that got to Lydia's body and bypassed the Nightmare's control of her mind, altogether. Pheromones, maybe.'

'Harry,' Michael said, 'I really don't mean to discourage your scholarly pursuits, but would you mind, very much, helping me with these broken ribs.'

We took inventory. I had some nasty bruises on my throat, but nothing more. Michael had one rib that was definitely broken, and one more than might have been cracked, tender as it was. I got him wrapped up pretty well. Thomas came out of my room, dressed in some of my spare jogging clothes. They hung off of him, and he had to roll the sleeves and legs of the sweatpants up. He slouched into a chair, his gaze settling on Lydia's sleeping form with a rather disconcerting intensity.

'It all fits now,' I told them. 'I know what's going on, so I can finally do something about it. I'm going to go to the town house, and get everyone out.'

Michael frowned at me. 'What fits?'

'It wasn't the demon that crossed over, Michael. We were never fighting the demon. It was Kravos himself. Kravos is the Nightmare.'

Michael blinked at me. 'But we didn't kill Kravos. He's still alive.'

'Dollars to donuts he isn't. I figure the night before the Nightmare's attacks started, he puts together a ritual and takes himself out.'

'Why would he do that?'

'To come back as a ghost. To get revenge. Think about it – that's all the Nightmare has been doing. It's been rampaging around, avenging Kravos.'

'Could he *do* that?' Michael asked.

I shrugged. 'I don't see why he couldn't, if he had raised a bunch of power, and if he was focused on getting his vengeance and turning himself into a ghost. Especially . . .'

'. . . with the border to the Nevernever as turbulent as it was,' Michael finished.

'Exactly. Which means that Mavra and Bianca helped him out, specifically. Hell, they probably put together the ritual that he used. And if someone in federal custody here in Chicago suddenly turned up suicided in his cell, it would cause a big stir in local police — and would be serious news for the media. Which is why Murphy was being so hush-hush, and Susan was so distracted. She was working on a story, finding out what happened. Following up a rumor, maybe.'

Thomas frowned. 'Let me get this straight. This Nightmare is the ghost of the sorcerer Kravos. The cult murderer in the news several months ago.'

'Yeah. The turbulence in the Nevernever let him get made into a badass ghost.'

'Turbulence?' Thomas said.

I nodded. 'Someone began binding the local spooks with torment spells. They went wild and started stirring the border between the real world and the Nevernever. I figure it was Mavra, working with Bianca. That same turbulence let Kravos hit everyone he could in their dreams. It's how he got to me, and how he got to poor Malone, and how he got to Lydia just now. Lydia knew what he was doing. That's why she never wanted to go to sleep. I didn't see it coming, when he hit me in my dreams. I wasn't ready for a fight, and he kicked my ass.'

'But now you can defeat him?' Michael asked.

'I'm ready for him now. I beat this punk when he was alive. Now that I know what I'm dealing with, I can do it to his shade, too. I'll go to the house, take out the Nightmare, Bianca if I have to, and get everyone out.'

'Did you get hit on the head when I wasn't looking?' Thomas asked. 'Dresden, I told you about the guards. The machine guns. I did mention the machine guns, didn't I?'

I waved a band. 'I'm already past the point where a sane man would be afraid. Guards and machine guns, whatever. Look, Bianca has Susan, plus Justine, and maybe twenty or thirty kids being held captive, or getting set to get turned into fresh vampires. The police's hands are tied on this. Someone has to do something, and I'm the only one in a position to—'

'Get riddled with bullets,' Thomas interjected, his tone dry. 'My, how very helpful that will be toward attaining our mutual goals.'

'Oh ye of little faith,' Michael said, from his place in my easychair. He swung his head back toward me. 'Go ahead, Harry. What do you have in mind?'

I nodded. 'All right. I figure Bianca will have security all over the outside of the house. She'll cover all the approaches to it, any cars that go in are going to get searched, and so on.'

'Exactly,' Thomas said. 'Dresden, I thought maybe we could pool our resources. Work something out with our contacts and spies. Perhaps disguise ourselves as caterers and sneak in.' He paused. 'Well. *You* could pass for a caterer, in any case. But if we simply assault her house, we'll all be killed.'

'If we walk up where they can see us.'

Thomas frowned. 'You have something else in mind? I doubt we could veil ourselves with magic. In familiar surroundings, she's going to be difficult to fool with those kinds of glamour.'

I lifted an eyebrow at the vampire. 'You're right. I had something else in mind.'

I came through the rift between the mortal world and the Nevernever last. I bore my staff and rod, and wore my leather duster, my shield bracelet and a copper ring upon my left hand matched by another upon my right.

The Nevernever, near my apartment, looked like . . . my apartment. Only a bit cleaner and brighter. Deep philosophical statement about the spirituality of my little basement? Maybe. Shapes moved in the shadows, scurrying like rats, or gliding over the floor like snakes – spirit-beings that fed on the crumbs of energy that spilled over from my place in the real world.

Michael bore *Amoracchius* in his hand, its blade glowing with a pearly luminescence. As soon as he had picked up the blade, his face had regained color, and he had moved as though his bandaged ribs no longer pained him. He wore denim and flannel and his steel-toed work boots.

Thomas, dressed in my castoffs and carrying an aluminum baseball bat from my closet, looked about the place, amused, his dark hair still damp and curling wetly over his shoulders.

In a sack made of fishnet, Bob's skull hung from my fist, the orange skull-lights glowing dimly, like candles. 'Harry,' Bob asked. 'Are you sure about this? I mean, I don't really want to get caught in the Nevernever if I can avoid it. A few old misunderstandings, you see.'

'You aren't any more worried about it than I am. If my godmother catches me here, I've had it. Take it easy, Bob,' I said. 'Just guide us through the shortest path to Bianca's place. Then I tear a hole back over to our side, into her basement, we get everyone and get them out again, and bring them home.'

'There is no shortest path, Harry,' Bob said. 'This is the spirit world. Things are linked together by concepts and ideas and don't necessarily adhere to physical distance like—'

'I know the basics, Bob,' I told him. 'But the bottom

line is that you know your way around here a lot better than I do. Get us there.'

Bob sighed. 'All right. But I can't guarantee we'll be in and out before sundown. You might not even be able to make a hole through, while the sun's still up. It tends to diffuse magical energies that—'

'Bob. Save the lecture for later. Leave the wizarding to me.'

The skull swung around to Michael and Thomas. 'Excuse me. Have either of you told Harry what a brainless plan this is?'

Thomas raised his hand. 'I did. It didn't do much good.'

Bob rolled his eyelights. 'It never does. So help me, Dresden, if you die I'm going to be very annoyed. You'll probably roll me under a rock at the last minute, and I'll be stuck there for ten thousand years until someone finds me.'

'Don't tempt me. Less talk, more guide.'

'Sí, memsahib,' Bob said, seriously. Thomas snickered. Bob turned his eyelights toward the stairs leading out of the Nevernever version of my apartment. 'That way,' he said.

We passed out of the apartment, and into a sort of vague representation of Chicago, which looked like a stage set – flat building faces with no real substance to them, vague light that could have come from sun or moon or streetlights, plus a haze of grey-brown fog. From there, Bob guided us down a sidewalk, then turned into an alley, and opened a garage door, which led to a stone-carved staircase, winding down into the earth.

We followed his lead, into the darkness. At times, the only light we had was the orange glow of the skull's eyelights. Bob turned his head in the direction required, and we passed through a subterranean region that was mostly blackness and low ceilings, eventually rising up a slope that emerged in the center of a ring of standing dolmens atop a long hill. Stars shone overhead in a fierce blaze, and lights danced in the woods at the base of the hill, skittering around like manic fireflies.

I stiffened in my boots. 'Bob,' I said. 'Bob. You blew it, man. This is Faerie.'

'Of course it is,' Bob said. 'It's the biggest place *in* the Nevernever. You can't get to anywhere without crossing through Faerie at one place or another.'

'Well hurry up and cross us out,' I said. 'We can't stay here.'

'Believe me, I don't want to hang here, either. Either we get the Disney version of Faerie, with elves and tinker-bell pixies and who knows what sugary cuteness, or we get the wicked witch version, which is considerably more entertaining, but less healthy.'

'Even the Summer Court isn't all sweetness and light. Bob, shut up. Which way?'

The skull turned mutely toward what seemed to be the westernmost side of the hill, and we descended down it.

'It's like a park,' Thomas commented. 'I mean, the grass should be over our knees. Or no, maybe like a good golf course.'

'Harry,' Michael said, quietly. 'I'm getting a bad feeling.'

The skin on my neck started to crawl, and I looked back to Michael, nodding. 'Bob, which way out?'

Bob nodded ahead, as we rounded a stand of trees.

An old, colonial-style covered bridge arched up over a ridiculously deep chasm. 'There,' Bob said. 'That's the border. Where you're wanting isn't too far past that.'

In the distance, came the notes of a hunting horn, dark and clear – and the baying of hounds.

'Run for the bridge,' I snapped. Thomas sprinted beside me without apparent effort. I glanced at Michael, who had reversed his grip on the sword and held it pommel-first, the blade laying against his forearm as he ran. His face was twisted up in effort and pain, but he kept pace.

'Harry,' Bob commented. 'If it's all the same, you might want to run a bit faster. There's a hunt coming.'

The horn belled again, backed up by the dolmens, and the cries of the pack rang out sharp and clear. Thomas whirled to look, running a few paces backward, before turning again. 'I could have sworn they were miles away a moment ago.'

'It's the Nevernever,' I panted. 'Distance, time. It's all fucked up here.'

'Wow,' Bob commented. 'I hadn't realized that they *grew* hellhounds that big. And look, Harry, it's your godmother! Hi, Lea!'

If Bob had a body, he'd have been jumping up and down and waving his fingers at her. 'Don't be so enthusiastic, Bob. If she catches me, I get to join the pack.'

Bob's eyelights swung toward me and he gulped. 'Oh,' he said. 'There's been a falling out, then. Or a falling further out, at any rate, since you weren't on such great terms to begin with.'

'Something like that,' I panted.

'Um. Run,' Bob said. 'Run faster. You really need to run faster, Harry.'

My feet flew over the grass.

Thomas reached the bridge first, his feet thumping out onto it. Michael got there a pace later. With a broken rib and twenty years on me, he still outran me to that damn bridge. I've got to work out more.

'Made it!' I shouted, taking a last long step toward the bridge.

The lariat hit me about the throat before my feet had quite touched down, and jerked me back through the air with a snap. I lay on the ground, stunned, choking for the second time in two hours.

'Uh-oh,' Bob said. 'Harry. Whatever you do, don't drop me. Especially under a rock.'

'Thanks a lot,' I gasped, reaching up to jerk the rope from its constricting hold on my throat.

Heavy hooves sank into the turf on either side of my head. I gulped, and looked up at a night-black steed with black and silver tack. Its hooves were shod with bladed shoes of some silvery metal. It wasn't iron or steel. There was blood on those shoes, as though the horse had trampled some poor, trapped thing to death. Or else sliced it apart.

My gaze slid on up past the horse, to its rider. Lea rode the beast sidesaddle, perfectly relaxed and confident, wearing a dress of sable and midnight blue, her hair caught back in a loose braid of flame. Her eyes gleamed in the starlight, the other end of the lariat held in one lovely hand. The hellhounds crowded around her steed, all of

them focused on yours truly. Call it a wild impression of
the moment, but they looked hungry.

'Feeling better, are we?' Lea asked, with a slow smile.
'That's wonderful. We can finally conclude our bargain.'

33

It only takes a couple of these rough little episodes of life to teach a man a certain amount of cynicism. Once a rogue wizard or three has tried to end your life, or some berserk hexenwolves have worked really hard to have your throat torn out, you start to expect the worst. In fact, if the worst doesn't happen, you find yourself somewhat disappointed.

So really, it was just as well that Godmother had caught up to me, in spite of my best efforts to avoid her. I'd hate to find out that the universe really wasn't conspiring against me. It would jerk the rug out from under my persecution complex.

Therefore, working on the assumption that some sadistic higher power would make sure my evening got as complicated as it possibly could, I had formed a plan.

I jerked the lariat from about my throat and croaked, 'Thomas, Michael. Now.'

The pair of them produced small cardboard boxes from their pockets, palm-sized and almost square. With a shake, Michael cast the contents of the first box forward, slewing the box left and right, like a man scattering seeds. Thomas followed his lead, on the other side of my body, so that objects began to rain down atop and nearby me.

The faerie hounds let out startled yelps and leapt away. My godmother's horse let out a scream and pranced back several steps, putting distance between us.

I scrunched up my face and did my best to shield my

eyes from the scattering nails. They fell over me in a sharp-toothed shower, prickling as they struck, and settled around me. Godmother had to let out on the rope that had looped about my throat as her horse backed away, giving me a bit of slack.

'Iron,' hissed my godmother. Her lovely face turned livid, furious. 'You *dare* defile the Awnsidhe soil with iron! The Queen will rip your eyes from your skull!'

'No,' Thomas said. 'They're aluminum. No iron content. That's a lovely horse you have. What's its name?'

Lea's eyes flashed to Thomas, and then at the nails all over the ground. While she did, I dipped a hand into my pocket, palmed my contingency plan, and popped it into my mouth. Two or three chews and a swallow and I was finished.

I tried not to let the abrupt surge of terror show.

'Not steel?' Lea said. She beckoned sharply at the ground, and one of the nails leapt up to her hand. She gripped it, frowning, her expression abruptly wary. 'What is the meaning of this?'

'It's meant to be a distraction, Godmother,' I said. I coughed, and patted my chest. 'I just had to eat something.'

Lea laid a hand on her horse's neck, and the savage beast calmed. One of the shadowy hounds nosed forward, nudging one of the nails with its snout. Lea gave the rope a little jerk, taking up the slack again, and said, 'It will do you no good, wizard. You cannot escape this rope. It is bound to hold you. You cannot escape my power. Not here, not in Faerie. I am too strong for you.'

'All true,' I agreed, and got to my feet. 'So let's get cracking. Turn me into a doggie and show me which trees I can pee on.'

Lea stared at me as though I'd gone mad, her expression wary.

I took hold of the rope and shook it impatiently. 'Come on, Godmother. Make with the magic already. Do I get to pick my color? I don't think I want to be that charcoal grey. Maybe you could do a nice sandy pelt for me. Or oh, I know, winter white. With blue eyes, I always wanted blue eyes, and—'

'Be silent!' Lea snarled, and shook the rope. There was a sharp, stinging sensation, and my tongue literally stuck to the roof of my mouth. I tried to keep talking, but it made my throat buzz as though bees were in it, angry, stinging. I kept silent.

'Well,' Thomas said. 'I'd like to see this. I've never seen an external transformation before. Do proceed, madame.' He waved his hand impatiently. 'Dog him, already!'

'This is a trick,' Lea hissed. 'It will avail you naught, wizard. No matter what hidden powers your friends are preparing to cast at me—'

'We're not,' Michael put in. 'I swear it on the Blood of Christ.'

Lea sucked in a breath, as though the words had brought a sudden chill over her. She rode the horse up to me, close, so that the animal's shoulder pressed against mine. She reeled in on the braided leather of the lariat as she did, until she held it by a length of no more than six inches, jerking hard against my throat, hauling me almost off balance. She leaned down close to me and whispered, 'Tell me, wizard. What are you hiding from me?'

My tongue loosened again, and I cleared my throat. 'Oh. Nothing much. I just wanted a bite to eat before we left.'

'A bite,' Lea murmured. Then she jerked me over toward her and leaned down close, dainty nostrils flaring. She inhaled, slow, the silken mass of her hair brushing against my cheek, her mouth almost nuzzling mine.

I watched her face, her expression changing to slow surprise. I spoke to her in a quiet voice. 'You recognize the smell, yes?'

The whites showed around her emerald eyes as they opened wider. 'Destroying Angel,' she whispered. 'You have taken death, Harry Dresden.'

'Yep,' I agreed. 'Toadstool. *Amanita virosa*. Whatever. The amantin toxin is going to show up in my blood in about two minutes. After that, it will start tearing apart my kidneys and liver. A few hours from now, I'll collapse, and if I don't die then, then I'll apparently recover for a few days while my innards fall apart, and then drop into arrest and die.' I smiled. 'There's no specific antidote for it. And I kind of doubt even you could use magic to put me back together again. Stitching closed a wound is a lot different from major internal transmutation. So, shall we?' I started walking in the direction Lea had come from. 'You should be able to enjoy tormenting me for a few hours before I start vomiting blood and die.'

She jerked the lariat tight, halting me. 'This is a trick,' she hissed. 'You are lying to me.'

I looked up at her with a lopsided grin. 'Now, Godmother,' I said. 'You know I'm a terrible liar. Do you think I could really lie to you? Do you not smell it yourself?'

She stared at me, her face twisting slowly into an expression of horror. 'Merciless winds,' she breathed. 'You have gone mad.'

'Not mad,' I assured her. 'I know precisely what I'm doing.' I turned to glance back at the bridge. 'Goodbye Michael. Goodbye Thomas.'

'Harry,' Michael said. 'Are you sure we shouldn't—'

'Shhh,' I said, shooting him a look. 'Ixnay.'

Lea's eyes flickered back and forth between us. 'What?' she demanded. 'What is it?'

I rolled my eyes, and gestured at Michael.

'Well,' Michael said. 'As it happens, I have something here that might help.'

'Something?' Lea demanded. 'What?'

Michael reached into the pocket of his jacket and produced a small vial, capped at one end. 'It's extract of St Mary's Thistle,' he said. 'They use it in a lot of hospitals in Europe, for mushroom poisoning. Theoretically, it should do quite a bit to help a poisoning victim survive. Provided it's taken in time, of course.'

Lea's eyes narrowed. 'Give it to me. Now.'

I *tsked*. 'Godmother. As your faithful pet and companion, I feel I should warn you about how *dangerous* it is for one of the high sidhe to accept gifts. It could bind you to the giver if you don't return a gift in kind.'

Lea's face slowly flushed scarlet, sweeping up from the creamy skin of her collarbones and throat over her chin and cheeks and up into her hair. 'So,' she said. 'You would drive a bargain with me. You would take deadly toadstool to force me to release you.'

I lifted my eyebrows and nodded, with a smile. 'Essentially, yes. You see, I figure it's like this. You want me alive. I'm not of any use to you dead. And you won't be able to undo the poisoning with magic.'

'I *own* you,' she snarled. 'You are *mine* now.'

'Beg to differ,' I said. 'I'm yours for the next couple of days. After that, I'm dead, and I won't be doing you any more good.'

'No,' she said. 'I will not set you free in exchange for this potion. I too can find the thistle.'

'Maybe,' I admitted. 'Maybe you can even do it in time. Maybe not. Either way, without a trip to the hospital, there's not much chance of me living, even with the extract. And none at all, really, if I don't get it soon.'

'I will not trade you away! You have given yourself to me!'

Michael shrugged one shoulder. 'I believe that you wrought a bargain with a foolish young man caught in the heat of the moment. But we aren't asking you to undo it altogether.'

Lea frowned. 'No?'

'Naturally not,' Thomas said. 'The extract only offers Harry a chance at life. That's all we'd ask from you. You'd be obliged to let him go – and bound for a year and a day to do no harm to him or his freedom so long as he remains in the mortal world.'

'That's the deal,' I said. 'As a faithful pet, I should point something out: If I die, you *never* get me, Godmother. If you let me go now, you can always give it a shot another night. It isn't as though you have a limited number of them, is it. You can afford to be patient.'

Lea fell silent, staring at me. The night fell silent as well. We all waited, saying nothing. The quiet panic I already felt, after eating the toadstool, danced about my belly, making it twitch and jerk.

'Why?' she said, finally, her voice very quiet, pitched

only for me. 'Why would you do this to yourself, Harry? I don't understand.'

'I didn't think you would,' I said. 'There are people who need me. People who are in danger because of me. I have to help them.'

'You cannot help them if you are dead.'

'Nor if I am taken by you.'

'You would give your own life in place of theirs?' she asked, her tone incredulous.

'Yes.'

'Why?'

'Because no one else can do this. They need me. I owe it to them.'

'Owe them your life,' Lea mused. 'You are mad, Harry Dresden. Perhaps it comes of your mother.'

I frowned. 'What's that supposed to mean?'

Lea shrugged. 'She spoke as you do. Near the end.' She lifted her eyes to Michael and straightened on the horse. 'A dangerous play, you made tonight, wizard. A bold play. You cut the traditions of my people very close to the bone. I accept your bargain.'

And then, with a casual flick, she removed the lariat from me. I stumbled back, away from her, gathered up my fallen staff and rod, and Bob in his net sack, and made my way to the bridge. Once there, Michael gave me the vial. I unstoppered it and drank. The liquid within tasted gritty, a little bitter. I closed my eyes and took a deep breath, after swallowing it down.

'Harry,' Michael said, watching Lea. 'Are you sure you'll be all right?'

'If I get to the hospital soon,' I said. 'I've got some-where between six and eighteen hours. Maybe a little longer. I drank all that pink stuff before we left to line my stomach. It might slow down the rate of digestion on the mushroom, give the extract a chance to beat it to my guts.'

'I don't like this,' Michael muttered.

'Hey. I'm the one who ate the deadly poison, man. I don't much care for it myself.'

Thomas blinked at me. 'You mean, you were telling her the truth?'

I glanced at him, nodding. 'Yeah. Look, I figure we'll be in there and out again in an hour, tops. Or else we'll be dead. Either way, it will happen in plenty of time before the first round of symptoms sets in.'

Thomas just stared at me for a moment. 'I thought you were lying,' he said. 'Bluffing.'

'I don't bluff if I can help it. I'm not too good at it.'

'So you really could die. Your godmother is right, you know. You are mad as a hatter. Nutty as a fruitcake.'

'Crazy like a fox,' I said. 'All right. Bob, wake up.' I shook the skull, and its empty eye sockets kindled with orange-red lights, somehow too far back inside them.

'Harry?' Bob said, surprised. 'You're alive.'

'For a while,' I said. I explained to him how we'd gotten me away from my godmother.

'Wow,' Bob said. 'You're dying. What a great plan.'

I grimaced. 'The hospital should be able to take care of it.'

'Sure, sure. In some places, the survival rate is as high as fifty percent, in the case of amantin poisoning.'

'I took extract of milk thistle,' I said, a little defensive.

Bob coughed, delicately. 'I hope you got the dosage right, or it could do more harm than good. Now, if you'd come to me about this to begin with—'

'Harry,' Michael said, sharply. 'Look.'

I turned to look at my godmother, who had ridden a little way off and sat still upon her dark steed. She raised in her hand something dark and gleaming, maybe a knife. She waved it to the four corners, north, west, south, east. She said something in a twisting, slippery tongue, and the trees began to moan as the wind rose, washing through them. Power washed out from the sidhe sorceress, from the dark knife in her hand, and raised the hairs on my arms, the nape of my neck.

'Wizard!' she called to me. 'You have made bargain with me tonight. I will not seek you. But you have made no such bargain with others.' She threw back her head in a long, loud cry, somehow terrifying and beautiful at once. It echoed over the rolling land, and then was answered. More sounds came drifting back, high-pitched howls, whistling shrieks, and deep, throaty coughing roars.

'Many there are who owe me,' Lea sneered. 'I will not be cheated of you. You have had the potion. You would not have placed your life in such jeopardy without a cure to hand. I will raise no hand against you – but they will bring you to me. One way or another, Harry Dresden, you will be mine this night.'

The wind continued to rise, and overhead sudden clouds began to blot out the stars. The howls and calls came closer, carried on the rising wind.

'Shit,' I said. 'Bob, we have to get out of here. Now.'

'It's still a pretty good walk to the spot you showed me on the map,' Bob said. 'A mile, maybe two, in subjective terms.'

'Two miles,' Michael noted, clinically. 'I can't run that far. Not with my ribs like they are.'

'And I can't carry you,' Thomas said. 'I'm amazing and studly, but I have limits. Let's go, Harry. It's just me and you.'

My mind raced, and I struggled to put together a plan. Michael couldn't keep up. He had managed the sprint before, but his face looked a little greyish, now, and he carried himself stiffly, as though in pain. I trusted Michael. I trusted him at my side, and at my back. I trusted him to be able to take care of himself.

But alone, against a wrathful faerie posse, how would he do? I couldn't be sure – even with the sword, he was still a man. He could still lose his life. And I didn't want another life on my conscience.

I glanced over at Thomas. The handsome vampire managed to wear my castoff clothes and make them look like some kind of fashion statement. Slouch nouveau. He returned my glance with a perfect, shining smile, and I thought about what he had said, about what a good liar he was. Thomas had sided with me. Mostly. He'd been friendly enough. He even, apparently, had every reason to want to help me and work with me to get Justine back.

Unless he was lying to me. Unless she hadn't been taken at all.

I couldn't trust him.

'The two of you are staying here,' I said. 'Hold the bridge. You won't have to do it for long. Just slow them down. Make them go around.'

'Oooo,' Bob said. 'Good plan. That should make it a real pain for them. Harry. I mean, until they kill Michael and Thomas and come after you. But that could take minutes! Hours, even!'

I glanced at the skull, and then at Michael. He shot Thomas a look, and then nodded to me.

'If there's trouble, you'll need me to protect you,' Thomas objected.

'I can watch out for myself,' I told him. 'Look, this whole plan is based on surprise and speed and quiet. I can be quiet better alone. If it turns out that fighting has to be done, one or two people wouldn't make a difference. If we have to fight, this whole thing is over.'

Thomas grimaced. 'So you want us to stay here and die for you, is that it?'

I glared. 'Hold the bridge until I can make it out of the Nevernever. After that, they shouldn't have any reason to come after you.'

The wind rose to a howl, and shapes began to crest the top of the hill with the dolmens, dark things, moving swift and close to the ground.

'Harry, go,' Michael said. He took *Amoracchius* into his hands. 'Don't worry. We'll keep them off of your back.'

'Are you sure you wouldn't rather I come with you?' Thomas asked, and took a step toward me. The shining steel of Michael's sword abruptly dropped in front of Thomas, the sharp edge of it pressing against his belly.

'I'm sure I'd rather not leave him alone with you, vampire,' Michael said, his tone polite. 'Do I make myself clear?'

'As water,' Thomas said, sourly. He glanced at me and said, 'You'd better not leave her there, Dresden. Or get killed.'

'I won't,' I said. 'Especially that second part.'

And then the first monstrous thing, like a mountain lion made all of shadows, bounded past Lea, and a set of

dark talons flashed toward me. Thomas shoved me out of
the way of the strike, crying out as the thing tore into his
arm. Michael shouted in Latin, and his sword flared into
argent light, cutting the vaguely catlike beast and dropping it into two squirming, struggling halves to the floor
of the bridge.

'Go!' Michael roared. 'God go with you!'

I ran.

The sounds of fighting died behind me, until I could
only hear my own laboring breaths. The Nevernever
changed, from sculpted, faerie-tale wilderness to dark, close
forest, with cobwebs hanging down across a narrow trail
through glowering trees. Eyes flashed in the shadows,
things that never quite could be clearly seen, and I stumbled on.

'There!' Bob called. His orange eyelights swung to shine
upon the split trunk of a dead, hollow tree. 'Open a way
there, and it will take us through!'

I grunted, and came to a halt, gasping. 'Are you sure?'

'Yes, yes!' Bob said. 'Hurry! Some of the awnsidhe will
be here at any moment!'

I cast a fearful glance behind me, and then started gathering in my will. It hurt to do. I felt so weak. The poison
in my belly hadn't started tearing my body apart yet, but
I almost thought that I could feel it stirring, moving,
licking its chops and eyeing my organs with malevolent
glee. I shoved all of that out of my thoughts, and forced
myself to breathe steadily, to gather in my strength and
reach out to part the curtain between worlds.

'Uh, Harry,' Bob said suddenly. 'Wait a minute.'

Behind me, something broke a branch. There was a
swift, rushing sound, of something moving toward me. I

ignored it and reached out a hand, sinking my fingers into the friable border substance of the Nevernever.

'Harry!' Bob said. 'I really think you should hear this!'

'Not now,' I muttered.

The rushing noise grew closer, the rattle of undergrowth shunted aside by something large. Behind me, a warbling bellow shook the ground. Holy brillig and slithy toves, Batman.

'*Aparturum!*' I shouted, thrusting out with my will and opening a way. The rent in reality shone with dim light.

I threw myself forward into it, willing the way closed behind me. Something snagged at one corner of my leather duster, but with a jerk I was free of it and through.

I tumbled forward, onto the floor, the smell of autumn air and damp stone all around me. My heart thudded painfully with the effort of both the running and the spell. I lifted my head to look around me and get my bearings.

Bob had been good to his word. He had brought me out of the Nevernever right into Bianca's mansion. I found myself on the floor at the head of a staircase down, away from the front doors and the main hall.

I also found myself surrounded by a ring of vampires, all of them in their inhuman forms, the flesh masks gone. There had to be a dozen of them there, dark eyes glittering, their noses snuffling, drool spattering out and dripping from their bared fangs to the floor while their talons clawed at the air or ran lightly over their flabby black bodies. Some of them showed burns on their rubbery hide, patches of shrunken, wrinkled, scar-like tissue.

I didn't move. Anything, I sensed, would have set them off. Any motion, any move to flee or fight or escape would have ignited a frenzy, with myself on the receiving end.

While I watched, frozen, Bianca came up the stairs dressed in a white silk nightgown that whispered around her shapely calves. She carried a single candle that bathed her in soft radiance. She smiled at me, very slowly, very sweetly, and the bottom dropped out of my stomach.

'Well,' she purred. 'Harry Dresden. Such a pleasant surprise to have you visit.'

'I tried to tell you,' Bob said, his voice miserable. 'The curtain felt weak there. Like someone had just gone through it. Like they had been watching this side.'

'Of course,' Bianca murmured. 'A guard for every door. Did you think me a fool, Mister Dresden?'

I glowered at her, despairing. There wasn't anything I could say. I saved my breath, and began to draw in my will, to throw everything I had left into taking that smug smile off of her pretty, false face.

'Dears,' Bianca purred, watching me. 'Bring him down.'

They hit me so fast that I never saw them move. There simply came a hideous, rushing force. I have memories of being passed from claw to claw, thrown, carried into the air, toyed with. Snuffling, squashed snouts, and staring black eyes, and hissing, terrible laughter.

I was driven down, carried, tossed about, everything torn from me, Bob disappearing without a sound. They pressed me down while I struggled and screamed, all useless, my mind too full of terror to focus, to defend myself.

And there, in the dark, they tore my clothes from me. I felt Bianca press her naked flesh to me, a heated, sinuous dream-body that unraveled into a nightmare. I felt the skin split and burst apart around her true form. The sweetness of her perfume gave way to a rotten-fruit reek. Her purring voice became a whining hiss.

And their tongues. Soft, intimate, warm, moist. Pleasure that struck me like hammers while I tried to scream against it. Chemical pleasure, animal sensation, heartless and cold, uncaring of my horror, revulsion, despair.

Darkness. Horrible, thick, sensual darkness.

Then pain.

Then nothing.

34

I have very few memories of my father. I was about six years old when he died. What I do remember is a careworn, slightly stoop-shouldered man with kind eyes and strong hands. He was a magician – not a wizard, a stage magician. A good one. He never made it big, though. He spent too much time performing for children's hospitals and orphanages to pull down much money. He and I and his little show roamed around the country. The memories of the first several years of my life are of my bed in the backseat of the station wagon, going to sleep to the whisper of asphalt beneath the tires, secure in the knowledge that my father was awake, driving the car, and there to take care of me.

The nightmares hadn't started until just before his death. I don't remember them, specifically – but I remember waking up, screaming in a child's high-pitched shriek of terror. I'd scream in the darkness, scrambling to squeeze into the smallest space I could find. My father would come looking for me, and find me, and pull me into his lap. He would hold me, and make me warm, and soon I would fall asleep again, safe, secure.

'The monsters can't get you here, Harry,' he used to say. 'They can't get you.'

He'd been right.

Until now. Until tonight.

The monsters got me.

I don't know where real life left off and the nightmares began, but I thrashed myself awake, screaming a scratchy, hollow scream that made little more noise than a whimper. I screamed until I ran out of breath, and then all I could do was sob.

I lay there, naked, undone. No one came to hold me. No one came to make it all better. No one had, really, since my dad died.

Breathing first, then. I forced myself to control it, to stop the wracking sobs and to draw in slow, steady breaths. Next came the terror. The pain. Humiliation. More than anything, I wanted to crawl into a hole and pull it in after me. I wanted to be not.

But I wasn't not. I hurt too much. I was very painfully, very acutely, very much alive.

The burn still hurt the most, but the sweeping nausea running through me came in a photo finish second. My hands told me that I was lying upon a floor, but the rest of me thought I had been strapped into a giant gyroscope. I ached. My throat felt tight, and burned, as though seared by some hot liquid or chemical. I didn't want to dwell too long on that.

I tested my limbs, and found them all present and functional. My belly twisted and roiled, and for a moment locked up tight, jerking me into a tight curl around it.

The sweat on my naked body went cold. The mushroom. The poison. Six to eighteen hours. Maybe a little more.

I felt thick, dry mouthed, fuzzy with the same aftereffects of the vampire venom that I'd felt before.

For a minute, I stopped fighting. I just lay there, weak and thirsty and hurting and sick, curled up into a ball. I would have started crying again if I'd had that much feeling left in me. I would have wept and waited to die.

Instead, some merciless, steady voice in my head drove me to open my eyes. I hesitated, afraid. I didn't want to open my eyes and see nothing. I didn't want to find myself in that same darkness. That darkness, with hissing things all around me. Maybe there, still, just waiting for me to awaken so that they—

Panic swept me for a moment, and gave me enough strength to shiver and push myself up into a sitting position. I took a deep breath, and opened my eyes.

I could see. Light seared at my eyes, a thin line of it surrounding a tall rectangle – a doorway. I had to squint for a moment, so used were my eyes to the darkness.

I looked around the room, wary. It wasn't big. Maybe twelve by twelve, or a little more. I lay in a corner. The smell was violently rotten. My jailors, apparently, had no problems with letting me lie in my own filth. Some of it had crusted onto me, onto my legs and arms. Vomit, I guessed. There was blood in it. An early symptom of the mushroom poisoning.

There were other shapes in the dimness. A lump of cloth in one corner, like a pile of dirty laundry. Several laundry baskets, as well. A washer and dryer, on the far wall from the door.

And Justine, dressed in as little as I, curled up and sitting with her back to the wall, her arms wrapped loosely around her drawn-up knees, watching me with dark, feverish eyes.

'You're awake,' Justine said. 'I didn't think you'd ever wake up.'

Gone was the glamorous girl I'd seen at the ball. Her hair hung lank and greasy. Her pale body looked lean, almost gaunt, and her limbs, what I could see of them, were stained and dirty, as was her face.

Her eyes disturbed me. There was something feral in them, something unsettling. I didn't look at her for too long. Even as bad off as I was, I had enough presence of mind to not want to look into her eyes.

'I'm not crazy,' she said, her voice sharp, edged. 'I know what you're thinking.'

I had to cough before I could talk, and it made pains shoot through my belly again. 'That wasn't what I was thinking.'

'Of course it wasn't,' the girl snarled. She rose, all lean grace and tension, and stalked toward me. 'I *know* what you were thinking. That they'd shut you in here with that stupid little *whore.*'

'No,' I said. 'I . . . that isn't what—'

She hissed like a cat, and raked her nails across my face, scoring my cheek in three lines of fire. I cried out and fell back, the wall interrupting my retreat.

'I can always tell, when I'm like this,' Justine said. She gave me an abruptly careless look, turned on the balls of her feet and walked several feet away before stretching and dropping to all fours, watching me with an absent, disinterested gaze.

I stared at her for a moment, feeling the heat of the blood welling in the scratches. I touched a finger to them, and it came away sprinkled with scarlet. I lifted my gaze to the girl and shook my head. 'I'm sorry,' I said. 'God. What did they do to you?'

'This,' she said, carelessly, thrusting out one hand.

Round, bruised punctures marked her wrist. 'And this.' She held out the other wrist, showing another set of marks. 'And this.' She stretched out her thigh to one side of her body, parallel to the floor, to show more marks, along it. 'They all wanted a little taste. So they got it.'

'I don't understand,' I said.

She smiled with too many teeth, and it made me uneasy. 'They didn't do anything. I'm like this. This is the way I always am.'

'Um,' I said. 'You weren't that way last night.'

'Last night,' she snapped. 'Two nights ago. At least. That was because *he* was there.'

'Thomas?'

Her lower lip abruptly trembled, and she looked as though she might cry. 'Yes. Yes, Thomas. He makes it quieter. Inside me, there's so much trying to get out, like at the hospital. Control, they said. I don't have the kind of control other people have. It's hormones, but the drugs only made me sick. He doesn't, though. Only a little tired.'

'But—'

Her face darkened again. 'Shut *up*,' she snapped. 'But, but, but. Idiot, asking idiot questions. Fool who did not want me when I was willing to give. Nothing does that. None of them, because they all want to take, take, take.'

I nodded, and didn't say anything, as she became more agitated. It might have been politically incorrect of me, but the word LOONY all but appeared in a giant neon sign over Justine's head. 'Okay,' I said. 'Just . . . let's just take it easy, all right?'

She glowered at me, falling silent. Then she slunk back to the space between the wall and the washing machine and sank into it. She started playing with her hair, and took no apparent notice of me.

I got up. It was hard. Everything spun around. On the floor, I found a dusty towel. I used it to sweep some of the grime off of my skin.

I went to the door and tried it. It stood firmly locked. I tested my weight against it, but the effort made a sudden fire of scarlet flash through my belly and I dropped to the floor, convulsing again. I threw up in the middle of it, and tasted blood on my mouth.

I lay exhausted for a while after that, and might have dropped off to sleep again. I looked up to find Justine holding the towel, and pushing it fitfully at my skin, the fresh mess.

'How long,' I managed to ask her. 'How long have I been here?'

She shrugged, without looking up. 'They had you for a while. Just outside this door. I heard them taking you. Playing with you, for two hours, maybe. And then they put you in here. I slept. I woke. Maybe another ten hours. Or less. Or more. I don't know.'

I kept an arm wrapped around my belly, grimacing, and nodded. 'All right,' I said. 'We have to get out of here.'

She brayed out a sharp laugh. 'There is no out of here. This is the larder. The Christmas turkey doesn't get up and walk away.'

I shook my head. 'I . . . I was poisoned. If I don't get to a hospital, I'm going to die.'

She smiled again, and played with her hair, dropping the towel. 'Almost everyone dies in a hospital. You'd get to be someplace different. Isn't that better?'

'It's one of those things I could live without,' I said.

Justine's expression went slack, her eyes distant, and she became still.

I stared at her, waved my hand in front of her eyes. Snapped my fingers. She didn't respond.

I sighed and stood up, then tested the door again. It was firmly bolted shut from the other side. I couldn't move it.

'Super.' I sighed. 'That's great. I'm never going to get out of here.'

Behind me, something whispered. I spun, putting the door at my back, searching for the source of the sound.

A low mist crept out of the wall, a smoky, slithery mass that whirled itself down onto the floor like ethereal lace. The mist touched lightly at my blood on the floor where I'd thrown up, and then began to swirl and shape itself into something vaguely human.

'Great,' I muttered. 'More ghosts. If I get out of this alive, I've got to get a new job.'

The ghost took shape before me, very slowly, very translucently. It resolved itself into the form of a young woman, attractive, dressed like an efficient secretary. Her hair was pulled up into a bun, but for a few appealing tendrils that fell down to frame her cheeks. Her ghostly wrist was crusted with congealed blood, spread around a pair of fang-punctures. Abruptly, I recognized her, the girl Bianca had fed upon until she died.

'Rachel,' I whispered. 'Rachel, is that you?'

As I spoke her name, she turned to me, her eyes slowly focusing on me, as though beholding me through a misty veil. Her expression turned, no pun intended, grave. She nodded to me in recognition.

'Hell's bells,' I whispered. 'No wonder Bianca got stuck on a vengeance kick. She literally was haunted by your death.'

The spirit's face twisted in distress. She said something, but I could hear it only as a distant, muffled sound accompanying the movement of her lips.

'I can't understand you,' I said. 'Rachel, I can't hear you.'

She almost wept, it seemed. She pressed her hand to her ghostly breast, and grimaced at me.

'You're hurt?' I guessed. 'You hurt?'

She shook her head. Then touched her temple and drew her fingers slowly down over her eyes, closing them. 'Ah,' I said. 'You're tired.'

She nodded. She made a supplicating motion, holding out her hands as though asking for help.

'I don't know what I can do for you. I don't know if I can help you rest or not.'

She shook her head again. Then she nodded, toward the door, and made a bottle-shaped curving gesture of her hands.

'Bianca?' I asked. When she nodded, I went on. 'You think Bianca can lay you to rest.' She shook her head. 'She's keeping you here?'

Rachel nodded, her ghostly, pretty face agonized.

'Makes sense,' I muttered. 'Bianca fixates on you as you die tragically. Binds your ghost here. The ghost appears to her and drives her into a vengeance, and she blames it all on me.'

Rachel's ghost nodded.

'I didn't kill you,' I said. 'You know that.'

She nodded again.

'But I'm sorry. I'm sorry that me being in the wrong place at the wrong time set you up to die.'

She gave me a gentle smile – which transformed into a sudden expression of horror. She looked past me, at Justine, and then her image began to fade, to withdraw into the wall.

'Hey!' I said. 'Hey, wait a minute!'

The mist vanished, and Justine started to move. She rose, casually, and stretched. Then glanced down at herself and ran her hands appreciatively down over her breasts, her stomach. 'Very nice,' she said, voice subtly altered, different. 'Rather like Lydia, in a lot of ways, isn't she, Mister Dresden.'

I tensed up. 'Kravos,' I whispered.

Justine's eyes flooded with blood through the whites. 'Oh yes,' she said. 'Yes indeed.'

'Man, you need to get a life in the worst way. That was you, wasn't it. The telephone call the night Agatha Hagglethorn went nuts.'

'My last call,' Kravos said through Justine's lips, nodding. 'I wanted to savor what was about to happen. Like now. Bianca has ordered that you should receive no visitors, but I just couldn't resist the chance to take a look at you.'

'You want to look at me?' I asked. I tapped my head. 'Come on in. There's a few things in here I'd like to show you.'

Justine smiled, and shook her head. 'It would be too much effort for too little return. Even without the shelter of a threshold, possessing even a mind so weak as this child's requires a considerable amount of effort. Effort,' she added, 'which was made possible by a grant from the Harry Dresden Soul Foundation.'

I bared my teeth. 'Leave the girl alone.'

'Oh, but she's fine,' Kravos said, through Justine's lips. 'She's really happier like this. She can't hurt anyone, you see. Or herself. Her ranting emotions can't compel her to act. That's why the Whites love her so much. They feed on emotion, and this little darling is positively mad with it.' Justine's body shivered, and arched sensuously. 'It's rather exciting, actually. Madness.'

'I wouldn't know,' I said. 'Look, if we're going to fight, let's fight. Otherwise, blow. I've got things to do.'

'I know,' Justine said. 'You're busy dying of some kind of poisoning. The vampires tried to drink from you, but you made some of them very sick, and so they left you more or less untapped. Highly miffed, Bianca was. She wanted you to die as food for her and her new children.'

'What a shame.'

'Come now, Dresden. You and I are among the Wise. We both know you wouldn't want to die at the hands of a lesser being.'

'I might rank among the wise,' I said. 'You, Kravos, are nothing but a two-bit troublemaker. You're the stupid thug of wizard land, and that you managed to live as long as you did without killing yourself is some kind of miracle in itself.'

Justine snarled and lunged for me. She pinned me to the door with one hand and a casual, supernatural strength that told me she could have pushed her hand *through* me just as easily. 'So self-righteous,' she snarled. 'Always sure that you're right. That you're in command. That you have all the power and all the answers.'

I grimaced. Pain flared through my belly again, and it was suddenly all I could do not to scream.

'Well, Dresden. You're dead. You've been slated to die. You'll be gone in the next few hours. And even if you aren't, if you live through what they have planned, the poison will kill you slowly. And before you go you'll sleep. Bianca won't stop me, this time. You'll sleep and I'll be there. I'll come into your dreams and I will make your last moments on earth a nightmare that lasts for years.' She leaned up close, standing on tiptoe, and spat into my face. Then the blood rushed from Justine's eyes and her head fell loosely forward, as though she'd been a horse struggling against the reins, to find their pressure gone. Justine let out a whimper, and sank against me.

I did my best to hold her. We sort of wound up on the floor together, neither one of us in much shape to move. Justine wept. She cried piteously, like a small child, mostly quiet.

'I'm sorry,' she said. 'I'm sorry. I want to help. But there's too much in the way. I can't think—'

'Shhhhh,' I said. I tried to stroke her hair, to soothe her before she could become agitated again. 'It's going to be all right.'

'We'll die,' she whispered. 'I'll never see him again.'

She wept for some time, as the nausea and pain in my belly grew. The light outside the door never wavered. It didn't know if it was dark or light outside. Or if Thomas and Michael were still alive to come after me. If they were gone, and it was my fault, I'd never be able to live with myself in any case.

I decided that it must be night. It must be fullest, darkest night. No other time of day could possibly suit my predicament.

I rested my head on Justine's, after she fell quiet, and

relaxed, as though she were falling asleep after her weeping. I closed my eyes and struggled to come up with a plan. But I didn't have anything. Nothing. It was all but over.

Something stirred, in the shadows where the laundry was piled.

Both of us looked up. I started to push Justine away, but she said, 'Don't. Don't go over there.'

'Why not?' I asked.

'You won't like it.'

I glanced at the girl. And then got up, unsteadily, and made my way over to the piled laundry. I clutched the towel in my hand, for lack of any other weapon.

Someone lay in the piled clothing. Someone in a white shirt, a dark skirt, and a red cloak.

'Stars above,' I swore. 'Susan.'

She groaned, faintly, as though very much asleep or drugged. I hunkered down and moved clothing off of her. 'Hell's bells. Susan, don't try to sit up. Don't move. Let me see if you're hurt, okay?'

I ran my hands over her in the dimness. She seemed to be whole, not bleeding, but her skin was blazing with fever.

'I'm dizzy. Thirsty,' she said.

'You've got a fever. Can you roll over here toward me?'

'The light. It hurts my eyes.'

'It did mine too, when I woke up. It will pass.'

'Don't,' Justine whispered. She sat on her heels and rocked slowly back and forth. 'You won't like it. You won't like it.'

I glanced back at Justine as Susan turned toward me, and then looked down at my girlfriend. She looked back up to me, her features exhausted, confused. She blinked her eyes against the light, and lifted a slim, brown hand to shield her face.

I caught her hand halfway, and stared down at her.

Her eyes were black. All black. Black and staring, glittering, darker than pitch, with no white to them at all to distinguish them as human. My heart leapt up into my throat, and things began to spin faster around me.

'You won't like it,' Justine intoned. 'They changed her. The Red Court changed her. Bianca changed her.'

'Dresden?' Susan whispered.

Dear God, I thought. This can't be happening.

'Mister Dresden? I'm so thirsty.'

35

Susan let out a whimper and a groan, moving fitfully. By chance, her mouth brushed against my forearm, still stained with drying blood. She froze, completely, her whole body shuddering. She looked up at me with those dark, huge eyes, her face twisting with need. She moved toward my arm again, and I jerked it back from her mouth.

'Susan,' I said. 'Wait.'

'What was that?' she whispered. 'That was good.' She shivered again and rolled to all fours, eyes slowly focusing on me.

I shot a glance toward Justine, but only saw her feet as she pulled them back to her, slipping back into the tiny space between the washing machine and the wall. I turned back to Susan, who was coming toward me, staring as though blind, on all fours.

I backed away from her, and fumbled out to my side with one hand. I found the bloodstained towel I'd been using before, and threw it at her. She stopped for a moment, staring, and then lowered her face with a groan, beginning to lick at the towel.

I scooted back on all fours, getting away from her, still dizzy. 'Justine,' I hissed. 'What do we do?'

'There's nothing to do,' Justine whispered. 'We can't get out. She isn't herself. Once she kills, she'll be gone.'

I flashed a glance at her over my shoulder. 'Once she kills? What do you mean?'

Justine watched me with solemn eyes. 'Once she kills. She's different. But she isn't quite like them until it's complete. Until she's killed someone feeding on them. That's the way the Reds work.'

'So she's still Susan?'

Justine shrugged again, her expression disinterested. 'Sort of.'

'If I could talk to her, though. Get through to her. We could maybe snap her out of it?'

'I've never heard of it happening,' Justine said. She shivered. 'They stay like that. It gets worse and worse. Then they lose control and kill. And it's over.'

I bit my lip. 'There's got to be something.'

'Kill her. She's still weak. Maybe we could, together. If we wait until she's further gone, until the hunger gives her strength, she'll take us both. That's why we're in here.'

'No,' I said. 'I can't hurt her.'

Something flickered in Justine's face when I spoke, though I couldn't decide whether it was something warm or something heated, angry. She closed her eyes and said, 'Then maybe when she drinks you she'll die of the poison in you.'

'Dammit. There's got to be something. Something else you can tell me.'

Justine shrugged and shook her head, wearily. 'We're already dead, Mister Dresden.'

I clenched my teeth together and turned back to Susan. She kept licking at the towel, making frustrated, whimpering noises. She lifted her face to me and stared at me. I could have sworn I saw the bones of her cheeks and jaw stand out more harshly against her skin. Her eyes became drowning deep and pulled at me, beckoned to me to look deeper into that spinning, feverish darkness.

I jerked my eyes away before that gaze could trap me, my heart pounding, but it had already begun to fall away. Susan furrowed her brow in confusion for a moment, blinking her eyes, whatever dark power that had touched them fading, slipping unsteadily.

But even if that gaze hadn't trapped me, hadn't gone all the way over into hypnosis, it made something occur to me: Susan's memories of the soulgaze hadn't been removed. My godmother couldn't have touched those. I was such an idiot. When a mortal looks on something with the Sight, really *looks*, as a wizard may, the memories of what he sees are indelibly imprinted on him. And when a wizard looks into a person's eyes, it's just another way of using the Sight. A two-way use of it, because the person you look at gets to peer back at you, too.

Susan and I had soulgazed more than two years before. She'd tricked me into it. It was just after that she began pursuing me for stories more closely.

Lea couldn't have taken memories around a soulgaze. But she could have covered them up, somehow, misted them over. No practical difference, for the average person.

But, hell, I'm a wizard. I ain't average.

Susan and I had always been close, since we'd started dating. Intimate time together. The sharing of words, ideas, time, bodies. And that kind of intimacy creates a bond. A bond that I could perhaps use, to uncover fogged memories. To help bring Susan back to herself.

'Susan,' I said, forcing my voice out sharp and clear. 'Susan Rodriguez.'

She shivered as I Named her, at least in part.

I licked my lips and moved towards her. 'Susan. I want to help you. All right? I want to help you if I can.'

She swallowed another whimper. 'But. I'm so thirsty. I can't.'

I reached out as I approached her, and plucked a hair from her head. She didn't react to it, though she leaned closer to me, inhaling through her nose, letting out a slow moan on the exhale. She could smell my blood. I wasn't clear on how much of the toxin would be in my bloodstream, but I didn't want her to be hurt. No time to dawdle, Harry.

I took the hair and wound it about my right hand. It went around twice. I closed my fist over it, then grimaced, reaching out to grab Susan's left hand. I spat on my fingers and smoothed them over her palm, then pressed her hand to my fist. The bond, already something tenuously felt in any case, thrummed to life like a bass cello string, amplified by my spit upon her, by the hair in my own hands, the joining of our bodies where our flesh pressed together.

I closed my eyes. It hurt to try to draw in the magic. My weakened body shook. I reached for it, tried to piece together my will. I thought of all the times I'd had with Susan, all the things I'd never had the guts to tell her. I thought of her laugh, her smile, the way her mouth felt on mine, the smell of her shampoo in the shower, the press of her warmth against my back as we slept. I summoned up every memory I had of us together, and started trying to push it through the link between us.

The memories flowed down my arm, to her hand – and stopped, pressing against some misty and elastic barrier. Godmother's spell. I shoved harder at it, but its resistance only grew greater, more intense, the harder I pushed.

Susan whimpered, the sound lost, confused, hungry. She rose up onto her knees and pressed against me, leaning on me. She snuggled her mouth down against the hollow of my throat. I felt her tongue touch my skin, sending an electric jolt of lust flashing through me. Even close to death, hormones will out, I guess.

I kept struggling against Godmother's spell, but it held in place, powerful, subtle. I felt like a child shoving fruitlessly at a heavy glass door.

Susan shivered, and kept licking at my throat.

My skin tingled pleasantly and then started to go numb. Some of my pain faded. Then I felt her teeth against my throat, sharp as she bit at me.

I let out a startled cry. It wasn't a hard bite. She'd bitten me harder than that for fun. But she hadn't had eyes like that then. Her kisses hadn't made my skin go narcotic-numb then. She hadn't been halfway to membership in Club Vampire then.

I pushed harder at the spell, but my best efforts grew weaker and weaker. Susan bit harder, and I felt her body tensing, growing stronger. No longer did she lean against me. I felt one of her hands settle on the back of my neck. It wasn't an affectionate gesture. It was to keep me from moving. She took a deep, shuddering breath.

'In here,' she whispered. 'It's in here. It's good.'

'Susan,' I said, keeping the feeble pressure on my godmother's spell. 'Susan. Please don't. Don't go. I need you here. You could hurt yourself. Please.' I felt her jaws begin to close. Her teeth didn't feel like fangs, but human teeth can rip open skin just fine. She was vanishing. I could feel the link between us fading, growing weaker and weaker.

'I'm so sorry. I never meant to let you down.' I said. I sagged against her. There wasn't much reason to keep fighting. But I did anyway. For her, if not for me. I held onto that link, to the pressure I had forced against the spell, to the memories of Susan and me, together.

'I love you.'

Why it worked right then, why the webbing of my godmother's spell frayed as though the words had been an open flame, I don't know. I haven't found any explanation for it. There aren't any magical words, really. The words just hold the magic. They give it a shape and a form, they make it useful, describe the images within.

I'll say this, though: Some words have a power that has nothing to do with supernatural forces. They resound in the heart and mind, they live long after the sounds of them have died away, they echo in the heart and the soul. They have power, and that power is very real.

Those three words are good ones.

I flooded into her, through the link, into the darkness and the confusion that bound her, and I saw, through her thoughts, that my coming was a flame in the endless cold, a beacon flashing out against that night. The light came, our memories, the warmth of us, she and I, and battered down the walls inside her, crushed away Lea's lingering spell, tore those memories away from my godmother, wherever she was, and brought them back home.

I heard her cry out at the sudden flush of memory, as awareness washed over her. She changed, right there against me – the hard, alien tension changed. It didn't vanish, but it changed. It became Susan's tension, Susan's confusion, Susan's pain, aware, alert, and very much herself again.

The power of the spell faded away, leaving only the blurred impression of it, like lightning that crackles through the night, leaving dazzling colors in the darkness behind.

I found myself kneeling against her, holding her hand. She still held my head. Her teeth still pressed against my throat, sharp and hard.

I reached up with my other shaking hand, and stroked at her hair. 'Susan,' I said, gentle. 'Susan. Stay with me.'

The pressure lessened. I felt hot tears fall against my shoulder.

'Harry,' she whispered. 'Oh, God. I'm so thirsty. I want it so much.'

I closed my eyes. 'I know,' I said. 'I'm sorry.'

'I could take you. I could take it,' she whispered.

'Yes.'

'You couldn't stop me. You're weak, sick.'

'I couldn't stop you,' I agreed.

'Say it again.'

I frowned. 'What?'

'Say it again. It helps. Please. It's so hard not to . . .'

I swallowed. 'I love you,' I said.

She jerked, as though I'd punched her in the pit of the stomach.

'I love you,' I said again. 'Susan.'

She lifted her mouth from my skin, and looked up, into my eyes. They were her eyes again – dark, rich, warm brown, bloodshot, filled with tears. 'The vampires,' she said. 'They—'

'I know.'

She closed her eyes, more tears falling. 'I tr-tried to stop them. I tried.'

Pain hit me again, pain that didn't have anything to do with poison or injuries. It hit me sharp and low, just beneath my heart, as though someone had just shoved an icicle through me. 'I know you did,' I told her. 'I know you did.'

She fell against me, weeping. I held her.

After a long time, she whispered, 'It's still there. It isn't going away.'

'I know.'

'What am I going to do?'

'We'll work on that,' I said. 'I promise. We have other problems right now.' I filled her in on what had happened, holding her in the dimness.

'Is anyone coming for us?' she asked.

'I . . . I don't think so. Even if Thomas and Michael got away, they couldn't storm this place. If they ever even got out of the Nevernever. Michael could go to Murphy, but she couldn't just smash her way in here without a warrant. And Bianca's contacts could probably stall that for a while.'

'We have to get you out of here,' she said. 'You've got to get to a hospital.'

'Works in theory. Now we just have to work out the details.'

She licked her lips. 'I . . . can you even walk?'

'I don't know. That last spell. If there was much left in me, that spell took it out.'

'What if you slept?' she asked.

'Kravos would have his chance to torture me.' I paused, and stared at the far wall.

'God,' Susan whispered. She hugged me, gently. 'I love you, Harry. You should get to hear it t—' She stopped, and looked up at me. 'What?'

'That's it,' I said. 'That's what needs to happen.'

'What needs to happen? I don't understand.'

The more I thought about it, the crazier it sounded. But it might work. If I could time it just right . . .

I looked down, taking Susan's shoulders in my hands, staring at her eyes. 'Can you hold on? Can you keep it together for another few hours?'

She shivered. 'I think so. I'll try.'

'Good,' I said. I took a deep breath. 'Because I need to be asleep long enough to start dreaming.'

'But Kravos,' Susan said. 'Kravos will get inside of you. He'll kill you.'

'Yeah,' I said. I took a slow breath. 'I'm pretty much counting on it.'

36

My nightmares came quickly, dull cloud of poisonous confusion blurring my senses, distorting my perceptions. For a moment, I was hanging by one wrist over an inferno of fire, smoke, and horrible creatures, the steel of the handcuffs suspending me cutting into my flesh, drawing blood. Smoke smothered me, forced me to cough, and my vision blurred as I started to fade out.

Then I was in a new place. In the dark. Cold stone chilled me where I lay upon it. All around me where the whispers of things moving in the shadows. Scaly rasps. Soft, hungry hisses, together with the gleam of malevolent eyes. My heart pounded in my throat.

'There you are,' whispered one of the voices. 'I watched them have you, you know.'

I sat up, shivering violently. 'Yeah, well. That's why they call them monsters. It's what they do.'

'They enjoyed it,' came the whispering voice. 'If only I could have videotaped it for you.'

'TV will rot your brain, Kravos,' I said.

Something blurred out of the darkness and struck me across the face. The blow drove me back and down. My vision blurred over with scarlet and my perceptions sharpened through a burst of pain, but I didn't drop unconscious. You don't, as a rule, in dreams.

'Jokes,' the voice hissed. 'Jokes will not save you now.'

'Hell's bells, Kravos,' I muttered, sitting up again. 'Do

they produce a *Cliched Lines Textbook for Villains* or something? Go for broke. Tell me that since you're going to
kill me anyway, you might as well reveal your secret plan.'

The dark blurred toward me again. I didn't bother
trying to defend myself. It drove me to the ground, and
sat on my chest.

I stared up at Kravos. Forms and shapes hung about
him like misty clothes. I could see the shape of the shadow
demon, around him. I could see my own face, drifting
among the layers. I saw Justine there, and Lydia. And
there, at the center of that distorted, drifting mass, I saw
Kravos.

He didn't look much different. He had a thin, pinched
face, and brown hair faded with grey. He wore a full,
untrimmed beard, but it only made his head seem
misshapen. He had wide, leathery shoulders, and symbols
painted in blood, ritual things whose meanings I could
vaguely piece together, covered his chest. He lifted his
hands and delivered two more blows to my face, explo-
sions of pain.

'Where are your gibes now, wizard?' Kravos snarled.
'Where are your jokes? Weak, petty, self-righteous fool.
We are going to have a very good time together, until
Bianca comes to finish you.'

'You think so?' I asked. 'I'm not sure. It's our first date.
Maybe we should take this one step at a time.'

Kravos hit me again, across the bridge of my nose, and
my vision blurred with tears. 'You aren't funny!' he
shouted. 'You are going to *die*! You can't treat this as a
joke!'

'Why not?' I shot back. 'Kravos, I took you out with
a piece of chalk and a Ken doll. You're the biggest joke

of a spellslinger I've ever seen. Even I didn't expect you to drop like that; maybe the link with that doll worked so well because it was anatomically corr—'

I didn't get the chance to finish the sentence. Kravos screamed and took my dream self by the throat. It felt real. It felt completely as though he had me, his weight pinning my weakened body down, his fingers crushing into my windpipe. My head pounded. I struggled against him, futile and reflexive motions – but to no avail. He kept on choking me, the pressure increasing. Blackness covered my dream vision, and I knew that he would hold it until he was sure I was dead.

People who have near-death experiences often talk about moving toward the light at the end of the tunnel. Or ascending toward the light, or flying or floating, or falling. I didn't get that. I'm not sure what that says about the state of my soul. There was no light, no kindly beckoning voice, no lake of fire to fall into. There was only silence, deep and timeless, where not even the beating of my heart thudded in my ears. I felt an odd pressure against my skin, my face, as though I had pressed into and through a wall of plastic wrap.

I felt a dull thud on top of my chest, and a sudden lessening of the burning in my lungs. Then another thud. More easing on my lungs. Then more blows to my chest.

My heart lurched back into motion with a hesitant thunder, and I felt myself take a wheezing breath. The plastic-wrap sensation tugged at me for a moment, then lifted away.

I shuddered, and struggled to open my eyes again. When I did, Kravos, still holding my throat, blinked his eyes in shock. 'No!' he snarled. 'You're dead! You're dead!'

'Susan's giving his real body CPR,' someone said, behind him. Kravos whipped his head around to look, just in time to catch a stiff cross to the tip of his chin. He cried out in startled fear, and fell off of me.

I sucked in another labored breath and sat up. 'Hell's bells,' I gasped. 'It worked.'

Kravos struggled to his feet and backed away, staring, his eyes flying open wide as they looked back and forth between me and my savior.

My savior was me, too. Or rather, something that looked a very great deal like me. It was my shape and coloring, and had bruises and scratches, mixed with a few burns, all over it. Its hair was a wild mess, its eyes sunken over circles of black in a pale, sickly face.

My double peered at me and said, 'You know. We really look like hell.'

'What's this?' hissed Kravos. 'What trick is this?'

I offered myself a hand up, so I took it. It took me a moment to balance, but I said, 'Hell, Kravos. As flexible as the boundaries between here and the spirit world have been, I would have expected you to figure it out by now.'

Kravos looked at the two of us, and bared his teeth. 'Your ghost,' he hissed.

'Technically,' my ghost said. 'Harry actually died for a minute. Don't you remember how ghosts are made? Normally, there wouldn't be enough latent energy to create an impression like me, but with him being a wizard – a real wizard, not a petty fake like you – and with the border to the Nevernever in such a state of flux, it was pretty much inevitable.'

'That was very well said,' I told my ghost.

'Just be glad your theory worked. I wouldn't be very good at this, solo.'

'Well, thank Kravos here. It was him and Bianca and Mavra who stirred things up enough to make this possible.' We looked at Kravos. 'You aren't getting to sneak attack me while I'm doped unconscious, bub. It isn't going to be like last time. Any questions?'

Kravos hurled himself at me in a fury. He overpowered me, and bore down on me, far too strong for me to overcome directly. I thrust a thumb into his eye. He screamed and bit at my hand.

And then my ghost came in. He wrapped his arms around Kravos's neck and leaned back, hard, tugging the man's body into a bow. Kravos strained and struggled, his arms flailing, strong as any maddened beast. My ghost was a little stronger than I, but he wouldn't be able to hold Kravos for long.

'Harry!' my ghost shouted. 'Now!'

I gripped Kravos by the throat, letting all the frustration and fury inside well up. I held up my left hand, and my dream self's nails lengthened into glittering claws. Kravos stared at me in shock.

'You think you're the only one who can play in dreams, Kravos? If I'd been ready for you the last time, you'd have never been able to do to me what you did.' My face twisted, mouth extending into a muzzle. 'This time I'm ready. You're in my dream, now. And I'm taking back what's mine.'

I tore into his guts. I ripped him open with my claws and wolfed into his vitals, just as he had to me. Bits of him flew free, dream-blood splashing, dream-vitals steaming.

I tore and worried and gulped down bloody meat. He

screamed and fought, but he couldn't get away. I tore him to pieces and devoured him, the blood a hot, sweet rush on my tongue, his ghost-flesh hot and good, easing the ache of emptiness inside of me.

I ate him all up.

As I did, I felt power, surety, confidence, all rushing back into me. My stolen magic came raging back into me, filling me like silver lightning, a tingling, almost painful rush as I took back what was mine.

But I didn't stop there. My ghost fell away as I kept going. Kept tearing Kravos apart and gulping down the pieces. I got to his own power when I ate his heart – red, livid power, vital and primitive and dangerous. Kravos's magic had been for nothing but causing harm.

I took it. I had plenty of harm to start causing.

By the time I'd finished tearing him to shreds, the pieces were vanishing like the remnants of any foul dream. I crouched on the dream-floor as they did, shaking with the rushing energy inside of me. I felt a hand on my shoulder, and looked up.

I must have looked feral. My ghost took a step-back and lifted both hands. 'Easy, easy,' he said. 'I think you got him.'

'I got him,' I said quietly.

'He was a ghost,' my ghost said. 'He wasn't really a person any more. And even as ghosts go, he was a bad egg. You don't have anything to regret.'

'Easy for you to say,' I said. 'You don't have to live with me.'

'True,' my ghost answered. He glanced down at himself. His bruised limbs grew slowly translucent, and he began vanishing. 'That's the only bad thing about this gig as a

ghost. Once you accomplish whatever it was that caused
you to get created, you're done. Kravos – the real Kravos
– is already gone. Just his shell stayed behind. And this
would have happened to him, too, if he'd killed you.'

'Do unto others before they do unto you,' I said. 'Thanks.'

'It was your plan,' my ghost said. 'I feel like hell anyway.'

'I know.'

'I guess you do. Try not to get killed again, okay?'

'Working on it.'

He waved one hand, and faded away.

I blinked open my eyes. Susan knelt over me, striking
my face with her hand. I felt wretched – but that wasn't
all. My body almost buzzed with the energy I held, my
skin tingling as though I hadn't used a whit of magic in
weeks. She struck me twice more before I let out a strangled groan and lifted a hand to intercept hers.

'Harry?' she demanded. 'Harry, are you awake?'

I blinked my eyes. 'Yeah,' I said. 'Yeah. I'm up.'

'Kravos?' she hissed.

'I pushed his buttons and he lost control. He got me,'
I said. 'Then I got him. You did it just right.'

Susan sat back on her heels, trembling. 'God. When you
stopped breathing, I almost screamed. If you hadn't told me
to expect it, I don't know what I would have done.'

'You did fine,' I said. I rolled over and pushed myself
to my feet, though my body groaned in protest. The pain
felt like something happening very far away, to someone
else. It wasn't relevant to me. The energy coursing through
me – *that* was relevant. I had to release some of it soon or
I'd explode.

Susan started to help me, and then sat back, staring at
me. 'Harry? What happened?'

'I got something back,' I said. 'It's a high. I still hurt, but that doesn't seem to be important.' I stretched my arms out over my head. Then I stalked over to the dirty laundry and found a pair of boxers that fit me, more or less. I gave Susan a self-conscious glance, and slipped into them. 'Get something on Justine, and we're out of here.'

'I tried. She won't come out from behind the washing machine.'

I clenched my jaw, irritated, and snapped my fingers while saying, '*Ventas servitas.*'

There was an abrupt surge of moving air and Justine came tumbling out from behind the washing machine with a yelp. She lay there for a moment, naked and stunned, staring up at me with wide, dark eyes.

'Justine,' I said. 'We're leaving. I don't care how crazy you are. You're coming with me.'

'Leaving?' Justine stammered. Susan helped her sit up, and wrapped the red cloak around her shoulders. It fell to mid-thigh on the girl, who rose, trembling like a deer before headlights. 'But. We're going to die.'

'*Were,*' I said. 'Past tense.' I turned back to the door and reached into all that energy glittering through me, pointed my finger and shouted, '*Ventas servitas!*' With another roar of wind, the door exploded outwards, into a large, empty room, splinters flying everywhere and shattering one of the two lightbulbs illuminating the room beyond.

I said, voice crackling with tension and anger, 'Get behind me. Both of you. Don't get in front of me unless you want to get hurt.'

I took a step toward the doorway.

An arm shot around the edge of the door, followed swiftly by Kyle Hamilton's body in its masquerade costume, his flesh mask back in place. He got me by the throat, whirling me in a half circle to slam me against the wall.

'Harry!' Susan shouted.

'Got you,' Kyle purred, pinning me in place with supernatural force. Behind him, Kelly followed him in, her once-pretty face twisting and bulging beneath her flesh mask, as though she could barely contain the creature inside her. Her face was warped, twisted, distorted, as though whatever was beneath it had been so horribly mangled that not even a vampire's powers of masquerade could wholly conceal its hideousness.

'Come along, sister,' Kyle said. 'Tainted or not, we shall tear open his heart and see what a wizard's blood tastes like.'

37

Fury surged through me, before fear or anxiety, a fury so scarlet and bright that I could scarcely believe it was mine. Maybe it wasn't. After all, you are what you eat — even if you're a wizard.

'Let go, Kyle,' I grated. 'You've got one chance to live through this. Walk away, right now.'

Kyle laughed, letting his fangs extend. 'No more bluffs, wizard,' he purred. 'No more illusions. Take him, sister.'

Kelly came at me in a rush, but I had been waiting for that. I lifted my right hand and snarled, '*Ventas servitas!*' A furious column of wind slammed into her like a bag of sand, catching her in midair and driving her across the room, into the wall.

Kyle screamed in fury, drawing his hand back off of my throat and then driving it at me. I dodged the first blow by jerking my head to one side, and heard his hand crunch into the stone. The dodge cost me my balance, and as I teetered, he lashed out again, aiming for my neck. All I could do was watch it come.

And then Susan came between us. I didn't see her move toward us, but I saw her catch the blow in both of her hands. She spun, twisting her hips and body and shoulders, letting out a furious scream. She threw Kyle across the room, in the air the whole way, and with no noticeable trajectory. He slammed into his sister, driving them both into the wall once more. I heard Kelly scream, incoherent and bestial. The black, slime-covered bat-thing beneath the pleasant flesh mask tore its way out, shredding damply flapping skin with its talons as it started raking at Kyle. He struggled against her, shouting something that became lost in his creature-form's scream as he too tore his way free. The two of them started clawing at one another in a frenzy, fangs and tongues and talons flashing.

I snarled, and rolled my wrist, flipping my hand toward them in a gesture wholly unfamiliar to me. Words spilled from my lips in thundering syllables, '*Satharak, na-kadum!*' That scarlet, furious power I had stolen from Kravos flashed over me, following the gesture of my right hand, lashing out in a blaze of scarlet light that spun around the maddened vampires. The scarlet blaze whirled about them, winding too swiftly to be seen, a ribbon of flame that cocooned them both, burned brighter and hotter, the spell enfolding them in fire.

They screamed as they died, sounds like metal sheets tearing, and somehow also like terrified children. Heat thrummed back against us, almost singeing the exposed hairs on my legs, my chest. Greasy black smoke started to spread over the floor, and it stank.

I watched as they burned, though I could see nothing beneath the blazing flame-cocoon. Part of me wanted to dance in malicious glee, to throw my arms up in the air and crow my defiance and scorn to my enemies while they died, and to roll through their ashes when they'd cooled.

More of me grew sickened. I stared at the spell I had wrought and couldn't believe it had come from me – whether or not I'd taken the power, maybe even some primal knowledge of this spell, from Kravos's devoured spirit, the magic had come from *me*. I had killed them, as swiftly and as efficiently as with as little forethought as one gives to crushing an ant.

They were vampires, some part of me said. *They had it coming. They were monsters.*

I glanced aside, at Susan, who stood panting, her white shirt stained dark brown with blood. She stared at the fire, her eyes dark and wide, the whites filled in with black. I watched her shudder and close her eyes. When she opened them again, they were normal once more, blurred with tears.

Within the confines of my spell, the screams stopped. Now there were only cracklings. Poppings. The sound of overheated marrow boiling, bursting out of bone.

I turned away, toward the door, and said, 'Let's go.'

Susan and Justine followed me.

I led them through the basement. It was large and unfinished and damp. The room outside the washroom had a large drain in the center of the floor. There were corpses, there. Children from the masquerade. Others, dressed in rags and castoff clothes. The missing street people.

I stopped long enough to send my senses questing out over them, but there was no stirring of breath, no faint pulse of heartbeat. The corpses showed no lividity at all. The floor lay damp beneath our feet, and a hose still ran out a trickle of water, to one side.

Dinner had already been served.

'I hate them,' I said. My voice rang out too loud, in that room. 'I hate them, Susan.'

She said nothing, in answer.

'I'm not going to let them keep this up. I've tried to stay out of their way before. I can't, now. Not after what I've seen.'

'You can't fight them,' Justine whispered. 'They're too strong. There are too many of them.'

I held up a hand, and Justine fell silent. I tilted my head to one side, and heard a faint thrumming, at the very edges of my magical perception. I stalked across the room, around the bodies, to an alcove in the wall.

Cheap shelving had been installed in the alcove, and on the shelves sat my shield bracelet, my blasting rod, and Bob's skull, still in its fishnet sack. Even as I approached, the skull's eyes flared to life.

'Harry,' Bob said. 'Stars and skies, you're all right!' He hesitated for a second, and then said, 'And looking *grim*. Even dressed in boxers with yellow duckies on them.'

I glanced down, and did my best to picture a vampire wearing boxers with yellow duckies. Or a wizard wearing yellow duckies, for that matter. 'Bob,' I said.

Bob whistled. 'Wow. Your aura is different. You look a lot like—'

'Shut up, Bob,' I said, my voice very quiet.

He did.

I put on my bracelet, and took up my rod. I scanned around and found my staff wedged into a corner, and took it out as well. 'Bob,' I asked. 'What is all my stuff doing here?'

'Oh,' Bob said. 'That. Well. Bianca got the idea, somewhere, that your stuff might explode if anyone messed around with it.'

I heard the wryness in my voice, though I didn't feel it. 'She did, did she.'

'I can't imagine how.'

'I'm doubling your pay.' I took Bob's skull and handed it back to Justine. 'Carry this. Don't drop it.'

Bob whistled. 'Hey, cutie. That's a real nice red cloak you got there. Will you let me see the lining?'

I swatted the skull on the way past, drawing an outraged, 'Ow!' from Bob.

'Stop goofing around. We're still inside Bianca's, and we still have to get out.' I frowned, and glanced at Justine, then swiftly, left and right. 'Where's Susan?'

Justine blinked. 'She was right here behind—' She turned, staring.

Water dripped.

Silence reigned.

Justine started trembling like a leaf. 'Here,' she whispered. 'They're here. We can't see them.'

'What's this "we" stuff, kimosabe,' Bob muttered. The skull spun about in its fishnet sack. 'I don't see any veils, Harry.'

I swept my eyes left and right, gripping my blasting rod. 'Did you see her leave? Or anyone take her?'

Bob coughed. 'Well. Truth be told, I was looking at Justine's luscious little—'

'I get the point, Bob.'

'Sorry.'

I shook my head, irritated. 'They snuck in, under a veil maybe. Grabbed Susan and went. Why the hell didn't they stick around? Just put a knife in my back? Why didn't they take Justine, too?'

'Good questions,' Bob said.

'I'll tell you why. Because they weren't here. They couldn't have just carried Susan off that easy. Not now.'

'Why not?' Bob asked.

'Trust me. She'd be a handful. They couldn't do it without making a fuss, which we'd notice.'

'Assuming you're right,' Bob said, 'why would she just walk away?'

Justine glanced back at me, and licked her lips. 'Bianca could make her. I've seen her do it. She made Susan walk into the laundry room on her own.'

I grunted. 'Looks like Bianca's been hitting the books, Bob.'

'Vampire wizard,' Bob said. 'Black magic. Could be very tough.'

'So can I. Justine, stay behind me. Keep your eyes open.'

'Yes, sir,' she said, her voice quiet. I strode past her, toward the stairs. Some of the energy I'd felt before had faded away. My pain and weakness grew closer to me, more noticeable. I did everything I could to shove it to the back of my mind. A swift little thrill of panic gabbled in my throat and tried to make me start screaming. I shoved that away, too. I just walked to the bottom of the stairs, and looked up them.

The doors at the top were elegant wood, and standing open. A soft breeze and the smell of night air flowed down the stairs. Late night, faint with the traces of dusty dawn. I glanced back at Justine, and she all but flinched away from me.

'Stay down here,' I told her. 'Bob, some things are going to start flying. Give her whatever help you can.'

'All right, Harry,' Bob said. 'You know that door's been opened for you. They're going to be waiting for you to walk up there.'

'Yeah,' I said. 'I'm not getting any stronger. Might as well do it now.'

'You could wait until dawn. Then they'd—'

I cut him off, short. 'Then they'd force their way down

here to escape the sunlight. And it would still be a fight.'
I glanced at Justine and said, 'I'll get you out, if I can.'

She chanced a swift glance at my face, and back down.
'Thank you, Mister Dresden. For trying.'

'Sure, kid.' I flexed my left hand, feeling the cool silver
of the shield bracelet there. I gripped my staff tight. Then
rolled the blasting rod through my fingers, feeling the
runes carved into the wood, formulae of power, fire, force.

I put one foot on the stairs. My bare foot made little
sound, but the board creaked beneath my weight. I squared
my shoulders, and went up the next stair, and the next.
Resolute, I guess. Terrified, certainly. Seething with power,
with a simmering anger ready to boil over again.

I tried to clear my mind, to hang onto the anger and
to dismiss the fear. I had limited success, but I made it
up the stairs.

At the top, Bianca stood at one end of the great hall
through the open doors. She wore the white gown I'd seen
her in before, the soft fabric draping and stretching in
alluring curves, creating shadows upon her with an artist's
conviction. Susan knelt beside her, shaking, her head
bowed. Bianca kept one hand on her hair.

Spread out around and behind Bianca were a dozen
vampires; skinny limbs, flabby black bodies and drooling
fangs, the flaps of skin between arm and flank and thigh
stretched out, here and there, like half-functional wings.
Some of the vampires had climbed up the walls and perched
there, like gangly black spiders. All of them, even Susan,
had huge, dark eyes. All of them stood looking at me.

In front of Bianca knelt a half-dozen men in plain suits
that bulged in odd places. They held guns in their hands.
Great big guns. Some kind of assault weapons, I thought.

Their eyes looked a little vague, like they'd only been allowed to see some of what was in the room. Just as well.

I looked back at them and leaned on my staff. And I laughed. It came out a wheezing cackle, that echoed around the great hall, and caused the vampires to stir restlessly.

Bianca let her lips curve into a slow smile. 'And what do you find so amusing, my pet?'

I smiled back. There was nothing friendly in it. 'All of this. For a guy with two sticks and a pair of yellow ducky boxer shorts, you must think I'm a real dangerous man.'

'As a matter of fact, I do,' Bianca said. 'Were I you, I would consider it flattery.'

'Would you?' I asked.

Bianca let her smile widen. 'Oh. Oh, yes. Gentlemen,' she said, to the men with guns. 'Fire.'

38

I lifted my left hand before me, pouring energy into the shield bracelet, and shouted, '*Riflettum!*'

The guns roared with fire and thunder. Sparks showered off of a barrier less than six inches away from my hand. The bracelet grew warm as the security men poured a hail of gunfire at me. It stopped, just short, and bullets shot aside, chewing through the expensive woodwork and bouncing wildly around the room. One of the vampires let out a yowl and dropped from the wall to splat on the ground like a fat bug. One of the security men's guns suddenly jumped and twisted, and he cried out in pain, reeling back, blood streaming from his hands and the ruins of his face.

Technology doesn't tend to work too well around magic. Including the feeding mechanisms of automatic weapons.

Two of the guns jammed before dumping their full clips, and the others fell silent, spent. I still stood, one hand extended. Bullets lay all over the floor in front of me, misshapen slugs of lead. The security men stared, and stumbled away from me, behind Bianca and the vampires, and out the door. I don't blame them. If all I had was a gun, and it had just been that useless, I would run, too.

I took a step forward, scattering bullets with my bare feet. 'Get out of my way,' I said. 'Let us out. No one else has to get hurt.'

'Kyle,' Bianca said, stroking Susan's hair. 'Kelly. She

was quite mad in any case. Not all of them make the transition well.' Her gaze traveled down to Susan.

The smile I wore sharpened. 'Last chance, Bianca. Let us out peacefully, and you walk away alive.'

'And if I say no?' she asked, very mild.

I snarled, my temper snapping. I lifted the blasting rod, whirled it around my head as I drew in my will, and snarled, *'Fuego!'* Power exploded from the rod, circular coruscations following a solid scarlet column of energy that lanced forward, toward the vampire's head.

Bianca kept smiling. She lifted her left hand, mumbled some gibberish, and I saw cold darkness gather before her, a concave disk that met my energy lance and absorbed it, scattered it, sent smaller bolts of fire darting here and there, splashing on the floor in small, blazing puddles.

I just stared at her for a moment. I knew that she'd known some tricks, maybe a veil or two, a glamour or two, maybe how to whip up a fascination. But that kind of straightforward deflection wasn't something just anyone could do. Some of the people on the White Council couldn't have stopped that shot without help.

Bianca smiled at me, and lowered her hand. The vampires laughed, hissing, inhuman laughter. The hairs on the back of my neck stood up, and a cold shudder glided gleefully up and down my spine.

'Well, Mister Dresden,' she purred. 'It would appear that Mavra was an able instructor, and my lessons well learned. We seem to be at something of a standoff. But there's one more piece I'd like to put on the board.' She clapped her hands, and gestured to one side.

One of the vampires opened a door. Standing behind it, both hands on a stylish cane, stood a medium-sized man, dark of hair and coloring, brawny through the chest and shoulders. He wore a tailored suit of dark grey in an immaculate cut. He made me think of native South Americans, with a sturdy jaw and broad, strong features.

'Nice suit,' I told him.

He looked me up and down. 'Nice . . . ducks.'

'Okay,' I said, 'I'll bite. Who's that?'

'My name,' the man said, 'is Ortega. Don Paolo Ortega, of the Red Court.'

'Hiya, Don,' I said. 'I'd like to lodge a complaint.'

He smiled, a show of broad, white teeth. 'I'm sure you would, Mister Dresden. But I have been monitoring the situation here. And the Baroness,' he nodded to Bianca, 'has broken none of the Accords. Nor has she violated the laws of hospitality, nor her own given word.'

'Oh come on,' I said. 'She's broken the spirit of all of them!'

Ortega tsked. 'Alas, that in the Accords it was agreed that there is no spirit of the law, between our kinds, Mister Dresden. Only its letter. And Baroness Bianca has strictly adhered to its letter. You have instigated multiple combats in her home, murdered her sworn bondsman, inflicted damage to her property and her reputation. And now you stand here prepared to continue your grievance with her, in a most unlawful and cavalier fashion. I believe that what you do is sometimes referred to as "cowboy justice."'

'If there's a point in here, somewhere,' I said, 'get to it.'

Ortega's eyes glittered. 'I am present as a witness to the Red King, and the Vampire Courts at large. That is all. I am merely a witness.'

Bianca turned her eyes back to me. 'A witness who will

carry word of your treacherous attack and intrusion back to the Courts,' she said. 'It will mean war between our kindred and the White Council.'

War.

Between the vampires and the White Council.

Son of a bitch. It was unthinkable. Such a conflict hadn't happened in millennia. Not in living memory – and some wizards live a damned long time.

I had to swallow, and hide the fact that I had just gulped. 'Well. Since he isn't running off to tattle right this second, I can only assume that you're about to offer me a deal.'

'I never thought you were slow on the uptake, Mister Dresden,' Bianca said. 'Will you hear my offer?'

I ached more with every moment that went by. My body was failing. I had ridden the rush of magic through the last several moments, but I had spent a lot of that power. It would come back, but I was running the batteries down – and the more I did it, the more I couldn't ignore my weakness, my dizziness.

Legally speaking, the vampires had me over a barrel. I needed a plan. I needed a plan in the worst way. I needed time.

'Sure,' I said. 'I'll hear you out.'

Bianca curled her fingers through Susan's hair. 'First. You shall be forgiven your . . . excesses of bad taste of the last few days. But for the two deaths, none of it is unworkable – and those two would have died shortly, in any case. I will forgive you, Mister Dresden.'

'That's so kind.'

'It gets better. You may take your equipment, your skull, and the White bastard's whore with you when you leave. Unharmed and free of future malice. All accounts will be called even.'

I let the dry show in my tone. 'How could I possibly say no.'

She smiled. 'You killed someone very dear to me, Mister Dresden – not directly, true, but your actions mandated her death. For that, too, I will forgive you.'

I narrowed my eyes.

Bianca ran her hands over Susan's hair. 'This one will stay with me. You stole away someone dear to me, Mister Dresden. And I am going to take away someone dear to you. After that, all will be equal.' She gave Ortega a very small smile and then glanced at me and asked, 'Well? What say you? If you prefer to remain with her, I'm sure a place could be made for you here. After suitable assurances of your loyalty, of course.'

I remained silent for a moment, stunned.

'Well, wizard?' she snapped, harsher. 'How do you answer? Accept my bargain. My *compromise*. Or it is war. And you will become its first casualty.'

I looked at Susan. She stared blankly, her mouth partially open, caught in a trance of some kind. I could probably snap her out of it, provided a bunch of vampires didn't tear me limb from limb while I tried. I looked up at Bianca. At Ortega. At the hissing vampire cronies. They were drooling on the polished floor.

I hurt all over, and I felt so very damned tired.

'I love her,' I said. I didn't say it very loud.

'What?' Bianca stared at me. 'What did you say?'

'I said, I love her.'

'She is already half mine.'

'So? I still love her.'

'She isn't even fully human any longer, Dresden. It won't be long before she is as a sister to me.'

'Maybe. Maybe not,' I said. 'Get your hands off my girl-friend.'

Bianca's eyes widened. 'You are *mad*,' she said. 'You would flirt with chaos, destruction – with war. For the sake of *this* one wounded soul?'

I smote my staff on the floor, reaching deep for power. Deeper than I've ever reached before. Outside, in the gathering morning, the air crackled with thunder.

Bianca, even Ortega, looked abruptly uncertain, looking up and around, before focusing on me again.

'For the sake of one soul. For one loved one. For one life.' I called power into my blasting rod, and its tip glowed incandescent white. 'The way I see it, there's nothing else worth fighting a war for.'

Bianca's face distorted with fury. She lost it. She split apart her skin like some gruesome caterpillar, the black beast clawing its way out of her flesh mask, jaws gaping, black eyes burning with feral fury. 'Kill him!' she shouted. 'Kill him, kill him, kill him!'

The vampires came for me, across the floor, along the walls, scuttling like roaches or spiders – too fast for easy belief. Bianca gathered shadow into her hands and hurled it at me.

I fell back a pace, caught Bianca's strike with my staff, and parried it into one of her flunkies. The darkness enfolded the vampire, and it screamed from within. When the fog around it vanished, nothing remained but dust. I responded with another gout of fire from the rod, sweeping it like a scythe through the oncoming vampires, setting them aflame. They writhed and screamed.

Spittle sliced toward me from above and to one side, and I barely ducked away in time. The vampire clinging to the ceiling followed its venom down, but it met the end of my staff in its belly, the other end solidly planted against the floor. The vampire rebounded with a burping sound and landed hard on the floor. I lifted the staff and smote down on the thing's head, to the sound of more thunder outside. Power lashed down through the staff, and crushed the vampire's skull like an egg. Dust rained down from the ceiling, and the vampire's claws scratched a frantic staccato on the floor as it died.

I had done well for the moment – the vamps nearest me were falling back, teeth bared. But more were coming, from behind them. Bianca hurled another strike at me, and though I interposed both staff and shield, the deathly cold of it numbed my fingers.

I was running out of strength, panting, my weariness and weakness struggling to claim me. I fought off the dizziness, enough to send another flash of fire at an oncoming vampire, but it skittered aside, and all I did was plow a blazing furrow in the floorboards.

They fell back for a moment, separated from me by an expanse of flame, and I struggled to catch my breath.

They were coming. The vampires would be coming for me. My brain kept chattering at me, frantic, panicked. They're coming. Justine, Susan, and I might as well be dead. Dead like all the others. Dead like all their victims.

I leaned against the wall by the stairs, panting, fighting to hold on to some sense of clarity. Dead. Victims. The victims below. The dead.

I dropped the blasting rod. I fell to my knees.

With my staff, I scratched a circle around me, in the

dust. It was enough. The circle closed with a thrum of power. Magic ran rampant in that house, the sea of supernatural energy stirred to froth.

I had no guide for this kind of spell. I had no focus, nothing to target, but that wasn't the kind of magic I was working with. I shoved my senses down, into the earth, like reaching fingers. I blanked out the burning hall, my enemies, Bianca's howling. I shut away the fire, the smoke, the pain, the nausea. I focused, and reached beneath me.

And I found them. I found the dead, the victims, the ones who had been taken. Not just the few piled below, like so much trash to be discarded. I found others. Dozens of others. Scores. Hundreds. Bones hidden away, never marked, never remembered. Restless shades, trapped in the earth, too weak to act, to take vengeance, to seek peace. Maybe on another night, or in another place, I couldn't have done it. But the way had been prepared for me, by Bianca and her people. They'd thought to weaken the border between life and death, to use the dead as a weapon against me.

But that blade can cut both ways.

I found those spirits, reached out and touched them, one by one.

'*Memorium,*' I whispered. '*Memoratum. Memortius.*'

Energy rushed out of me. I shoved it out as fast as it would go, and I gave it to them. To the lost ones. The seduced, the betrayed, the homeless, the helpless. All the people the vampires had preyed on, through the years, all the dead I could reach. I reached out into the turmoil Bianca and her allies had created, and I gave those wandering shades power.

The house began to shake.

From below, in the basement, there came a rumbling sound. It began as a moan. It rose to a wail. And then it became a screaming mob, a roar of sound that shattered the senses, that made my heart and my belly shiver with the sheer force of it.

The dead came. They erupted through the floor, and took forms of smoke and flame and cinder. I saw them as I swayed, weakened, finished by the effort of the spell. I saw their faces. I saw newsboys from the roaring twenties, and greaser street punks from the fifties. I saw delivery people and homeless transients and lost children rise up, deadly in their fury. The ghosts reached out with flaming hands to burn and sear; they shoved their smoky bodies into noses and throats. They howled their names and the names of their murderers, the names of their loved ones, and their vengeance shook that grand old house like a thunderstorm, like an earthquake.

The ceiling began to fall in. I saw vampires being dragged into the flames, down into the basement as burning sections of floor gave way. Some tried to flee, but the spirits of the dead knew no more pity than they had rest. They hammered at the vampires, raked at them, ghostly hands and bodies made nearly tangible by the power I'd channeled into them.

Vampires died. Ghosts swarmed and screamed everywhere, terrible and beautiful, heartbreaking and ridiculous as humanity itself. The sound banished any thought of speech, hammered upon my skin like physical blows.

I was more terrified than I had ever been in my life. I struggled to my feet and beckoned down the stairs. Justine stumbled up them, Bob's eyelights blazing bright orange, a beacon in the smoke. I grabbed her wrist and tried to make my way around the trembling house, the gaping hole in the floor that led down to an inferno.

I saw a spirit leap for Bianca with blazing hands reached out, and she smote it from the air with a blast of frozen black air. She seized Susan by the wrist and started dragging her toward the front door.

More spirits hurtled toward her, the eldest of the murderers of this house, fire and smoke and splinter — even one that had forged a body for itself out of the spent bullets laying upon the floor.

She fought them off. Talon and magic, she thrust her way through them, and toward the front door. Susan began to wake up, to look around her, her expression terrified.

'Susan!' I shouted. 'Susan!'

She began to struggle against Bianca, who hissed, turning toward Susan. She fought to drag my girlfriend closer to the front door, but one of the ghosts clawed at the vampire's leg, setting it aflame.

Bianca screamed, berserk, out of control. She lifted one hand high, her claws glittering, dark, and swept it down at Susan's throat.

I sent my spell hurtling out along with Susan's name, the last strength of my body and mind.

I saw her rise. Rachel's ghost. She appeared, simple and translucent and pretty, and put herself between Bianca's claws and Susan's throat. Blood gouted from the ghost, scarlet and horrible. Susan tumbled limply to one side. Bianca started screaming, high enough to shatter glass, as the bloody ghost simply pressed against her, wrapping her arms around the monstrous black form.

My spell followed on the heels of Rachel's ghost, and took Bianca full in the face, a near-solid column of wind, which seized her, hurtled her up, and then smashed her down into the floor. The overstrained boards gave way beneath her with a creak and a roar, and flame washed up toward me in a wave of reeking black smoke. I felt my balance spin and I struggled to make it to the exit, but fell to the ground.

Spirits flooded after Bianca, fire and smoke, following the vampire sorceress down the hole. The house itself screamed, a sound of tortured wood and twisted beam, and began to fall.

I couldn't get my balance. I felt small, strong hands under one of my arms. And then I felt Susan beneath the other, powerful and terrified. She lifted me to my feet. Justine stayed by my other side, and together, we stumbled out of the old house.

We had gone no more than a dozen paces when it collapsed with a roar. We turned, and I saw the house drawing *in* upon itself, sucked down into the earth, into an inferno of flame. The fire department, later, called it some kind of inverted backblast, but I know what I saw. I saw the ghosts the dead had left behind settle the score.

'I love you,' I said, or tried to say, to Susan. 'I love you.'

She pressed her mouth to mine. I think she was crying. 'Hush,' she said. 'Harry. Hush. I love you, too.'

It was done.

There was no more reason to hold on.

39

I regard it as one last sadistic gibe of whatever power had decided to make my life a living hell that the burn ward was full, and I was given a room to share with Charity Carpenter. She had recovered in spirit, if not in body, and she started in on me the moment I awoke. The woman's tongue was sharper than any sword. Even *Amoracchius*. I smiled through most of it. Michael would have been proud.

The baby, I learned, had taken an abrupt turn for the better in the hours before dawn the morning Bianca's house had burned. I thought that maybe Kravos had taken a bite of the little guy, and I had gotten it back for him. Michael thought God had simply decreed the morning to be a day of good things. Whatever. The results were what counted.

'We've decided,' Michael said, stretching a strong arm around Charity, 'to name him Harry.'

Charity glowered at me, but remained silent.

'Harry?' I asked. 'Harry Carpenter? Michael, what did that poor kid ever do to you?'

But it made me feel good. And they kept the name.

Charity got out of the hospital three days before me. Michael or Father Forthill remained with me for the rest of my stay. No one ever said anything, but Michael had the sword with him, and Forthill kept a crucifix handy. Just in case I had some nasty visitors.

One night when I couldn't sleep, I mentioned to Michael that I was worried about the repercussions of my workings, the harmful magic I had dished out. I worried that it was going to come back to haunt me.

'I'm not a philosopher, Harry,' he said. 'But here's something for you to think about, at least. What goes around comes around. And sometimes you get what's coming around.' He paused for a moment, frowning faintly, pursing his lips. 'And sometimes you *are* what's coming around. You see what I mean?'

I did. I was able to get back to sleep.

Michael explained that he and Thomas had escaped the fight at the bridge only a few moments after it had begun. But time had stretched oddly, between the Nevernever and Chicago, and they hadn't emerged until two o'clock the following afternoon.

'Thomas brought us out into this flesh pit,' Michael said.

'I'm not a wizard,' Thomas pointed out. 'I can only get in and out of the Nevernever at points close to my heart.'

'A house of sin!' Michael said, his expression stern.

'A *gentlemen's* club,' Thomas protested. 'And one of the nicest ones in town.'

I kept my mouth shut. Who says I never grow any wiser?

Murphy came out of the sleeping spell a couple days later. I had to go in a wheelchair, but I went to Kravos's funeral with her. She pushed me through a drizzling rain to the grave site. There was a city official there, who signed off on some papers and left. Then it was just us and the grave diggers, shovels whispering on earth.

Murphy watched the proceedings in complete silence, her eyes sunken, the blue faded out until they seemed almost grey. I didn't push, and she didn't talk until the hole was half filled in.

'I couldn't stop him,' she said, then. 'I tried.'

'But we beat him. That's why we're here and he's there.'

'*You* beat him,' Murphy said. 'A lot of good I did you.'

'He sucker punched you. Even if you'd been a wizard, he'd have gotten to you – like he damn near did me.' I shivered, remembered agony making the muscles of my belly tight. 'Karrin, you can't blame yourself for that.'

'I know,' she said, but she didn't sound like she meant it. She was quiet for a long time, and I finally figured out that she wasn't talking because I'd hear the tears in her voice, the ones the rain hid from me. She didn't bow her head though, and she didn't look away from the grave.

I reached out and found her hand with mine. I squeezed. She squeezed back, silent and tight. We stayed there, in the rain, until the last bit of earth had been thrown over Kravos's coffin.

On the way out, Murphy stopped my wheelchair, frowning at a white headstone next to a waiting plot. 'He died doing the right thing,' she read. She looked down at me.

I shrugged, and felt my mouth curl up on one side. 'Not yet. Not today.'

Michael and Forthill took care of Lydia for me. Her real name was Barbara something. They got her packed up and moved out of town. Apparently, the Church has some kind of equivalent of the Witness Protection Program, for getting people out of the reach of supernatural baddies. Forthill told me how the girl had fled the church because she'd been terrified that she would fall asleep, and gone out to find some uppers. The vampires had grabbed her while she was out, which was when I'd found them in that old building. She sent me a note that read, simply, 'I'm sorry. Thank you for everything.'

When I got out of the hospital, Thomas sent me a thank-you letter, for saving Justine. He sent it on a little note card attached to a bow, which was all Justine was wearing. I'll let you guess where the bow was. I took the note, but not the girl. There was too much of an ick factor in sharing girls with a sex vampire. Justine was pretty enough, and sweet enough, when she wasn't walking the razor's edge of an organic emotional instability – but I couldn't really hold that against her. Plenty of people have to take some kind of medication to keep stable. Lithium, supermodel sex vampires – whatever works, I guess.

I had woman problems of my own.

Susan sent me flowers and called me every day, in the hospital. But she didn't ever talk to me for long. And she didn't come to visit. When I got out, I went to her apartment. She didn't live there anymore. I tried to call her at work, and never managed to catch her. Finally, I had to resort to magic. I used some hair of hers left on a brush at my apartment, and tracked her down on a beach along Lake Michigan, on one of the last warm days of the year.

I found her laying in the sun wearing a white bikini that left maximum surface area bared to it. I sat down next to her, and her manner changed, subtly, a quiet tension that I didn't miss, though I couldn't see her eyes behind the sunglasses she wore.

'The sun helps,' she said. 'Sometimes it almost goes away for a while.'

'I've been trying to find you,' I said. 'I wanted to talk to you.'

'I know,' she said. 'Harry. Things have changed for me. In the daylight, it's not too bad. But at night.' She shivered. 'I have to lock myself inside. I don't trust myself around people, Harry.'

'I know,' I said. 'You know what's happening?'

'I talked to Thomas,' she said. 'And Justine. They were nice enough, I guess. They explained things to me.'

I grimaced. 'Look,' I said. 'I'm going to help you. I'll find some way to get you out of this. We can find a cure.' I reached out and took her hand. 'Oh, Hell's bells, Susan. I'm no good at this.' I just fumbled the ring onto it, clumsy as you please. 'I don't want you far away. Marry me.'

She sat up, and stared at her hand, at the dinky ring I'd been able to afford. Then she leaned close to me and gave me a slow, heated kiss, her mouth melting-warm. Our tongues touched. Mine went numb. I got a little dizzy, as the slow throb of pleasure that I'd felt before coursed through me, a drug I'd craved without realizing it.

She drew away from me slowly, her face expressionless behind the sunglasses. She said, 'I can't. You already made me ache for you, Harry. I couldn't control myself, with you. I couldn't sort out the hungers.' She pressed the ring into my hand and stood up, gathering her towel and a purse with her. 'Don't come to me again. I'll call you.'

And she left.

I'd bragged to Kravos, at the end, that I'd been trained to demolish nightmares when I was younger. And to a certain extent it was true. If something came into my head for a fight, I could put up a good one. But now I had nightmares that were all my own. A part of me. And they were always the same: darkness, trapped, with the vampires all around me, laughing their hissing laughter.

I'd wake up, screaming and crying. Mister, curled against my legs, would raise his head and rumble at me. But he wouldn't pad away. He'd just settle down again, purring like a snowmobile's engine. I found it a comfort. And I slept with a light always close.

'Harry,' Bob said one night. 'You haven't been working. You've barely left your apartment. The rent was due last week. And this vampire research is going nowhere fast.'

'Shut up, Bob,' I told him. 'This unguent isn't right. If we can find a way to convert it to a liquid, maybe we can work it into a supplement of some kind—'

'*Harry,*' Bob said.

I looked up at the skull.

'Harry. The Council sent a notice to you today.'

I stood up, slowly.

'The vampires. The Council's at war. I guess Paris and Berlin went into chaos almost a week ago. The Council is calling a meeting. Here.'

'The White Council is coming to Chicago,' I mused.

'Yeah. They're going to want to know what the hell happened.'

I shrugged. 'I sent them my report. I only did what was right,' I said. 'Or as close to it as I could manage. I couldn't let them have her, Bob. I couldn't.'

The skull sighed. 'I don't know if that will hold up with them, Harry.'

'It has to,' I said.

There was a knock at my door. I climbed up from the lab. Murphy and Michael had shown up at my door with a care package: soup and charcoal and kerosene for me, as the weather got colder. Groceries. Fruit. Michael had, rather pointedly, included a razor.

'How are you doing, Dresden?' Murphy asked me, her blue eyes serious.

I stared at her for a moment. Then at Michael.

'I could be worse,' I said. 'Come in.'

Friends. They make it easier.

So, the vampires are out to get me, and every other wizard on the block. The little wizardlings of the city, the have-nots of magic, are making it a point not to go outside after dark. I don't order pizza for delivery anymore. Not after the first guy almost got me with a bomb.

The Council is going to be furious at me, but what else is new.

Susan doesn't call. Doesn't visit. But I got a card from her, on my birthday, Halloween. She only wrote three words.

I'll let you guess what three.